THE ADVENTURES OF TOM CONLEY

R. C. Thom

Library of Congress registration number: TXU 2-281-746
Registration effective date: Sept 27, 2021

ISBN for Print ISBN: 979-8-9861808-4-7
ISBN for Ebook ISBN: 979-8-9861808-7-8

Disclaimer:
The characters you will meet here are not real people and they do not directly mimic any people I know living or dead. None of the scenes they appear in were actual. Some places and events are close to being historically accurate. The details of events, real or not, in this book were entirely invented by me. This work of fiction is not meant to be factual. Some of my fictional people are shown within a historical context but don't rely on that being accurate. What these characters say and do is fictional unless stated otherwise. When I mix science with fantasy that is where I really make stuff up. I also employed a light sprinkling of actual sciences and scientific methods as well.

Content Editor: Lisa Cross
Cover art: Rachel Thompson
Book Design: Gayle F. Hendricks
Line editing and proofreading:
Angel Ackerman, Parisian Phoenix Publishing, angel@parisianphoenix.com

For editing and publishing services:
Parisian Phoenix Publishing Company, angel@parisianphoenix.com
Check out Parisian Publishing: ParisianPhoenix.com, X: ParisBirdBooks

Books by Rachel C. Thompson *aka* R.C. Thom.

Available in print and e-book.

Soul Harvest: Print ISBN number: 798-1-7321459-1-7
Or in E-book: 798-1-7321459-0-0

Aggie in Orbit: Print ISBN number: 798-1-7321459-7-9
Or in E-book: 798-1-7321459-6-2

Aggie in Space: Print ISBN number: 798-1-7321459-8-6
Or in e-book: 798-1-7321459-9-3

Dragon Fire: Print ISBN number: 798-1-7321459-2-4
Or in e-book: 798-1-7321459-3-1

Stalking Kilgore Trout: Print ISBN: 798-1-7321459-4-8
Or in e-book: 798-1-7321459-5-5

Book of Answers: Print ISBN Number:979-8-9861808-0-9
Or in e-book: 979-8-9861808-1-6

Another Anthology: Print ISBN.979-8-9861808-2-3
Or in e-book: 979-8-9861808-3-0 (International)

The Adventures of Tom Conley Print ISBN 979-8-9861808-4-7

Or in e-book: ISBN 979-8-9861808-7-8 (International)

Amazon only three satirical short stories in each three pack for $1.99

President's Three Pack

GLBT 3 Pack

Heretic's 3 Pack

Rachel's Email: humanrights4all@aol.com
RCThom.com or RCThom.net for info about her books

INTRODUCTION:

This action-adventure tale is based in archeology, paleontology, and ancient esoteric concepts. Unlike *Indiana Jones*, this story uses real science mixed with a healthy dose of science fiction, fantasy, and magic. Professional shovelbums will no doubt notice inaccuracies. This is intended for a general audience who may have limited knowledge of the sciences mentioned. I do believe the pseudoscientific aspects of this story ring true. The experts I consulted with agreed, but please don't take these real-world technologies and techniques shown within as gospel. I also consulted persons familiar with autism regarding my special needs character.

In this volume, I limited my usual satirical treatments of fictional situations. However, this will thematically resonate with some of my earlier books. You will notice I tap into parts of the alternative history memes and narratives prevalent among speculative thinkers on the topic of human history. Writers like Graham Handcock, Cremo and Thompson, Robert Temple, and many others were my inspiration. I have read a great many books from alternative history authors. I have also read large amounts of information based on actual science and scholarship from qualified experts in the sciences mentioned above. To be clear, I'm not a believer in what the speculators are selling. I'll stick with the best evidence until better evidence is brought forth. There remain copious unanswered questions regarding our past and the history of our extinct human relatives. I twist what's real with make-believe. I hope you enjoy my mixture of fact and fiction. Love it or hate it, please leave a review anywhere you can.

PRELUDE:

ANATOLIA 12,700 YEARS AGO

Two Ergaster men grounded their submersible vehicle on a temporary river's mud-bank midway between receding shores. The recent roaring torrents had subsided, but too soon. They had not yet reached their destination farther inland. Sudden new rivers had flowed from Mountainlands. Such flooding rendered new waterways between the sea and inland lakes. Tormented oceans had recently rushed upland against meltwater rivers. Freshwater lakes far inland had breached and drained while other lakes nearer the sea became one with the larger body. Those greater bombastic days had passed thus Jardel and Micmore chanced the new rivers while they lasted.

This team's goal was to locate distant relatives of their kind. Other races were too far removed from them in intelligence and industry to rely upon. Micmore's people had no desire or interest in living among the lesser races. His were the Sea People. Their land-bound relatives, The Uplanders, people of his race, rejected coastal living preferring their high and mighty mountain observatories. These Sky Watchers were the ones who created the meteorite impacts. The Watchers had lost control. The Watchers, against all advice, had gone too far.

"And now we seek our destroyer's help," muttered Mic as he made ready to disembark.

The pyramid dwellers fared best. Upland's great female artists, in ancient times, had mixed lesser homo-types with Ergaster DNA. It was not the women's intention to make slaves but to uplift a lesser race. Ergaster men, fearful of the Primitives' advancements, forced the lesser people into bondage in order to control them.

It didn't work.

Sapiens' intelligence grew. They overbred and everywhere they lived free. They multiplied too fast and had to be put down.

Mic had always said, 'So few of us cannot rule so many.' The great culling had to be. Micmore agreed with the reasoning but not the method. Of course, the Primitives had to die, but calling meteorites? Far too radical.

"Too few of us and so many of them," Jardel often said, as he did again.

Jardel and Micmore's mission was to reestablish relations with the Uplanders. Micmore didn't care about the fleet. He volunteered to save himself. The mountains were far safer than the ships. Nothing was left of the Sea People's coastline cities.

With the submarine grounded, Micmore donned his water-walker suit and carry-pack. He waited while fat Jardel huffed and grunted squeezing into his suit. Lacking room inside the craft, they dressed on the topside deck of their small submersible with little room to maneuver.

"Will you hurry?" Micmore said. "Hatch is open and floods may come any time, satellites have that ice-dam ready to burst."

"I am of the court," Jardel said in his high fashion way. "I am not used to gallivanting in the wilds as you…er…science-types are wont to do," he said, huffing.

"This is necessary. There is no wont," Micmore said.

Neither were men of travels. He and Jardel, being young, were volunteered for not having transmuted. They still resemble homo sapiens. Mature Ergaster men were monsters to sapiens' eyes and greatly feared. The politician finally managed to get the one-suit over his fat belly.

"This is not my calling. Why did they have me go? This is not my vocation."

"Have you not heard anything?" Micmore spoke curtly, tired of Jardel's whining. "The killer returns, another impact. The fleet cannot stay afloat. Every ship is old and most are damaged. All with improper repairs! We must establish ourselves inland."

"Do not treat me as a child."

Jardel sat on the hatchway while dressing. He stood up fast rocking the little craft in its mud cradle. Had the craft not been stuck, Jardel would have gone overboard. *Even a child has better sea legs. I would not have him, except Jardel can talk anyone out of anything, even the Primitives.* Mic had pressing survival questions such as: Will the locals help us or kill us should we encounter them? Will sweet words soothe the savages? Finally, after many swearing complaints, the politician was ready.

"Would you be so kind and lead the way," Jardel said.

Mic was compelled to step off the deck and walk on the water first. No point arguing, Jardel wouldn't have it otherwise. Jardel skated and wavered atop the muddy water. Mic had to help him but the two made it to shore unscathed. The ground in every direction was muck and mire. They needed higher ground before removing their suits.

"What now? There is no land here. Why did you bring me to a swamp? Are you thickheaded?"

"We go up," Mic said, stating the obvious. While the fat man struggled to exit the water onto land, Mic stood onshore taking stock. "There is a distant fire uphill. Survivors or made-people. I don't know. It's a start. Adjust your suit for land."

"I am not made for this. Can't you assist me? How will I climb?" Jardel said, stumbling onto a muddy but solid shore.

Mic refused the bait. Yet, he had to admit that Jardel walking uphill any distance, even in a G-suit, was beyond his ability. The politician was not a man accustomed to carrying his own weight. The pleasure of Jardel's suffering was too small a payment for tolerating this complainer's presence.

"Get used to it, Jadel, we have a long way to go."

Mic ignored Jardel's grunts and proceeded. A little onward the bank became steep and high. The water-walker equipment had been modified for land use and it handled the incline well enough, but the mechanism required the user's physical effort. All along the way, Jardel moaned about doom and failure. A long, muddy gully was soon reached and that made going easier. The rift had recently passed meltwater.

Mic quickened his pace, flash floods being an imminent threat. Jardel's grips increased with the pace. Mic paid no heed.

They gained flat land which laid between rifts after forty minutes of slow climb. The higher plains appeared unaffected between torrent cuts. Amazing that any of these hills and grasslands survived.

"Look there," Mic said. "A fire. The local race. Come along Jardel, let us investigate. Perhaps they can point our way out of here."

Mic's maps weren't going to be of help in a destroyed landscape. Approaching the fire, the people there ran away except for a young woman. The female, crouched close to the fire, talked to herself, rocking. Mic recognized the species and realized he and Jardel were safe.

"She invokes her gods for protection against the likes of Mic and Jardel," Jardel said. "That is rich, indeed."

Mic moved in closer to the fire and took his headgear off to show the Primitive that he was true-human. He couldn't hear Jardel yammering with his helmet removed. Too bad Jardel managed to get his lid off as well.

"Look at her," Jardel said, "This is our forebears' created race? Disgusting creature."

"I don't know which variety, but yes," Mic said. "One of the wild ones, perhaps a distant relative of escaped slaves thousands of years removed. The lesser races mixed freely before Women's Magic woke their minds."

The girl wore fine-made animal skins, her hair was orderly. She wore a necklace of teeth and shells.

"Ancient runaways make good breeding stock."

"I cannot believe we must copulate with such animals, how low have we become? They have short loins…how do you do it?"

Only Jardel would think of that base aspect first while standing on the brink of extinction. The bigger effort was to reestablish Ergaster's decimated numbers. Ergaster man, vaguely related to lesser humans, made breeding through proxies possible. Ironic that Ergaster's attempt to wipe out sapiens invited Ergaster's own demise…*and now we need them.* A great number of the upstarts remained on Earth. Primitive populations rise quickly while Ergaster stagnates. Women's Magic made procreation possible, but in captivity, the Goddesses refuse to employ their blessing. The Goddesses did not bestow fertility onto half-breeds, not even to save the Goddess's own race.

"We will find a way," Mic muttered to himself.

"What did you say?" Jardel asked with a seething voice.

"We are a dead people if we don't increase our numbers." Mic lamented. "Our women still refuse us."

Forcing Ergaster women to bear children was impossible. Forcing magic more impossible. Controlling women became survival. Jardel fought the High Council's judgment. Jailing the Goddesses was a mistake in Jardel's view. Mic agreed with the Council.

"Crossbreeding will never work. Mules can't reproduce," the politician said. "We should release the Goddesses. Belock is wrong."

"Be of good cheer, Jardel," Mic said. "Our science will use such proxies as this girl. And you, for your part, will have the Primitives willing and thinking of us as gods. You think of yourself that way already. We will rule as before and without need of the Goddesses. Belock is wise."

Mic tried to communicate with the girl between debates with Jardel. But she did not understand. Seeing another fire in the distance, the team pressed on and reached it. As before, the Primitives fled. No one stayed behind. The Primitives had made ready a tomb in a shallow natural cave. The natives had bashed away enough interior space to form a slab table to hold the body. Hay and grass covered the altar. A body did not yet lay there.

"Such a bizarre way of disposing of the dead," Jardel said.

The idea made Mic feel a little ill. Ergaster incinerated their dead.

"Let us get out of these suits, I am hot," Mic said. "See how we scared them. We must go about as they do. We'll never obtain cooperation wearing G-suits. The observatory is a long way and we must eat. They aren't starving. They will help us. We'll leave the equipment and don the local attire."

"What of our water-walkers, Mic? Will we not want them, should we need an escape?"

That was the first intelligent question Jardel asked on this excursion. Mic entered and searched the tomb for supplies. Artifacts left by fleeing sapiens were of no help. The food pots were empty. The grave's contents were not advanced although the copper ax-head was curious. *The lesser people are more sophisticated than I thought.*

They stored the gravity boots, power packs, and walker clothing. Their best protections were too cumbersome. Powerpacks didn't last if relied upon. Capacity was an issue. *Jardel will waste power every opportunity and what if weapons need charging?* Powerpacks lasted indefinitely unused. He shoved them inside his boots and left them on the platform. They rolled the ready door-slab into place and melted the edges with the portable sonic welder sealing the cave's entrance.

"Not a bad job, if I do say so myself," Mic said.

The natives were not as primitive as Mic was taught. That girl at the fire might have been a practitioner of rudimentary magic. Mic's joke to Jardel about godhood may be a prophetic guess. Pretending godhood was one means of survival. Magical thinking must have developed naturally as proven by the tomb and that fire girl. *Magical thinking without magic is useful.* He was certain Ergaster would soon win back control over their former slaves. The lesser ones were programmed to fear their makers. Fear is useful. Ones without fear, such as that firewoman, were anomalies, random genetic variations, nothing more, not a threat. Still, this discovery was worrisome. Eons removed from captivity allowed advancements. Yet fear of Ergaster remained.

Mic took up his pack with hope. The end of the world had not come after all. Mic felt certain Ergaster will rise again.

"Fleas cannot kill the boar."

CHAPTER ONE:

Ten-year-old Tommy Conley gripped the bow rail too hard. That birthmark on his chest kept itching. He watched the ocean beyond the bowsprit for trouble as *The Finder* made way on its engines. He pretended to be a lookout but an unease ruined his game.

"Nothing's gonna happen," he said to convince himself.

The sea was a relaxing azure blue and flat-calm but anticipation had the crew of Captain Richard Wailer's salvage ship charged. Tommy had caught the treasure bug too when *Finder* entered the target zone. He wasn't the only kid onboard but the others weren't interested. Weeks at sea homeschooling took the wind out of the other kid's sails. They ignored progress, but not him. Tommy was just like his old man. *We're adventurers!* But this wasn't a real adventure. Tommy had read enough comics to know the difference.

Captain Rich side-scanned his way through the Sargasso Sea slow and steady following the path of the Spanish galleon, *Regal*. Whatever they found in international waters was theirs, be it *The Regal* or another wayward ship. Wailer's ace was an antique logbook written on *Regal's* escort ship, *The Bell*. She witnessed the sinking and Captain Wailer had their log. Dad's legendary good-luck also excited expectations. Captain Rich said *The Regal* had struck a submerged protrusion where none had been recorded then or since.

Tommy left the bow and found his way to the auxiliary sonar room where operator and ship's photographer, Amy Parks, was on look-out for real. A nagging feeling came over Tommy as he watched Amy's big screen. It was almost like what Dad described as his lucky feeling. Tommy ignored it and focused harder on the screen.

"Something's there…like a pixel ghost. What is that?" Tommy said, pointing at the screen. Gooseflesh pricked his forearms and that splotch on his chest felt hot.

Amy listened with headphones without watching the screens while awaiting pings to bounce off uncharted obstacles. She didn't expect to find anything. Amy removed her headgear and adjusted the scanner's image.

"It's shaped like a shark. It's too big, must be a whale shark," she said.

"Can you get a better picture?" Tommy asked. "There aren't supposed to be any around here."

"Good point, Squirt. The biology guys will think it's interesting. Adjusting side-scan." Amy had all eyes forward to avoid a collision. She adjusted the sonar pod's direction and followed the creature checking relative distance on scope. "Boy, that thing's huge," she said. "Bigger than our mini-sub…Hey, wait a minute. Pay dirt."

"What? What's that? It's a crown," Tommy said. A fuzzy submerged peak formed on screen showing long objects sticking up from the top. Amy adjusted until she ran out of dials. "Can't you get more?"

"Nope," she said. "Side-scans are mounted in blisters on the hull which limits rotation. The ship's sonar reaches wider but it's fixed. Doesn't give fine details anyway."

Tommy drew closer. "What'cha think that is?"

She didn't answer. Instead, she plucked a microphone off the bulkhead.

"Hey, I got something, it's off starboard three hundred yards plus. It's a pinnacle." PA speakers all over the vessel spilled the message. She let go of the microphone and mussed Tommy's hair. "Good eye, Squirt. We almost steamed right by it."

"I didn't do anything," Tommy said. But he felt strange. His heart beat funny. A new sensation, nothing like a lucky feeling, made his stomach jitter.

"You're a natural, just like your old man." Amy said.

Tommy didn't think so.

Dad was first to enter the topside auxiliary sonar room. He wasn't a big man but he filled the small room.

"Jesus Christ," Dad leaned in toward the scope. Tommy ducked. "There ain't supposed to be anything here. We're outside the banks. That's a freaking mountain."

"Underwater volcano," Amy Parks said. "Not on the charts, for sure. Maybe it's what sunk the Regal. I don't know…It's too deep. The peak is tiny, too. Erosion? It could've shrunk. If Regal hit it, she slid into the trench."

"Move aside, Tommy boy," Captain Rich said coming in. He gently pushed Tommy away but didn't make him leave. Now, the room was really stuffed. The captain's breath smelled like pickles. "That's it, gotta be. Amy, gin up the signal."

"Already did," she said.

Captain Rich picked up the com mic and called the bridge. He had them come about dead slow. Amy sent her refined coordinates to the bridge. The pilothouse confirmed a lock on it. Whatever Amy's equipment saw, the bridge got it too.

Amy tapped the sea chart screen mounted above the main scope. "We haven't reached our destination yet…It's too small to hold a wreck…Hey, that's weird…" Amy fiddled with the computer. "There's a structure on it, maybe a lifeboat. What're the chances?"

"What do you think, Bert?" The captain asked Thomas the Older. Everyone called Tommy's dad, Bert. People said he looked like Bert Lancaster, the old-time movie star.

Even in this dark tin-can room, Tommy saw bumps emerge on Dad's forearm as Dad scratched that birthmark on his chest. *Everyone says Dad's got a special talent but he's scared.* Tommy wasn't worried though. Dad found stuff nobody could. That's why Captain Rich hired him. *Dad has tons of Irish luck.*

Salvage ships go out for months on end and Dad wouldn't leave Mom and him behind. Only because Captain Rich let families come did Dad agree. *The Finder* was 180 feet long—a refit 1904 sailing and motorized ocean liner with art nouveau trim and room for three hundred. Dad called it, 'a floating city on a wild goose chase.' Dad was uneasy about boarding on departure day. He shifted from foot to foot scratching that birthmark over his heart on the dock saying, 'It's good money, easy money. It'll be fine, just fine.' Dad's invisible fleas were worried then the same as now.

Dad didn't answer the captain's question. He scratched his birthmark mumbling instead.

"Worth a look?" Captain Rich said, pressing for an answer. "What do you say? You're the good-luck charm. What's the problem?"

"Something's there. But I don't know." Dad said. "Something ain't right, can't put a finger on it." Dad patted his smoldering birthmark which got hot when he was uneasy. "I'm thinking there're bodies on it," Dad said. "Man, I got the willies. I'm a divemaster, not an undertaker." Dad's arm hair hackled. Tommy's neck hair stood in response.

Tapping his lower lip with one finger, Richard Wailer stared at the screen. He wore a well-trimmed gray-streaked beard, while Dad's was brown, scraggly, and disorganized. *Captain Rich got it together. He knows what he's doing.* The captain was a husky, imposing man over six-two while Dad was a 'half-pint' toothpick with a movie star's face. 'Nobody gets to be captain doing dumb things.' Dad always said. 'What the captain says goes. Always obey the captain' had been drilled into Tommy's head before boarding. At sea, safety is first.

Amy's equipment showed relative position. Coming about, the ship closed in. Captain Rich pulled the microphone off a bulkhead and hailed the bridge. "All stop. Ready stations, standby." He released the switch. "Amy, what're the numbers, can we anchor? What's the draft?"

"Peak's sixty feet below, the hull will clear room to spare. We're drafting thirty feet."

"Nothing ventured, nothing gained," the captain said. He slapped Dad's back before leaving.

Dad didn't look right, sweat beaded on his forehead, and his face went pale like somebody getting sea-sick and Dad never got sea-sick. Tommy felt woozy, too, but that was nothing new. He got sick when the seas were rough—no big deal. But this was the first time his knees went goofy on a dead-calm day.

Everyone exited the shed with Dad and Tommy last. Captain Rich took off striding aft along the promenade deck. Dad stopped, knelt, and addressed Tommy.

"You know this is risky business, diving, right?" Dad checked around but nobody was in ear-shot. "If anything happens…you'll take care of Mom for me, won't you? Can you do that? Promise."

"Come on, Dad. You're the best. Nothing can happen to you. You're special, you're… You're like Superman—"

"Stop. I'm not. Get that out of your head. This is real. This ain't magic. Its science. We're doing science. That's what keeps divers alive." Dad stood, dug out his pocket knife, and pulled off his Rolex. "Here, hold these for me."

"Bert! Shake a leg, will you?" Captain Rich called. Tommy felt the edge of Wailer's voice cut. Tommy's birthmark started itching.

Dad shoved his items into Tommy's hands. "Remember, I'm counting on you."

Dad took off for Captain Rich. He didn't have the captain's long legs but Dad was plenty quick. Tommy stuffed Dad's things deep into his cut-off jeans pocket.

"Shake a leg," The captain yelled.

Dad's legs were fine, it was Tommy's legs shaking. Dad hot-footed it aft. Tommy couldn't stop quivering long enough to follow. A dread came over him he never felt before. *But Dad's the lucky one?* He remained there alone midship battling confusion. Tommy's fears ground against reality. He didn't move until the launch's away crew swept him into their midst as they proceeded to the fantail.

The crew went to work. Tommy, tagging along, felt better by keeping busy. The crew asked him to spot the cables as they lowered the launch. Captain Rich didn't mind him rowing in the crew's wake. Tommy always helped when asked. The ship couldn't anchor so Captain Rich used an alternate plan.

Word was passed around. The anomaly rested on the entire head of that rise. The ship's anchors were too massive for it. The waters were otherwise too deep. Anchoring on the side of the volcano wouldn't work. The captain gave orders to hold station with the docking jets saying everything over the PA. He finished with, "It's not the best solution, but fine for a quick dive." Captain Rich was good about telling the crew everything.

The crew sent down *Finder*'s Remotely Operated Vehicle first for safety. Operations chatter came over the ship's PA system. The ROV pilot reported a local rip making it hard to hold station. Amy responded over the PA that the pictures were good. Once the ROV came back, Captain Rich called for a quick on-deck meeting. The away-crew met under the shade of the promenade deck's overhang. Amy Parks presented the images on her laptop.

"What's that look like to you?" Wailer asked the team archaeologist, Doctor Morgan.

Morgan was a marine biologist with a master's degree in archeology which impressed Tommy a lot. Morgan had spent half his teaching life on archaeological dives for Seaside University. Morgan liked to talk and he said his school 'needed divers more than jellyfish repairmen.' They made him dive so he quit. They didn't pay him enough to take risks. The captain touted his luck to have Morgan—two for the price of one. Marine biologists were common but ones with wreck diving experience weren't. Captain Rich said the grant money for biological sampling would come in handy.

Tommy heard the scuttlebutt about Richard Wailer's money so he didn't believe Captain Rich, the famous treasure hunter, would ever run out of cash.

"It doesn't look like any shipwreck I've seen," Morgan said. "See that?" He put a finger on Amy's screen. "That's not a ship's rib and it's too big to be a beam. This structure is rectangular, as in golden ratio. It's an offering building, a little chapel, similar to what we recovered off Crete. Wherever it was, it's on a sunken barge."

"Are you sure?" Wailer said. "A Greek temple?"

"I'm telling you, Rich, that's stone. It's not natural, either. You don't get flora growing on old wood like that. Wood doesn't last. The barge is gone but not its contents. Call it what you will, but it's stone, it's been worked, and it doesn't belong."

The captain eyeballed his geologist, Doctor Clark, and blew out a stream of air.

"Morgan's right," Doctor Clark said. "However, volcanoes do form similar deposits." He had piloted the ROV. "Columnar basalt can't form on peaks, however. Columns are normally hexagonal, not round. I've never seen vertical samples on a crater face, never in spaced rows. Flood basalt doesn't form this way. It's not natural."

"I see it," Amy said. "I'm bouncing signals. There's an outline under the silt." She scrolled the images. "That's a Greek column, it's fluted. This is crazy. Clark's right."

"Why would anyone tow a barge this far out of shipping lanes?" The captain asked himself aloud. "To hide something," he answered. "Must be worthwhile. Some well-moneyed son of a bitch—sorry Tommy—bought himself a Greek temple and lost it. Temples have statues worth more than brass cannons. Easy money. Objections? No? That's it. Let's hit it people."

The meeting broke up. *The Finder* had cranes midsection and, on her fantail, but they weren't normally used for salvage. The fantail was once tennis courts until Wailer had it refitted for deck storage. He parked his twenty-six-foot sailboat and launches there. Everything was blocked up and chained to the deck. The aft crane lifted the mini-sub out of the hold and moved the other crafts into the sea with ease. The lift had enough power to hoist statues if it had to.

The dive-boat hit water. It carried a smaller salvage crane. Tommy's excitement grew as the operation came together. The process was exactly like the underwater excavations he had read about in *Marine Archeology Digest*. Pictures of huge, submerged Egyptian statues were in the magazine. Tommy followed along and watched Captain Rich watching his people. The captain barked like a sea-dog and got no sass from the crew. Dad, on the other hand, waddled from leg to leg tapping that birthmark on his chest, sweat running down his long nose.

"Bert, not convinced?" Wailer said.

"I've been wrong before."

The captain eyed Dad while tapping his lip until Dad gave a thumb up. "That's it, we'll dive. Drop float anchors, ball weights. That rip is trouble. Recharge the ROV, we'll use it to record the dive. Restock the dive-boat. Test your gear. Report when all is ready."

Wow, this is a real adventure and I'm in it. Tommy should have been excited, but Dad's worry worried him. Tommy's chest felt funny, and he should say something, but Mom was busy, as usual, in the map-room. Her job had to do with reading old scrolls. He wished Mom had come to the dive meeting, but she didn't dive, so what the heck, why bother?

****

Wailer played the procedures over in his mind looking for red flags as the dive-boat loaded gear. *The staging crew will set marker floats attached by strong tethers to less destructive ball anchors. Next the ziplines get attached to the mains for transporting finds. After, they'll send down baskets on ziplines. Pull a ripcord and the balloon's gas-charge fires sending the basket topside. Ziplines run parallel to float anchor lines. The first dive team will ready the basket lines before they return. No need to decompress loads—airbags send them fast. Setup divers should only stay long enough to avoid decompression. Divemaster Bert will take his time safety checking and installing the search grid to maximize recovery divers work-time. Sixty feet requires a decompression hold at the first knot, thirty-two feet. Decompression time depends on the length of stay.*

That's Bert's territory. Richard didn't have the timing down like Bert. The captain called down to the launch crew after he finished racking his brain before they shoved off.

"Make sure the balloon gas charges are full. Eyes open. No mistakes!"

The depth at sixty feet wasn't bad. Holding time at mid-station won't be long. No sharks on sonar, nothing nasty hitting the outbound chum pots, no shark cage needed. One less issue. His divemaster was the kind to max site-time. He didn't like Bert's habit of cutting it too damn close, but if that's what it took to safe-off, so be it. *If he's late he'll pay. How Conley survived that cave dive without getting the bends makes him either lucky or a mermaid.*

***

Tommy rode over on the dive-boat, S*ea Flower*, and stayed out of the way. He knew Mom watched him from *The Finder* on camera. *Sea Flower's* wide beam and 35-foot length made it stable for winches. Lots of room on board for Tommy to keep out of the way. He knew the drill. When baskets are hauled on board midship, Amy takes pictures before the find is touched. More pictures again after it's removed and processed. She ran the ROV's cameras remotely while Doctor Clark drove it. Everything done according to convention. Ship's archaeologist supervised the recovery. *Everybody's busy, all-hands-on-deck.*

Captain Rich lets people do their jobs without hanging on them. Tommy's job was to stay clear. He hung out while Dad dressed on the bench next to the ROV control station. The anchor setup divers were back. Tommy helped Dad check everything. Safety comes first, but rechecking that many times seemed silly.

"Dad, you alright?" Tommy asked. "Maybe you shouldn't go? What if something happens?"

"I'm going, it's my job. I'll be fine." Dad said testing gear for the sixth time. "Not that deep. I'll be fine. It's fine, just fine. I've free-dived deeper."

"Watch with me," Amy said. "ROV's down. Camera's good, visibility 80 feet, we'll watch your dad work, OK, Squirt?"

Amy's ROV camera station was inside a small booth on deck next to the operator. Her 35MM camera was on the dash waiting to take photos. This little stand-in cabin was open to the air but hot inside the booth. Even so, Tommy shivered. *What if Dad gets tangled in the cables?* Diving is dangerous. Dad wore only one tank. He wasn't supposed to stay long. What if he got stuck? Someone sent down the stake-out materials, spikes, ropes and a hammer, in a recovery basket.

The all-go was given. Dad and his dive partner, Dave, stepped off the aft platform and proceeded down. Tommy watched the divers descend by way of the ROV's camera. Amy's monitor caught everything. Fish ignored the divers. Tommy wished he could fish, but nothing that might entangle a diver was allowed over the side. The ROV didn't get close either, rather, it hovered twenty feet off the structure in open water. They had to push against the rip which sailed up and over the top. Kelp wavered on the rise like flags in the wind.

Dad and his dive-buddy had still water closer to the mountain's surface. Marking out the perimeter went easy. The fluorescent border ropes stood out sharply. They got the grid-lines set in under twenty minutes. Dad earned a thin slice of spare time to check things over.

Captain Rich's voice came over the com once in a while after he took the dinghy back to *Finder*. Tommy wasn't the only one listening and watching the ROV's live feed. It played on every monitor. The archaeologist gave directions in the diver's headsets but everyone heard. Dad reported the perimeter had paving blocks, a collapsed wall, maybe. The columns supported a rock slab roof. It didn't seem stable to Tommy. It was hard to know the true condition with everything covered in seaweed. Finally, near the end of the timed dive, Dad asked Morgan if he could go inside. The ROV's camera zoomed. A white-stone altar deep within the structure came into focus. Nothing on it, not even kelp.

Moran's voice came on. "Quick look then you get the hell out, copy?"

Dad's voice came on. "Timing out. I'm going in while I can."

"What about Dave?" Captain Rich said of the other diver.

The other driver didn't have a transmitter. Dad tapped his wrist. Dave checked his watch. He indicated assent and Dad gave a thumb's up. Dave started up the rope on his way to decompress at the 32-foot knot.

"I got three minutes, going in," Dad said over the PA.

"Amy, Ted, move the ROV in," The captain said. "Bert, be careful."

The ROV camera zoomed in but Tommy couldn't see much. Encrusted stonework disappeared and the back of Dad's headgear filled the shot. Amy adjusted as the ROV moved sideways. Dad reached under. Tommy could swear he saw a little green light under the table.

"It's an altar for sure." Amy said over the com.

Dad moved in deeper. "Got something. Going in for it…What the hell?…Inside…Tight hole. Shit! I'm stuck. I can't let go."

"Let it go," Wailer said over the PA.

"Screw that! Send a tank…Wait…It's moving…I have never seen…Got it, I got it! Coming up."

The ROV backed out just ahead of Dad but the video feed blinked in and out. Amy reported on com the ROV's camera cord came loose. The next thing Tommy made out was Dad pulling a basket's ripcord sending it skyward.

"I got thirty seconds. I'm going back. Might be more."

The balloon broke the surface. Deckhands scrambled trying to gaff the basket to winch it aboard. Somebody hooked the swinging basket and lost it. The basket had cleared the water but out of nowhere, the sea rolled pitching the boat. A sudden gale blew. The basket swung outbound spinning wildly over the ocean. Tommy, distracted by deck activities, ignored the monitors.

"Watch the screen for me, Squirt," Amy said, grabbing her film camera, "Be right back."

Tommy took the ROV's camera joystick and zoomed to where Dad should be, but he wasn't there. The camera switched off and on as Tommy widened his search.

"Time, Bert! Come up, you're done. We got it. Bert…Bert? Respond!" The captain said, "Where the hell he'd go? Goddamn it, sweep the cameras!"

Tommy frantically moved the camera around, finding nothing until something big, some kind of fish, swam too close filling the camera's view. It collided with the ROV and the camera winked out. Tommy blinked, clearing his eyes in disbelief while deckhands yelled back and forth all at once. Captain Rich screamed orders over the

PA. Tommy let go of the joystick and backed out of the booth leaving Doctor Clark muttering curses.

"Rover's main cable detached!" Doctor Clark yelled from the remote-control station.

"Blow the tanks," Wailer ordered over the PA.

Tommy turned to the gunwales. Just aft new divers frantically suited up. Dave broke the surface. The water below churned from the ROV's blown ballast. Below surface visibility zero. The ROV's cables retracted spooling fast. The sub was out of control. A diver mounted the platform to help Dave. Seconds ticked. Bubbles boiled at the surface. The basket swayed out of control. The wind had stopped after that first blast but rogue waves continued. Somebody yelled, "shark!" Everything happened all at once and in slow-motion at the same time.

"Secure that basket before somebody gets killed!" the PA blared.

Tommy's heart thumped out of time with the swinging basket as he clung to the gunwale waiting for Dad to reach the surface. Hoping, crying, he looked on. The basket slipped the crewman's pole-hook and swung inboard, nearly taking Tommy's head off. He fell backward hitting the deck hard. *Sea Flower* yawled the other way. A glint of gold and green flashed in the sun as the basket passed over again. More men engaged gaffs and pulled the basket in. It cleared the rails and somebody lowered it. It hung a foot above deck banging on the sidewall. The swells ceased, but the boat still rocked. Amy rushed in snapping pictures but the boat pitched and she lost her balance. Amy fell and landed face first on the deck just missing the basket.

A diver went in. Tommy leaned way over the top rail but was unable to see below. He searched until the diver resurfaced. The diver wasn't gone long. Captain Rich had come over in a fast dingy and boarded without Tommy's notice until Wailer joined Tommy's vigil at the rail.

"Goddamn it, Bert! Where in the hell are you!" Captain Rich kicked a sidewall.

Tommy remained fixed on the gunwale. Wailer paced, yelling orders. Tommy couldn't move. His hands gripped so hard he marked the teak with his fingernails and it hurt. But he couldn't let go. Amy laid a hand on his shoulder, breaking Tommy's grip on the rail. He turned inboard. The sun backlit her and she glowed. Power radiated from her like a goddess. He blinked tears from his eyes and the goddess was gone.

"I'm sorry Tommy," Amy said, wiping tears away, "He's not coming back, he's down too long."

"What the hell are you doing?" Wailer boomed as the rescue diver lifted himself onto the platform. "You can't leave him, go get him!"

The diver spit out his mouthpiece. "No way! Biggest shark I ever saw! No freaking way," He kicked off his fins and let them float away before stepping into the splash-well. "I hate sharks!"

Captain Rich ran forward and punched the control shack. "Damn it, damn it all." Turning to the basket: "This, all this, for a trinket!" He snatched the glowing artifact out of the basket. "Ouch, it burned me! It burns!" He dashed it on the deck. It bounced and flew through the scupper port, next to Tommy, and into the sea.

That artifact leaving the ship jolted Tommy to his core. Sadness and grief had glued him to the rail, but that thing shooting out of the scupper broke his heart.

Without a thought, Tommy mounted the gunwale even as a Great White bumped the *Flower* just under him. Tommy dove. *I gotta save Dad's piece.*

What came over Tommy was a compulsion he did not understand. He wasn't brave. He liked the safety of his cabin cocoon stuffed with dinosaur books, and puzzles. The other kids had climbed the mainmast up to the crow's nest but he refused. He wouldn't take the risk. He read adventure stories never expecting to have one himself. This wasn't supposed to be an adventure.

Tommy swam fast. Even though the artifact glinted gold, somehow, he reached the heavy object. He snatched the chain and its medallion as it fluttered above an abyss. His lungs begged. He never dove this deep before. His chest burned on deck but forty feet below it felt like lava. He rolled on his back, out of air.

The sun seemed too far above; the dive boat's shape was very small. The water had cleared. Tiny faces looked over the side. *I'll never reach it.* A shark bumped him from below, testing its food. He imagined the shark pushing him toward the surface.

Tommy accepted his dying dream. *See you soon Dad.* 'Everything's fine, just fine.' He exhaled. Bubbles encased him. Behind closed eyes, a beautiful goddess adorned in gold and silver armor beckoned him. Her green robes floated, hailing him. He reached for her with the chain wrapped in his fingers and blacked out.

***

"Darndest thing I ever saw, Doc," Captain Rich said. "Shark launched him clear out of the water. Landed on deck."

Tommy opened his eyes and found himself in bed surrounded by crewmen, Mom holding his hand. The ship's doctor, Jane Smith was bent over him. The captain stood behind Mom. Tommy was in the infirmary.

"I'm not dead." He whispered.

"He checks out," Doctor Smith said. She shrugged. "Could have been worse. Plenty of bruises, no cuts, no bites. You're one lucky young man."

Mom embraced him. They cried together over Dad's passing. Captain Rich stood back with a stiff face, but he cried, too. After a time, the ship's doctor, fighting tears herself, asked them all to leave. The captain and Smith remained as the rest filed out.

"Do what the doctor says, "Mom said, stopping at the door before leaving.

"Tommy, it's OK. You can let go now," Doc said. "Your hand. Release your fist."

Tommy clutched something. His hand was shut tighter than a seafood market clam. With effort, he let his fingers relax one by one. That fluttering jewel wasn't a dream.

Tommy lifted it by its chain. An amulet dangled before him but it was smaller than he remembered in the basket. Tommy held it further away, a dime-sized green gemstone set in a quarter-size gold disk. The rim had four raised points spaced like a compass. The outer ring held symbols in between raised points.

"What's this writing?" Tommy said. "There were two. What gives?"

He could have sworn there were two disks in the recovery basket. But he wasn't sure. Doc Smith held an open hand under it waiting for Tommy to drop it. Instead, Tommy drew it back, gathered it close to his chest and closed his fist tight.

"I'm never letting it go, never," Tommy cried.

The captain bent closer. "Tommy, that's ship's-property, but you keep it. Don't tell anyone or they'll all want souvenirs. Get some rest." Captain Rich backed away and stopped at the door. "I swear, Tommy, I'll make this up to you. I'll cover your education, all of it, whatever you need. I promise."

Wailer hung his head and left. The doctor followed.

They made landfall two weeks later at St. John. Tommy and Mom flew home. He and Mom got the full story of what took place from the crew as the weeks passed on their way into port. Before landfall on St. John, Mom made Tommy promise to never do anything so risky again. Over and over Mom had chided him, "Diving into shark-infested waters! My word I almost lost you! Never, never, do anything like that again! You must swear it to me."

Tommy made the promise but an oath wasn't necessary. Dad had starkly set the example of what not to do. Besides, Mom became his responsibility. What would happen to her if something happened to him? *Take no risks, safe is best.* Dad's mandate churned inside him. 'Take care of your mom, promise.' Dad's last words echoed in Tommy's soul.

****

Tommy took to wearing the amulet every day once home. He didn't think magic was real but he had a silly notion that the charm protected him. It didn't like being left behind in his junk box with the old coins, fossils, and odd rocks he collected. After Tommy settled in at a middle school, Mom wanted his jewel gone.

"It's too hard on me," she said. "It reminds me of that dreadful day. We…I need to move on. You'll get mugged. I'll get rid of it if you insist on wearing it."

"Fine, alright Mom, you win. I'll put it away." Tommy said, but he wasn't ready to lay it aside.

That argument went on for two and a half years. His solution was to wear it so she couldn't see it until she caught on. After that, he kept it at home, but somehow it always showed up on him. She saw that too. He had to leave it home or she'd get mad, but leaving it, he hid it away from her. He didn't know why but he was afraid she'd do something to it.

On the night she got serious about taking it, they had a big fight. He wore it to bed one last time. The chain belonged around his neck. It gave him energy or something. Yet when he woke, the charm was gone. He should have been angry, but he felt released instead.

Mom had enough problems. Tommy didn't want to add troubles to her plate so he kept his trap shut. He thought then that she had taken it while he slept.

Since *Finder*, that birthmark on his chest grew. Only natural, Tommy thought. A few weeks after losing the amulet and turning age thirteen, his birthmark darkened. It appeared the same as Dad's. Same pinkish brown, raised a little, and disk-shaped. He didn't tell Mom it had changed or that he was proud of it.

The amulet never left Tommy's mind. When he occasionally asked to see it, Mom swore up and down, she didn't have it. He wasn't one to argue. His policy was to avoid conflicts. He wanted to remember Dad by it. It was the last thing Dad had touched. Tommy wasn't convinced it was gone. Feeling brave, after high school graduation, he pressed her hard and asked for it back. He accused her of taking it. That stopped her cold.

"Dad's mark is enough, uncanny you have one like his. You inherited his splotch," she said. "That's all the reminder you need. Dad's inside you. He's there over your heart. He's with us…in spirit. He lives on in you. I gotta believe that.'"

She cried and cried. He let her answer stand although it wasn't the answer he wanted. Tom didn't believe in spirits, ghosts, or gods, but, in a way, she was right. It was better to move on. Money was tight, maybe she sold it. University isn't cheap. Wailer's scholarship didn't cover everything. Besides, he had Dad's watch and penknife. Tom knew himself as practical. He didn't believe in chasing ghosts.

"It's better this way." He told her. "You're right, Ma. I gotta move on."

Tom thought his life was straight ahead and not in the past. But he was wrong.

CHAPTER TWO:

FIFTEEN YEARS LATER

Tom couldn't stand hanging around the apartment where he and Mom lived. After Dad died Mom became unstable. He spent his home-time in his beat-up class-C camper out in the parking lot of the apartment complex. He parked it next to his Jeep project junker. Mom's place was on the second floor. Her balcony was in sight of the 1978 Dodge. He had to keep an eye on her. But they both needed space. The camper had been Dad's so Tom kept it running although it was well past its prime.

As a child, he and his skater friends played in the old camper. In his teen years, the plan switched to inviting girls inside. The girls weren't convinced and he couldn't blame them. The old truck was ugly on the outside although decent inside. He had driven it for his driver's license test. The driver's ed teacher wasn't amused. He drove it whenever he had gas money. Why not? Tom loved old things. Robbers didn't bother with his rolling junk pile Jeep either.

The closer he got to finishing at university, the more time he spent inside the old truck. *Mom does better when I'm not around.* Mom would bounce back when he went away on field trips. Living with her bipolar wasn't easy for either of them.

Tom checked the wall clock. The battery had died. He didn't wear the wristwatch. It was Dad's watch and sacrosanct. Mom insisted it was lucky, but Tom didn't want to get mugged by wearing it. Dad's good-luck piece wasn't lucky for Dad. He left it behind the day he died. *There's no magic in anyone's watch or anything else.*

Luck didn't exist. One makes his own luck was Tom's attitude. Tom wore the watch when it was safe to do so. He liked it too much to risk losing it. How many poor people wear a Rolex? It didn't impress his advisor but he had a need for its luck today. No getting around it, he had to go upstairs and get it. *Why not borrow the car while I'm at it?*

Tom let himself in and found Mom vibrating in her chair. Her oversized sweat suit hid her skinny frame but not her mania. The do-rag enhanced her poverty ensemble. The house wasn't a mess for a change. Mom's depression had abated. Her height of five foot ten inches didn't show with her sunk into the rocker. Depression folded her down so small she'd pass for a leprechaun. Uncoiled mania brought on hurricane cleaning jags. Energy radiated off her.

"Thought you were going to school?" Mom said.

"Forgot my watch. I have an appointment with Dithers. The truck needs gas I was hoping—"

"Ellen called. You're supposed to stop by the protest with brochures. I'm going out today."

"Going out?" *Crap, I need her car.* "I guess I'll drive the truck, it's hard to park on campus and—"

"Relax, Speedy. I got a ride," she said with snap in her voice. "You know where the keys are."

She's pissed but not at me. Tom's walking on eggshells dance wasn't over yet. There were plenty of eggs left. Her unpredictable phase usually kicked on right after switching moods.

Tom proceeded into his old bedroom. He hardly ever stayed there, even in winter. All his kid stuff was stashed in the closet except for the cartoon character linens. His meager adult belongings were in the camper. The Rolex, the only valuable thing he owned, was kept on the dresser for safety. Mom put it there whenever he left it out. It ended up in his room no matter how messy the house. Mom kept a better track of it than he did. He put it on and set the alarm for his appointment. No point hanging around. He figured he'd drop by the protest early, hang out, and maybe do a few other things at Old U before seeing Dithers.

"You sure it's fine to take the car?" Tom said coming out into the living room.

"It's not the car, it's my car. Your inheritance has not yet come." She rocked out of the chair and stood in one motion. "I must get my ass in gear. Don't forget to set the car alarm."

Tom grabbed the keys but stopped before the front door and got his skateboard out of the coat closet.

"Oh no, you don't," Mom said. "That thing makes a bad impression. I swear, Tom. You're twenty-five. Don't you think it's time to knock off skateboarding?"

Tom held onto his board anyway. "I'll leave it in the car."

She went into her room and shut the door but called out. "Tommy, don't forget to set the car alarm."

Set the car's alarm? That Honda was too old. It had no value. Nobody wanted parts off a 15-year-old, four-door. She bought it with the life insurance settlement and loved that car more than it deserved. It took years to get the money out of the insurance company. If Wailer hadn't fronted the cash, she'd still be riding buses. Tom left without saying goodbye.

Her key fob was a coin medallion, a gift from Wailer to him when Tom graduated high school. He got his driver's license that same week. Tom trashed Wailer's little gift but Mom pulled it out of the can. It was real gold. Tom told himself, I'm not into treasure like Wailer. Tom hated to admit it but that fob was cool as hell. Its mounted coin came off a sunken Spanish Galleon.

Tom still hated Wailer and he chastised himself for thinking that way—that fob wasn't cheap. It wasn't Wailer's fault Dad died. The man had made good on his promise. Wailer was a decent man. He supported good causes, and Tom's education, but Tom couldn't let go.

Tom's chest hurt whenever reminded of Wailer. Thinking about school brought ill feelings for the patron of his education. He stuffed the hate back where it belonged into his despair pit. Mom called depression her pit. He wouldn't let the pit defeat him the way it did Mom.

CHAPTER THREE:

MARY AND RICHARD

Mary rocked in her thrift store lounge chair clamping down anxiety. Richard had called asking to come over. She moved the lounger around to face the door. Not easy when her small apartment was cluttered. Tommy wasn't home. She planned it that way. Her boy kept his room neat even when the rest of the house resembled an explosion in a mattress factory. Tommy wasn't the disorganized type.

"Must be magic," she joked to herself. "He didn't get it from me."

Her son was out more than in lately and that improved her nerves. He didn't need to be underfoot. Did his shoebox full of boyhood treasures hold him? Tommy spent his days at school or in the field. But he invented reasons to stay home when he should be out partying and chasing coeds.

"You're too damn responsible, Tommy."

His excuses were timing out. Mary couldn't wait for him to get out on his own. *I'm the one who never leaves. I'm who needs her things around her.*

"You gotta stop swimming in quicksand," she told herself.

Bipolar wouldn't allow her a normal existence. Richard's stipend was a life line. She couldn't hold down a job. The life insurance ran dry and disability didn't pay much. She owed Richard for that and a lot more. She hated depending on him. Embarrassed, she didn't want to see him, but he had asked.

"Begging dogs must heel."

Mary had had enough therapy to know herself. Meds made her mind into mashed oatmeal so she stopped using them. She needed to think, especially now. A level head suited better dealing with Richard. But unmedicated, the chest-hammer of mania floated just below her surface threatening a panic attack. Mania beat the hell out of The Pit. When the door knock came her insides jumped but she didn't move.

The knock came again, harder. *He is a forceful man.* "Mary, you in there?"

"Yes, yes. Coming."

Mary rocked upright out of the chair and flattened the wrinkles of her mint green skirt. She dressed today: white silk blouse, light summer skirt, and makeup. She used oversized sweatpants and loose tops to hide her anorexic tendencies. Going out, and not for therapy, felt damn good even if it was with him. She checked her hair in the mirror by the door. She had stopped growing it long. It was still silk-pretty although worry had eroded her fertile scalp. Her hair wasn't as thick and strong as it used to be.

Opening the door, her breath caught. She had expected his driver. Richard, as tall and handsome as ever, produced an authentic smile. Dapper in a sports jacket and tie, he had hardly changed–only a little grayer around the temples. His square jaw hadn't sagged. His hair and beard had only gotten sexier over the years. *I'm a dish-rag and he's a fresh, hot towel. I'm forty-five and used up. Why isn't he?*

Mary straightened her back and extended a hand. Years in that chair watching soap stories on TV made her spine weak, yet it was her knees threatening to give out.

"You look well," he said, taking her hand and kissing the back. "The place is much less…chaotic."

He remained in the hall.

"I'm off meds, if that's what you mean. Last time I saw you, I was a zombie." Most of their communication over the years had been by phone. She resisted touching her face, not wanting to smudge the makeup. "Will you come in?"

"No, we don't have time. Amy might not make it through the day."

"Why Richard? Why are we doing this? I haven't seen her since Bert died."

Richard flinched at the mention of Bert's death but didn't answer. That day still pained him the same as it did her, she assumed. *Good, let him suffer.*

"I'll be right with you," she said.

She didn't need his answer. Mary got her handbag and spare keys off the hook, although she didn't need the handbag. Richard will pay for lunch like everything else. She kept that to herself. Richard's scholarship wasn't a family secret, but she didn't want Tommy depending on him for everything. Living with a beggar's hand outstretched isn't any way to live. *I won't let Tommy step into Richard's snare the way me and Bert did.*

Downstairs, his driver stood ready and opened her door on the sedan. She entered the back seat. Richard didn't bring the limo, but this common sedan had a glass partition. The driver couldn't hear them. One didn't drive a limo into this part of Midhurst, not if one valued the hubcaps and everything else attached to them.

Richard slid in next to her. "Mary, I'd like you to consider—"

She put a hand over his mouth. "I know what you want, you can't have him. Tommy graduated. He'll find something on his own. I need…He needs independence. He's not working for you. Got it?"

Richard had agreed to pull funding to force Tommy off his ass and into life, but of course, Richard would also provide a job for Tommy if she let him. She was surprised Richard went along with stopping the money. If Richard had any other ideas about Tom's future, she didn't want to hear it.

"That's not why I'm here." Richard exhaled a puff of air. "Amy, remember? Listen, she is more than sick. Amy's dying and she has something she needs to tell us, both of us."

"I'm sure it's in the back of your mind. You paid for Tommy's schooling. You'll want something from him. You can't have it. My husband died chasing your wild dreams. You owe us this."

Richard winced, and in doing so, he looked 100 years older. His crows' feet ran deep.

"I'm not arguing that with you, Mary. I'll help Tommy any way I can, you know that. Out of respect for you, I won't have him join my expeditions. Those were the conditions you set. I'll honor it. Yet, I can still—"

Mary held up a hand. "Stop, just stop."

Richard had that look, that all-knowing look. Filthy rich Richard knows all and sees all but he is still blind. The moneyed get what they want. He raised a finger. *Here it comes.*

"Look, Mary. I promised him. I know people in academia. What about a good job not working for me? It's tough out there. His grades aren't good."

"I know. Universities and governments, that's how you get what you want…" She flipped her hand dismissively.

Mary's suspicions were well-founded. Richard Wailer had claws into everything, a regular blood-sucking capitalist octopus. All that for his stupid spiritual quest—his big secret. Everything he did was associated with it. Below the skin, he wasn't a business-man doing business. She had figured him out, but intuition doesn't pay the bills. Jobs were hard to find. The car proceeded on for a few minutes in silence.

"Come on, Mary. I owe him."

"I suppose…If you stay away from him. Sure, fine. Do what you can. Nothing dangerous. I won't have you put him at risk. It's bad enough you…" *Killed my husband,* she finished in her head.

Richard had been leaning toward her, now he pushed back. The leather seat squeaked like a rat fart. The smell of his resentment wafted in the air.

"I told you I won't do that. Have I ever lied?"

"All the time," she said under her breath.

His face changed from angry to thoughtful. The anger evaporated fast. He leaned toward her again. "Cards out, I have a request. I'd like to see that amulet, the one Tommy brought up. I gave it to him, remember?"

"How can I forget?" Mary snapped. "I told you years ago. It's gone, lost. Okay?" This was about his spiritual quest. A lot of bullshit in her mind, but she owed the patron some respect. "I'm sorry, Richard. I wish I could help."

"Tell me again. How it was lost?"

"He wore it all the time. I didn't like it. It reminded me of what happened. He had it on that same gold chain. He wore it every night. I swear that medallion shrank."

Don't feed his mythology. She paused to rearrange her skirt. His relentless blue eyes remained on her.

"I told him he'd get ripped off. He saw the wisdom. After, he'd only wear it to bed, his dream-catcher. Never had nightmares wearing it but one night he had a big one, a night terror, a real doozy. I went in. He woke up crying. That's how I knew it was gone. Ridiculous, I know. Next day, I searched. It was well and good gone, disappeared. He accused me! Maybe he tossed it in his sleep. Windows were open."

"How did he react once he realized it was missing? What did he feel? Hormones aren't all a 13-year-old feels."

"I don't know. He never said anything about it. I was in a bad way… Things weren't clear to me. Over-medicated. I think he accepted it. Tommy didn't make a stink… He knew I was hurting. He's a good boy."

Richard listened, carefully tapping his lower lip with a finger all the while, but his eyes seemed far away as if he was piecing a distant puzzle together. Did he regret giving it away? It can't be worth more than he can afford to lose? Mary wouldn't ask. Asking opened doors. She wasn't interested in crossing new thresholds. There was a time when she would have barged on through. Richard shrank into his seat without another question.

The rest of the ride went quiet. She had nothing more to say other than arguments. How many times can one thank the patron of her son's education? When the car entered the hospice's long driveway, he pushed upright and adjusted his cuffs.

Mary's mania was stark but she wasn't out of control yet. Rather, she was in a good place for the moment. A panic attack wasn't coming soon. In this state, her mind became needlepoint sharp. Even so, the idea of facing Amy's deathbed threatened to drag her back into the pit. She hoped not. She wanted to hear what Amy had to say. Amy was kind to Tommy when he was a boy.

CHAPTER FOUR:

TOM AT SCHOOL

Tom wheeled Mom's old Honda into the faculty parking lot slow and easy. His days of hotrod driving were over. He had to show respect. But still, he wasn't ready to cut his scruffy skateboarder's hair short. He still felt like more of a student than a teacher. If he got his way, this wouldn't be the last time he parked there. He planned to trade that adjunct's spot for a regular staff parking space. Until then, it was the far end of the lot for him. He also had a long walk across campus. He shut the motor off, reached back, ignored his skateboard, and grabbed the box of brochures.

"This isn't good." He had meant to bring a suit and change in his basement office. He wanted to look decent for his meeting with Dithers.

His dress shoes were there but that's all. Loafers didn't work with his regular duds. His worn-out skate shoes matched the rest of him. The suit didn't matter. His jeans and cowboy shirts were as much a part of the scenery at Old U as the antique university buildings. Six years on campus made him a fixture. Why not make it permanent?

He crossed the lower grounds and mounted the stairs up to the old section of campus, built on high ground before canals and water management began. He didn't like the newer campus buildings put up in the 1960s. Light tan bricks the color of baby poop and the buildings' blocky forms had the appeal of a monochromatic Lego set.

At the head of the stairs, he stopped to drink in the old. Tom loved old. The smell of dust pumping out of the roof vents of the 19th century buildings floated his boat. Tom often wondered what was inside those forgotten attics. Lights never shone out of Old U's doghouse-dormers.

Campus's original six stone buildings were spread around a 150-yard circle. Typical of the era, wood timber framing maxed out at five stories, steel frame buildings didn't exist yet. Stone and big timber construction ruled the era. The field stones were local. The limestone stairsteps were imported but native woods took care of the rest. Tom was in love with the neoclassical corneous work. He didn't care for Victorian gingerbread. Greek pediments were his cup of tea. Old U's original hard-pine dentil moldings, freeze boards, and egg-and-dart fascia topped the walls below wide overhanging eaves. The original Yankee gutters made of native copper still worked. Neoclassical was all the rage in the 1840s and that spice fit Old U.

He inhaled again tasting fresh-cut grass, ivy, flowers, and moss before setting foot on the only modern intrusion of the old campus, a concrete walkway. Great for skateboarding but Tom preferred the cobblestones. He had no plans to go anywhere.

Leaving's too hard, why do it? He dropped the box of leaflets under his arm thinking it was his skateboard.

"Oops," He picked up the brochures and set out.

The Round was situated in the middle of Old Campus with giant oaks hiding the modern buildings beyond. Tom rounded a low stone utility building and took the Parkway to the Round where the weekly protests were held. Tom and his crew called it the Parkway because skaters had used it for a freeway since the 60s. He should knock off skating. Sweaty and carrying a skateboard wasn't the best way to arrive at class.

Ellen and Bob were at the anti-war table on the grass under a big oak. The protest space wasn't much of a protest. A dozen fold-up canopies were usually spread around with different groups spouting different gripes but the place was nearly empty being late summer. It seemed more like a sideshow-barker complex than a serious effort to make a difference.

The Peace Project's booth wasn't the only tent there. A few others were dotted around the cement pad's perimeter. School had designated the Round as the free-speech zone. Every cause had petitions on hand when campus was busy. Tom hadn't manned the booth for a while and he felt guilty. Although, at this time of year, getting signatures and handing out pamphlets was harder than extracting bone from hard rock.

"Leave it to a business major to overdress," Tom said arriving. Bob wore a light-blue summer weight Brooks Brothers suit. Why not? His rich parents paid for it. "What's next, trick paint on your skate deck?" Bob's new board, already well scuffed, leaned against the table.

"How's it hanging man?" Bob said. Tom stuck out his hand. "Where's your ride?"

"The car. It's hanging, I guess. I hope it hangs on long and hard," Tom said thinking of his academic career.

"This is not the place to masturbate," Ellen said dead-pan. "That bush over there isn't occupied, I know, I just used it." Her light flowery summer dress and girl-next-door face juxtaposed her remarks.

"That's what I get for dating a theater major," Bob said. "Bad jokes. How's the job prospects?"

"Berkeley hasn't called," Tom said. "They want doctorates which gave me an idea. I'll get there yet."

He said it to them, but not to Mom. Let her think he's moving on. He wasn't budging. He'd hang there, near Chicago, and keep an eye on her. *She's pushing me out for my sake but what about her?* Mom needed help, true. But he had to admit he just wasn't ready to leave Old U, his home away from home.

"What's the plan?" Bob said.

"I'm sticking around. But, if Berkeley calls, I'm gone like a hotdog fart."

"You do make plenty of hot wind," Ellen said. "Tommy, for real, back off the beer-nuts and hotdogs."

"She has a point," Bob said. "How do you stay so thin eating that crap?"

"Lucky, I guess. You guys need a bathroom break, better do it. I've got a meeting. Here're the brochures." He dropped the box on the table.

Tom stayed with the booth long enough to allow Ellen and Bob to go for chow. The student cafeteria wasn't bad. Tom ate there often and mostly the same fare, whatever was cheap, usually hot dogs. As an adjunct, even part-time, he could use the faculty lunchroom but he wasn't comfortable there being a recent graduate. Tom stayed with Bob and Ellen until his Rolex chimed.

Why's my birthmark got to start itching now? Dithers will think I smoke crack.

Teaching the summer adjunct slot was great but the job ended too soon. Professor Cross came back from maternity leave. Tom had a plan and felt good about what he'd ask Dithers for once his knees stopped knocking. *How can he say no?* Having worked at Great Lakes University summer programs, he figured he had a lock with his freshly achieved double master's degrees. He took the summer fill-in with high hopes. Nobody on staff wanted it. He took the substitute job expecting inroads. But somehow, his will-do attitude failed to morph into a fall placement.

"Dithers loves me," he told his friends in parting. "He won't pass me up." Tom took off for Dithers' office playing over everything in his mind.

His archeology and paleontology degrees were wrapped up. He had his teaching certification. Ready for work although he wasn't crazy about classroom teaching, being the field instructor type. *With a doctorate, Berkeley will beg me to come.* All he needed was a thicker sheepskin. He applied to Berkeley three times and got nowhere. *I'm not ready anyway and more school's a perfect excuse to stay.* He had a clearer vision. Tom thought he finally had it together. Admin didn't have a job for him so why not stay anyhow? Why not push for the doctorate? Tom wasn't ready for a full-time job with its risks and responsibilities. Staying was safe.

Tom's advisor, Doctor Dithers, had his door open when Tom arrived in the reception area. Dithers, on the phone, frowned when Tom plopped into one of the waiting area's vintage chairs.

Tom admired the ancient paneling while waiting. Admin was in the oldest university building of the Midwest. The imported paneling came out of a 14th-century French rectory. The founders began shipping in old world materials soon after commissioning the campus, over land, before the Erie Canal was dug, while the Indian Wars raged.

Dithers waved Tom in. Tom took a chair. "What can I do for you, Professor Conley? I trust you received your last payment? I wish GLU had something more for you. I was going to call and—"

"I'm not here about a job, I have this idea," Tom said.

"That's not what I meant. I mean funding. Too bad you aren't seeking employment. I have something here for you. It's a temp position at a local high school. I know the principal. They need a fill-in. One of the special-ed teachers is on medical leave. It only runs for a few weeks. I told them yes. I have more," Dithers dug into the pile of papers on his desk.

"I appreciate that Doctor Dithers. I'd like to stay busy until next session. I haven't worked it out yet, but I'm gonna stay. I want a doctorate. I have most of the necessary credits. In a year or two… Maybe something here will open? I'm told Berkeley wants a man with deep paper. More bang for their buck. So, I'm—"

"Hold on," Dithers raised his hand, palm out like a crosswalk guard. "That is not going to happen. Your funding has run dry. Didn't you hear me?"

Tom stood up. "But I got… you see… I mean… Oh, shit."

Dithers waved him to sit. The administrator's stink-eye destroyed Tom's resolve. He fell back into the chair with heat rising in his chest.

"That's better. I have a teaching post for you as well. A temporary field assignment. You know the place, your former field-study location. You asked for field work and I arranged it."

"But I have this idea and—"

"See here young man. You signed off on the job search. I quote, you said. 'I'll take anything you got,'" Dithers' chubby cheeks flushed. The light shining off his bald head reflected pissed-off red. "I committed you. You are going to the Badlands. If you ever want funding, or a job reference, you best not cross me. You are meddling in my reputation. You'll take the job and like it."

"But Doctor, substituting high school kids sucks. Can't I skip that? I'll wait for the field work—"

"You can't stay here. There's no post-grad money for you. It's time you move forward with your career. Take the jobs, or I assure you, you'll get nothing more from Old U."

Tom leaned way back in his chair and chocked angry words back rather than spit them at Dithers. Subbing high school kids was the last thing he wanted, but the Badlands dig was welcome. To survive in academia, Tom knew well, one played by the rules, the rules Administration set. Leaving Mom would be hard. On the upside, The Badlands' dig season ends early. *I won't be gone long.*

In the back of his mind a bell rang. He enjoyed bone digs. The Badlands beat sitting on campus in a stuffy office marking papers for the lead paleontologist. Subbing high school can't be that bad. Dodging spit balls for a few weeks was better than hanging around the apartment.

"Doctor, I'll do it." Tom said. "After this… Any grants I can apply for?"

"Possibility, depends on your performance. Your primary funding foundation keeps changing the rules and the others aren't interested in your career."

"About that substitute job? Is it local? But won't I miss the dig's start date?"

"You'll have time. You don't need to go in for setup. It's handled. I have calls to make. I'll send you the details via email. Good day, Assistant Professor."

The word 'professor' rang his ear-bells. He didn't care for the handle 'doctor,' maybe higher education wasn't for him. Doctors live in ivory clouds and he was a groundhog. Tom had a knack for shovel bumming. He enjoyed scratching raw earth for tiny puzzle clues and he was good at it, too. Dad had been a finder of things, but Tom's talent was the process of extracting artifacts rather than finding them. He didn't see himself as the explorer type, too risky. Shovel bums were worker-bees.

Tom walked away from Dithers thinking things weren't that bad.

The school job was close by. The dig-job is only eight hours drive away. Mom had encouraged him to get a job but what if she tried suicide again? If Mom got sicker, he could run home from either job. The building super lived on the same floor and he'd watch out for her whenever Tom went away. The best part, there was nothing dangerous about South Dakota. Nothing to worry her. Mom will approve. *That'll give us both a break.*

Tom took his time going back to his little, cubby-hole office in the back of the archeology department's storage basement. He didn't need anything there except his excavation kit. Dithers didn't tell him to clear out, so there was hope. He left the rest of his effects in place. If he ever got to Berkeley, he'd relocate his belongings. *Yeah, right.*

"May as well face it, Conley, this place is home."

CHAPTER FIVE:

HOSPICE

———

Richard's car pulled into the no-parking zone like Richard owned the place. Maybe he did. Mary didn't understand how wealthy this man was when she and her husband joined his crew fifteen years ago. Richard and Bert were pals from college. Before that trip, she was as wild and care-free as Bert and just as willing to take chances. She went so far as to drag her son along on adventures. Such things would be good for Tommy, she had justified. Was it a good experience for her boy? No, it was a mistake. Trusting Richard Wailer was a mistake. Signing onto his ship was a mistake. *Coming here with him is…is that a mistake?*

Richard himself hurried to open her door. She didn't want that. She didn't want to owe him anything more. Bad enough he paid Tommy's way. He reached for her hand to help her out of the car.

"I'm not an invalid," she said, snapping at him.

"Have it your way, sorry," He spoke with a sad, quiet voice.

"I don't need help," she whispered, more to convince herself than him. *That isn't true, I've been incapacitated for years.*

Her degree from university remained unused. *What good is an ancient manuscript scholar who can't get out of bed?* She had layers of problems. Depression had kicked her down hard recently. She hardly ate. She had a feeling human life was drawing down. Power got sucked out of her. Bert used to have feelings and dreams, too, but his dreams came true. Hers never did. *Again, not true.*

Depression's lying to you. It always lies. It's a lie, all lies. She often repeated that mantra to keep the pit at bay. Depression ate at her soul like the shark who ate her husband. If that's what had happened. Bert's body was never found. *I won't let it swallow me today.*

Richard went straight to the visitor's desk. Mary followed him dragging ass. The nurse knew him and after a brief exchange he led on to a room. *He knows where he's going and what he's doing.* I wish I did. Arriving at Amy's private room, he went in while Mary hung back at the door. The place smelled of ripe fish and seawater. Whatever made the room stink wasn't pleasant. Medication? *They don't treat cancer with sushi.*

"Mary, come on. She's awake."

Mary shuffled in. Richard pulled another chair to the bedside. Amy sat up with some effort. She brightened. Her face glowed with a kind halo. Mary rubbed her eyes. Why is she lit? Is Amy glad to see him? Mary shook it off. *I'm seeing things?*

"Mary Conley…I'm happy you came," Amy said. "It's been years…Bert's memorial service…Sorry, I lost touch."

Mary and Amy fell in together and talked like old friends. Small things were said, common things. Mary didn't know Amy had lived in the area all this time and was very close to Tommy's university. Amy had a son, too, but she never married. She was a few years younger than Mary but cancer made Amy appear ancient.

"When you get out of here, we'll get together, lunch or coffee," Mary said meaning it.

She felt a kinship with Amy she couldn't explain. Amy, fine-glass frail, took Mary's hand. Amy's soft touch sizzled electric upon giving Mary's hand a little squeeze. Power flowed between them until Amy let go.

"When you're released…I…I…" Mary's voice trailed off.

"I'm not leaving here alive," Amy said. Her voice weaker. "I've something to tell you. Wish I had long ago." She paused to cough. "See what harboring secrets does to you? Don't worry. I didn't have an affair with Bert." She mustered a tiny, humorless laugh. It sounded far away.

"What is it? What have you to say?" Mary asked leaning closer. Richard leaned in as well. Mary forgot him until then. That ocean smell became stronger. It must have been the medication but the odor emanated from Richard. *Essence of seadog aftershave.*

"I have to tell you…It's hard…I can't die with this on my heart."

Amy had a coughing fit. With each hack more life drained away. Her halo dimmed. When Amy stopped, she resembled a corpse. Mary shivered. Amy squeezed Mary's hand again, but there wasn't any force behind it.

"That amulet, the one Tommy went after…do you still have it?" Amy asked.

"No, I'm sorry. It's lost, lost a long time ago. He wore it but one morning it was gone. Must've lost it before that…Anyway, it's gone."

"I would have liked to see it," Amy said. "You see…" she coughed a while, sweat beaded on her face, the smell increased. "You see…There was another charm," She leaned upright off her stacked pillows. "I had it. When the basket came up on deck, there were two on that chain. When Rich snapped it up out of the basket, one pendant got caught…fell on the deck. I took it." Amy started hacking again. "I stole it. It made me."

Amy took air and lowered herself deeper into her pillows. Richard rocked back into his chair as if rebuffed by a gale. He didn't speak. Mary didn't think him angry but staggered. He spoke under his breath tapping on his lower lip with a finger until his brow rose. Time returned. Mary let herself breathe. Richard leaned forward. His expression thoughtful.

"Where is it, Amy?" Richard said evenly. "It's important. I must know."

Amy laughed with real humor despite her hollow death rattle. Mary never thought she'd hear such a thing in her life. It made her heartsick. Mary wiped away a tear.

"Lost," Amy said, "lost as can be. It haunted me. You know. I should have gotten rid of it, but I couldn't let go. Instead…I gave it to my son. He's different, you know, autistic. He lost it. It didn't last a day. I wore it when I was pregnant…it made him different."

"Oh, Amy…What about your son?" Mary said, thinking to volunteer as a guardian. But with her bipolar, that wasn't going to happen. They don't let people in her condition adopt.

"He's cared for," Richard said. "I…The authorities have him in a group home. Amy's been here a while…Not much longer, I'm afraid. Her boy is well cared for."

Amy's hand had less than nothing behind it—no power at all, no life, as if the telling had drained the last of her battery.

"Had to get it off my chest," Amy said trying to sit up. "It's good you lost it… Look what it did to me." With that, Amy collapsed backward into her pillows. "I can rest in peace. So tired…Better this way…No secrets…is better."

Mary noticed Richard tapping his lip, gearing up to ask another question. Mary had enough of him. Amy was worn, see-through thin. Mary had a sense…She read people better than most. It was time for them to go.

"Amy's done, said what she needed to say," Mary said. "We're finished here."

When Richard opened his mouth, Mary put a hand over it. His whiskers pricked her palm.

"Tired, so tired…" Amy moaned.

"We're going," Mary said, getting up. "Rest Amy. Come on, Richard."

Mary turned to Amy to say goodbye, but Amy had fallen asleep. Her shallow breathing was nothing more than a whisper floating on seaweed. She and Richard left without a word to each other. When they reached the foyer, the bad smell was replaced with flowers. She hadn't noticed them on her way in. Mary bent to sniff a flower and an alarm rang.

"Crash Cart, room nine," came over the PA.

Mary dropped the rose and stepped onto the door-opener mat. Amy's gone, really gone. Mary's tears poured out and she let them. Bipolar taught her one thing: tears are good. Let the grief out before it eats you alive.

"Tears held are acid to one's soul," she said getting into the car.

Mary's storm cloudy eyes rained buckets. She didn't expect it but Richard cried, too.

CHAPTER SIX:

DITHERS' CALL

A few hours after Conley left, Dithers took a moment to make the call. He waited until long after the boy exited. Five minutes after he hung up, Richard Wailer strolled into his office. Wailer had an air about him that forced Dithers to pay attention. The perfume of old money always commanded his attention. If Conley knew Wailer was behind cutting the funding, the boy would blow his lid. Wailer, as usual, came straight in without a knock or a hello. Rich men are real assholes.

"Did you convince him to take the Badland offer?" Wailer said.

"He didn't argue," Dithers said. "Frankly, I don't understand why you pumped so much money into him. His grades are barely passable. If you hadn't made such a generous donation, he'd have washed out. I doubt his doctorate request will ever fly given his grades. What do you see in this man?"

"I owe him this. His father died in my service."

"He wants yet another degree which won't enhance this unremarkable thinker. How did you know he would ask? I did as you requested, but I would have denied him otherwise."

Wailer's cell phone chimed and he took the call. Dithers was aware his own voice carried an edge of contempt and he let it ooze. He had earned every milestone himself and put himself through school the hard way. That this low-class billionaire favored such a mundane manchild was an affront to Dithers' hard work. So, Conley's daddy had died, it happens. Pay the money and move on. Why the continued interest?

"Sorry," Wailer said, "You were saying?"

"At any rate, Conley will go as you arranged. The high school assignment first and then off to the Badlands. He'll be working under Berkeley's Doctor Mede as an assistant professor. Berkeley's running the field study program this term."

"Mede's a good man. I've worked with him before. And you're sure Tommy doesn't know I pushed his placement?"

"I told him the Antiquities Fund hired him. He doesn't know you provide money for that as well."

"Let's keep it that way. He won't take my aid. He hates me."

"Can't say as I blame him," Dithers said under his breath.

"What's that?"

Wailer heard. That telltale smirk confirmed it.

"Nothing," Dithers said. "Why hate one as generous as you?" Dithers held out his hand.

Wailer dropped an envelope onto the desk. Dithers grabbed it. Judging by the weight, it was the usual payment and still inadequate.

"If he comes begging again, I'll send him packing," Dithers said.

Wailer left without a hand-shake or goodbye, slighting Dithers as before. Dithers smelled Wailer's disdain although the benefactor presented himself even-faced. A man of Wailer's riches should spread it wider. Wailer could do better, but there wasn't any point in asking. He only gives enough grease to keep his wheels turning. Big-shots get more lubricant and Dithers wasn't in that club. But he was also in another club that paid better. He picked up his private cell phone and punched in a memorized number.

"CIA," someone said on the other side.

"Agent Mulder, please. Dithers here," he said.

Not the agent's real name, of course. Dithers didn't think phone-Mulder was the same man who had visited him to make arrangements. Same or not? He guessed not.

Mulder picked up and said, "Shoot."

"Wailer was just here. He arranged for his protégé, through me, of course, to attend Mede's T-rex dig. I sent the info in an email to Conley, you'll pick it up there, no?"

Mulder didn't answer other than, "Humm."

Dithers, a curious man, wasn't likely to get an answer but he asked anyway. "Why are you so interested in Wailer? What are you after? Maybe I can help."

The man laughed heartily which wasn't expected. G-men never smile. It wasn't a nice, friendly sound of good humor, rather it chilled Dithers.

"Doctor Dithers, we're interested in every man of Wailer's status." The phone went dead.

A minute later Dithers' phone chimed. His bank received a deposit. Bigger than the previous one. He guessed it was the last payment concerning Conley. The Finder Foundation will continue granting as always with or without Wailer's nod. The Foundation operates autonomously. The organization's interest in the arcane won't abate. Wailer had the board stacked.

Wailer insisted on digging things up the CIA didn't approve of. Wailer's snooping where he didn't belong was the tip-off. Dithers wasn't one to rock the government's boat unless money fell out of it. Dithers needed another corrupt patron to keep the river flowing.

CHAPTER SEVEN:

TOD MURPHY

Tod Murphy saw the writing on the wall early in his career and it wasn't cuneiform on hardened clay. It had quickly become obvious. His geological career in support of archeology wasn't going anywhere. The CIA offered and he threw in with them. It wasn't hard to do. The government watched every interesting site and he thought the watcher may as well be him. It paid better. But, the money cost him his integrity.

Murphy pushed the pile of folders on his desk aside. "I got to get out more."

His people showed up whenever a dig became important. Before taking the job, he asked what the government's interest was in anomalous finds. A CIA field agent with a social psychology degree had explained it.

'It's like this,' he had said. 'Education is a social control vehicle to manage the population. That's a positive. What if the masses learned of the uncomfortable realities' governments must perform? There'd be chaos. Chaos can come from any direction. We plaster over touchy ideas for the public's best interest. As Henry Clay, the industrialist, said, and I quote, "If people understood what was happening there would be blood in the streets." Think about that.'

Murphy thought before signing on. He didn't buy the agent's rationale of 'the public's best interest.' He jumped in out of curiosity. There were many more layers behind social engineering than admitted. New evidence took a generation to ferment and consensus came hard. The old guard must die before the new is acceptable. He didn't have the patience to wait. The real deal, in his view: the oligarchs lose money when paradigms shift. Rewritten textbooks cost money and careers. Obsolete doctorates must stretch the truth to stay employed.

Glad it ain't me. New ideas sour them but its sweet for me.

Director Murphy had been collecting doubts of late. Who were they really protecting? He tried to convince himself he made the right move, but it seemed less right after eighteen years.

Murphy's archaeological-geologist career proved a dead-end. That agent wasn't fooling. Murphy had since witnessed many career-enhancing finds plastered over. They would have done it to him giving what he had found, which reminded him of the hatchet job they did to Doctor Cory although the hatchet didn't bite. Murphy despised weak academics. He admired Cory's balls. The official narrative wasn't where reality is at. He joined the Company to see the truth and he wasn't disappointed.

"So, why do I feel like shit?"

One of his agents stuck his head into Murphy's office. "Boss, pick up line three, one of your contacts."

Line three, I'm Mulder on that line. Murphy punched the button. "Shoot."

It was Dithers. Wailer's pet project was going out to Badlands. No problem, Murphy had a man there, and besides, he wasn't concerned with Thomas Conley. That sad sack was just another of Wailer's beholding tools. *The real question is; what is Wailer after?*

Murphy hung up on Dithers before his informant finished.

Murphy had a feeling about Conley. Conley wasn't one of Wailer's key men like Mede or Cory, not a person of interest to the CIA, and yet something was off. Wailer supported a lot of students. Even Murphy got a Finder Foundation grant while in Egypt. If Wailer knew what Murphy had found, he'd shit himself. Ironic that discovery drove Murphy into the arms of the CIA. Wailer had been the best way to answer Tod's questions.

Murphy was a bird feeding around the buffalo's feet. There to snatch whatever the behemoths kick up. Fear forces people out of character, himself included. But the CIA position worked for him…for now, but for how much longer?

"Back to work." Murphy called his pursuit-hound with the intercom. "Billings get in here."

Billings worked for Homeland Security assigned to Antiquities. The man had connections. Murphy didn't trust him but he still used him. Murphy's Antiquities Department had been pushed into using one of Wailer's mental health facility for the research project. Having the project nearby was good but the arrangement was risky. Higher-ups had contracted with Wailer's group home. Not smart. Overlap complicated Murphy's job. Billings walked in.

"What's Wailer up to right now?" He asked Billings.

"Wailer's here in Chicago. Came in from Patagonia. He checked in on the Conleys. Seems another of his ex-employees is or was in hospice. Amy Parks is dead."

"He's hard on his people, make no mistake," Murphy said. "That'll put a dent in his pocket."

"How's the research team doing with the Parks kid, anything there yet?" Billings asked.

The Parks Project wasn't Billings' assignment. Antiquities was only interested in what info Parks might provide. The Psy-ops people had other concerns. *Billings is digging. By habit, side job, or curiosity?* Office people talk. The Parks Project wasn't a secret. Too many people outside of Murphy's department knew about it. Murphy hated leakers. He wanted such lips sealed. It dawned on him. *There's a mole in-house.* Homeland perhaps, but there was more to it, there's always more. *Why is he asking?*

"What do you think of Kenny?" Murphy asked.

"From what I hear, that kid's amazing," Billings said trying for a smile. The man resembled a weasel with shit stuck in its teeth. "How's Wailer figure in?"

"The boy has talents," Murphy said, careful to keep his cards close. "Interesting ideas, insightful. He's autistic. Must be why the treasure-hunter lends a hand. Wailer doesn't know what we know."

"I don't get why Wailer's involved at all."

"He helped the kid's mother, a former employee, so he helps the kid, too," Murphy said. "Wailer's doing charity. He owns the group home chain. He doesn't know why…the government is studying autism." *Right under his nose.*

"That's good," Billings said. "If anything happens…Wailer won't care. The kid's just a test subject as far as he knows."

"Who the hell knows what Wailer cares about?" Murphy said. The idea of the boy getting hit disturbed Murphy but he kept a straight face. Murphy sensed his department flying off the rail. "I don't know what the man is after."

"I know a way to find out," Billings said cryptically.

"Do you?"

Murphy drummed his fingers on his desk. Billings tracked America's moneyed elite who collected what was better left buried in the ground. That Wailer supported research in archeology and paleontology gave Murphy and Billings a common-case file. Murphy located artifacts and removed what troubles came out of the ground while Billings ran down what had already come out and into the hands of elite collectors.

"We've taken down bigger men," Billings said. "We know he has rare manuscripts."

"Procurement hired Wailer's research group knowing he's a person of interest. They have a reason. That info is above my paygrade," Murphy said. "Lay off Wailer until upstairs green-lights it."

Billings should chase that question—what are the Bigs really after? The usual task was to set up a mark to take a fall. Knocking Wailer off his golden perch won't help the cause or be easy. Wailer has too much money and influence. Besides, Wailer hunts for what the Antiquities Department wants. Let him do the work. Mechanics don't abuse their tools.

"You're right, above my paygrade as well," Billings said. "I'd like to know what the honchos see in Parks."

Murphy's Homeland agent was a little man with a big ego but not big enough to take on Wailer. Billings snooped where he didn't belong seeking what weren't his concerns. *That's not liaison work.*

"What's your take on Wailer?" Murphy said, snooping a bit himself. "What about the boy?"

"Wailer isn't interested in the boy, as you said. He owns the franchise so it makes sense he'd help a friend. His contract lab won the bid fairly. He'll get paid on both ends, smart." Billings said. "I doubt he knows we're looking at the kid for salvage advantages."

"Cozy arrangement. What else?"

"Of course, Homeland is officially hands-off the Parks child. Mental research is not in our purview. Catching Wailer crossing the line is what Homeland is after. Bust him so it sticks, and we'll get everything he collected. I'm gathering evidence."

"Keep it going," Murphy said. "Parks is mine for the time being. Keep after Wailer. Later we'll combine notes and add up the charges."

Murphy dismissed Billings and went back to his computers. The Japanese discovered new geoglyph lines in Nazca, older ones, lines that needed covering up. The image he uploaded would stagger the uninitiated mind. Someone carved an airplane into the desert 15,000 years ago and that wasn't approved for public consumption. He had a team on its way. A new thought crossed Murphy's mind concerning that problem.

"The Japs will play ball."

He picked up his secure phone to call Tokyo.

***

Mark Billings took lunch across the street a few blocks away in a greasy-spoon diner on the outskirts of the industrial park, as usual. He didn't like the food, but he ate there regularly. After ordering coffee, Billings went to the payphone in the back by the restrooms, the only old fashioned, hard-wired payphone nearby. It cost too much for the Company to tap hardwires. Communications had gone all digital. Leg-work became passé.

He dialed a memorized number and hung up. A moment later the phone rang. He hunched over the receiver with his face inside the phone's side panels. Somebody picked up the other end and said nothing. They never said much.

"Go," Billing said.

"We want Parks. Group home buses him to the high school," the voice said.

"Wailer's been around…You think he's interested in Parks? He had relations with Amy Parks…Right, the kid might be useful…Wailer's love child?…I'll look into it."

Billings hung up and turned. Murphy stood there grinning.

"Thought I'd grab a bite with you," Murphy said. "Who was on the phone?"

Billings kept cool. "Beats me, Boss. It rang so I took it. I fucked around, goofed on her. Had the wrong number."

Murphy wasn't a trained agent and easy to read. He didn't catch the lie. The Company hired amateur spies for the Antiquities Department which made Billings' job easier. Working around mugs like Murphy was simple. Murphy didn't care about security. Curiosity drove him, same thing that killed the cat.

"Whatever. What's good here?" Murphy licked his lips.

The man is hungry. He didn't follow me. Billings needed to take a leak but he held it.

"Forget the meatloaf," Billings said. "Fries aren't bad. I usually get the B.L.T."

"Sounds good, I'll meet you in the booth. Got to wash up," Murphy said and vanished into the restroom.

Billings ordered his and Murphy's lunch and paid for it. With the side money the Watchers provided, he could well afford to treat the director to lunch. Billings didn't care about money anyway. Boss Man's plate was too full. He didn't have time to pick fly-shit-details out of Mark's hodge-podge. Even so, Mark Billings decided he needed to find a different phone booth for next time.

CHAPTER EIGHT:

HIGH SCHOOL TEMP

Tom pulled into one of the regional high school's many parking lots dragging his reservations. He hated being forced. That spot on his chest throbbed. He hated to leave Mom alone but she was stable, even cheerful this morning.

He should have taken Mom's old Honda but it needed gas. Dad's vintage RV might be mud-ugly but it ran well and everything worked. He felt secure in his rolling home away from home. The old Dodge provided the confidence of familiarity. He needed reassurance having never taught disabled kids before. He taught site-surveying and excavation techniques to adult students on dig projects and had only worked with young kids a few times. Substituting high school was an animal with teeth and he wasn't a lion tamer.

He stopped at one of the staff lots entrances and sat there too long. "You can't stay here forever." He said and proceeded into a maze.

It took twenty minutes to find a place where his 21-foot-long truck fit. He had to park way in the back along a high fence. This regional school was the size of a village.

Reading the site map, he didn't know where he was. A sense of doom smacked him. *My first day and I'm late.* He wanted to run, call out, and go home, but he needed the money. He checked the schedule again. He was to start after morning homeroom.

He got out and started walking uphill. "Looks like I'll make it." The first session's bell rang. "Guess not…How'd I get so far behind?" Already sweating, Tom picked up the pace. "Better late than never is a crock."

He slowed down and followed another late teacher which brought him straight into the wrong building. The secretary spotted his problem. Instructions said to park in lot M, he chose lot W. The sign mounts broke and hung the M upside-down. He, the professional observer, missed it and parked on the wrong side of the complex.

I'll get it right tomorrow if they don't fire me.

CHAPTER NINE:

PETE AND KENNY

High school senior Pete "The Blaster" Brenner and his main-bro hung out at Pete's hall-locker eyeing Kenny Parks.

"Look at that," Pete said to his sideman Randy Pike. Pete closed his locker. "Ten minutes till lunch and he lines up. Special-ed shouldn't let the 'tards go early. They could get hurt."

"Look at him waiting at the cafeteria door talking to a stupid dinosaur toy," Randy said.

Pete play-punched Randy and said, "Cover me."

Randy got the message and showed his yellow-brown teeth. Pete caught a whiff of rot wishing Randy would brush once in a while. Pete had an opportunity for a little fun. Pete's point-man hung back by the intersection just in case some teachers came along. Randy whipped out his cell phone to record. Randy in place, Pete started the party.

"Hey Webber-tard, what you doing? Got any money?"

"What? What's that mean, Mr. Webber?"

"No stupid," Pete said and laid his backpack on the ground. "A Webber-tard means a dumb retard that goes to Webber's class, see?"

"I'm not. I'm smart, really smart. You're too dumb for Mr. Webber's class."

Kenny said it like an everyday fact. Pete hated how his dad called him stupid all the time and now this jerk does it. Pete almost hauled off and punched the kid. "Asshole" sprang out instead of a right hook. Pete's rage flared but he wouldn't do Dad's trick, haul off and sucker-punch the A-hole. Forget impulse. He was smarter than that. Screw that kid. I'm smarter.

"Can't let him get away with that," Randy hissed.

"Smart? I'll make you smart," Pete said.

Pete grabbed Kenny's wrist and twisted it back around as he learned in karate classes. The whole body should follow but Kenny bent like a wet twig. Pete had an eel to handle. He finally managed to force Kenny to let go of the plastic toy which fell into Pete's free hand. Pete stuffed it into one of his backpack's outer pockets.

"'Tard's never gonna see that again." Pete boasted.

Kenny dropped to his knees.

"If you're so smart, why you have a dinosaur toy?" Pete said looking down at Kenny. "Man, he's dumber than a three-year-old."

Pete let Kenny up and put more pressure on Kenny's wrist expecting Kenny to freeze but Kenny went limper. Pete lost grip again.

"Not a dinosaur. You're stupid," Kenny said and stood up. "It's Dimetrodon. A reptile from before them, like way before in the Permian, like not even—"

"Shut up, give me your money."

Pete, foot out, twisted Kenny's arm the other way and spun him toward the lockers. Parks tripped but didn't face-plant. *That's weird. I gotta work on that move.* Kenny's welfare glasses flew off but didn't break.

"Pete! Trouble. Cool it." Randy called in a high rasp.

"Got off easy this time, Webber-tard. You still owe me lunch money."

Pete let go of Kenny and quickly moved back out of range behind Randy. Kenny got on all fours and didn't get up. Pete's hands smelled like a swamp.

"That 'tard should take a bath and get some clean clothes," Pete whispered to Randy.

Foster kids were the worst. Some were okay, like Randy. When the chips were down, Randy would step in and take the heat. He didn't care about getting into trouble. Pete couldn't afford to take a hit the way his parents were.

***

Mr. Webber rounded the corner of the side hall and saw Kenny on the floor adjusting his glasses. Webber's star student waved to him but remained on the floor, looking for something. Webber closed in and pulled his spectacles down half-mast and projected hard disapproval at Pete and Randy.

"Kenny, are you alright?" Webber asked.

"I lost Dimetrodon. He was right here…Right here, maybe he went to the…the…the before time… the Permian, maybe he went home. Oh, yes, he was the big shot, biggest back then."

"That's alright Kenny. We'll get you another dinosaur."

Webber resisted the urge to react quickly. He didn't grab Kenny to help him up. Autistic Kenny was funny about being touched. He liked to do things for himself.

"Not a dino," Kenny said while getting on his feet. "He's a reptile. Reptiles, reptiles were more, always more, but everyone thinks they're not so great. Wrong, wrong, wrong. Dimetrodon was the top predator 230 to 297 million years ago. He was a non-mammalian synapsid and—"

"I'm sure you 're right, Kenny. When it comes to that, regularly spot-on," Webber said without enthusiasm, still angry at the bullies. He immediately regretted his tone. Kenny was sensitive to voice tonalities. Webber had said similar things a million times before, but with gusto. Kenny's bottom lip quivered and turned down.

"I'm sorry, Ken. I'm sure we will find him later."

Webber carefully checked Kenny for injuries. Kenny didn't mind being touched when he anticipated it. The boy was none the worse for wear. Kenny's appearance was not a measure of condition. One could never tell what Kenny thought or felt. He didn't react to pain. His facial expressions seldom changed. His eyes were forever diverted as if he observed things far away others did not see. Webber and Kenny proceeded into the cafeteria together.

****

"He's way stupid," Pete said. "You wanna bet he gives me his lunch money twice tomorrow?" Randy's yellow teeth agreed. Pete backed away from the smell. "His new mom's stupid, too, gives the 'tard enough cash for three lunches."

"He's a free-lunch kid, anyhow," Randy said. "What's he need money for?"

The rest of Webber's class came with an aide and went inside. More kids came and got in line. Pete's grade lined up for lunch Period One every day along the west corridor. Pete was already at the head of the line. He could be first or last to show up but it didn't matter. Nobody ever stopped Pete the Blaster from cutting ahead.

CHAPTER TEN:

LUNCH ROOM

Teachers Mr. Paul Webber and Mrs. Pat Frances stood lunch duty with each one stationed at an exit. Webber got word his temporary teachers' aide would join them this period and so he had an eye out for Mr. Conley. Webber didn't mind showing a new man the lunch-ropes, what little there was to know.

"It's nice to have another cow-poke helping corral these wild colts," he said to Pat before they split up. "He should be here already."

"No doubt he got lost." She returned.

The new man was late, not a problem. Everyone got lost on his first day. Lunch Room One hosted 180 at each of three lunch periods and each period seated an entire grade plus making it rodeo-loud. Webber wished Administration would place his students with the freshmen, rather than the seniors, but then again, the freshmen were rough this year.

Webber saw Mr. Conley hurrying toward the cafeteria door. The new man was a tall, sandy-haired fellow, wiry-thin but energetic and robust, fresh out of college. Maybe the new man played sports. He had an athletic demeanor with nerdiness layered on. Webber thought of himself as a good observer. Such skill was necessary to work with his charges. He should have been observing in the other direction.

A crash ripped the air. The special education table flipped over just as Mr. Conley stuck out his hand in greeting. Both men rushed to the scene. Webber's kids were in a panic. Food was flung everywhere. They who did the dirt blended into a laughing mob before Webber crossed the room. He and Conley righted the table. There was no time for investigations. Sherry was crying. Susie tossed her cookies, real cookies, the ones she just ate, and Timmy was on the floor licking soup off the next table's bench seat. The other five students were in various states of shock or hysterics.

"Mr. Conley," Webber said, pointing. "Get Timmy off the floor, then the others, one at a time. Safety first. Don't worry about liabilities. Handle each as I say."

Webber had seen how many new teachers were afraid to touch a student, but certain of his special-ed charges required physical contact, and the ones that needed it, got it. Some, like Kenny Parks, were limited in that way.

"Right. Right. Fine. Got it," Conley said with a tight voice.

Conley didn't hesitate getting things in order. The new man checked everyone for injuries like a pro and pushed jeering students back without losing his nerve. Webber went directly to the students who needed the most attention, glad that Sherry wasn't screaming. That tiny girl had an inordinately shrill voice.

Webber did a quick head count. One missing. Paul Webber spotted his star student leaned against the back wall. Kenny resembled an out-of-kilter Easter Island Moai. Mr. Conley stood nearby turning pale. Conley had picked Kenny up off the floor like a sack of potatoes before Webber could stop him.

"It's alright. Don't touch him," Webber said with intentional calm. "It'll make him worse."

"What should I do? Is he having a seizure? Shouldn't we call—"

"No, it's alright, Mr. Conley. He, Kenny—"

"He was shaking violently. I thought he swallowed his tongue. I grabbed him and—"

"You did alright, really," Webber said with a soothing voice. "Kenny has episodes. He'll freeze like that when he panics. He calls it 'going away.' He'll be alright. Help me guide him into a seat so he can't fall."

A little color migrated back into Conley's face.

"What I do wrong? My first day…Gees, I don't want to get fired."

Conley's youthful vigor deflated before Webber's eyes. Teaching will age you before your time. Webber patted Conley on the shoulder.

"Not your fault. You don't know about Kenny's oddities. Each of my students has special needs. How would you know them? Kenny will reboot shortly. He'll come out of it on his own. But here's the thing, Kenny doesn't like being embraced. He'll tolerate being touched. Lightly, or in small ways, that's acceptable when he knows it's coming. He's improved much. I'm teaching him how to shake hands."

"I hoisted him up like a hay bale. He looked terrified. I messed up."

"Only natural, Mr. C. You are fine."

Mrs. Frances was busy getting the regular kids seated without much success. Thus, Webber said, "Mr. C, please stay here and keep Kenny company. If you talk gently to him, he may come out of it. I must go help Pat, ah…Mrs. Frances."

Webber joined the effort to restore order. Lunch being a short forty minutes came and went, but Kenny didn't move. Mrs. Frances had called the office for cover before the warning bell rang because Kenny showed no sign of budging.

Webber rejoined Mr. C at the special-ed table when the dismissal bell rang. Special-ed kids were first in, last out which helped prevent trouble. As mainstream students filed out, Webber chatted with Mr. C. They talked of careers and colleges and Webber learned that Mr. C had achieved three degrees at university including a teaching certificate. Foremost Tom, holding masters in paleontology and archeology, aimed for a career teaching field work. He didn't put on airs. Webber felt quite comfortable with Mr. Conley.

"So, why aren't you digging dinosaur fossils or some such?" Webber asked. Kenny stirred on the word dinosaur.

"I will soon," Conley said. "I have a dig coming up. I'm waiting to start. I can't sit home with bills accruing. This job popped up and I jumped. I'm a shovel bum through and through. Can't wait to taste dirt again."

"The fossil hunting business sounds exciting," Webber said with real interest. "Have you found anything exciting in your field study days?"

Kenny's leg started. He tapped his foot when interested in something, but not always. Webber wasn't yet sure what made Kenny react. Excitement or frustration? Kenny's file hadn't fully described his spells.

The bell rang once more and Webber had his students rise to exit. Vice Principal Evans arrived to assess conditions. The event reached Evans by way of CCTV before Frances called. Seeing things well in hand, Evans had Conley stay to watch Kenny until he recovered.

Webber said before going, "Mr. C, when he comes out of it—"

"Tom, please call me Tom."

"Off duty, of course, but here I'll use Mr. C. I'm Paul when students aren't about. When he comes around, walk him down to me. You may have a long wait. Don't touch him much. You saw why. You'll love Kenny. He's an encyclopedia of dinosaurs. Ask him about fossils and he'll surprise you."

***

Tom sat with Kenny until halfway through Lunch Two. All the while, Tom talked paleontology and the boy responded in increments: faint smiles here, a lifted finger there, his foot-tapping increased. The more Tom talked shovel bumming, the more the kid came to life.

Early on, Tom had done a bit of field work with younger kids. Old U sponsored a summer lakeside trilobite fossil hunt for grade-schoolers. University enrollment required participation in volunteer projects. That summer's job with young kids, and their excitement over common fossils, had supercharged Tom's enthusiasm. The memory brought back what first captured his interests as a youngster. Later, as a summer-session classroom instructor, he had more responsibility and less joy. This gig wasn't so bad. Special-ed kids are older but childlike. *If I can work with 5th graders, I can work with Kenny.* Kenny regained mobility and shuffled in his seat.

"Hey Kenny, how're you? Want to go to class? What do you say partner?"

"Oh yes, Mr. Conley. Oh yes. Feeling good, good, good."

They set out for Mr. Webber's classroom. The ten-minute walk became twenty. Tom didn't know where he was going. He got distracted talking about dig sites. Kenny never stopped talking bones. Nothing he said was wrong and a few things he said were cutting edge.

To satisfy his curiosity, Tom followed up later that first day between assignments. He read Kenny's blog on Webber's computer. Tom was surprised and impressed. *Where did a kid who can barely write a sentence get this stuff?* Kenny knew all about Mesalands Community College's rare finds. Nobody knew the place, too many paleontologists included.

Tom had read about autism while working on his certificate. What he read amazed and baffled him. Kenny, as an autistic in person, was far more interesting and surprising than any case file he had read. Tom felt a connection with the boy that he didn't see coming.

Tom dug into Kenny's blog archive and brought up an article about feathers. Kenny understood what few people outside the field knew. He wrote that Hadrosaurs were the largest of all the Ornithischians and evidence suggested they had feathers. Tom checked the posting date. Kenny had reasoned out feathers based on known evidence, fine, but he did it first. His paper detailed the logic. How did Kenny extrapolate the data ahead of peer-reviewed papers? Professional researchers only reached Kenny's conclusions long after Kenny proposed them.

"Kenny is unbelievable, righter than rain," Tom said to Webber after break.

"I told you so, Mr. C. Kenny is a very special lad, indeed." Webber laid a hand on Conley's shoulder. "I believe you go next door for this period. I'll see you again last period."

Over the following weeks, Webber had Tom's help, but Tom was also a roving aide and didn't get to know Webber's kids well. He knew Kenny best as he and Kenny tread common ground. Scheduled for the fall and spring's T-rex dig in the Badlands, Tom had no choice but to go when it was time. Kenny was excited about Tom's dig and promised to follow progress on the internet.

Tom stayed at a nearby RV park rather than drive back and forth wasting gas every day and went home on weekends. Mom's manic jag had mellowed but she remained energetic and bounced around with the car a lot. Her wheels weren't available and that was fine with him.

"This job feels like home," he said to Mr. Webber on the morning of his last day. "I hate to leave. Regional feels like home."

"I must say, Mr. C, it was good to have you with us. The students actually like you. You have a knack for teaching."

"Going is hard," Tom said, "but somebody's gotta dig them bones."

Word had gotten around. With many congratulations, his fellow educators wished him well all that last day. It wasn't like finishing his master's degree. Many of his contemporaries acted like back-biting bastards. One doc candidate openly celebrated Tom leaving Old U. Contrary thoughts haunted him all day.

Crazy ideas came to mind. I could stay. They love me. I should apply. A permanent job solves my problem. If not here, some other local school. I'll need a different certification for high school, maybe history. How do I get around Dithers?

Tom decided to go for it toward the end of the day and he worked on mustering the courage to do it. He talked himself into staying and tried to talk himself out of the old shovel bum dream but the dream wouldn't stop hammering his heart. He had a good excuse to go back to Old U without chasing a doctorate. He only needed a few more credits. He'd go to community college if no other way. It wouldn't take long. Dithers didn't have any say over the history department. Tom ran that thought through his mind over and over but logic didn't drive back emotions. Dirt had him by the soul.

"Who am I kidding?" Tom asked himself after his last class.

The thought of giving up the dig made his birthmark hurt. He loved shovel bumming and that T-rex dig was tasty…but leaving Mom…but Mom's better than in years…but what if she relapses?

When he got the email confirming Badlands, he ignored it until Dithers called with threats. Tom relented just to get him off the phone. Forces not under his control were pushing and he didn't like it. Pissed off, he ginned up enough balls to face Dithers. But Mom had called last night pleading with him to take the dig. She anticipated his reservations. Tom felt he had guts enough to confront Dithers but not Mom. Accepting his fate, that splotch on his chest left him alone. His birthmark had its own ideas which never seemed to match his.

"Stress reaction. I'm no good in a conflict," Tom said to the empty hallway on his way to sign out.

The buses and kids had gone. Tom approached the office for the last time. Mr. Webber and Mrs. Frances swooped in from the intersection. One on each side, they took his elbows and steered him off track.

"What's this?" Tom said. "I'm getting the heave-ho?"

"No, no," Pat answered with a laugh. "It's party time."

She and Paul guided him into the Faculty Room. A small group of teachers cheered as he entered. Tom struggled to keep tears from bubbling out. He was on the verge of bawling when Kenny burst into the teacher's room and ran to Tom, took Tom's hand and gripped it hard. Kenny locked eyes on Tom's mouth. It was the closest to eye contact the child could manage. Tom was so moved he didn't know what to say. Kenny should have been on his bus returning home.

"Gonna miss you, Mr. Conley," Kenny squeaked.

"It's okay, we'll meet again," Tom mumbled choking on emotions. "You'll see."

"Got to tell you goodbye, Mr. C. Nobody listens, you…you, you listen. You know I know…I have to tell you. You'll find eggs. Baby T-rex! BA-hill, look under him. He's protecting eggs. He's got momma's eggs! That's new! T-rex's a lion pride, you'll see."

"Keep digging, Kenny," Tom said. "You'll do fine. Keep writing that blog you have and I'll keep reading it." Tom mussed Kenny's hair and the young man didn't have a cow. More evidence Tom belonged. "Keep digging, kiddo."

"I'm digging, Mr. C. I dig it. I dig it all up. Don't forget T-rex eggs. BA hill."

"I don't know, Kenny. I might hang around. Maybe I'll work here."

"No, no, no…has to be you! You have to go. Nobody else can do it…You have to go."

"Alright. You got it, partner," Tom said, not sure what to make of Kenny's speech. But Tom felt released. "Watch me on the internet, kid. The site's wired." Tom's internal debate ended. "I'm gonna miss you, too, Kenny."

The kid has more confidence in me than I do. His chest warmed without burning. That sense of hidden forces sweeping him along blanked out. Streams of time flashed and vanished in an instant. He wiped his eyes. A new excitement for the Badlands came over him.

The hall monitor caught up with Kenny saying, "Mr. Parks' guardian will be here to pick him up soon." She quickly ushered him away.

Tom had met Kenny's guardian once while punching out. She didn't sit right with him. She didn't seem like anyone's mother. She had the bearing of a cop. Kenny never missed the bus this way before. Rather, it was because he went 'away' inside his head to that land only Kenny knew. Tom saw it as the only place Kenny had where the other kids couldn't hurt him. Tom suspected Kenny spent more quality time away than in reality.

Tom said his goodbyes to staff and proceeded to the parking lot with Kenny on his mind. He was glad to have known Kenny. *Doing good feels good.* Tom figured he had a positive effect on Kenny although, as yet, unseen. Kenny reminded Tom of his calling. That desire for discovery smoldered under everything. Kenny had bellowed fresh air into Tom's muted fire. His future was indeed ahead searching for puzzle pieces, 'yet to be discovered,' as Kenny often said. Tom decided he'd work the Badlands with gusto to make himself indispensable.

"Maybe this'll lead me somewhere? Berkeley runs it. Could be my back door."

CHAPTER ELEVEN:

DULLES BROTHERS

Albert Dulles preferred his reception room bright. Eighty years underground did not remove his need for the sun. He bathed his personal spaces with sunlamps. But he preferred harsh fluorescent for his workspace.

He had grown three heads taller. His skin had gone pale, his jaw wider, his brow protruded, and his hair was gone. To a human he resembled Frankenstein's monster except for a round head. He didn't mind the price. His long-lived species detested their human-like childhoods as he did.

Young Ergaster men appear as normal homo sapiens. Alas there weren't any young ones to work and blend on the surface. That was no longer possible for the Dulles Brothers. They were the last full-breed to have lived above. Freak shows had gone out of vogue. The inability to live above did not preclude them from controlling the nations for Ergaster's purposes. They relied on half-breed operators and human greed. Ergaster men and sapient women produced only mules.

Brother Jacob didn't care for his adult Ergaster ugliness. The younger Dulles preferred low lights. Albert didn't adjust the lamps to appease his brother. He lowered them for the guest. The expected one, a half-breed, won't change. Many agents like him were out of control having gone native. *Such tools shall die.* But not Amos the Faithful. Amos called the underworld home although he must remain above until the missing Goddess is captured. Albert would rather host Amos than the CIA agent who was late.

Jacob spoke while fiddling with his computer. "Albert, dismiss the female. Our CIA man is near."

"No," Albert said. "Let him see how women ought to be." Albert himself was once in the half-breed's position, that of an important government official.

"Your call. What if he has news about Artemis?"

Females of the Watchers had been made captive. For 300,000 years before their imprisonment, women had been equal until Ergaster man subjugated them. Twenty thousand years had since passed. Their magic had been greatly reduced in the world. The Watcher men caged them under an energy shield to push down Women's Magic and yet their magic still leaked.

"The missing one is a catalyst but not for long. She is without her keys," Albert said. "She still draws magic."

Sapient women were gaining power. Free Creation Magic gave Albert little choice but to take drastic action. Ergaster man must prevail. The rats will be wiped out again. Albert's recent attempt had failed when the keys escaped shutting off the device. Despite that loss, Albert found a way to restart the machine. The project had only been delayed.

"Her keys would have quickened the process," Albert said.

"True, but we only need the one we have," Jacob said.

"When our agents find them," Albert said, "humankind's slow death won't be so slow. Smart of her to separate herself from her keys. She knows we developed a key detector."

"We raised a volcano with her key set, of course she sensed it. Waste of our time. I say we draw in another meteorite as we did before." Jacob said. "You will never find her keys."

"Are we not spymasters?" Albert said. "Without keys, her power is diminished. We are closing on her. Keys or not, she won't get away this time."

Jacob had lobbied to retry that failed cosmic action, but with more finesse. The Dulles Brothers weren't there thirteen thousand years ago, but their living relatives were. Manipulating an asteroid nearly killed his race along with the sapiens. The megafauna's ruin had caused an Ergaster famine. They depended on the wooly mammoth for meat. Predators designed for population control were made to crave human flesh but Ergaster's man-eaters had died out. Adaptable sapiens had mastered the new environment despite the megafauna collapse.

Sapiens were out of control again. If left alone, humans will develop enough technology to detect and destroy them.

"Imagine having a planetoid strike Washington?" Jacob laughed like a hyena. "We should do a small hit for the sake of fun."

"We will not, get over it. The machinery is defunct," Albert lied. "However, the need is ripe. One city is not enough. They all must die this time. The wars we create are not enough."

"The parasites are more dangerous than ever," Jacob said. "We can't tolerate a resurgence of Women's Magic. It grows with the key-set lost in the world."

Magic did more than grow. Evidence showed human females becoming magical as if copious power leaked from the Goddess's prison. Had Ergaster not captured them, by this time, all humanity would be infected with Goddess wisdom making wars impossible.

"We shouldn't have started the vent system there," Albert said of his mistake in sending the keys to a remote location. They had since devised a way to engage the machine from there. "It's lost but not done. We must find it before Artemis does."

"Too late for her. The time to act has come," Jacob said. "Kill them before they kill us."

"I put everyone on it." Albert said. "It shall come to pass."

Albert's influence was ingrained into America's deep-state. His controls continued to be operational but less stable. Every year more threads snapped. Social constructions failed one by one. His plagues, wars, and political interventions no longer did the required work. Humanity began pulling together. Keeping them divided became a battle. More evidence of Women's Magic in the world.

"I'm sure a smaller space rock—"

"No," Albert said. "This is better. We can shut these machines off before they kill us, too. This time humanity dies and we will remain untouched."

"Shut them off?" Jacob chuckled. His deep rumble echoed. "Shut them off…if ever we start them. What if our operatives can't locate the keys?"

"We have volcanic venting. They die slower but faster than you think. One key is enough. Even so, we'll recover them before Artemis can. Keys can't be destroyed. They drew that ship to them to make an escape. Our men will find whoever has them…" Albert drew a bent finger across his throat.

"What if the restart fails?"

"The piles have started. It has begun. The keyset? If found, lava for everyone. Until then, we gas the rats. Black smokers will smite the sun. They die slower but they die. What is a year or two to us?"

"Sooner is better," Jacob said looking up from the computer. "Our CIA man has arrived. Get the door."

He pointed at the old lady. The woman who waited on them ambled from her service cart to the door dragging Albert's contempt. She had become bent by a third. Her hands nearly touched the floor. The hump of her back pushed her down where she belonged. She reminded him of a Neanderthal with her rat's nest hair. It did his heart good to see a Goddess, such as the great Athena, in her proper place. She swung open the heavy oak door and retreated to her corner with haste. In came Jason Thompson, the CIA's shadow director. The current political hack in the director's chair being Thompson's lapdog.

"It is confirmed?" Albert asked.

"Yes, fifteen years ago, a research ship called *The Finder,* stopped there. They stumbled onto the first vent injector. It sank first and the rest followed. Richard Wailer's salvage ship is known. He's a minor celebrity. From what I gathered; they didn't recover anything. They lost a diver. Cause of death is listed as shark attack. The body was never recovered."

"Why did you not dig deeper?" Jacob said.

"I did. The crewmen I interviewed said the captain, very pissed off, took the only find and pitched it over the side. No one saw exactly what it was but a gold chain was mentioned. If it sank to the bottom, it's out of reach. Only a specialized ROV goes that deep. Wailer didn't have that equipment. They made best speed back to port after the death. Shall I arrange a deep-water recovery? If it's there, we'll find it."

"Wailer had them and cast them into the sea!" Jacob said.

"It seems so," Thompson said.

Thompson is wrong. If the keys were thrown back the machine would not have stopped. Keys seek cradles. Artemis' temple was its home. Someone from that ship took them. The prime suspect, Amy Parks, recently died. Another mistake. Thompson should have kidnapped her. No more mistakes.

"This is what we do," Albert said. "Track down every crewman. This Wailer fellow…well monied isn't he? Find out where he is and where he goes. Assume that pair of amulets made landfall. Find them. Release your dogs."

"Don't wait," Jacob said, "Pick up Wailer first. Question everyone."

With a wave Albert dismissed Thompson. Albert remained silent until the cadence of Thompson's steps faded out of hearing within the rock-hewn passages. The mention of a shark was unexpected. They had not put one of their mechanical monsters in place there. Odd coincidence?

"Good work on Thompson's part," Albert said.

"So, the mystery is resolved," Jacob said. "You're right. The key escaped. Have him go after the crew women first."

"Too overt. We can't tip our cards. Thompson will dig into everyone. If his mind is intent on finding a woman, she may read it. Better if he remains neutral," Albert said with confidence. "Even so, we will proceed. The machines will run and when they do—"

"That'll make the Siberian Traps seem like a playground," Jacob said with a chuckle.

Long had the Dulles' studied Women's Magic to understand the enemies' ways and means. The Watchers' path was clear. The idea was proven. The lava flows of the Siberian Traps could have wiped out a huge portion of Earth's human population. If only they were able to start it again. The device was made to build land, preserve life, and not destroy it. The vent system was not designed for what the Watchers intended either. They found a way to subvert it.

Losing the keys was a gift. It gave Albert time and a new plan. The process may be less immediate but also inescapable once the vent system reaches temperature. There will be no shutting it down once peak is achieved, not even if the control board amulet is removed.

Albert's plan was the best solution. Wailer did him a favor. Earth will be wiped clean of vermin without resistance. Once more and for all time Ergaster man will prove Men's Magic—technology—the superior force. Thinking of magic, Albert realized Athena had remained in her place at the tea cart. Her very existence disturbed him. He called Borek, who stood guard outside his chambers, and had her removed.

***

"Borek, remove this dirty rag from my office."

Athena didn't wait and labored out the door. The shield was heavy there making every step a challenge. In the hallways moving was less trouble. Her escort exuded less evil which restored her a little.

"Darkness feeds on itself," she mumbled in a language Borek did not know.

Athena had placed herself in the presence of the Dulles Brothers by intent. Pretending humility was her chosen tactic. She tolerated stays within the men's compound but it wore her down. Earthmen would fear to tread there. Remaining close to her enemy delivered tiny payments of information among the insults. The sacrifice is well worth it. She suffered them to learn.

Signs were mounting. Her plan wormed its way closer to fruition. Albert made it clear. The senior Goddess was a flea on the wall careful not to bite the dog that feeds lest she cause an itch of curiosity.

"Our masters seem irritable this evening," she said openly.

Borek, seven feet tall, loomed two feet above her head. She lost his face in the dim hall light. No words were necessary. He grunted in agreement.

Athena was able to walk upright outside of Albert's personal shield. She proceeded with quick bear-footed slaps between Borek's long stride boot thumps. The closer to her chamber she came, the more power returned. She ventured to plant another seed.

"Borek, remember the elder days of freedom? You were honorable. You need not follow the young upstarts. Are not Ergaster men free?"

"I made my oath. I am not free, as you say. I am sworn, is fealty nothing?"

"You were once sworn to uphold mankind."

"They are not men. They are animals of our invention."

"And you are not the invention of Gia? Your bones, this rock, your sinew, the minerals. Who made them?"

"Enough! You lost your place, Creationist."

The odd pair arrived. Borek opened the heavy oak door for her but did not go inside. Her labyrinth of rock-cut domiciles would drive him mad. The foyer was safe for him but not the inner depths charged with Women's Magic against males.

"In you go," Borek said.

"Won't you come in and have tea?"

Borek didn't answer but stepped back. Her domicile's magic would kill an Ergaster man. Magic is oppressed under an energy jail but not gone. What little the Goddesses mustered was enough to keep Borek at bay and he knew it well. No male that entered the Goddesses' chambers survived. The stalemate held twelve thousand years but it could not hold much longer without Artemis. Her magic had gone mute. Artemis must have given her keys out.

Earthborn slave-girls came as needed bringing food, but no others had gone beyond the inner door. The Goddesses were not slaves. Men once called them sprites, Earth spirits, fairies, and many other names. They had been the keepers of life and life above suffered by their absence. Athena wondered if an Earth man could survive her chambers. Have they all lost the sacred feminine within them? Has balance been driven out of them completely? She had questions, but this she knew: Earth won't survive under Men's Magic.

Several of the ladies came from the inner chambers to greet her. They gathered around her and put hands on her. Athena felt her power grow.

"Here we are, branches torn from the Tree of Life," Athena said.

Borek grunted and shut the door. He did not lock it. There was no escape. Athena allowed herself to expand. She straightened to full height. Age fell off like shed scales. Her ragged clothing remained yet the decrepit woman beneath emerged radiating, glowing with timeless beauty.

"Come to me, sisters. I need healing."

The ladies surrounded her again. Their forms were that of old women, bent and gray, dressed in Bedouin scraps. That was an illusion. Let Ergaster think them powerless. They assume it takes all of our power to stay them. Power was reserved for the plan. They accumulated it for the end-time which the coven sensed had come.

"What did you learn?" Inanna said. She was first behind Athena. The sisters were at odds.

"He cannot help but gloat," Athena said. "I have news. The keys escaped. She imbued them to do so. They rest now, hidden."

"A lot of good it will do if they don't find their way here. Artemis is hiding. Not a peep of her magic to trace. Who will guide the plan? How can we know? Did it divide?" Annona said in low tones. Her link to Artemis had been severed. "It can't remain hidden from them long. They always find our devices."

"It has divided and it will come," Athena said in the faintest whisper.

She could not risk exposing the secret lest Borek overheard. Artemis' spell to hide them, one never tried before, must have worked.

Annona disliked the plan although it was long in motion. Giving Ergaster access to the vent system was too risky in her opinion. A device made to form planets can also destroy one. Her jailers didn't understand its power. They will kill themselves and Earth in their ignorance. What choice did we have but to try it? Desperation birthed a desperate action. They let Ergaster taste a bait they could not resist.

"This will not work," Annona repeated.

"The Faiths guide it. Did they not imbue it?" Athena said in defense.

Athena had designed Artemis's escape. But their free agent could be dead. Goddesses can die when they choose. Artemis would give up her life to protect the mission. But did she sacrifice herself? This unknown worried them. Amulets keep power as long as the owner lives. Does she yet live? In death, will her spirit continue to power the key?

"Artemis is yet free in the world," Athena said. "Albert indicated this."

"There is hope," Annona said. "The Faiths' magic is strong."

"We are," three women spoke as one. "We cannot see, but we feel it, it comes, it will come. Even now it seeks a way. We see a sword's edge. Life hangs by thin fibers."

"This is fair news," Inanna said. "I concede, Athena. It may come but what if it does? We can never be free while Ergaster men remain. Womankind cannot hide from them."

"We fulfill the oath," Athena said. Murmurs rippled around the coven. That's Ann's real objection. She doesn't want to die. "If we cannot remove them, we remove ourselves. They can't procreate. Our powers keep them. They will age and die."

"If we ever get out from under the yoke. 'The power of three' breaks the door's seal. Only two are driving forward."

"Yes, a problem," Athena said. "Yet, we have hope. Life will find a way."

The Goddesses were inventors, keepers of life, creators but not all-seeing, not all-knowing, and least of all, not all-powerful. Their time of guiding life on Earth ended when they were captured, yet life perpetuates itself. The Goddesses set the world in motion, but now it was on its own. Death cannot be made within a Goddess' heart. Ergaster women cannot kill but Ergaster men must die in order to preserve life on Earth, the highest goal.

Women's devices had long been captured. Such life-givers are only viable as long as the Goddesses remain. .

"Men's Magic cannot preserve them."

"Our kind must pass," Sibel said.

The coven cannot kill but it must. A way was found if luck held. Dead Goddesses don't bear children. One mated with a human man and produced a fertile offspring. Albert must never know that. A hundred years ago preparations for the next Ergaster man's child facilitated Artemis' escape. *Sibel will be raped next.* She will soon be fertile. Better to die and that choice can only be done in daylight.

CHAPTER TWELVE:

THE BADLANDS

Students called Assistant Professor Thomas Conley 'Skinny Tom.' There were other Toms on site between students and staff. Conley didn't mind the handle. Shovel bums don't do formalities. Several weeks into the dig, he felt at home although he wasn't able to do much digging himself. He had been there twice before as a student and his inner landscape hadn't changed but teaching was the job which compelled him to stand back. The long view felt strange. He preferred swinging a spade but the dig super's job was filled.

What a puzzling site... Long after him, the project will continue. Understanding T-rexes' environment alone will take lifetimes. The current research task was to explain why so many rex tracks were laid at the same time, in the same place, if that turned out to be true. If so, the situation was odd. T-rex was supposed to be a lone hunter/scavenger, but the footprints disagreed.

Exposing prints was tedious work. The trackway had been laid down in mud that later became shale which disappeared under a sandstone hill. They could not remove the overburden haphazardly, rather, they had to excavate top-down as not to disturb what might present itself above the shale. *Good experience for students.*

Over the years, tons of materials were removed with no end of the pathway in sight. T-rex feet ran half a mile along a former stream in between a series of low hills. Waterways were interesting places to excavate otherwise. Students had the opportunity to make their first significant discoveries.

By individual word-of-mouth, dig leader Doctor Jonathan Mede of Berkeley called for an early meeting to discuss progress. No one told "Big John" Callahan. Nobody trusted Big John, especially Mede. Big John treated students like slave labor. Tom entered the main tent, calling out a happy greeting.

"Stifle it," Mede answered.

Callahan, six-foot-five and just short of overweight, sported a wild coif of hair on his head which had a mind of its own. He slept late, drank more than his share of the hard-to-get beer at night, and did very little else but watch over everyone's shoulder. When Tom first met him several weeks before, the hair on Tom's neck stood up. His birthmark flared hot.

"Come around people. Quick now. Quietly, please," Mede said from his seat. "We have a mystery to solve."

Callahan was another mystery. Callahan intimidated others like an ego-driven academic, but Tom sensed malice behind it. *Yet, the man's subtle and thoughtful at times like a lioness considering her quarry.* Callahan had a lightning-flash mean streak, too. One never knew when or why Big John would lash out.

"Callahan's only interest is what we find," one of the students whispered as people settled at the long table. "He took my crocodile bone yesterday."

"I'll put you down anyway," Mede said.

Early meetings gave students time to claim finds and credit. Mede had his logbook open. Tom agreed with the consensus. Big John had dirty hands and it wasn't from digging. He'd glom onto anything not recorded. Mede posted obvious disdain whenever Big John stuck his nose in. Nobody knew what Callahan's actual qualifications were. Callahan came without explanation by way of an obscure government research facility. The Finder Foundation had filed an objection but didn't withdraw its financial support.

Dawn in the Badlands is beautiful but no one paid attention to morning's glories. Chunky Doc Mede nervously scratched his salt-and-pepper beard between log entries. Tom resisted touching his birthmark. Tom got up, poured a coffee, and noticed Mede's laptop. The Shovel Bum blogsite was open as usual. *I'll have to read it. Mede sure finds it interesting.* The last student stumbled in.

"All here, good, so let's talk prints," Mede said. "Keep your volume down."

Serena, a doc candidate with a specialty in footprints, spoke up. "It must be different animals at slightly different times, maybe offspring returning to their birthground generation to generation to mate, lay eggs as birds do. I know, radical idea, but this many T-rexes can't be grouped. They're solitary creatures."

Pete Rosco, as always, had to disagree. "No reason they could not be here together, they were scavengers, after all. Any big dead thing brings them together. Why wouldn't they get along? There's plenty of food. When a big sauropod—"

"Where are the remains then?" Someone said with an angry tint.

"Where are the Hadrosaurs? Isn't this their migration route—"

"They did have a fantastic sense of smell," the biologist chimed in.

The usual debate took off: predator V. scavenger. But something else was going on with rex. Tom felt it more than thought it. This assemblage was like no other yet discovered. There had to be a reason for it. Everyone talked at once forcing hushed tones to rise while Tom shut off his intuition to consider the evidence.

"No, no, no… Stifle now," said Mede. "Let us not revisit that. Geology, what have you?"

Dick didn't like the spotlight and flinched when called upon. "My data suggests incursions are all of the same layer. I don't see enough differentials in the stratum's content, so it's not that tricky. What's curious is I'm detecting heavy sulfur with cyanide concentrate in the immediate covering layer. We saw that same soil condition on the undisturbed crest of T-tot's hill, and only traces below it where I'd expect soil washed down from above. Diluted, of course. The silt had been poisoned just above the trackway. I'd bet volcanic gas killed them all at the same time. It's not the KT boundary, it's too old. No tracks or bones above the mud pan until much later."

Does that confirm a large group of rexes cohabitating? Can't be. If so, where are the bodies?

"No way it's that," Eva said. "We have two adult females, different ages, a big male and a smaller one. The small ones might be contemporaries of the same clutch, but I don't see how they all could have lived together in this small valley. Too big, limited resources and…"

That yearling we finished removing last week makes a case.

Tom heard all these arguments before and drifted off thinking about the big find. An entire young animal, still articulated eroding out of a hilltop, was found last season. They finished excavation soon after he arrived. Huge find. The team christened it T-tot. T-rex wasn't the lone hunter going around killing smaller rexes like a Hollywood B-movie. T-tot should have been somebody's lunch and not preserved so well. The standard T-rex lone-hunter theory is losing credibility.

One big sauropod keeled over would feed a hundred of them for a year. No work or risk involved, but what explained the scattered herbivore bones? Tom didn't buy the competition for food angle. Slow-moving, stupid food on the hoof were as thick as mosquitoes in a swamp on the nearby plains. If rex hunted at all it had to be pack hunting. That's the best strategy, but how to prove it?

Tom got up and poured himself another cup. Mede always sat by the stove. From behind, Tom read Mede's open laptop. The Shovel Bum's blog lead-in read, *"T-rex cared for its young, but it was a family effort."*

"Who wrote that tripe," Tom asked looking past Mede's unruly gray hair. Mede, busy playing debate moderator, didn't answer.

Tom bent closer and recognized Kenny Parks' byline. "I know that name."

He set his tin mug down. Knees protesting, Tom leaned on the stainless-steel field sink for stability. *Where did he come up with that, T-tot isn't even close to publication-ready?* Tom didn't have time to think about it.

The camp cook/ hired lead digger hurried in. An old Mexican-American past retirement age, Jorge Rodriguez, gave the cut-neck signal. Callahan was coming. Mede brought his man Jorge on all his digs. The meeting was effectively over. The cook/ dig master got to work at the stove while Mede directed each one to his day's work. Students jumped up and helped with food. Everyone got occupied.

Tom regained his legs after a while and resumed sipping coffee. Trying for casual, he slid into the chair next to Mede uninvited. Tom noticed Mede wore the same aftershave his dad had used. Jorge set down Mede's plate and the old man attacked his eggs and potatoes. One of the visiting doctors usually sat with Mede. People gravitated to each other according to social status. Tom was way out of Mede's league.

Tom checked the tent. Callahan was busy pawing samples at the finds table out of hearing range. Tom worked up a reason to approach Mede.

"Doc Mede, have you read this blogger before?"

Mede chuckled. "Kenny Parks? Every day. He's a high school student—brilliant. Fantastic insights, he's right more than wrong. He's better than any freshmen at Old U."

Mede cast eyes toward a freshman washing yesterday's dishes. Mede wasn't above friendly school vs. school banter.

"Parks answers questions on the forum page. I try to stump him, but he's good. Still, he goes way out on a hypothesis's limb. What fun, eh Conley?"

Mede's an expert observer. Nobody read the ground better, except maybe, Jorge. But Mede was also apt at reading people. Stunned, Tom forgot to close his mouth and drooled a little.

"What's wrong, Conley? You look like you saw an anomaly."

"I had Kenny subbing high school. He told me something…never mind. That reminds me. I might have left my pick behind when we lifted T-tot off that hill. What hill was that?"

"Number six, what a badass hill that was, steep approach—"

"Badass, BA… I need to go." Tom got up with his head reeling.

Mede grabbed Tom's vest and pulled him back, bending Tom's face close.

"If you see Callahan," Mede stopped, looked around, "or he sees you, go the other way. You get me?"

"I think so."

Tom stepped back on weak legs. The cook stood idle-by behind them. Jorge looked right at Tom and winked before turning back to the stove. *That's weird.*

This project was wired with live internet cameras. Old U took care of communications. Media majors ran the satellite link and camp power. When the generator ran, the world watched them dig. It was PR, and by Tom's standards, wasted money. But then again, lots of people, people such as Kenny enjoyed watching discoveries as they occurred. One benefit of the live feed was it made it harder for Callahan to screw people.

Tom took off, stopped at his camper, and grabbed his excavation kit and rock hammer. Equipped, he hurried to Hill Six. *Kenny's BA Hill.*

Callahan was nowhere in sight. Tom climbed BA Hill. The grid pins were gone. He went to the divot where T-tot was extracted. They had plastered the little dino for removal where he lay. Tom removed some residual plaster then scratched and picked under where the young T-rex had expired. *The camera's still here but not recording, too bad.* The cams were wired together but this hill's feed had been switched off.

"Nobody's recording Hill Six anymore." Tom said going deeper. "Site is tapped out. Nothing's here… I hope."

Tom lost track of the time. He heard the generator fire but ignored it. He should have gone to the active site. An hour later he found an egg, then another, and another. His mind wrenched sideways. Just as Kenny said!

All around the eggs he found fern and twig impressions as if this was a giant nest. *Maybe young-rex was stealing eggs. But the eggs aren't broken?*

That was his snap judgment until he saw the connection: the entire hill, eighteen feet around descending fifteen yards, all the same color and texture.

"This is a…a giant nest!"

Tom's mind raced. It had been reused for generations and grew bigger with each new layer of lining. Tom felt stupid and staggered at the same time. He pushed upright from his bent forward position. *Why didn't I see it before? This is a grant money bonanza.*

"Looks like she had an appetite for eggs, of course," Callahan said from behind.

Tom twisted half around. Callahan extended a meaty hand and pulled Tom up onto his feet as easy as a bundle of dry sticks. Big John's grip was painful. Callahan pushed dirt into the hole with his size 14 army boot.

"No need to play with Diplodocus eggs, common as dirt, we have T-rex tracks to uncover."

Callahan's voice came laden with menace. *I know rex eggs when I see them.* Tom had an intuitive urge to bite his tongue. Going off on Callahan could kill his baby career before it got going.

"Don't you think I should—"

"I'll cover them for another day. Get going, Conley. I'll take it from here."

Tom hadn't seen the bully with a shovel before. It looked more like a weapon than a tool in his hands. Tom stumbled back to basecamp hot, tired, dirty, and disconcerted. The more he thought as he walked the deeper his career hopes collapsed. *I should have stood up to him, so why didn't I?* His birthmark throbbed in response.

"Because I need this job."

Back at the big tent, he resisted the urge to rip the flap open and entered lightly. Students might be cleaning and prepping finds but nobody was home, just the cook. *Why isn't the dig supervisor on-site?* Anger flared. *That old man's too close to Mede. What an exalted place for an unqualified hanger-on, waste of grant money.* The inequities of life piled on him like dino shit, Callahan and now this.

"Where's Mede?" Tom said, aware his voice seethed.

Jorge put one finger to his lips and pointed to his ear with the other hand. "Boss is scouting north gully on way to Dig One. He will be there soon."

Jorge pointed to the back of the tent. Tom didn't move. The ravine back there, out of camera range, was where students smoked pot and did everything else staff isn't allowed to do. Every teaching dig-site had its traditional no-teacher zone. Professors politely went the other way. Jorge pointed his chin forcefully toward no-teacher land.

"I don't get it," Tom said refusing to take the hint.

"Sorry, *señor*, he has gone."

Jorge tossed his head toward the back like a Punch and Judy doll.

"That's fine." Tom begrudgingly took his meaning. "I'll catch up with him later. I'm going to Three anyway."

Jorge turned around and resumed cleaning the cast-iron griddle with an oil stone and no oil. The stone screeched like a Velociraptor. Tom used the diversion and ducked under the tarp and descended into the narrow ravine which opened into a wide series of washes. He spotted Dr. Mede downrange scratching a rock in his hand with his straight brass pick.

Tom marched to Mede. "I've got a bone to pick with you—"

"That's why they hired you, my boy. Surely, you can dig it?" Mede's pun carried no humor.

A joke? Mede never jokes. It took Tom aback and snuffed his wick at the same time. But Tom's complaint didn't dissipate.

"Callahan," Tom said, "He covered rex eggs and told me to get lost. T-tot was guarding a rex nest. My God that entire mound is a nest, must be many generations built up." Tom's chest itched like a flea-bit demon. "T-tot was protecting eggs, alone, this must be a rex family pride, like lions! It's important. It's—"

"Off the table, son." Mede carefully put his dental pick back into his pocket-protector. His safari vest's breast pocket was stuffed with small implements but no pens. "You'll find, in this business... You are new, of course. You'll see that if you want a career, certain things our donors are concerned with won't come to light, not if you value your professional neck."

Tom was aghast. "But this is a major discovery! This must be published. It's, it's—"

"It's not worth your life, Tom. There'll be others. Things slip through. They don't man every dig, only when they think there's something important. How they know, I don't know. After Christmas break, before spring season starts, there won't be a T-rex nest here to study."

Tom fell to his knees. He wanted to ask, who the hell is Callahan anyway? But he didn't get a chance. The man in question came out of another ravine. Tom heard his massive boots crunching gravel before seeing him. Mede rolled the rock in his hand around.

"See anymore?" Mede said as Callahan closed in. "I think you may be right. It could be a baby rex coprolite. Good eye, Professor Conley. Big John, what do you make of this?"

Callahan took the specimen. The man wore an antique jeweler's loop on a silver chain around his neck, a pretty thing of flora engraved silver, but not effective although the primitive magnifying glass was intact. Nineteenth-century technology was useless there. Big John morphed into a Cyclops reading the bumps on Jason the Argonaut's head.

Callahan handed the sample back. "Nice coprolite. It doesn't warrant attention, but log it for future study."

"Of course. Good idea Professor Callahan," Mede said with tight lips. "I'll make a note."

Mede pulled out his small side-pocket notebook and pretended to write with a pencil stub. Callahan turned and proceeded upslope.

Tom played along and pushed dirt around with his finger. Mede had a long history of good finds, some considered uncanny. Tom wondered how many more finds Mede could have published. As Callahan proceeded toward camp, Mede helped Tom to his feet and handed the specimen over, but Tom didn't need a closer examination to know it wasn't a coprolite—wrong color and consistency.

"Fossilized plant stem," Tom said. "Tumbled down as upper grades eroded."

"Right you are," Mede said.

Such samples were everywhere. Callahan wasn't qualified. Tom marched back up the ravine with a new appreciation of his position. There was more to Mede than shown. Another revelation also stuck: Kenny was right. Tom also sensed an ally in Mede. Tom felt like he had crossed into the world of co-seekers. Each on different paths but moving in the same direction. Mede, like him, wanted the truth. The truth can set you free or crush you. Dancing between the lines is how Mede survived.

"Lesson learned, Doc," Tom said and proceeded to the dig. Tom had stepped over the line into truth-land, and there was no going back for him.

That night in the mess tent, Tom pulled up Kenny's blog, but the post about T-rex family values was gone. A moderator's chat window popped open on his screen. He hadn't instant-messaged the moderator. It said, *"Saw him cover the eggs. He'll pay. I'll let you know where something good is next time."*

The window vanished. Tom tried to respond but Callahan came in just then, the last man he wanted to see. It was time to shut the generator down anyway. Tom went to his camper and opened the pint of good whiskey he had saved to celebrate his first big find and poured two fingers into an Old U coffee mud.

"Here's to you Kenny Parks." He didn't have anyone to click glasses with so he tapped his skateboard and took a sip. "What am I getting myself into?"

He took another taste, intending on getting good and drunk. But he set it aside after a couple of half-hearted sips. Whiskey didn't relieve that bitter heart-twisting taste Callahan left in his mouth.

CHAPTER THIRTEEN:

MARY ESCAPES

No one ever knocked on her triple-locked door unless she expected it.

"Landlord?" Mary whispered.

Recent paranoia abated, but Mary Conley wasn't going to be stupid and open any entry on faith. She didn't believe in faith.

"Faith is for fools." Leaning to the eyehole, she couldn't believe who she saw.

"Richard?" *Two visits in a month, I must rate. What's he doing here? Amy isn't dead three weeks and he's still around?*

She expected the funeral to be the last time she'd see Richard Wailer. Tommy was done with school so his patron had no business there. If Tommy wasn't off at his field job, she wouldn't open up for Richard. She could have ignored his tapping but something nagged her to let him in.

"All right, already. I'm doing it," she said and swung the door wide open.

"I see you cleaned the place deep. Looks nice," Richard said. His head swung left and right before stepping inside. "Nice lamp, looks antique."

"You would notice anything old. Got it at the thrift shop. I'll clean when I'm manic, okay? I'm not ashamed of my bipolar ways. Mania has its moments."

"You aren't manic. This isn't that," Richard said, spreading his hands. "It's something else. You're naturally high energy. Something was forcing you down."

"How would you know? When did you become a psychologist? Better question: why are you here?"

"Saving your life and mine, too, I hope."

Mary wanted to laugh but held it. Save my life? I've been trying to die since you killed my husband... That isn't fair. Not Richard's fault.

"Alright Captain Cryptic, spill it," Mary said.

"Sit Mary, let's talk. Have you noticed that when Tommy's away you feel better?" He shut the door. "He wasn't home last spring, and you felt better. He was home at the end of summer and you hit bottom. Your mood picked up after he left. Am I right?"

Mary backed up and lowered herself into Tommy's spot on the sofa. She caught a whiff of Tommy's shaving cream. *I love my son. He's wrong.* She avoided the rocker when not depressed. She had put on a nice dress and wanted to keep it that way. The rocker was filthy from her stewing there in clothes well past their laundry date. Her chair-hole smelled of distress and tear-salt. Tommy having something to do with her moods rattled her skull. Richard might be right and she didn't like it.

"You are better when he's gone."

She had poured a fresh cup of tea before he showed. Hands shaking, she managed a sip but didn't offer Richard a cup. "You don't know what you're talking about. Unless… You're keeping tabs on me? Admit it."

"I keep track," Richard said. He pulled a chair out of the kitchen. "I have men watching, that's part of why I'm here, things they've seen. I keep an eye on you and Tom. Guilty, shoot me."

"Guilt, I suppose so. We have that in common. I let Bert sign onto your ship. I let Tommy see his father die. Guilt all around. It's eaten the center out of me."

"No, it's not that." Richard ran a hand through his hair. "Look, you're ill because Tommy held the amulet, it's gone now but…Tommy had it. So did Amy's son, Kenny. She told me he swallowed it. Kenny didn't lose it. He still has it. They killed her to get it, but…They think it's lost. I'm not sure who they are, not yet. Somebody powerful wants it. They know Kenny is a special ed case. He's more special than they can imagine."

"What are you saying? Why're you always so damn cryptic? Who are they?"

"I'm not sure, but I have a few ideas. That volcano wasn't there two weeks before we arrived. It's gone now. It wasn't the only one. There were many like it all around the world. Had they gone off…but they're gone, sank to the bottom. They're controlled…an extraordinary force beyond understanding, such as, dare I say…"

"Magic. You're telling me it's magic? I don't believe in magic." Mary was incredulous. She knew enough geological science to know volcanoes aren't seasonal flowers. Every ocean vent could not have been surveyed. "Tell me the gods are returning and you'll have to leave."

"It's not magic. It's technology and it's dangerous," Richard spoke waving his hands around. "I'm working on who's behind it… That shark wasn't a shark. It's a machine. I have video." He leaned forward. "It went after the amulet. By chance, it pushed Tommy to the surface. Somebody wants it bad and when they figure out Tom has it or had it…" Richard spread his hands.

"Nobody knows about Tommy's jewel. I never talked about it. You lost your mind, Richard! And I thought I was nuts… What's this to do with me? We don't have it. It's gone."

Mary took her cup off the end-table but didn't drink. She missed the coaster putting it back. A wave of cold truth slapped against her soul. She braced herself for more.

"Will you please hear me," Richard said.

"I'm listening."

"Amy's son still has half of it. They think it's MIA. They don't know it split. The CIA has or had him under observation. My people were onsite with Kenny…" Wailer gritted his teeth but kept talking. "He's been renditioned. He should have been safe there. My fault, though I had it covered. Amy's cancer wasn't natural… You must come with me. They'll research who was on board if not already. They'll make you talk. Then, Tommy is a target. They won't go after him if we make them think… They'll assume you have it if you make an unannounced move. We have to run."

"You're crazy! I can't…I can't," She reached for her now cold cup of tea, knocking it over. "I know you're right. Damn it! I can't explain it. I'm not crazy. This is real. I get that. It's always been real. Odd sensations. I don't want to go, but I must. What about Tommy?"

"My people will keep an eye on him."

"It's always been this way for me, second sight," Mary said, hardly believing she finally voiced it. "I never told anyone. Bert had it, another kind, stronger, more focused. You knew that…Poor Bert. I get feelings…I feel the truth. I'll go. I need to get ready."

"That's what they're after, special abilities. The government and someone more dangerous. They aren't in it for the greater good. The CIA observes and learns before they take. They're careful. The Watchers have no moral compunction. They will kill you, Mary. I'll see that they don't. But you have to come with me now. Right now."

"Now? Today? I've got to call Tommy. What about our things? I need my books."

"I'll have my men pack you," Richard said. "They'll forward anything you need later, but we must go." Richard handed Mary his phone. "It's shielded. Press one and it goes directly to the dig site's satellite phone. I have connections there. You need a cover story."

"I got it." Mary took the phone. *Of course, he's got connections there, I should have known.* His phone didn't have a brand name. Mary covered the mouthpiece. "Got an answering machine. I'll leave a message."

It beeped.

"Tommy, it's Mom, listen, I have an opportunity. I'm going on a peace mission. You know I always wanted to do this. I checked and Doctor Hillman says I should go. I'm doing well and still off meds. He says I should do it and I am. I'll be gone for a while. Don't worry. I'm in good hands. Call back later. If I'm not home, you'll know why."

She hung up thinking, *Tommy's going to flip when he gets that message.*

"Did it like a pro," Richard said. "Great idea. Quick-minded isn't manic. They won't move too fast. They'll wait until you're distracted or sleeping. Good thinking."

"Butter me up, why don't you." She had felt an unspoken tension between them for years, emotional poker. She laid down her wild card. "You aren't doing this to get into my panties, are you?"

"I had a thing for you, sure… but, out of respect for Bert…"

"Ha, you admit it!"

Richard's face turned red. She'd never seen that before. "Relax, my sense of romance is closed for renovations. I admire your honesty. I don't see why people think you're an asshole. I gotta pack, won't take long. I need—"

"No, we got to go." He checked his watch, got up, and looked out the kitchen's small window. "I'll buy whatever you need."

"How about a Harley Davidson?"

"If you like, but there isn't any room to ride it on the *Finder*. We're doing the L. Ron Hubbert act. We'll stay out at sea."

"From the Midwest? The Great Lakes?"

Richard checked outside using the balcony's sliding glass door by peeking around the curtain. He pointed out his limo parked below and the two police cars on a side street and one outside of the parking lot's main exit.

"They followed me here, perfect. We'll use it," Richard said. He opened his phone and said, "Go."

They watched from either side of the sliding door through drawn curtains. The limo backed up to the building's main door. A few seconds later it took off like a moonshine rocket ship. Cop one pulled the limo over. The cops got out of the car and walked up to the limo with one officer on either side. Each man had a hand ready on his gun. The limo driver hammered it when the first gun came up. The policemen jumped aside. Before the patrolmen reentered their car, the other cruiser tore-ass after the limo.

"They were going to shoot us!" Mary said.

"Best driver in the business," Richard said, ignoring Mary's distress. "That'll do but not for long. Let's go."

Richard spoke with his usual confidence. His earlier display unnerved her. His calm side was better for her mental health. She felt more able under his umbrella.

He isn't scared so why should I be. Because they want you dead, dumb-ass.

Mary's mind raced with wild fears while running down the back stairwell. The fire escape alarms were active. Management was good about that. But the emergency door's alarm didn't scream. A blacked-out, ratty, decommissioned police sedan sat waiting. Mary and Richard slipped in with no witnesses in sight. Richard donned a hoodie, baseball cap, and sunglasses. He slunk low behind the wheel and drove them out of the complex slowly. He looked a hundred years old with his face in shadow.

Mary wanted to roll the window down but he said no. The car smelled like beer farts. Mary pulled her wool cap low and hunched down.

CHAPTER FOURTEEN:

KENNY AT HOME

The Antiquities Department agent, Jane Brower, watched Kenny on her computer from the Chicago office. She relaxed. After school, as usual, Kenny went online to watch dig sites. She also had eyes on the Foundation's group home staff who ran the facilities. The researchers doing psychology experiments under contract to the government, another of Wailer's shell operations, were under surveillance as well. It was a lot for one observer to track, but she did her best.

Director Murphy knew about this child's desirable attributes, and he wanted to know more. Jane's primary task was to identify and classify Kenny's odd findings by way of her off-site observations, and steal the contractor's findings ahead of official reports.

"Let's see what we'll bury next," Jane mused while scanning several screens. Kenny was busy so she had time to download the researcher's latest without them knowing it.

The Antiquities Department didn't only cover up problematic truths, they neutralized them, and the problem-people who exposed anomalies. Jane signed on accepting the need as worthy. Should such a discoverer refuse to join the government's efforts to expel shocking facts, his or her career would be over. Not many refused the call to cooperate. Murphy provided either sugar or salt, their choice. Kenny couldn't make that decision.

In Jane's mind, there were natural forces at play not yet understood. Some of these were akin to magic. *But of course, it isn't magic.* Foreign technologies only look like magic. That was the official line, but she didn't buy it. Jane's theory was that people like Kenny have natural energetic powers beyond sciences' current perceptive capabilities. All due to his unusual brain, she believed, be it magic or biology. She'd find the answer. She thought science sometimes asked the wrong questions.

"It's extra physical, not metaphysical" fell out of her mouth. She didn't have evidence to back it but rather enjoyed considering the idea.

Jane told co-workers that she didn't believe in magic although she didn't exclude the possibility. Murphy's team dealt in the arcane. She was hired for her open mind and sealed lips. Her department saw what should not be seen.

Kenny's got more going on than interesting insights. She read Kenny's text as it scrolled on her screen in real time. Checking the CCTV camera, Kenny stood five feet from the computer typing midair as if playing air-piano. He didn't touch the keyboard at all—no wires, no apparatus, eyes closed.

"That computer can't interrupt hand movements." A chill went down her spine. She rubbed her eyes and looked again. "Boss isn't going to like this." She called out from her desk. "Hey, Tod, you gotta see this."

Kenny usually had the live cameras at Berkeley's Badlands dig on. He'd run two or three live-dig websites on split-screens while writing his blogs. Multitasking was proven ineffective for regular people, but it worked for him. Kenny concentrating on one thing was rare.

"Weird," Jane said as Murphy looked over her shoulder. "Now he's writing in the third person. It's hard to keep up. He types too fast." Jane blew up the text to follow better.

"Recording, right?" Tod said. "Assess it later. Take screenshots. I'm swamped." Tod left.

He must have seen Kenny do this before. Jane turned back to her computer to confirm the recording. She checked playback. She'd clean up the grammar later for the transcript. She caught up to Kenny typing. She didn't get the chance to show Murphy Kenny's air-typing trick. Kenny slowed down. Jane read along.

Kenny doesn't mind his travels, oh no. When he wants, when things are not nice mostly, he can go and he does and he did. The dinosaurs weren't glad to see Kenny. Oh no, not happy. Not anything like Mr. Conley happy, but they didn't mind either. Kenny isn't stupid, oh no. He didn't go all the way in mostly. Mostly, he likes to watch. I know them all by name and many kinds that other smart people like Kenny, that's me, don't know at all—yet to be discovered! Kenny knows, yes, always avoid other smart people. And, oh yes, Kenny you can go all the way in if you want to.

She stopped the player and clicked her voice recorder on. "He says that a lot, often repeated, that he's going or went somewhere. How's he going anywhere? Who's Conley?"

Jane underlined the name "Conley" on her paper notes before resuming.

Kenny did it a few times just to see but he never stays long, oh no. Die and there you are forever. It's safe unless you get stepped on. Big predators have pea brains. They run on instinct but they are really smart too, and if you don't smell like something they eat, they leave you alone, long as you don't do something dumb, like run or hang around after a fresh poopy. Poop is a magnet. If it makes a poo, it's food.

"Poop is a magnet?" She said and stopped the playback and clicked on her voice recorder program. She set it to type her voiced comments into the body of Kennys' text, in brackets for future review, rather than scribbling notes.

"Interesting idea but where did he hear that? If it craps, it's edible? That's original. The mention makes him laugh. Everyone at the school assembly laughed when he said it there but he didn't think it was funny at the time. He has a selective sense of humor, hum." Jane backed the onsite video up and as expected, Kenny laughed like crazy after he wrote about poop. Well behind Kenny's live typing, she hit play again. She'd get caught up eventually.

Lately, he didn't want to go away, oh no. Kenny has a blog spot! His new mommies let him. He's on a real dino blog and people ask him about things and he tells them, people on the airwaves need Kenny a lot, a real lot. He gets to see Mr. Conley and that dirty CIA guy on the Internet. I'll fix him. Computers are easy. Kenny follows webs, looks at people on their cameras. Kenny doesn't need software, oh no. He watches Pete the Blaster a lot. A real lot, the other bullies, too. When Kenny goes away, they leave him alone. Easy breezy.

But that Pete, oh no, he won't let up and it's Pete's fault anyway. In the future, the CIA man, will ask, 'How did you discover sending people back?'

Jane stopped the playback and pressed record. "That's interesting, he's confused about time, past, and present. He thinks the CIA will interview him. Do we have a man at the Badlands dig? Need to check that and see if he knows we're inside the group home as well. He's predicting his future. The child has an overdrive imagination."

Ha, Kenny wasn't stupid. He'd play dumb, and that is smart. He will tell them, years and years ahead from now, when they know anyway. 'Never trust the government.' That's what Mommy used to say before she died. Too bad, too bad, she is nice, nice, nice. New mommy isn't nice!

Jane paused to record. "He often gets the past and current confused. He may not understand time, or perhaps, the way he uses language is the issue. His memory and imaginings must overlap. He thinks the Foundation's lead behavioral psychologist is his mother."

In the future, Kenny tells the President how he was walking in the hallways really, fast. That's what he did. Mr. Webber let him go one minute, just one minute, always one, just one, before the bell. Oh, he would fly. Kenny walks so fast, not run, you're not allowed to run in school, oh no, 'Don't you run in the hall, Kenny.' Everyone says it.

Kenny, that's me, was walking and around the corner, Pete jumped out, but too late to stop. Kenny jumped away to the Jurassic because Kenny is thinking about it, for his blog. We crashed. Kenny left and Pete came with him. In the future, the future.

Kenny is there and a giant spider right there, oh four feet across, spinning a dead tree-glider, the size of a cat, into a ball, a ball, not a basketball, a dino-ball. Fascinating but something's distracting, something is screaming, a flying reptile? Nope, it's dumb, stupid Pete. This is my place. Me, Kenny, says, 'No Pete allowed, oh no.' Kenny goes back. People are there. A real short trip. We're on the ground from the crash, the crash, the crash of 29, 29, 29. People want us to go to the nurse, but the new mommy wouldn't like that. Oh no, she doesn't like a lot. Pete didn't want to go either. He messes in his pants. Pete runs to the restroom. That's the first time, after Mr. Conley left. Kenny found the way. Easy Breezy.

"Strange," Jane said into her recorder. "He's writing past-tense third-person as if he saw this from the future but if it's past, hum…or maybe it's in the recent future but he's looking at it from the extreme future. Then he does it the other way."

Jane saved another screenshot and Kenny's text blanked out.

"What the hell!"

She tried a few things but it was gone. She checked everything again to be sure. The videos were also gone, no audio or visual. She pulled out her notebook to write what she could remember.

"I'm screwed. Tod's gonna piss blood. That little hacker!"

Her paper notes were fine but what she recorded on her pocket device got wiped clean. She wrote down what she remembered such as 'Kenny knows the CIA watches him' which is creepy as hell. What else does he know?

She switched tabs and the first screenshot she took was still there. As she reread gooseflesh rose on the back of her neck. Her hand hovered above the 'save' hotkey. The previously saved page had blanked out. *I ain't risking my cell phone.* More unease piled on. She pressed save, and like the other tabs, it evaporated. Pressing 'save' also kicked her chair away from the computer desk.

"Too much coffee," she said rolling back to the desk with rubbery legs. Her mind reeled with questions.

Is this my imagination? Did Kenny overhear something? What's with Conley? Conley's associated with that thorn in Murphy's side, Richard Wailer. There's more to Conley.

Jane's intuition clicked on. She wanted to shut it off but couldn't. Conley's worth more attention. But he wasn't in the job profile. Steer-clear of innocent bystanders. Don't waste budget money. *'I'm only after what Antiquities can use,'* Murphy had said. Kenny's the one with potential. Conley the half-ass academic is nothing. Just another of Wailer's hopeless nerds. She felt compelled to ignore him.

Jane checked older notebook entries. She didn't dare open electronic files without an eye witness. From her cubicle, she searched the office pool for a super. Billings was out, but Tod was in his office. Hating to do it, she grabbed the laptop and proceeded through Tod's open door with a lump in her throat. Boss didn't mind walk-ins unless the news was bad. Jane didn't trust Billings anyway. Tod's wrath was easier. Something about Billings wasn't right, but she couldn't finger it. Jane's intuition jazzed her with a low voltage tingle as she opened the laptop for Tod. She explained what had happened to the files.

"Kenny deleted what he just wrote," she said opening the backup file. "I'm thinking it'll happen again. It's a hack, but how and when did he send a worm?"

As she and Tod watched, the next picture of Kenny's essay melted away. The image of lava pouring on paper filled the screen and quickly evaporated. Another page popped open unannounced and melted. One after another followed.

"Crap, it won't stop. I only opened one page," she said.

"Christ, we'll lose it all!"

Tod didn't look happy. Jane's temples pulsed. Bad time for a migraine. As each file opened, be it audio or film, the lava melts continued. Tod's frantic attempts at screenshots with his phone failed to save a picture.

"What'll I do with this?" Jane said about her empty job folder. A bolt of ice-lighting stiffened her spine.

Tod rolled his chair back. He checked the backup server behind his desk. Kenny's new stuff was gone and everything related to him corrupted. What text was left resembled liner-A Greek. The department hadn't yet followed up on Kenny's latest leads. Her paper notes weren't good enough to reconstruct.

"Let's hope the Foundation has copies," Murphy said and cringed.

"He hacked us. Nobody hacks the CIA," Jane said with a sharp edge. She hated losing data. "Now what? We take him out? Bring him in? Chemically pick his brain clean? How the hell does he do it?" The word traitor flashed in her mind but not her heart. Her anger flipped off. Rendition is horrible. "You want me to pull the trigger?" She said what was expected and didn't like it. "I'll send the paperwork."

"Not yet. He's in a safe-house," Tod said. "We need more. From now on, everyone takes handwritten notes. The hacker can't be him. Somebody else did it. I'll set a trap."

Thank God he's in thinking mode. Tod remained leaning way back in his chair rubbing his big, block chin. *This is huge and he acts like it's just another puzzle?*

"Maybe Antiquities should back out?" Jane said. "Send in the tech boys."

"Hate to do that. He's productive, found us all kinds of interesting things," Tod said. "You exposed our weakness, that's useful. We'll take Parks in deeper before the hacker beats us to it. I got to get around Wailer first. Jane, send in a deep-cover request. Watch Parks more carefully, forget the researchers. Alert the Foundation people, I have one on the payroll. Tell 'em we'll need a closer look at their machines. They'll cooperate. Mention me."

"I'll make the arrangements," Jane said.

"Setup the deep cover application. Hold it until I see it," Tod said as she crossed his threshold. "I hate contractors."

Tod's words and attitude followed Jane into the office pool. *He hates contractors. Sorry Tod, there's more of them than there are of us.* The Antiquities Department was a minor consideration inside the bureaucracy. Her office didn't get to act fast or do anything extraordinary outside of their budget without a ream of paperwork in place. Antiquities didn't have rendition money or the authority to execute one.

Billings, the Homeland rep, and others had to sign off before moving Kenny to a secure facility. It took time. The proof of a direct attack was weak. It could have been any hacker snooping around. Accidental intrusions would force them to cover their tracks. Jane felt dead-sure Kenny needed to get out of there fast. She had an odd desire to protect him…*but from who?* Jane normally ignored intuition but it wouldn't leave her alone.

"Okay fingers, do your magic." Jane cracked her knuckles. "Let's save Kenny."

Moving Kenny depended on paperwork. Jane faced her PC sensing the planet's rotation. Her life was bolted down yet everything felt like riding a rogue wave. She gripped the edges of her desk. Black-boxing this boy is wrong. Lately, her inner voice proved true. She'd never say it to her colleagues but intuition predicted bad-times ahead for this child. An idea came out of the heavens.

"Memo time." She started her text to speech program. "Justification: the honchos need evidence. Kenny doesn't use the computer without supervision. He's not the hacker. Possible inside counter agent? Relocations take time. The application won't be approved in time. Paperwork is the anchor. He's not safe." She clicked off the recorder. "Bad's coming for this boy and I can't prove it."

Jane slumped in her chair.

"Staring at a blank screen doesn't get nothing done," Murphy called from his office.

She proceeded with the paperwork and acquired a blazing headache in the process. Something inside her feared for Kenny. Like magic, once the application left her desk, her skull stopped pounding, but a deep pain in her chest began.

CHAPTER FIFTEEN:

GRADUATION

Why'd you let that Webber-tard get off, man? School's out next week. Get it while you can, Pete."

Randy the Junior was already taking over, smelly teeth and all. Randy had been acting more and more like the big man the closer they got to graduation.

"That kid messed with you. Ya gotta do something," Randy pressed.

"Yesterdays' news," Pete said.

"Today man. What'cha gonna do about it? Revenge man. Can't let it slide."

Pete didn't have an answer. *What I'd say? Yo man, I'm scared. No way.* He didn't know if it was real or that moron drugged him somehow, but every time he screwed with that retard, he'd fall into a nightmare and snap out of it screaming. Mom had him at the doctor's three times and they said it's seizures. Dad slapped him around for it, too. But yesterday it changed. Dared to do it, he tripped Kenny in the lunchroom. That crayon-eating moron smiled at him like a weasel. Thank God he didn't do anything. That a-hole plucked Pete's nerves big time. Pete rode the bus home yesterday sweating in his sneakers.

Horror struck yesterday late afternoon at home. Pete had checked his email and got one from his own account. He hadn't messaged himself. He opened it and read, *'Are you ready for the Permian Extinction?'* and nothing else. It had to be Kenny.

Pete had started talking. "That kid's screwing with me, I'm gonna—"

His mouth slammed shut. He couldn't move. He blinked and materialized in a swamp with mud up to his knees, dog-sized crawlies in every direction. The smell of plant-rot was strong enough to even make Randy sick. A giant dragonfly's wings ripped the air like a chainsaw hovering in front of him. He almost shit, but managed to clinch his cheeks tight.

"I'm really here! Kenny!" Pete cried, not expecting help.

Boom, he was back in his chair. The carpet an instant soaking mess. His muddy jeans stank worse than a dumpster. He had peed his pants. He screamed like never before. Mom rushed in scared but not because of him. Dad would have flipped. They cleaned up before Dad got home. Mom bitched the whole time. Cleaning was better than taking a beating. Dad didn't care who he hit when he got pissed.

Pete got through last night in one piece. Thinking of it made his legs rubbery. He staggered a little and leaned on a locker. Randy talked but Pete didn't hear him. Pete came back to himself before anyone saw him shaking, but the jitters were still there under his skin. Pete refocused.

Randy was saying, "Finals end next week. Webber's crew won't be here. Make your move. You a pussy or what?"

Pete couldn't back down. No way. He had to set the example. "Watch what happens at lunch."

The next period came and went and Pete wasn't up on hitting the cafeteria. He planned to skip but he got swept up with the gang and they flooded into lunch together. They got food, ate, did what they do, spitballs and insults flew, and all were good distractions. Randy didn't forget.

"Go for it. You're the big man," Randy said. "Me and Bing will distract the teach. Lay that mo-fo down, bro."

Pete got up slow. Took his backpack and dragged his ass toward Webber's table. Bing and Randy took their trays up. Bang, crash! They knocked the pile over and started a fake fight. Kenny stood and took a step forward as Pete neared the 'tard-table.

"Don't touch me! Look, Ken, old buddy..." Pete started.

"Don't run when you get there," Kenny said, bouncing in place without moving.

"It's like this, Ken. The guys will think I'm a puss. Do me a favor and play like I'm messing with you, but I'm not, we're friends now and—"

"You can live there, plenty to eat," Kenny's voice sounded far away. "But...Oh no, don't run. Nothing shiny is good. Shiny attracts them."

"So, we good? You and me, right buddy?"

"If you don't smell like food they know, they won't eat you. Remember—don't poop!"

Kenny held out his arms, stepped closer, and hugged Pete. Pete, surprised, didn't back up. He transported instead. A distant volcano vented hot gas. A lush valley of giant conifers and ferns lay around the base of where Pete stood. He stood on the top of a swimming pool-sized nest of sticks and ferns twenty feet high. Huge eggs lay at his feet. A giant bird jumped and landed six feet in front of him on the other side of the nest. The way it moved...He thought it was a bird but it was too big, seven-feet-tall with its head high. No feathers on its reptilian face, no beak but its head was surrounded by a collar of fiery red, black and yellow feathers protruding in every direction.

"Don't run. Don't run. Don't move. Oh God, oh God, oh God..."

The creature cocked its head, lowered its nose to Pete's, eye-level, swaying with its big nostrils flaring. Air rammed in and out of its snout-holes with a rasp. If a monster could look puzzled, it'd look like that, like a German shepherd hating the dog-whistle. It lifted one chicken-foot slightly.

"Don't move, don't move..."

It jumped and landed face to face with Pete, nostrils dripping, slime hanging off its teeth, fish-rot breath worse than Randy's. Pete took half a step back. Its jaws snapped. Pete almost let it rip. That retard had said, 'If it poops, its food.' Pete laughed when Kenny said it but he wasn't laughing now.

"Oh, no. Don't shit. Hold it, hold it..."

The dam broke. Pete's jeans flooded with brown soup.

The creature came on hard, head first, smashing Pete's face. Pete's front teeth flew out. It happened all in one fast motion. It clapped onto Pete's shoulder with its mouth and tossed Pete, leaving his backpack behind. Pete landed thirty yards away in a ditch full of mud and giant piles of shit. He hit the ground head first but lived, his arm barely attached, his shoulder raw hamburger. He resisted passing out, fought it. Pete thought that if he closed his eyes, he'd never wake again. That was the first and last well-reasoned thought Pete the Blaster ever had.

****

That strange bi-ped was a missed opportunity. It could have been a nice meal. Its weak bones broke easy. But the little one was left at home for a purpose. He guarded the nest while the rest of his group were away hunting. He was told to stay in the nest and he didn't argue. If the bi-ped had walked away, there was nothing he could have done. He obeyed orders but wanted food. Curious, T-tot tore the backpack to shreds seeking edibles and so he swallowed a tiny plastic Diplodocus. T-tot enjoyed Pete's meatloaf sandwich.

Rex's gastro system had no enzymes to digest plastic. T-tot didn't know when or where, but he crapped out the toy.

The next morning the hunting party returned dragging the hindquarter of a Hadrosaur. T-tot told his tale. The pride's senior female announced that T-tot earned his meal and she let him have it alone. The body in the ditch had bloated. The matriarch sniffed the dead thing thinking it was vaguely familiar but decided it wasn't safe to eat. Rain fell hard that night and washed the odd creature into a deep catch where other discarded meals accumulated.

Bone pit ten, yet to be discovered, gained more fill. Pete's bones didn't fossilize but traces of him remained.

CHAPTER SIXTEEN:

BADLANDS LATE SPRING

Late spring, the dig moved along miserably until Big John Callahan disappeared. Then, Tom's job shifted. Tom arrived at breakfast with the theme from Jaws swimming through his brain. The excitement had passed but a lingering unease dogged him. Whatever happened to Big John could happen to anyone. Mede reported him missing promptly to no avail. The National Park Service assumed he got lost, not uncommon in the wilds.

Three days after the search, a tow truck came, hooked up the camper, and took all Callahan's effects away including the bones he stashed. The wrecker came with a fleet of blacked-out SUVs. Men in suits crawled all over everyone, tossed everything, and asked stupid questions while the Park Service did a proper search. G-men had swept away every trace of Callahan like a flash flood.

Hotter weather came as the investigators withdrew and the event was quickly forgotten. The man wasn't missed. Tom felt one pressure lift as new pressures fueled his tanks.

Early starts and afternoon naps were the late season's order of operations. Breakfast came with the rising sun. Tom took in the Shovel Bum blog with coffee. Many posters offered essays but Kenny's stuff was the most interesting. Tom read Kenny's Corner first. The boy wrote poorly but Kenny presented important ideas with logical arguments. He followed what's new in real-time. Kenny's blogs gave Tom ideas on where to apply for jobs. He had no offers. Berkeley wasn't happening.

Mede and Rodriguez were in a corner deep in talk. With the generator running and pots clanging with food prep, eavesdropping wasn't possible. Tom needed to make his move. He hated being pushy. He didn't have enough balls to ask, but he needed a job. He thought it easier to go home and beg Old U for a job, even a janitor's spot. Yet he had to admit there was nothing back there for him but a shabby, empty apartment. Mom's message said nothing about when she'd be back.

As the season's end drew near the students' late-night activities increased. Only a few of them had dragged ass into the mess tent so far. Students partied more and cared less while Tom's worries piled up.

Watching Mede and Rodriquez sparked jealousy. Tom closed his laptop. *How's that old laborer and Mede have such intimacy?* Tom wanted to get closer to Mede to explore the growing connection he sensed. Mede wasn't a snob like the visiting professors who came and went. Mede didn't have Callahan's bloated ego, rather Mede cared about students. Tom admired Mede's ways of teaching and imitated the man's methods. But Tom, admittedly, had deeper reasons to mount Mede's inside track. Tom hoped for a leg-up on his applications.

Tom needed a job, any job, so why not the dream job? He hadn't done anything important in his career yet, nothing he could prove, nothing to warrant anyone hiring him, nothing to offer, no discoveries, nothing published or worth publishing. Tom was invisible.

Ask him about Berkeley, you idiot. You got nothing to lose.

Food wasn't up yet so Tom reopened his laptop rather than interrupt the head honcho. An instant message popped on saying: "Move camera six, ten degrees south and down two degrees. Big find today."

Somebody's idea of a joke? Mede's computer was left open. Tom rounded the table and checked the screen, same crap. There were a few other hired staff in house drinking coffee and reading computers so he ask the group a question.

"Did anyone get hacked?" Tom called.

Nobody answered yes. The IT girl looked at him like his head was on upside down. He rechecked. The message was gone.

"I'm seeing things," Tom said quietly.

Morning presented Tom's best opportunity to get on the old man's good side. Next season's team wasn't posted yet and Tom wanted in. If not an adjunct, any position, even dig labor. His extraction and bone processing skills were solid. He had desirable field attributes such as a fine touch. He was good with students. He had to refile applications and job-hunt all over again. It was too late in the season for summer call-backs. Tom sipped cold coffee building steam, and his whistle blew when Jorge left Mede. Jorge took off fast and nearly knocked over the geologist at the tent's flap.

"Now or never."

Tom got up choking down butterflies and approached Mede. Mede closed his laptop and looked past Tom.

"Debbie, take over cooking," Mede said so everyone heard. "Quick, let us eat and clean up, we're late. It'll be hot today. Latecomers are on their own."

Debbie and Bob, the interns, cracked eggs into a stainless-steel bowl. A student got the bacon going. Bacon-smell watered Tom's coffee mouth. Worried about increasing chest pains, he avoided junk foods, but bacon's salt was a necessary exception in this heat. Tom hovered near the stove too long debating with himself what to say to Mede.

Mede fell in with a visiting professor. More people filed in. The tent came alive with conversations, toaster's popping, and hurried food consumption. Tom and Van, the new staff guy from Berkeley, went over the day's plan. Tom forgot about that odd instant message. Mede remained busy. Tom's opportunity for the big ask faded into kitchen smoke.

Tom, lab staff, and Mede lagged behind as students and assistant professors moved out. Mede delegated well. The site leader's duties featured paperwork, site management, and occasional over-the-shoulder supervision. Mede wasn't there to teach, but Tom learned a lot from him. As the first assistant in Callahan's absence, Tom became Mede's roving eye. Tom had no time for shovel work, and he loved getting personal with dirt, but he had no option but to resist dirt-diving. Students learned by doing.

He and Mede ambled toward the main dig together in silence. *Here's my shot.* Mede was in thinking mode. He rubbed his beard around his mouth and twisted his mustache. *I shouldn't broach the topic.* The life of an adjunct required begging for jobs, thus, Tom interrupted Mede's reflective state.

"Doctor, I wanted to ask you about next season."

"Not now, Conley. I know, I know. Dig's winding down. Your time's coming. Shush, let me think."

My time's coming? What's that supposed to mean?

They arrived together at the mud-pan wash located below and south of where T-tot was found. They stopped to overlook the operations in progress. Students were chipping away sandstone above the shale in various locations, while others sifted overburden.

Here water runoff had once moved through a gully or creek carrying silt resulting in seasonally layered sediments. Over time, it became clay which became the shale littered with T-rex footprints of all sizes and, apparently, contemporaneous. There must have been a waterhole nearby which was the temporary consensus. Tom thought today was the day they'd find the source. A freshwater spring would explain a lot. Kenny's dangerous idea—that rex was a pride keeper—lingered in his thoughts.

Jorge was busy with students when Tom and Mede arrived. Everybody was scraping and brushing in the same general area under Jorge's direction. It wasn't where Tom would have focused. *He's on the wrong track. Why does Mede put so much faith in him?*

"Conley, keep the cameras off my back, will you?" Mede said before they parted. "I have enough on my plate. I'll watch the main dig. Stay back and distract Sara for me, won't you?"

"Anything you need, Doc. I'm your man," Tom said.

They proceeded in different directions. Exposing rex footprints was ongoing in several locations. One team engaged with the day's primary effort of following a depression that may have passed floodwater. Mede headed there.

"Today's the day," Tom called after Mede. Mede waved a dismissive hand. "Tracks gotta lead to a water source," Tom said aloud to himself, but even he wasn't convinced. He made his way to the site's web camera which was mounted on a tall fixed post.

"Hey, Prof Conley's here," Sara from media studies shouted. She waved at him with too much enthusiasm. She seldom used the title professor. All staff was Doc or Pros or Prof to her, no matter their actual position. Tom didn't mind.

Sara ran the live-feed program and often presented onsite live interviews for the inter school website system. Her activities weren't Tom's concern. He avoided her, having nothing in common. Mede tolerated the media department's presence, but he didn't like it either. Paleontology wasn't Sara's major. Keeping her out of Mede's hair earned brownie points.

She marched straight up to him. "Pros, how about a few words for the blogosphere?" Sara said, gushing sparkles. "Can ya show us your stuff?"

Tom cleared his eyes, a trick of the light. It was hard to fault her moxie. She put the word "personality" into the term media personality. *She's made out of spunk.* Tom ignored the media people, but when Sara wanted your attention, she got it. Mede did the required interviews, otherwise, Mede ran for the hills whenever she came around.

"Come on, what do you say Prof? This is your time to shine!"

"Sure, why not," he said evenly.

Tom addressed the fixed camera. It had been adjusted to overlook the new grid of suspended ropes not yet under excavation. Mede worked twenty yards beyond and was in the shot. Tom addressed the site-cam and pushed the lens downward. "How's this?"

"I don't know. We'll see." Sara used a tablet-cam to record and monitor the other cameras. "I love it! Students in the background brushing, perfect!"

"Where do I go?"

"Okay Doc, move left…a little back…There you are. One, two, three… action! Take it away, Professor Thomas Conley."

"Take what away…Oh, I see. Fine. Thank you, Sara. Hello, shovel bums. Today, we hope to find a waterhole or some other reason why so many T-rexes have left their prints here. As you can see… Check our website for detailed stills…rexes crossed paths often here. Was it mating behavior? But why all sizes? So far there are no indications of bird-like dance displays as others have noted of other species on other digs. Thanks to Kenny Parks for posting that article on the Shovel Bum Blog. Check Old U's homepage for links. We have a lot more there on the latest theories regarding raptor mating behaviors. Thanks, Sara."

Tom half-turned to leave but she waved him back to the spot.

"Pros, can you show us your techniques? Demonstrate for us how you look at the ground. Explain what you see. I'm told you are an expert excavator. I'll bring the tab-cam in close. We'll go split-screen."

"Right-o, to use Doctor Mede's phrase," Tom said, "Let's move away from the active search grid for this demonstration."

"Right. Why disturb progress? We don't want to distract the diggers. Yeah, lead the way, Doc."

He had a spot in mind behind the work area and out of Mede's line-of-sight. He adjusted the stationary camera's angle southward and further downrange. Dropping to the ground, Tom unrolled his canvas tool organizer. Tom extolled the virtues of his homemade kit. He was especially proud of Dad's vintage pocket knife. Every one of Tom's hard or soft brushes had a specific purpose as did his many small picks. Sara stopped him before he got too deep into his make-do excavation set.

"Pros, can you go back up a bit? More left. I wanna get some diggers in the back-drop, but out of microphone range, yeah?"

"Sure thing."

Sara explained to the online audience how she worked her hand-cam and switched back and forth between close shots and long shots from the mounted web-cams as she did it. Meanwhile, Tom moved his field kit to the new spot. He had a *deja vu* feeling of being drawn to the ground where she indicated. Sara exuded more energy than her usual radiation. Sparks shot out of her. He stopped, rubbed his eyes. *I gotta get that checked, something is wrong with me.*

He spread out his tools for the second time arranging them for demonstration. On Sara's cue, he talked about how he used what and why. He had developed a combination of household items consisting of wood carving tools, tiny demolition bars, dental picks, soft and hard brushes, toothpicks, toothbrushes with sharpened to a point handles, and a very old multi-blade Boy Scout pocket knife. The only purpose-made tool was his light rock hammer.

"Okay, Pros, show us your stuff in action!"

He wanted to scratch his birthmark. *Bad time to get an itch.*

"The matrix is soft here," he said. "I'll begin with a medium-stiff brush like so. This area is unusual in that it's not sandstone and not the typical hard-rock sedimentary material where we find encased bones. Hardness depends on the strata."

"That's good info, Doc."

Sara moved in closer with the handheld camera.

"Look at that, a coprolite and it could be a baby T-rex." He brushed more and started with a small dental pick. "Yes, definitely raptor feces. See the bits of bone? This looks remarkably like a human tooth…"

Tom reeled off his knees, falling backward onto his ass. He crawled back baby-style. He had never seen a dino tooth like that before. Sarah closed in. *Maybe a new species.* He discovered it on a live camera. *Let's see them kill this. Berkeley, here I come.* Discovery brought opportunities. Tom excavated around the specimen too fast for a professional. He couldn't stop himself. He felt compelled to lift it out while the live feed lasted.

"I'm ready, Sara. Come in closer. This is the big moment."

His birthmark burned like hell. The camera's lens motor whorled.

"Zooming in. Great stuff, Prof."

"This is a fine example, not smashed or broken," Tom said trying to keep a level tone. "It's exactly where it was placed seventy million years ago."

He was about to lift it out when Mede came and bent over Tom's shoulder.

Mede whispered, "Told you, your luck would change."

Tom took up the specimen but not careful enough. It broke in half. Within it, a small face emerged. Dimetrodon, but magnitudes smaller than any egg-bound sample can be.

"Dimetrodon is180 million years older. This can't be here."

A bit of its sail shone, too. Tom was vexed. Dimetrodon went extinct forty million years before dinosaurs existed and T-rex was a latecomer. The lens's motor strained. Tom's chest radiated heat. Sweat dripped onto the sample washing the tiny, white-bleached face cleaner. Tom's eyes weren't lying.

"What am I looking at?" Tom blurted in his shock.

He rocked back on his heels.

"Plastic toy," Mede said. "We should talk."

Jorge, a few yards back, smiled like a jack-o-lantern as Mede and Jorge walked away. The old digger had a full set of white teeth Tom hadn't noticed before. Later that afternoon Mede visited Tom at his camper. The old man had never done that before.

"I'm retiring, Tom, my boy," Mede began. "I was worried about you finding a finder. I see that you have. You'll do nicely. Stick to Jorge until you get a handle on things. But I won't lie. This is dangerous."

"The last thing I want is danger. I don't understand," Tom said. "Why're you leaving now? There are only a few weeks left?"

"You'll get it, my boy…when you're ready," Mede said. "Timing can't be helped. My internal walking papers tell me it's time I leave. Not everyone with your talent gets this opportunity. It's your site now, for a short time, at any rate."

Tom tried questioning Mede about his meanings but Mede gave no straight answer. Rather, Mede spoke in riddles and mythologies pontificating about special talents. He alluded to magical practices, more like magical thinking in Tom's mind.

Tom didn't believe in anything esoteric. Mede insisted that fate was at work. Tom didn't buy it. There had to be a better explanation besides Mede's wild speculations. Some kid lost it, that's all. Tom saw why the man was retiring. Mede had surely lost his mind. It struck Tom that it'd be better for him if Mede didn't put a word in for him at Berkeley. Mede offered to send a standard letter of recommendation. Interviewers ignore references from crack-pots.

The last thing Mede said before leaving Tom's camper was: "Watch your computer. I'll be here for a few more days."

He marched off to his tent singing. Singing! Mede never sang. Yeah, he lost his mind. Tom opened his laptop after Mede left and an instant-message was there waiting.

'I said it's downrange, down where I said, downrange yet to be discovered. They're mad… really mad… mad, mad. I think… think… I'm in trouble.'

No address, no source where it came from. Getting an instant-message without a messenger-application is strange but Kenny's message stranger still.

"Kenny Parks," Tom said and his burner lit. "Kenny's in danger?"

Wild thoughts struck, visions of Kenny under torture. Tom pushed back from the laptop. An overwhelming compulsion to do something for Kenny hammered him. But he had no idea what to do or how to do it. Emotional pain clawed its way around his ribcage seeking escape.

"I'm losing it. Just a panic attack. I'm turning into Mom. Breathe, Tom, breathe… This isn't real…it's not real…" He took a dozen deep breaths. "First step, get the facts. Kenny uses school computers. He doesn't have one at home. He's gotta be at school."

Tom checked. Too late, school had closed. Tom flunked Computer Science. He had no clue how Kenny accessed his machine, but he took a guess.

"He's got a smartphone?"

The horn blasted. Tom closed his laptop and went to dinner in a sober daze. His brain would not stop spinning, like how Mom described mania. He could not get Kenny out of his mind. This mental merry-go-round gave him a new understanding of what Mom suffered. He felt otherworldly, detached. He hardly touched his food.

He left camp directly after dinner and drove 600 miles overnight back to Central Regional. He had to tell the police something but he had no evidence. He didn't know what to say. Tell the cops a kid he hardly knew sent a cryptic message? No way. What if Kenny is fine? Kenny's supposed to attend summer school, all of Webber's kids do. Didn't he graduate this year? Tom had to know if Kenny was safe or not. Knowing, he thought, would seize his thought centrifuge. Internal debates kept him up all night on the eight-hour drive.

"It's nothing, just my imagination. It'll be alright. Kenny will be fine. I'm not crazy," Tom said. "Then why am I talking to myself?"

Tom pulled into the school's parking lot W just before dawn. He slept fitfully for a little while in the camper. No calls came in from work, no calls at all. Back at the dig everyone was up. His body wasn't rested, but his mind sizzled. He was pie-eyed awake and ready when Central Regional's doors opened. He would not sign in. He didn't want them to know he had come, and he didn't know why. He waited fearing cameras, but security didn't have one there.

Webber pulled in, still driving his old, faded Volvo. Tom ran and intercepted him near the lot's exit.

"Mr. Webber, it's me, Tom Conley," he said huffing for breath.

Webber, turning, put his hands up as if deflecting a blow.

"Surprised the crap out of me. Strange to see you here—"

"Kenny. Kenny Parks, do you still have him?"

Tom's chest throbbed. Webber confused, backed up.

"He wrote me," Tom said, "Kenny said he was in trouble… is he in trouble?"

"I'll say." Webber's whole body slumped. "The FBI… I guess it was them, men in black suits, came and asked questions about his absence. Everyone on staff was interviewed. Kenny missed graduation ceremonies, if you can believe that. Can you imagine? He's supposed to stay the summer but I haven't seen or heard of him since Pete Brenner went missing. Rumors have it the police think Kenny did Pete Brenner in. It may be true judging by the police's questions."

"Guess I'll contact the FBI. You know, follow up."

Tom's energy leaked away. Depression pushed in. I'm too late.

"Don't do that Mr. Conley. I was warned. They warned us not to speak of this, very forcefully. It's to do with ongoing investigations. You should go. I never saw you."

Webber rushed toward the school.

Tom got back in his truck and left for the Badlands, hoping he still had a job. Mom's not around, no point going home. Getting fired face-to-face is better. He drove slowly, trying to come up with a story. Exhausted, he camped one night along the route after driving five hours. When he arrived late morning, after three days gone, Tom found Mede in the lab unperturbed. Mede didn't say a word about Tom's unexpected departure. Tom had to say something.

"Sorry, Dr. Mede. I had to run home for an emergency."

"I understand, my boy," Mede said. "No need to apologize. It is nice to have a special helper in your career corner, isn't that so?" He waved toward Jorge as he said it. "Good finds do slip through the cracks, if you know how to work such cracks. Sara's an impromptu crack-opener." He laughed. "You take what you can get, no? I didn't see that one coming." Mede chuckled. "Plastic toy. Well done."

"Callahan was here to plug holes, wasn't he? But why, who is he?" Tom asked.

"Was. A failed academic, sorry to say." Mede's voice reflected sadness. "An infiltrator, maybe FBI or some such thing. The government watches like regular intellectual property hounds. You'll soon see. A funding agency may have sent him to confirm how their money's spent. My guess, he wasn't on our patrons' payroll. G-men don't do missing persons."

It sank in. The authorities, be they oligarchs or governments, actively plaster over uncomfortable facts which disagree with public narratives. It was obvious in the media, but Tom never thought to see such manipulations within academia. Then again, the powerful do pay for a lot of research. Tom heard the rumors thinking them a load of crap. He had ignored it. Science was supposed to trump all, and he had believed it, until the evidence proved otherwise.

"Science doesn't matter, it's about money," Tom said sadly.

"Profit politics wins the day every day," Mede said.

Mede moved over to the finds table and looked over the specimens there.

Tom had read how Calico and other fascinating American early-man sites were snuffed. That all changed when enough evidence piled up against the Clovis First notion to crush it. Nobody in social science thought modern government mythologies were real, yet the worst of those stories often turned out true. Callahan was real.

"I don't get it. What're they afraid of?"

"Damned if I know," Mede said picking up a Dremel tool. He proceeded to change the bit while he talked. "It could be…I don't know, they can't admit certain facts that upset things, things counter to social engineering. It might be high technology of the past they're after. Maybe aliens, who knows? They squash anything that doesn't fit. Things like T-rex evolved higher intelligence, a thinking non-mammalian animal…You didn't hear me say that."

"That was Kenny's toy. I feel it in my bones but I can't prove it," Tom said.

His birthmark flared hot as if in confirmation.

"You have good bones, my boy. If you want a career, keep that to yourself. Such talent might well bring you harm. Do science slow and quiet and you'll go far, unlike my dear friend, Doctor Cory."

The last thing Tom wanted in life was dangerous situations, or worse, screwing up his career before it got started. Cory was formally a well-respected professor, until he published his madly popular alternative history books based on collected yet indeterminate artifacts. Cory's interpretations held his ill-informed fanbase's attention. Tom never met the man, only his critics. He didn't need to touch Cory's lava to know it burned careers into ashes.

"Your dear friend? I'm confused," Tom said.

"Cory's a good man," Mede said and selected a fossil which had been accidentally halved during extraction. "He likes the hot seat. His choices aren't how I do it. I'm for incrementalism and he's the catastrophist type. We're both right, but slow is the safer way."

"I concede your point, Doctor Mede. Mind if I help you with that?"

Mede didn't answer. Tom didn't need one. He picked out a mini rotary tool that ran on batteries and took up the other half of Mede's fossil. Tom slowly removed material from a small but remarkable crocodilian jawbone, an out-of-place fossil, but nothing earth-shattering. An interesting little mystery was Tom's speed. He got into the grind.

"Slow and steady wins the day," Mede said while picking his bone.

Mindful but simple tasks relaxed Tom. In the back of his awareness, the tool's droning became a group of old women wailing in the distance. He struggled against the thought when smokey images of deep caves came to mind. The song came from a tunnel, the sound of women calling him, pleading with him. He saw them in his mind. Tom never went caving. He hated enclosed spaces. Even his basement office at Old U gave him the willies at times. Caves are too dangerous. Caving and diving were two things he long ago decided he would never do.

He shook off the vision and lost himself in the work at hand.

CHAPTER SEVENTEEN:

AFTER MEDE

Three weeks before the site's scheduled closure, Tom was left on his own. Mede had gone. Jorge stayed longer but left before the end. Old U borrowed Mede's dig master for a short time. Tom supervised the last groups. Each class had two weeks infield. He had to stay longer to break camp once students departed. Managing on his own was a career and confidence booster. Tom's hopes grew. Rex City became his responsibility alone. Running a prestigious site, even for a few weeks, created career-lubricant.

Last week Tom and Jorge had stood near the ruminate of BA Hill surveying the grounds. Jorge's departure was scheduled, and Tom had questions. Students were off the footprint excavation, being too hot for hard digging. Rather, that day's lesson was on field surveys and how one should see the ground. Old man Jorge had an eye for terrain. Interesting stuff was recovered thanks to Jorge who never took credit. Tom hated to ask but the old digger's knack seemed unnatural. With the clock running down, Tom finally asked the question plaguing him.

'How do you do it, Jorge?' Tom had asked. 'Seems like magic.'

'*Señor*, I imagine. It is not magic. De past in my brain.'

'What do you see,' Tom asked knowing nothing about visualization. The answer was a relief.

'Look, de ground moves, it flows.' Jorge had said. 'This swale between hill. Rex made her nest high. She knew seasonal floods. Her nest she packed hard with clay and sticks down low, softer high up, this resisting washout. Smart girl. De meal-bones wash away, si. There is jungle all around, over de tree-line open plains.' He pointed in the other direction. 'Below a ravine, dense jungle all around. Good for rex. She smells de herds, no tangle in de jungle. Rains come and wash all clean. She no like filth. A bone pit must be downrange, *si*? Simple hydraulics.'

Tom had warmed up to the man by that time. He felt oddly let down to know the man's so-called secret. The old dig-master used logic and reason which Tom admired. Jorge's practical tips, Tom felt, will improve his skills. There was much more to Jorge than his cover. Mede had called Jorge a finder and it fit. However, Jorge found things the old fashion way. Or did he?

Dad was a real finder. I'm not.

Tom feared the finds would dry up after Jorge split. On the night Jorge took flight, the instant messages started again. Hints from Kenny, very short, as if he didn't have time or permission. Tom received useful ideas. Messages over the dig's last week were incomplete but made sense to him. Tom learned no charges were filed regarding the missing kid. Kenny had nothing to do with Pete's disappearance as far as the cops saw. Small but interesting finds continued thanks to Kenny.

This morning's message refreshed Tom's energy. Pressed for time, a million things on his plate, Tom decided to check on the location Kenny suggested anyway. He didn't mind a break from site activities. He had an intern take over before wandering off.

He tested the spot Kenny mentioned by scratching around in loose dirt with a brick trowel. That nagging sensation let go when he uncovered a size-14 boot track imprinted in hard shale…impossible. *Mistaken identity.* Not wanting to misstep, Tom kicked dirt on it before anyone saw. He made up his mind to only expose career-safe items. He felt confident in his academic survival plan. Rule one: Avoid controversy.

He took two steps west and stopped. He didn't have a permanent position. Berkeley provided the site managers and yet they turned him down. But if he played the game and impressed them, he'd gain a handhold. He had Mede's boiler-plate recommendation letter. Possibilities were forming. *But damn it, Kenny's right again.* Tom felt like Lot's wife. He needed a good find to wedge open a career-crack.

"Sorry, Kenny. I'm not touching this."

Tom walked away in the direction the print pointed. His chest-burn kicked on.

Part of that message rattled Tom's nerves. Kenny wrote, *'I have a present, a present, for you, just for you, under the juniper, six inches, just six, it's six.'* There weren't supposed to be any junipers anywhere near there. But he spotted one tiny example in the distance. He would have missed it if he hadn't turned his back on the boot print.

"Can't be. Son of a bitch."

How it survived the botanists might know, but it puzzled him. It grew down range where that footprint pointed. He never noticed it before. He proceeded on with his kit tucked under an arm determined to prove Kenny wrong.

The plant had grown in loose soil which it barely hung onto. He pulled it out leaving a divot. Tom saw a bone. He dropped, unrolled his kit, took a trowel and shoveled like a badger. He found himself inside the flattened belly of an adult T-rex in no time. The last rib bone above the gut emerged intact. *I should stop—call the team—but I can't.* He kept going against all reason. At six inches down, he saw an object poking out from under a gullet-stone.

The obsession broke. He brushed the dirt off it carefully and picked it up. The silver had turned black. The glass was gone but he recognized it.

"Floral engraving…Jesus, it's Callahan's."

Tom in discovery mode never noticed his surroundings. Students were everywhere doing ground searches. It was hard to avoid them. Tom worked excavations like a painter glued to his canvas. One of the students came in close from behind as Tom held Callahan's eyepiece high for a better look. Focused as he was, Tom didn't see Danny coming.

"Holy cow, that's metal inside a dinosaur. I don't believe it. If this is real…Oh my God!"

"Relax Danny, it's a geo-cash, somebody buried it," Tom said with a calm voice although his insides jittered. The chest pain quit. He took a deep breath. "It's nothing really, forget it."

"But I watched you dig undisturbed soil, and… and… it's… it's aliens I bet."

Tom laughed but not in condescending fashion. "Ever read the Shovel Bum Blog? Someone goes around and does this. They have a portable microwave. They restitch the soil into a passable matrix. It's a trick. I got tipped off. It doesn't take a rocket surgeon to pull this off. Too bad the tricksters decided on this spot."

Danny Peterson looked dejected, embarrassed. "I'm so dumb. God, I'll never get it right."

Tom put on a kind face. He wasn't one to embarrass students. The kid looked crushed.

"You're fine, Danny. I'm not making fun of you. Somebody worked at this deception but not too hard. That plant's an obvious landmark. Had you dug it yourself, you'd have felt the dirt's softness."

"Yeah, I see. Survey ain't that easy."

"You'll get the hang of it. Don't give up, Danny."

Boots crunching came from behind. It was the new staff guy. He had shown up out of nowhere yesterday with only a week left. *He's gotta be with the government.* But the late-comer didn't act like the government. Still, it didn't make sense to send anyone at this point.

"Danny, play along," Tom whispered as the spy approached. Tom stuffed the jeweler's loop inside a pocket of his tool-rollup.

"What'cha got there, dudes?" He said. "What's in the hole?"

Before Danny could respond, Tom spoke, "It's a T-rex. Danny here spotted a bone, told me where to look. I dug in, got a little carried away. Good eye, Danny, your first big discovery."

"But I…I mean I…It was nothing I just…" Danny stammered.

"It's a nice find, Danny. Congratulations," Tom said. "This is exactly why we do ground searches, right? Would you run back to the lab, get on the radio, and alert the team, please."

Danny took off running. Tom wondered if his feet touched the ground. Tom and the new man followed, walking slow. Tom didn't say anything about it. He'd talk with Danny later. The new man had a lot of questions, but Tom evaded the answers.

Staying out of the footlights is better, but new rexes didn't grow on trees. The way it was found unnerved him. Paranoia replaced reason. *Play it safe, no risks.* This grand career opportunity had bad timing. He needed a better look. That eyepiece spooked him.

Once back at camp, Tom put on the director's hat and organized a new effort. He started the procedures required to protect it for next season. Rex had to wait for better weather. Tom hoped he'd be back for it. It was a thin hope. He followed Jorge's example and didn't claim the find.

Later, after a quick chat, Danny was relieved. Of course, Danny and his school will take credit. Giving Danny the find already paid, Callahan's loop was forgotten. Tom figured his Mede-like attitude would eventually pay but not soon. He wasn't ready to trust his luck. Tom retired to his camper after chow with a lot on his mind, how that loop got there foremost. Drinking alone in his camper beat getting drunk with his students at the campfire celebration. *How did it get there?*

"Yet to be discovered, as Kenny would say," Tom said after a few gulps. "Give away your find, that's me." He raised his mug. "Here's to Mr. Congeniality."

Tom's tradition was to take a celebratory nip at night on the occasion of a student's discovery. His bottle lasted the season. T-rex required the rest of the bottle. *Good given comes back around is bullshit.*

One special-ed student proved the concept. Yet, was Kenny a gift or a curse? Tom gulped and wondered if that eyepiece had been a gift to Big John Callahan. Tom had doubts. People don't give bullies nice things. 'How did Kenny do it?' was Tom's big question and he reasoned out an Occam's razor answer.

"Acute observation skills. What else can it be?" Tom said, but it didn't feel right. "Okay, it's magic, real magic. I ain't good enough on my own."

Tom shuddered having said it. He hated to admit it.

There remained too many questions and very few answers. The danger hit home. What if Kenny turned on him? Tom shook off that fear. He refused to believe the kid has paranormal abilities until now. What made the boy tick, autism, special abilities, magic…which? Kenny did not… could not… send Callahan back in time.

"He's a watcher. He's glued to live feeds. He saw the geo-cash deposited."

But the matrix was hard. Tom shivered. The geo-cash lie came out of nowhere but it worked. Tom raised his mug.

"Thanks, Kenny, but no thanks."

Tom decided he must steer clear of Kenny Parks. If Kenny was behind Pete Brennon's disappearance…Impossible as that sounded…Tom wasn't taking any risks, no way. Tom pulled his phone, blocked Kenny's number, and trashed the Shovel Bum Blog link. He did the same on the laptop without checking first. *No more messages from Kenny.*

"Stand or fall on my own. If I can't, I'll do something else."

Tom felt heart-sick like turning tail on his drowning brother. Cutting Kenny off was necessary for his sanity. A worry had been growing on him—that he was becoming mentally ill like his mother, or worse. Nothing seemed right. He didn't trust his judgment. Mom always said, 'Feelings lie. Stick to the facts. Square things off.' But his well-rounded facts kept magically landing in square peg-holes.

"I gotta understand it or I'll go nuts."

CHAPTER EIGHTEEN:

CELEBRATION

The next day was a blur of elbows and ass cracks. Everyone worked like demons to protect the new find. Tom, hungover, dragged himself through the day, glad his task was oversight and not mixing plaster. Excitement was high, but not for him. Once the new find was isolated, students slathered on the protection. Afterward, the camp shifted into party gear. Rex was made safe in record time. Dinners were loud to begin with but the evening's clammer escalated when the dusty bottles of hard stuff, saved for such occasions, came out of hiding.

Tom went to the office yurt away from the excitement after dinner. The mess tent had transformed into party central. Tom preferred the quieter office. The chair smelled of Mede's aftershave, the same kind Dad had used. Dirty white canvas walls didn't kill the racket but it was private. He put his feet up and split open his cowboy shirt and stretched his T-shirt away to let air in. His birthmark had boiled all day, along with his thoughts. That disk of red skin above his heart finally stopped itching. The laptop was there but he ignored the urge to check for Kenny.

Next season there'll be a lot for students on T-rex number three.

"Them and not me. I wasn't asked."

Cheers in the distance went up. "Yeah, Danny! Go, Danny!"

Mede's words came to Tom's mind. *It is better for one's career to sidestep rather than embrace the spotlight'*

"Sorry to doubt your wisdom, Doc, but I think I just fucked my career."

Tom needed to collect himself. Questions spun. Too many things defied reason such as him sensing the CIA man before he heard footsteps. His chest had itched like mad until Kenny's item popped. After, and out of nowhere, his chest burned a warning, just before the CIA man showed. Something inside him wanted out. His heart beat wildly while he dug but it wasn't a panic attack. *I need my heart checked. This ain't good. Psychosomatic? Mental illness is hereditary.*

"I'm going out of my mind. Thank you, Mother."

He tipped his cup, saluting Mom, and eyed the laptop thinking he should find a local doctor. Basecamp was miles from nowhere, and he didn't know the area. His hands shook too much to type. He leaned back taking easy, slow, breaths and calmed his mind using Mom's technique. The heart seemed better but his mark was hot. No pain. *I'm not dying.* He took his pulse. Nothing wrong. He felt his wrist again. Heart rate ran steady although his chest thumped. Tom's first aid training didn't mention those symptoms.

A call came from outside. "Hey, yo! You in there, dude?"

"Crap, it's the CIA man." Tom quickly snapped his shirt buttons closed. "In here, come in."

The man ripped the flap open, entered, pulled up a chair opposite Tom, and sat on the edge pushing scraggly hair behind both ears with quick habit. His silver earrings reflected light. *Skater dude for sure.* The guy had Tom's haircut but darker and more overgrown.

"You're young for a spy," Tom said. "What do you want?"

The man passed for a freshman. A baseball cap and skate shoes were the only things missing.

"You've been sniffing around all day like a rat," Tom said. "You don't belong here."

"Ouch, you got me. You don't have to be a dick about it."

Tom treated everyone well but his chest burns refired and it worried him. Calling out the CIA man was stupid. This agent was a fish out of water whereas Callahan acted as if he was accredited.

"I got enough to do without babysitting the CIA," Tom said. "What're you doing here anyway? I know…the government's gonna bury anything interesting we find, right? I don't have time for games. Spill it already."

"Whoa, dude, come on," his companion said. "I'm working my way through school. It's a job, right? I'm supposed to write what I see, that's all. Geeze, you're paranoid. I ain't CIA."

The man-boy pushed his chair back, but the chair went over backward and so did he. Silicate sand is slippery, and the plastic carpet had bunched making a lump. The kid didn't bounce up. His skinny-jean legs got tangled in the chair's frame. Tom helped the boy up with a lighter heart.

"Since I'm holding your hand, you may as well tell me your name," Tom said. "You alright, man?"

"It's Bryon, dude. I'm sorry. It's just a job. I'm working on my anthropology degree. I need money. Foundation's media department sent me. I'm gigging for the magazine. They didn't give me a lead-in. They told me to stay out of your hair. I think they think someone here's a bone smuggler?"

The phrase struck funny and Tom laughed hysterically. "Bone smuggler, ha!"

He felt stupid. All this anxiety for nothing. *I worked myself into a heart seizure for nothing.* Anxiety had gotten the better of him. Callahan's eyepiece shocked him stupid.

"You aren't CIA?" Tom said. "Are you?"

"Oh, hell no. The magazine wanted a man-on-the-scene piece. You know, what it's like out in the wilds and junk. Wait," Bryon dug into his back pocket. "I got an envelope for you. They told me to give you this."

Tom opened the sealed envelope to find a one paragraph note. It said to expect a CIA man with an invitation and he should take the assignment. If Tom did this for the Foundation, they'll arrange a seat for him at Berkeley. Tom stuffed the note into his shirt's top pocket and closed the snap.

"Bryon, did you read this? This some kind of a joke?"

"Hell no, I'm not a snooper. Well, I am, sort of. I gotta list of questions." Bryon had a reporter's notebook Tom didn't notice before. "I was told to interview you before this honcho comes down here for final closeout. Admin dudes act like everything's a big secret."

"Are these your questions?" Tom asked, suspicious.

"Naw, the Foundation asked me to ask. I'll do my own thing, too, but they want this junk. They say you should be honest. They're paying for this, so they deserve answers, right? That's what they told me. They want the scoop before Berkeley, or whoever, publishes anything."

"Fire away," Tom said forgetting his chest problem.

Bryon flipped a few pages and found his list. He read the question to himself before asking.

"OK, they want to know about the T-rex eggs, like how you found them and where they were…says here it was early season."

"Rex eggs? We didn't find any." Tom lied. Something banged his ribs like a blacksmith's hammer. "Hate to cut this short…chest pains. I need a doctor. I was going to call 911."

"Wow, dude, bummer. I'll drive. I know where the walk-in clinic is."

That ended the interview. Bryon had a pickup truck and they made it to a small town called Drylake in half an hour. Bryon didn't have any more Foundation questions and, rather on the ride, he talked about his career path instead of doing the interview. He and Tom were both skaters so that topic dominated the conversation. *Bryon isn't CIA, confirmed.* The Foundation did deserve to know what they're paying for. When the conversation drifted back to the Badlands Tom kept the rex eggs buried, unwilling to expose his neck.

The one-horse town had a two-horse doctor with modern equipment setup inside one of the units in a 6-store strip mall. The ice cream store next door called Tom's name but he proceeded into the clinic and got checked inside and out, x-rays, the whole thing, and nothing was found wrong. When the doctor put Tom's digital sonogram up on screen, his birthmark looked weird. It had a pattern in it like a compass.

"What is that?" Tom asked. He traced the image on the screen with a finger. It reminded him of something he couldn't place. "Looks like writing."

"It's nothing," the doctor said. "No doubt an artifact from a previous shot. Somebody with a necklace. We get bleed through exposures from time to time. Your skin there is very thick, perhaps a calcium deposit. I'd have that biopsied if I were you."

"I'll do that after the dig's over. I'm leaving in a few days." Tom said. "I'll see my regular physician back home."

"I strongly suggest that you do," the doctor said.

Tom grabbed four cases of beer for the crew before heading back, given that the beer place was next to the ice cream place. The campfire celebration of Danny's big find was still going and short on stock. Tom's somber mood didn't want alcohol. Ice cream replaced his beer-lust, but his team enjoyed Tom's contribution.

Tom and Bryon made it back to camp in plenty of time to enjoy campfire festivities. Hotdogs were grilling. Bryon ate a grizzly-bear's share. *Maybe journalists store fat for the winter.* Tom's heart scare took a lot out of him and he retired early. A long foggy day blended into a foggier night. Tom escaped into slumber.

CHAPTER NINETEEN:

BACK HOME

The Badland's dig season ended. Tom meandered home in no hurry. The government man with a job offer didn't show. He didn't like the idea anyway and he didn't trust that nebulous message.

Federal field projects gave various participants turns managing sites in conjunction with privet partnering funding agencies. Money had everything to do with who ran what digs when and where. The Finder Foundation and the universities it sponsored had their turn. Next season, another school takes over. Tom lost his wedge. Adjunct slots were filled before he applied. Non-profits supported a lot of schools but it wasn't right how they bribed their way in. Tom shook it off.

"Intellectual property rights are what they're after." *Great, now I'm thinking like Mede, dark figures around every corner.* This line of thought had him worried about his mental stability. He felt more lost than usual on the long ride home.

"Get a hold of yourself. It's stress, all stress, only stress. Look at me, now I'm talking to myself."

Others on the highway talked in empty cars as well, but they were on phones. He didn't bother charging it. Nobody ever called.

He pulled into the parking lot of the ramshackle apartment complex he called home at midday. Nothing had changed. The complex's half dozen, 1960s two-story, walk-up buildings still needed paint. Stucco was still stained with rot-brown streaks wherever the rain gutters leaked and they leaked at every joint. Slime molds clung onto wherever the sun didn't strike. The weeds between tarmac cracks were fresh and green for late spring. Otherwise, the place was dead.

"Home, sweet home…if you can call a cell block home."

He backed into his old spot. His Jeep-project he had left there remained unmolested. Nobody would steal parts off a rust bucket. It needed too much and he didn't have the money or time for it. He had time now, so half the equation was solved. Mom said she left her car for him but it wasn't there, he thought, until he took a closer look at the only car in the lot uglier than his project. Mom's Honda had been stripped down to its unibody underwear, even the windshield was gone. A de-fleshed Macrocollum Itaquii carcass crossed his mind.

"She is not going to be happy," Tom said. He locked the camper. "Mom loves that car. Good thing she isn't here."

He took the exterior stairs to the upper floor and stopped before entering the interior's hallway. From the stairwell's balcony it was plain that the RV's roof needed serious attention. More problems, more expenses that he couldn't afford.

Entering, the apartment was uncharacteristically bright. The curtains were drawn open. He expected clean and organized but not toothbrush spick-n-span and hollow. She'd clean like crazy when manic but this was over the top. He went room to room inspecting.

All of her things were gone. Everything she cared about, and all her books, were gone. He didn't think it would be a long project when she announced going away. She'd take little trips sometimes but returned when her mood changed, and her mood changed often. He knew her pattern. She'd launch like a crusading rocket, burn out in orbit, and crash-land straight into her rocking chair.

This was different. She took her books.

"She's not coming back." The idea struck hard. Tom fell into a chair.

Mom studied dead languages and Egyptology in college and was good with Hieroglyphs. She loved deciphering texts. University basement storage materials that didn't dazzle and build careers was her playground. Her reference books made him fall in love with the past. Her collection had inspired him, but his interests were wider. Egypt was the tip of a planet-sized iceberg. Her lust for the past opened his intellectual doors yet she feared him crossing that threshold into a bigger world. He feared it, too. Foreign field work had its dangers. Tom thought paleontology was safe. He thought wrong. It wasn't safe for Callahan.

Her fallen scholar-apple took root in him while Dad's apple remained lost at sea. Dad was the adventurer, not her.

"That ain't me, either, or is it?"

Tom realized he'd have to test the hypotheses to know. His bedroom was empty. His adult things were in the camper. His childhood left-behinds were gone. She mentioned storage on the phone, but he didn't know the location. The idea of sleeping in his old bed, a real bed for a change, lost its appeal. His childhood dinosaur bedding was left folded atop his dresser. Slapping the mattress, a puff of dust rose.

"You really can't go home again."

The dining set was pushed against the balcony's sliding glass door. Its white plastic tablecloth glared with sunlight. The little balcony beyond had potted plants but they were dead. He found a note addressed to him on the table. He nearly missed the white envelope. Reading it, the note repeated what Mom had said on the phone. Good she wrote it down because he missed half of that conversation. Her doctors encouraged her involvement in outside activities. That advice took her far away.

"You really did it. How you gonna get psychiatric care on a peace mission?

He didn't think her trip would last, but her note changed his outlook. The last few lines kicked him in the balls. She had lied, and she never lies. Her exit wasn't for a peace mission. She went with Richard Wailer. No other way could she have moved out.

"Wailer! That son of a bitch."

Tom read it three times. She didn't give a reason, but Tom guessed Wailer needed her expertise. Why else would she take her books? But why her, a defunct practitioner? He must have hired her out of guilt. Wailer didn't deserve her. *We don't owe him.* Tom couldn't forgive Wailer, although Dad's death wasn't Wailer's fault. Dad's dying had shoved a harpoon into Tom, and he wasn't ready to tear that barb out.

She knows how I feel. How could she run out on me like this?

At the bottom of her note, a postscript said to open her lamp table. He figured Mom left him a present she didn't want the landlord to steal. The draw was full of crap but he searched and found a thick envelope under a stack of crossword puzzle books.

"What's this? Her will?" Fear gripped him. The envelope was fat. "Suicide note? Manifesto?"

She had tried suicide years before. After which she promised to stay alive to see him through. I'm on my own now. *Mom's reason to live evaporated.* He opened the package, trembling, and found it stuffed with money. Bad sign. He dug into the stack. No suicide note, but she left a message. The note said to spend it as he saw fit. The apartment's lease won't be renewed.

Relieved, he counted ten thousand dollars in large bills and two prepaid credit cards—a lot of money, more than he'd ever seen. Tom's fears buckled. He read the note again. The last lines read: *'Tommy, the cash won't last. Take the job. The Foundation will position you afterward. I have it on good authority. Love bunches, Mom.'*

"What is going on here?"

Tom rocked in Mom's chair, kicking down emotions. The chair smelled of dollar-store perfume and didn't help. He applied logic to this puzzle. The Federal Government was after something and The Foundation is after it, too—two users using each other. *And I'm caught in the middle.* Association with the Foundation could birth or abort one's career, and he didn't want that amniotic pressure.

I could say no. I should say no. I will say no.

Government attachments were too risky. *Take the cash and skate.* Nothing held him. Mom removed everything. His childhood was packed and gone. The apartment had nothing for him but secondhand furniture and mixed feelings. He had to admit it: he had had one foot out the door for a long time, ever since losing his amulet. He hadn't thought of that in years. The empty apartment brought back the worst days of his life. He lost Dad, and then he lost what Dad died recovering, and now, Mom's gone, too.

Next day, Tom hooked his dead Jeep to the camper with a tow bar and pulled it to a dealer. He traded it in with cash for a used Jeep but saved the towbar brackets. Next trip, if he ever got one, he'll tow the Jeep with him.

He decided to live on the road like a gypsy until the money ran out. With no offers pending, why not? Nobody from the CIA or anywhere else wanted him.

But for now, he stayed home in the empty place, undecided about where to go or what to do. Plenty of volunteer opportunities were online but nothing with career potential. The apartment's lease ran out while he lingered. He had to hit the road before management called the police. Ready to leave, he hesitated. Leaving the door open, he rocked in Mom's old chair one last time, pumping up courage. While Tom was sitting there facing the door, an official-looking fellow—dark suit, expensive sunglasses—walked in uninvited. He wasn't a donut-eater or steroid-infused, but the man read like a cop anyway.

Tom touched his birthmark and felt nothing.

"Let me guess, eviction notice, right?"

The man extended a hand. Tom, by habit, got up and took it. The intruder had a soft palm for the Dick Tracy type.

"Detective, right? I thought they sent sheriffs for evictions?"

"It's that obvious? I've changed since switching careers…Academia must have worn off." The corners of the man's mouth turned down. He withdrew his hand. "Doctor Tod Murphy, CIA, Antiquities Department."

"I know that name," Tom said. "You were on the geological survey team that refuted the Impact Hypotheses. Saw it in the periodical *Natural Science.* You argued against the obvious. It's since been widely accepted. The evidence is solid. Why'd you deny it?"

Murphy chuckled. "Simple, I protect the orthodoxy. I wrote that rebuttal before I signed on. It's, in part, how the Company noticed me. I agreed with them. When the public knows too much, shit hits the fan. Takes time for the masses to acclimate to alarming ideas. Even now people can't accept that meteorites smashed earth 13 KBP. Our species was lucky. If people think such things are repeatable…Bingo, social chaos, authority breaks down, not good. The state has an interest in keeping order, you understand. I see the wisdom in that. The masses are stupid."

"I read Voltaire, too," Tom said. "He wasn't half right."

Tom was familiar with that idea but didn't agree. Before his time, universities practiced open-source policies. Information flowed freely including controversial evidence and the world didn't stop rotating. Since then, important facts had been locked away within intellectual property jails, and Murphy was one of the jailers.

"Voltaire had a lot on the ball," Murphy said.

Tom cringed. He expected his chest to blaze but a stress-reaction didn't fire. So much for my early warning system. He began to think of his mark as a talisman but it seldom proved true. It didn't work when it should. Standing toe-to-toe with Murphy should have caused a reaction.

"So, you say. Whatever. I gotta hit the road," Tom said, leaning to the door.

Murphy didn't step aside.

"Hold on, let me explain." Murphy raised his hand.

Murphy rattled off three minutes of public trust justifications. Tom listened for what was behind it. Murphy spoke sincerely, voice even, demeanor neutral. Tom didn't sense an immediate threat but the smell of sweat and sour intentions floated in. Good-cop/bad-cop in one cop, Tom figured. He didn't want to see the other side of Murphy. Murphy spoke as if he believed that bullshit.

"What do you want from me?" Tom asked, not hiding his unhappy tone.

"There's a dig in Alaska. We'd like you to keep an eye on it for us. Sit, will ya?"

Murphy ducked inside and pulled a dinette chair into the living area. He sat leaning forward. "We lost our best field agent and until he's replaced, we'll need a little contract help." Murphy wiped the dust off the chair's arm with a finger. "The money's good. You're well recommended, can't say who. I'll need you to alert me, my agents rather, of anything that doesn't fit. We know your colleagues cover up things, and of course, you've seen them do it unless you're blind. Such things are career killers. But we—that is your government—need to know. Do you understand?"

"I suppose…alright," Tom said slowly. "I'll gig this one time, but after that, I'm done with you. I have a job lined up."

He didn't have any prospects. That note about Berkeley was bullshit. *Take Murphy's cash and put it toward the doctorate.* He wasn't going anywhere without one.

"I'll go but it'll cost you a lot. I want travel expenses, too."

Murphy leaned back. The old wooden chair creaked. "I think we can do that."

Murphy stood and slapped a thin folder down on the end table. Dust flew up. Tom's chest felt the blow. "Here's the info, address, contacts, some cash. Not much to read, but it gives you the facts surrounding Doctor Cory." Murphy wrote a dollar amount on the cover. "How's that?"

The amount Murphy put down was more money that Tom imagined.

"I'd take it, but Doctor Cory is a pariah. I don't want to be associated with the likes of him," Tom said aghast, already regretting he'd accept the offer. "I don't want my name on this."

"Fine, don't publish. We'll kick in another ten thousand, if that helps you out. You see why we need someone qualified up there." Murphy put a friendly hand on Tom's shoulder. "He's a wild one and crazy enough to publish things the public is better off not knowing, against official advice. But if there's nothing to report…you see where I'm going."

The man's countenance shifted into evil between breaths. "Don't cross me, you can't afford it."

"I take your point," Tom said without hiding his misery.

"Good, good," Murphy said. "You'll go. Any questions?"

"How'd you decide to use me? There are others more qualified. What about an ex-GI?"

Murphy chuckled but with a sharp edge. "Cory's a problem. I can't say who suggested you. You know him. He's a friend. A remarkable man."

Tom opened his mouth to ask if it were Kenny Parks but his mouth slammed closed on its own. It was better to say nothing. *Leave Kenny out of it.*

Murphy left. Tom picked up the folder. Nothing much in it but it weighed like a ball and chain. Murphy left him holding a bag of doubts stuffed with troubles. Tilt the wrong way and his career was over. Tom didn't trust instincts but one inner message was clear: Tod Murphy has career-crushing powers. Murphy could make Tom's life into a living hell. Good that Mom wasn't home to see how Tom's spine crumbled.

CHAPTER TWENTY:

KIDNAPPING

Keith Billings was losing at solitaire when the call he expected came in at his Antiquities Department desk. He took it unworried. "Billings here."

"Hold please," an operator said.

He was being watched, of course. His agency's eyes covered him, too. Homeland and the CIA watched everything and each other, two competing condors. He wasn't on either side. Billings threw in with the Watchers and a damn proud initiate was he. From the start, a powerful inner circle of the CIA, established by none other than Albert Dulles, functioned unmarked as real patriots wielding real power to do what must be done. He wasn't surprised to learn the Watchers killed the Kennedys. It had to be done. Dropping the Towers was radical, he thought at the time. He, an outside observer, saw where that was going. It made America stronger. His masters were right.

"Come on, I haven't got all day," Billings said.

"Holding for voice confirmation," the phone said.

Muffled speech in the background followed. The problem was on their end.

Billing's voice identifier ran sluggish. The speaker was his Homeland Security contact and one of the made-men. Billings was the go-between coordinating CIA and Homeland's joint activities…on paper.

He had another agenda. The Watchers placed him to eyeball the Antiquities Department. Various factions had the same objective to obtain what didn't belong. Murphy's mistake? He believed in the merits of his former profession. Murphy asked too many good questions. The only question Billings had was: how high should I jump?

Voice recognition beeped confirming a safe call.

"Go," Billing said.

"I'm texting the address," the voice on the phone said. "Rendition of Kenny Parks. A team is on its way to you."

"Details?" Billings asked. There was a ruffle of papers in the background. Smart using paper, nothing to hack. "I need confirmation."

"Target is autistic and housed at a private firm. A CIA contractor has him under surveillance. Antiquities' observers onsite. Expect resistance. Suit up. Take him alive."

The caller hung up. Billings pushed away from his desk phone in hand.

"Suit up. Where am I going to get a SWAT team?" He didn't wait long for an answer. Across the office, a beefy man in black fatigues stepped off the elevator and marched toward Billings' desk. Billings hung up. Everyone in the desk-pool stopped work. Bad idea, sending him here.

Director Murphy already moved on Billings' location. Murphy and the black-ops man met short of Billings' desk. Murphy eyed the war-clad operative with disdain written large. The ops man, all piss and muscles, returned the favor. This dude could have snapped Murphy's neck with one hand. Murphy didn't balk. More heart than brains.

"I hope you two have a lunch date," Murphy said. "I didn't ask for a rendition, no papers filed."

The uniformed man began to speak but Billings waved him off.

"I'll handle this. Homeland called just now. They want me to go with the team. I'm to ID a mark. It won't take long."

"You aren't going anywhere until I SIGN YOU OUT." Murphy moved in, squeezing his fists. Billings shrank in his chair. "If they want you that means they're after one of mine. Who is it?"

"Kenny Parks," Billing blurted out. He didn't mean to. Murphy's macho screw loosened. Murphy leaned into the armored man with a stiff finger.

"Back up, buttercup," the uniform said.

"Try it asshole," Murphy edged his cast-concrete chin closer. Murphy's jaw was known to have broken an attacker's hand.

A dozen agents jumped to their feet and moved toward the argument, pulling sidearms. Murphy was tough, but fair, and popular among his dozens of agents. Black-ops punched a bear in the nose. Musclehead stood ready to go a few rounds. He would lose. Three of Murphy's men had skills enough to filet that side of beef. Billings wasn't sure Murphy couldn't do it himself.

"Look here, Murphy—"

"That kid is mine." Murphy snapped. "He's important. I'm not giving him up." Murphy's voice could cut Kevlar. "He's where I need him. I've got a girl on him now. You go in shooting like the assholes you are, you'll kill my agent and the others. There are half a dozen mentally handicapped people in there, innocent doctors, too. Get me?"

The uniformed man staggered back half a step. "Christ, I didn't know that. Nobody told us. My file doesn't say anything about agents and retards."

Civilian shield. Murphy surprised Billings yet again. The Watchers placed Billings there to learn and he didn't see that. Murphy's thoughts ran deeper than shown. Lesson learned. He's slippery.

"What about it, Billings?" Murphy said. "Explain yourself."

"Look, Boss, I was told to bring him in, in here, just now, for an interview in our house. Homeland honchos are coming to question him," Billings lied. "I didn't ask why. I wasn't told. All I know is the big bosses want to talk with Parks."

"Homeland's woven out of morons," Murphy said eyeballing Agent Beefcake. "Scare-tactics shut him down. He's autistic. Your interviewer won't get anything by terrorizing him." He pointed at the SWAT man. "What's Homeland's big hurry? We're milking info slow but steady. It's paying off."

"We are? It is?" Billings said.

"Parks has the ability to find what we're after," Murphy said. "How? Who knows? The contractor's studying that. How his mind works isn't my concern, results are." Murphy stopped and scanned the uniformed man. "No name tag, eh?" Murphy continued in a softer voice. "Homeland interviews Parks here, here or nowhere, get me? Billings, go and see that they bring him here. I'm sitting in. Lose the uniforms. Kenny will shut off if you bust in ready for war. Don't touch him. He hates that."

The big man bristled until Murphy's demeanor clicked into cooperation. His words were logical, carried authority, and sucked the negative charge out of the warrior.

"We can do that," the special-ops man said. "Plainclothes, no problem. Nice and easy."

Kenny, Murphy's on a first-name basis with his mark. Interesting.

"See that you are," Murphy said. "Watch them, Billings."

"Will do, Boss," Billings said.

Murphy's agents backed away and he returned to his office. Billings and the agent made tracks but Billings smelled a rat. Rather than take his car and follow Mr. Jackboot back to his shop to change, Billings headed straight for Homeland's bullet-proofed troop carrier.

"What gives? Aren't we changing?" The lead SWAT man said.

"Screw that," Billings said. "No time. We go now. No guns, we grab the kid and get out."

"What about the house agent?"

"I'm sure Murphy's calling her now. Our party is expected. I'll bring him out. You bag him."

The military truck's entire iron-plated rear end opened by way of hydraulic rams. Billings walked the plank and got inside. Five other operatives sat waiting on hard benches. They weren't dressed in heavy gear yet. Guns, helmets, and vests hung under overhead racks. These men were steroid-infused sides of beef stuffed into Kevlar sausage casings without insignia. Cold heartless men. The vehicle was cold, too, like a slaughterhouse. Seemed right. Billings didn't mind the temperature.

***

Murphy waited until Billings had gone before picking up his secured cell phone. It came from Wailer's people, and Murphy had tested it himself. It was secure but he wasn't sure. Judging by the way Billings reacted to that new-to-him bit of information, Billings' phone tap didn't include Wailer's network. The liaison showed tells and Murphy needed to know why. Who is backing Billings?

Murphy entered a memorized number. A lady answered. Murphy used the code word first. "Sam, it's me, I have news. Homeland's going after Kenny, on the way now you better—"

"Got it," she said. The line went dead.

Sam must have monitored the exchange. Agencies spying on each other was expected, it didn't bother him, but why and how was Wailer in on this game? Murphy bought Sam time. Sending the rendition team away to change created a window, the garage being on the other side of Chicago. Murphy ran things over in his mind looking for clues.

Kenny's special-needs home was a Wailer property, but Wailer was far removed from his minor holdings. The Finder Foundation's social scientists didn't mind the

CIA's presence, rather, Wailer's people asked for protection with good reason—Kenny has value.

Murphy didn't find Wailer having a direct connection to the project. The researchers operated separately from the medical housing business. Wailer didn't mix businesses, but he did there. Murphy's Antiquities Department and Wailer's behavioral scientists shared the goal to understand Kenny. Murphy regarded the group home as an unofficial safe-house given that it was near the office. Murphy knew he was missing something. The plan to contract Wailer's eggheads to pick Kenny's brain for the CIA was tricky.

The phone rang. South America, he had to take it. Ten minutes slipped by before he called the home. It should have been enough time. Murphy punched into the site. On-screen Kenny stood a few feet back from the house computer typing in midair. Beyond, text scrolled on the computer.

"I've never seen him do that before," Murphy said.

He dialed the site. It rang but nobody picked up. On the main camera feed, the front door opened. Billings rushed in and manhandled Kenny, pulling him away. It was a wonder the kid didn't freeze solid. Murphy's agent picked up his call just as Kenny crossed the front door's threshold.

"Stay on the line with me," Murphy said as Agent Fox rushed into the reception room. "I'm on split-screen, outside camera is fuzzy." Murphy had problems adjusting the view. "Fox, front window. Narrate what you see. Record on your phone."

"Billings is approaching the SWAT carry-all. Men jumping out, shit! Kenny's screaming."

Murphy heard Kenny going off over the phone. Damn that kid has lungs.

"Those pirates! They forced a sack over Ken's head. They picked him up like a bag of seeds!" Fox's voice quivered.

She's scared and pissed. Murphy tried to get the long-view outside camera up without success.

"Keep talking," he said. "Keep calm, remember the plan."

"The carry-all is pulling out. They left Billings standing there. Wow, that was fast. I bet Billings is befuddled." The fire in her tone abated. "He's pulling his phone, walking back. He stopped. I better hang up. He's gonna call in."

"Fox, adjust Kenny's PC cam so I can watch. Talk to Billings like I said."

Murphy hung up. None of his phones rang. Whoever Billings called it wasn't him and it should have been. Homeland probably. Murphy suspected the agent served more than two masters, but who was number one? Something smelled.

That black-op man wasn't right, either. He never showed ID. *That's the first thing you do when visiting another departments' house.* No name tag bothered him. Murphy pulled up the offices' in-house security camera on another screen and isolated the man's picture and ran it through face recognition. No hits in Homeland's employee database. Murphy expanded the search while Billings talked on his phone.

"Son of a bitch!"

"What's that, Chief?" Fox added.

Murphy ignored her. The black-ops man worked for Watchtower Security, a mercenary outfit the CIA uses under the table. They're not on the official user list. Not associated with Wailer either. Whoever they work for wasn't in-network. *Some-*

one's either playing Billings or Billings is their man. Murphy didn't trust Billings to begin with and now Murphy didn't trust him at all.

"Be careful, Fox. Stay sharp."

"Right Boss, here he comes." She hung up.

Billings reentered the front room. The place was furnished like a typical parlor with a small computer desk, all designed pleasant for guests. The bay window allowed a view of the long front lawn and industrial park beyond. The computer's camera covered most of the room, the same computer Kenny used, which was wired into the house security system. Kenny didn't know the computer was there to study him. Murphy had people copying every word Kenny wrote by hand.

"I thought this is a group home," Billings said. "Where's the group?"

"The residence is back there," Fox said, pointing at the inner door. "Thank God nobody was up here. That's all they needed to see. We don't tolerate thugs here. What in the hell are you people doing?"

"Who are you to ask me? I ask the questions. Who are you?" Billings' voice rose in pitch. "If he belongs back there, why's he in the lounge? Who the hell are you anyway?"

She's flustered. I don't blame her. Billings didn't look alarmed. Who did he call? He's gaslighting her.

"Who am I? Who am I? I'm the director. I have Q clearance. I'm a doctor of behavioral science. Who the hell are you, besides a low-grade Brown Shirt enforcer?"

Billings is lucky that she didn't slug him.

"Hold up! Back down, lady. I'm an investigator doing my job."

"You have a funny way of investigating," Fox said in an angry voice. "It's doctor to you, and don't assume I'm a lady. You brought an army to arrest one skinny autistic boy?"

Billings backed up. She pounded his shoulder with a stiff finger. He didn't know about her Kung-fu until that finger delivered the message. Murphy had seen her split boards with that digit. Billings teetered off balance. Murphy stifled a laugh.

Billings can't tango with her. He is my leak!

"OK, I'm sorry. I give," Billings said. "Homeland assigned me. Nobody at Antiquities tells me snot. The goon squad wasn't my call. If I knew what was going on, I'd do better. I don't even know what you do here. Isn't this a disability home? I mean, why's CIA got a group home? That's gotta cost Uncle Sam."

Fox dropped her aggression and relaxed a few notches. Billings used a psychological trick on her. People love to talk about what they do. Fox sees it, she's playing into it. Good.

"The Company doesn't own this place," she said. "This is an operational health facility." Each word carried a little less juice. "Research started before we arrived. We moved in with permission. I'm here to work with Mr. Parks and share data. The Company has concerns. Our adversaries might use his talents. He's very good at locating what the public is better off without. It's a simple arrangement. The home allows us to look into him."

Good girl. She pushed Billings back as she spoke to where he had grabbed Kenny at the terminal. Everything Kenny did was on camera. Billings didn't know that. Billings noticed the screen. Kenny's email was still open and the boy was in the process of writing to Conley when Billings nabbed him.

"Mr. Conley, who's that?" Billings said pointing at the screen.

"Not sure," Fox said. "Kenny emails a lot of academics. He has a blog they frequent. He writes to them and they write back. He's a high-level theorist in paleontology."

"Parks ought to be at the shop by now," Billings checked his watch. "I better call in. I wasn't invited to the interview but still…They left me here. I'll need a ride."

Murphy blanked off his screen before his phone rang. Caller ID said it was Billings. Murphy picked up. "Murphy, shoot. I'm busy."

"Billing's here. Did the package arrive? I was left here. I need a ride in."

"Not yet, still MIA," Murphy said. "I don't have anyone to send. Walk or take a cab. I'm busy." Murphy hung up. *Let's see where my three-faced bandit turns next. He's the mole. The question is who is he tunneling for.*

On camera, Billings pocketed his cell phone. "Guess I'm walking. Nice to have met you, Doctor Fox. I don't know when they'll finish. I'll see you when I bring Parks back."

Murphy instigated the cell phone hack program from his desktop. Communications had set up a system to capture anything close. With the spy truck gone, mobile jamming left, too. *That's why the cameras went fuzzy.* Kenny was known in public forums. The kid was easy to find. Anyone could have gone after him. There was no telling when or if an opposing force might attack. *I should have been on top of it.*

"Whoever Billings called after the grab must be the unseen party," Murphy said drumming his fingers in thought.

Billings went outside on camera and stopped half-way down the walkway a few yards out. Fox moved to the window, recording with her phone. Murphy switched to the outside door camera. Billings was out of the camera's sound recording range but the phone-hacker zeroed in.

"Go on, asshole, make the call," Murphy whispered. "I'm ready for you."

Billings pulled his phone. Murphy's device blinked all go. *Got the son of a bitch.* Murphy couldn't wait to drain his mole's brain and force him to give up the others. Murphy's snoop-wear was the perfect hammer to crack Billings open. Murphy didn't get the chance.

Billing's head exploded. Brains hit the window on Fox's screen.

A sniper shot. That's when it hit Murphy. Parks was gone for good. Rendition wasn't by way of a subcontractor working for the government, hell no. Murphy's lead to identify the unknown party just got his skull splattered. Murphy smashed his coffee cup against a wall.

CHAPTER TWENTY-ONE:

ALASKA

Two CIA men observed Alaska University's campus from a blacked-out armor-plated Chevy SUV Field Surveillance Vehicle parked in AU's staff lot. The temperate, bright day there in Nome didn't cast light or warmth onto the car's occupants.

"Conley better do this right," the tall agent said. "File says he resisted our offer."

"He doesn't know Parks is…missing," The driver said. "Probably dead already. Conley got no reason to withhold cooperation. Don't mention Parks. Play dumb."

"Antiquities is behind this job." The passenger said. "I don't see why they brought us in. What's national security to do with archeology?"

"Justify their budget, what else." The driver tilted his fedora. "Job sheet doesn't say why we gotta lean on this guy."

"Need-to-know doesn't mean we can't speculate. Operations is confused about Parks' kidnapping—looks like an in-house job to me—wanna bet that's why there's a supervisor's car parked over there." He pointed his block-forged chin back right. "Parks was associated with Conley. Maybe they think Conley did it. And now they put Parks' buddy with Cory? It doesn't add up."

"That car's not one of ours." The driver pushed back his fedora ignoring the passenger's comments. "It doesn't look right."

"Don't be stupid, you think they'd tail us with a standard-issue?"

The driver leaned forward. "You're right. Tinted windows in Alaska?"

"Conley's pulling in. Let's rattle him. Flash the lights." The passenger pushed back his suit jacket exposing a sidearm. He positioned himself for Conley to see it. "He's coming."

The driver rolled down the windows and slid his seat back so Conley's line of sight wasn't impeded. Number One's badge gleamed gold while his black-matt auto remained dark and foreboding yet visible. Tricks of the trade.

Conley walked up in a huff. "What now," Conley said. "Standing on my neck ain't motivating me. I told you, not you, them, I guess, I'll do the report. Leave me alone or you'll get nothing."

"Just making sure you don't screw this up," the passenger said touching his Glock. Well-tanned Conley paled and stepped back. Psychological tricks, very effective. "You know what'll happen if you cross us?"

"Go scratch," Conley said. "I said I'd cooperate." He stomped off toward the Archeology Department.

"Not a happy camper," the driver said. "That's how we like it."

"I'll tune-in the remote ear. Let's see out how cooperative he is."

"No need, see that?" The driver pointed at the rear-view camera screen.

A dark figure exited the sedan and moved along the tree's shadow line outside the parking lot's border and out of campus camera's view. Hard to tell, but two others were in the car, trainees maybe. The operative employed Company techniques tailing the mark. No doubt a Company man.

"We have a ground man. Go figure. If the super wants it, let him have it." The driver said. "I'm not fucking with management. How about you?"

"No way. How'd you think I got promoted?" The passenger said. "Mouth shut, hands-off." The driver cracked a smile.

The listening device in the passenger's hand wasn't working. "Weird how it's fine everywhere but here. Cell tower interference must be cutting down range." The passenger tossed the parabolic mini-dish onto the backseat. It refused to hear Cory's office. "Piece of crap. Good thing we have a man up there."

He might have checked the connection but that wasn't his job. CIA agents on loan to HLS don't repair mobile technology—not authorized. Their asses were covered and that's what mattered. He unplugged the charger and tossed it back. It bounced off the seat's blood-proofed upholstery and hit the floor.

"What do we do now?" The driver asked.

"We get paid to watch so that's what we do. Take the first shift," the passenger said before lowering his seat into a lounger position. The driver did likewise. The Company didn't pay enough to stay up all night. No graft opportunities on this stakeout. No overtime money either. "Why should we bust our nuts?" The passenger yawned. "Management is on it."

"Aren't the big shots the ones who lost Parks?" The driver said. "Homeland screwed up."

The passenger didn't see the angle. What's a kidnapped mental-case got to do with the Antiquities Department? It wasn't his to know. Keep an eye on Conley, give him a nudge, that's the job profile. Unwilling informants require eyes-on. A simple, boring job. The passenger lowered his fedora and shut his eyes.

****

Professor Thomas Conley entered the outer office of Alaska State University's Archeology Department, walked up to the reception desk, and stuck out his hand.

"Hi, I'm here to see Doctor Cory."

The receptionist didn't look up. She waved him toward a pair of overstuffed leather English chairs with her tablet phone.

"Guess I'll take a seat."

Tall and thin, Tom didn't fit in either chair which had been made for short and fat 19th century industrialist. The greasy leather stank of cigars. He sank low into the chair's depths enjoying the feel of its age. Such furniture was four thousand miles out of place in Alaska. Paleontology and early man studies were Tom's primary interest, less so archeology although he had credentials for both. Cory's outer room's collection was a hodgepodge of eccentric archeology. Everything felt out of place. Tom admired the décor despite his mission.

What am I doing here? Keeping my career alive.

The room was long, rectangular, and cluttered. It smelled old. Shoe-horn stuffed bookshelves sat among crowded display cases between tall windows; papers were stacked on end-tables and carpeted floor throughout. Artifacts served as willy-nilly decorations. Everything haphazard, disorganized, but oddly homogeneous. Cory's waiting room felt like home.

"Doctor Cory has a good eye for unusual things," Tom said addressing the receptionist.

The girl at the desk didn't flinch. His pudgy, black-haired receptionist was busy on her phone. Tom enjoyed puzzles and the girl was easily solved. *A Native American local student.* Her short hair was the current lesbian standard. Tom had volunteered for Pride events although not gay himself. Her Hawaiian shirt in wild pink with green flamingos wasn't office attire. University staff dress code standards didn't apply. Hired secretarial staff don't work Saturdays. Universities won't pay overtime. Professionals showed interest in guests unlike her.

The file said Cory, short on money, relied on volunteers. Cory's tinfoil hat popularity forced the university to defunded his off-script efforts. Cory had paid for special projects out of his own pocket in protest. Volunteers loved it and embraced Cory's wild ideas.

"Cory ain't picky," Tom said, she didn't respond. "Beggars take what they can get."

The file reported Cory as an eccentric. Cory and Mede were psychic twins according to what Tom thought but didn't read. The file didn't make that connection. *The less psychic, the better.* Tom missed Mede. Mede would know what to do about the government's pressure. Still, Mede had been way off track. Mede suggested the CIA was after magic relics which Tom once thought foolish. Tom didn't know what the government wanted but lost technology was a possibility. The kind of ideas Cory's books promoted embarrassed establishment academics. The system hated him for that? Tom didn't buy it.

"That's cool." Tom pointed at the only fossil in the menagerie, a fist-size trilobite in a box-frame hung on the wall behind her next to a suit of armor. "I like that fossil, was it found locally?

The girl looked up, squinted, and shut her tablet. "Yeah, nice rock." Her attention shifted to the computer.

The modern hardware there was more out of place than he. Tom sunk deeper into the old chair admiring the rare suit of 13th-century armor standing next to Cory's door. The file called Cory's inner office 'the catacombs.' Tom decided to engage the receptionist for some tips about Cory. He tried starting a conversation again.

"I love the armor," he said. "It's complete, even an original long dagger. Every knight carried a dagger, you know. That one could stop a bear."

She looked over the top of her black-rimmed reading glasses. "Yeah, nice costume, whatever." She resumed clicking the mouse. "Stop a bear, right," she said under her breath. "I know how to stop a bear."

Tom gave up. He'd pick her brain later if given the chance. He enjoyed getting to know his students and co-workers before the CIA forced him into espionage.

Brain-picking was his handlers' profession and all they had in common. He had zero interests in spy-craft and precious few academic allies. If he didn't cooperate, the CIA would make sure he didn't have any professional friends. *This ain't a job interview; its infiltration.* Tom felt sewer-rat dirty. Disgusted with himself, he lost grip of his nerves and got up to leave but didn't get the chance.

The infamous Professor William Cory barreled out of his office door with a toothy smile. Tom thought of the Tasmanian Devil cartoon. The intern started pecking on the keyboard. Cory ignored her and came at Tom with a meaty outstretched hand.

"I'm Bill, Bill Cory. You must be Tom Conley." Cory took Tom's hand and shook it vigorously. "I see you've met Janis," he waved at the girl. "She's my tech guru. Good with a gun, too."

"We had the pleasure," Tom said dryly. "Gun?"

"Son, this is Alaska. Bears aren't polite."

Cory resembled what Conley expected. A stocky, solid man, gray crewcut, well-rounded gut. Forearms to make Popeye the Sailor jealous. Cory's book jacket photo matched the man right down to his tweed vest, rolled sleeves, and bolo tie. *I love bolo ties.* That unlikely combination fit Cory. Behind his girth lived a man who did his share of hard-earth digging and it showed. I respect that. Professor Cory wasn't a stay-in-the-tent man but more a hyperactive drill sergeant. The man buzzed standing still. Tom liked him on contact. That Mede spoke well of Cory only made sneaking around harder. Tom's chest flared with heat.

Cory stood back, looked him up and down. "You look like a special-ops guy I saw in the army: You in Desert Storm?"

"No sir," Tom said glad he didn't have to lie. "I never had the pleasure."

"Pleasure?"

"Iraq is old," Tom said. "Many things yet to be discovered. I'd love a few seasons on any one of those tells, better yet Turkey, endless possibilities."

"I agree," Cory said holding the door open. "That's why I volunteered for land-mine detection. You should have seen it, pot shards everywhere." He pointed at a five-quart pickle jar filled with pottery bits on the floor. "Best part, I didn't have to shoot anyone. Come on, let's get started."

A bead of sweat ran down Tom's long nose as he entered Cory's office. He hated lying but the game was on and he had to play.

Cory's office was cluttered worse than the reception area with books stacked higher and artifacts stuffed wherever they fit. A door marked "bathroom' was the only space unadorned. Cory filled the walls with shelves. His Victorian oak desk was massive. The laptop resting on it felt plain wrong. Two modern low-backed mid-century orange fiberglass chairs exaggerated the mishmash. Cory's chair was a 19th century congressional oak-roller.

"Don't stand there. Sit, sit, mind if I call you Tom?" Cory went on without an answer. "Let's get right to it, shall we? No sense in formalities. Call me Bill."

"Sure, Bill, nice to meet you," Tom said, "I prefer first names, that's fine."

"Good, good. Read your résumé, impressive. I did some checking. You've been on student archaeological and paleontology digs, good. I'm especially impressed by your recent fieldwork. Alaska might look open for paleontology but..." Cory ran a meat-hammer hand over his crewcut. "This situation ain't like that. Important to me is our tundra dig. It's old. Have you read my perspective? Says here…" Cory stopped, silently read a few lines, and waved Tom's introduction letter in the air. "I see you've seen my academic publications. That's good. Read my popular books and you'll better know where I'm coming from."

That's what I'm afraid of. Too bad his public consumption publications made him into an academic pariah. The man's record was first-rate before. *If readers knew how off he is, he'd never sell another book…but he was a great scholar.*

Cory leaned forward, squinting one eye.

"Say…I haven't seen your name in the journals? Credentials check out, but you haven't published anything? Nothing at all? Newbies deserve mention, supporting credits, something in print. That's how this business works. Grant money feeds on publications. Haven't you found anything worth financing?"

"Well, sir, I mean, I, I…" Tom took some air. "Dr. Mede asked that I—"

"Drop the sir. I'm outta the military. Mede's an old friend. What's he told you? I don't have to guess. He wrote to me about you."

Tom drew breath over slightly parted teeth to slow his heart rather than bite his tongue. The CIA ordered him not to speak of Mede. Mede taught avoiding unwanted attention. Unusual credits attract the wrong people. Obscurity is safer. Tom had bought into Mede's wisdom. Obscurity provides the ability to go unnoticed. Mede played cat Vs. mouse chess and Tom sucked at chess. The CIA got to him despite Mede's warning. It struck Tom that Mede had been forced out because Callahan vanished.

"Doc Mede forwarded his letter of recommendation?" Tom asked. He had a copy and nothing special was in it.

"No, he sent me a note unofficially. Mede likes things swept under the rug. He's a pro at vacuuming out grains. I don't do carpet sweepers," Cory said.

"There were a couple of…Doctor Mede encouraged me to wait."

"Why? What's your take?"

Tom cleared his throat and launched a rehearsed pitch. "My interest is in field work. Publishing brings accolades and politics and that means more time on campus and less in the field."

That wasn't a lie. He loved field work. With that out of the way, he uncoiled a bit and spoke from his heart. "I want to understand our past. The decent of man most interests me." He never said that out loud before.

"I see. The bullshit mixed in doesn't have anything to do with them two monkeys sitting in the parking lot, would it?"

Tom's heart squeezed the back of his throat and he couldn't even choke up a lie. He felt the blood drain from his face. Cory half-smiled.

"Not a problem. I know they're watching me. They got hooks in you, too, typical. Speak freely," the man chuckled. "I had my tech student wire up a white noise envelope. Janis cleared their bugs. She's got security talents. Mede and I were on the same wavelength, you know. We collaborated…unofficially, of course."

"But they, they'll, if they hear…" Tom's chin hit his chest. "I'm at a loss."

"They can't eavesdrop. I don't know how she does it, but I'm confident they can't hear us."

"I don't know what—"

"No worries, Son. Them goons aren't the only ones accessing nonpublic information. They got you up against a wall, I know, seen it before. Screw them, what do you say we do archeology?"

"That's my intent," Tom said meaning it.

"How're they putting the screws on you?"

"A former student. He's got special abilities…talents, I guess." Tom didn't mean to spill it. "I didn't find shit. It was all Kenny. They figured it out. If I don't help them, my career's over. They can prove I've cheated."

"Seen it before. Mede told me. Gaslighting bastards. Mede had his finder. Jorge is off-grid, smart man. Kenny's a new finder. Too bad they spotted him. This is how you end it. They'll stop once we provide what they're after. Mede was onto something big, too big. That's why they shut him down. Now we get to learn what they want. Screw-em. How about we fake you going along? Get me? Use the users. Take a chance? You want in?"

Cory's confidence and hard bearing instilled hope. The man was 4-wheel-drive tough and correct. Cory had survived serving in war and stood against enough mud-slinging to bury Einstein's career. Yet the man was still on all fours. Cory's books sold in huge numbers. Mede admired Cory's work and often mentioned it. Mede worked around the system. Cory plows through it. Same goals, different approach. Which was better?

"I'm not sure…Maybe…then again…Why not," Tom said relieved. His curiosity connected with Cory's and his heart agreed. His birthmark didn't protest.

"Good, good. Like you, I'm interested in anomalous finds but so are they. Pursuing such things is risky." Cory groused a hand over his crewcut.

"What about the future?" Tom said, thinking of his shaky career.

"As for me, I'll keep digging. Keep a lookout for anything the establishment ignores, or won't tolerate. I aim to know why, what they fear, what's behind it all. I wanna tackle the big questions. Get me?"

"I do," Tom said. His interests piquing.

Cory laid an old copy of The *Finder* magazine before Tom.

"Publishing there is what first brought trouble for me," he said. "Also opened new horizons."

Tom leafed through the back-issue. It featured one of Cory's uncomfortable theories based on good research which had instigated a raging academic row.

"I should have kept a lid on it until I had more. People were here in the Americas 250 thousand years ago, but I won't risk another paper on that unless its better supported. Too bad about Calico and Leaky. We need solid evidence. I'm tired of picking nits. I want the truth, what orthodoxy can't stomach and governments won't admit." Cory spoke drumming his fingers on old oak. "We'll keep our heads down until something breaks. Once we get it out, they can't squash it so easily. Get me."

"Limelight isn't for me," Tom said unintentionally supporting the hire-me speech. "Fame doesn't suit a diligent shovel bum."

Cory flipped Tom's letter to the resume page and read. *What am I getting myself into?* Cory rattled cages. Academic suicide. Nobody wanted on Cory's projects. But the man needs a qualified digger. Tinfoil-hat amateurs can't provide legitimacy. Tom didn't need to pander: He and Cory were on the same shelf. That the CIA wanted Tom made sense. Mutual interests build trust. Tom didn't see any commonalities with Cory until he met the man. That connection wasn't the government's intention. The feds grabbed Tom the pushover for his vague inside track. The CIA should have picked a better rube. Tom had a career to lose but he couldn't lose what he didn't yet have.

"What about Berkeley," Cory said looking up from the resume. "Says here in your note that's your aim. Stick with me and they'll hate you. Why them?"

Tom's mark pulsed. The question caught him short. He never told anyone. It was too crazy. His reasons weren't conventional and better left unsaid. He blurted it out anyway.

"Calico, Berkeley took over the site. I'm a fan. Leakey's data was good. He deserves vindication. Calico's lithic industry is 250K if it's a week. I want access to Leakey's collection."

Cory slapped his leather ink blotter. "That's the stuff, Son. I met Leaky, he was old, I was young. Leakey got a raw deal. Calico should have rewritten the books. Hot damn, am I right?" Cory chuckled deeply. His tone resonated with the past. "What do you think? Let's put it over on the government, eh? You and me, Son."

"We have similar concerns," Tom said. "You got the publishing guts. I don't have your fortitude. I think...I think we'd be good together. Should I find interesting evidence, will you publish it?"

"I'll rewrite goddamn history if you give me the goods. My publishers are on board. Screw academia. We'll go around them. Think about double crossing the feds before you confirm, it's risky."

Tom leaned back in his chair. Dangerously new won't happen, it will be squelched. Those two in the parking lot...but exposing real history was worth risking the government's ire. The prospect boiled with possibilities.

"Mede told me a tale, "Tom said, "He found a hundred-thousand-year-old bomb shelter in Iraq equipped with advanced technology," Tom said. "I didn't accept it, but his story rang true, impossible as it is. I feel sure he didn't lie."

"Mede got lucky. The CIA gave him a choice; support Operation Cover-Up or watch his career die. Mede and Jorge made the safe choice. All records of Mede's big dig were wiped off the planet. They went so far as to blow up the whole area." Cory said. Tom hadn't heard that part. "The war was a pretext."

Did I really see a plastic toy within rex shit? Callahan's silver eyepiece? Tom tossed the toy but he still had the jeweler's loop.

"I need to know what's real," Tom said.

"Our need for truth is common ground," Cory said, "No desire to publish yourself?"

"Later, if it doesn't rock the boat. I won't put my career in jeopardy." Or my life. "All I ever wanted was an interesting dig and a shovel."

"I need a man who wants the deep stuff. Take a minute and really think about what you are getting into." Bill Cory leaned back drumming his fish-stick fingers on hard oak. Tom had recited what Cory wanted to hear but he also spoke his mind and Cory listened. "It's yours if you want it."

Since Mede got sidelined, and Jorge disappeared, Kenny shut down. Without a dig-cam Kenny had no reason to communicate, or was there another reason? Digging goes harder with half a shovel. Working for the government sucked, but they provided his only opportunity. Without them there'd be no work for him. *I should walk. Tell them I'm out.* Cory would go along with it. *Who am I kidding, I don't have the balls.*

Cory took a minute to talk with the reception girl, it was getting late. Tom considered his position and knew he'd gladly double-cross the CIA given the chance which may well get him killed.

His mouth went dry. He wasn't good at deception. He wasn't wired for adventures. Cory called him to action. His chest itched over it. *I'm Cory's man alright and that's nuts.* On that thought, his birthmark stopped dancing. His career fears blew away like fine dust. He wants what Cory wants. Cory offered a path back to shovel bumming. Mede was smart to keep things buried, but they buried him anyway.

"What do you think," Cory said coming back into his office.

"If you'll have me, I'll do my part."

"Hell yes," Cory said. "You're hired!"

"When do I start?" Tom felt the skin around his birthmark un-crinkle with relief.

"Right now," Bill Cory said. "We have a project in southwest Alaska…I had some problems with the government. I need a top man on this. You up for trouble Professor?"

"What kind of trouble?" Tom said. He already knew Cory was too close to something the feds didn't want known. The CIA didn't tell him what that is.

"Let us make plans. This'll take a while, how about a drink; whiskey?" Cory got up, went to an old wooden file cabinet and pulled two dirty tumblers out of the bottom draw. The half-empty bottle of Wild Trumpet made Tom's mouth water.

"I'm going to enjoy working with you…Bill." Tom said. *He's a whiskey man.*

"To know the unknown," Cory said. They clicked glasses.

Cory explained the situation. The dig's location was in a shallow valley between gently sloping hills where a glacier had receded. At one section's base lay a series of bedrock outcrops like ratchet gears which preserved material deposited before the glacier developed. The "rachets" were shallow dead-end passages cut into bedrock. Such areas were exposed during interglacial periods thereby acquiring datable chronological sediments between warming events. Such rock formations, in antiquity, would have been ideal for migrating people to shelter in.

Sediments had filled in these alcoves between cycles of snow stacking. The latest receding glacier didn't disturb older sedimentary layers. Melt-water action had removed more recent deposits leaving older material frozen just below the surface. Such conditions provided a rare geological snap-shot.

"If people came through between maximums, as the theory goes, we'll know when and maybe who. Conventional enough." Cory said. "But we'll prove people came through before the ice ages if I have this right. I'd wager lithics found will match Leakey's Calico samples."

"That's dynamite!"

"Did I mention I worked landmine detail in the Army?" Cory said. "I don't mind a little dynamite. It's the claymores you gotta worry about."

Cory explained the geology and how cycles of global warming had exposed areas that were hidden off and on for two hundred and fifty thousand years. Had man come between ice flows these alcoves may well provide the evidence. The last glacier retreat before the present began twenty-four thousand years prior.

"That'll make it pre-Clovis no matter what we find," Tom said.

"Correct, "Cory said. "Nineteenth-century gold miners had explored the region and discovered, in the boulder fields' downflow, various lithic and bone industries, and a dozen intriguing unidentified spear points," Cory spoke as if this bomb shell was common knowledge. "Most of this evidence is held incognito, but I got hold of the original surveyor's journals and sketches. The ice has since retreated a few hundred yards more."

"I never heard of this," Tom said. "You're blowing my mind."

"Impossible to date back in the day. These artifacts have since been attributed to the accepted human migration theory of crossing the Bering Straits fifteen thousand years ago." Cory chuckled, stopped quickly, and leaned forward with a sly smile. "That stuff ain't Clovis, Son. That's faulty history."

Another round was poured and Tom sipped while Cory talked and gulped.

A military outpost had recently expanded and became a high-security base. The last thing the Army wanted was them snooping around. Of course, the Army and the CIA weren't really friends. The base was ready for further expansion but Alaska law demanded an archaeological survey first. The state, Army, and Homeland Security were at odds. In this confusion, an anomalous artifact could find its way into publication. That was Mede's way of cracking academic ice. Undatable lithic industries aren't too much for the mainstream. Bill wanted datable materials.

"It's a legitimate dig, not too risky," Tom mused.

"That'll depend on what we find." Cory took a sip.

Whatever is there, it deserves preservation, in Tom's view. Alaska and the Federal Wildlife Department also had conflicts. The oil lobby had a stake judging by the surveyors snooping around. Lots of distraction fingers were in this pie. Outside conflicts helped their cause. Tom would need to juggle and he didn't like that aspect.

"I've never dealt with the politics," Tom said. "I'm weak on that."

"You'll be fine," Bill said waving a hand dismissively. "Speaking of that, last summer we were constantly harassed by MPs. They watched closely. Commander Hodges claimed he was protecting us. Bears, he said." This notion tickled Bill. He slapped his desk with a hardy laugh before going on.

"Artifacts were confiscated in the field, goddamn military." The mirth ran out of Cory's disposition. "Anything advanced or metallic was taken as Army property. I went to Hodges and demanded they back off. Hodges wouldn't acquiesce. Got so bad, I canceled the dig in protest and walked off. Screw them. They can't drill or build anything until I sign off. I'm tenured."

"What a pissing match. So why go back?" Tom said.

"Feds are pushing for it," Cory said. "They needed someone they can control on site." Cory laughed. "That's you, my boy. The president's Energy Commission wants this finished. Army is unhappy, but the president is where the buck stops, eh? They offered unlimited funding." Cory blew air on his finger nails. "I had to call in a favor or two. That's how I got you. Don't look surprised. Me and Mede got our connections. He said I can trust you."

Cory accepted the invitation under strict conditions: no military within three hundred yards of the site and publication rights. It wasn't stated in negotiations, but the CIA had to have an inside man on the job to make it work and Tom was it.

"The feds need me more than I need them," Cory said. He sipped his whiskey. "I told them bastards to leave me alone or find someone else. State University has dig rights and AU can't replace me, not without a lawsuit. Time and tenure are on my side. They'll leave us alone or get nothing."

Cory spoke with passion and enthusiasm the way Tom had before the feds pressed him. Tom wished he could simply dig, and over time, fill in a few blanks. Earth's puzzle held countless fractured pieces. To uncover a few consolidating aspects of the big picture was a reasonable and safe professional ambition. Skating on thin ice in Alaska was the last thing he expected.

"This'll be tricky," Tom said. "I never had to deal with government before. Won't we need to give them something?"

"Not if I can help it." Bill said drumming his fingers. "I don't trust the Army. They're up to something and it ain't good. I'm guessing they want siloes. We got enough missiles already goddamn it."

"Why not do the survey themselves?" Tom said.

"Them oafs? They'll destroy important finds and make themselves look stupid doing it. Hodges knows that. He's gotta protect his ass. Law requires, federal and state, a legit survey. Wanna bet they lost something, a weapon maybe, a few dead bodies, who knows? The CIA's got to watch the Army, oil people and us. They can't see everything. Certified survey corked this bottle and we're the corkscrew."

"If we don't get screwed first," Tom said with half a smile.

Cory upended his drink. Tom drank a sip with his head spinning on possibilities. Cory probably knew more than he said. This will be more dangerous than Cory indicated. Tom's chest tightened on the thought. He downed his drink for relief. Cory poured another round.

"Could be the MPs were souvenir hunting," Cory said. "The Army doesn't give a seal-fart what we find as long as it ain't theirs and we get the hell out fast. That's my take. Sure, Hodges hates us. Worse scenario for them is if this turns into a dig they can't bulldoze. The press knows we have a unique site. This'll rip the over-the-land-bridge books into confetti if we confirm what I saw last year. Be that as it may, we're a problem for the Army."

"I'm not good at conflicts," Tom said, "But, I'm willing."

"Good man. Now, for something new: Can't let anyone see this until we're ready to publish. I hid a few little items before the goon squad riffled our tents."

Cory reached into a desk drawer and pulled a mortar and pestle set made of a fine white stone which he had bagged. It was dull but well-made as if cut on a lathe and engraved with runes unfamiliar to linguists. Tom had seen such characters on his long-lost amulet. Organic soil residue remained within the carvings of Cory's object. Datable material. Cory next laid down a primitive stone chopper encrusted with that same soil.

"These were found together," Cory said. "Not made from local stone."

"'Toto, I have a feeling we aren't in Kansas anymore.'" Tom said. His world shifted under him.

"Son, you aren't far off…"

Tom picked up the stone bowl still sealed in a dated find's bag.

"This is amazing, beautiful. I don't get it. No way Neolithic people made this fifteen thousand years ago, maybe late Neo. Certainly not Mesozoic. Are you sure this is original? The chopper fits, but not really?" Tom couldn't believe Cory smuggled these out. The man had stone balls. "Chopper doesn't fit. It's like a Rift Valley, Africa artifact, maybe Southeast Asia. Homo Ergaster, or Erectus...can't be that."

"Why not? I dug it myself. It's real." Cory said. "Found it under datable permafrost, outside alcove Number One, below the mudstone layer we removed. I'll email you photos. It was under—I said under—the surface of an undisturbed bog. Dated it myself. It's off the chart. Carbon dating tops out under a hundred thousand—it's older. Radiation testing and diatoms says it predates the ice ages. It wasn't made by late coming homo sapiens."

Tom whistled. He heard similar stories from Mede who never got to date his out-of-place items before the feds confiscated them. He took a moment to collect himself. Curiosity fed his beating heart. Cory's find locked in Tom's interests. *I can't back out, I'm hooked.*

"When can I leave?"

"That's my boy," Cory said as he poured another round. Tom had gulped his last drink. "Starts in three weeks, hardly enough time for preparations."

The two talked late into the evening developing plans. Cory will play the political games and process data from AU while Tom runs the dig. At one point Janis popped in to say she was going home. Tom got up to stretch his legs. Looking out the window, he noticed the second CIA car. The girl asked to stay late, feeling something was amiss, but Bill waved her off with a shoo-fly hand. The two got back to business which quickly digressed into more drinking and less organizing. Half in the bag, Cory called it a night.

"Eleven p.m.," Tom said standing up. Cory did the same. "I gotta get some sleep."

Tom pulled Cory's office door open and a man crashed onto the floor like a bag of bones.

"What the hell. What're you doing?" Bill said.

"I am Fredric Amos, Doctor Cory. Here for the interview. We talked on the phone. I was just going to knock. I called. The girl was to let you know I was on my way."

Cory turned red-faced. "She didn't mention you?"

Wild Trumpet must have exacerbated his color. Cory wasn't the kind to feel embarrassed. Tom swayed unsure on his feet, but Cory's sea-legs seemed to embrace alcohol and he stood unphased.

Tom revisited the window to give them privacy. Amos smelled like a mummy. From the anteroom window, Tom noticed that the CIA sedan moved and parked next to his Jeep. The SUV was gone. The lot served several departments. It could be anyone's car. Campus security typically uses recycled police cars, it might be that. He turned from the window.

"Damn, forgot you were coming," Cory said walking toward Tom speaking to the new man. "Listen, I'm closing shop. Time to git, the wife, you see. No need to interview. I hired Tom."

Tom nodded at Amos at the mention of his name. *I've seen that man before.* The applicant returned a hard stare with off-charcoal pupils surrounded by taupe. Strange eye color like Wailer. Bill and the man-come-late shook hands. Tom had no spy skills but something wasn't right. He hated feeling suspicious. CIA paranoia must have rubbed off on him. He shook the notion off as too much whisky.

"I might have something for you next season. Call Monday, I'll let you know." Cory told the applicant as they exited together.

The man took a stairwell. Cory and Tom, unsteady on their legs, opted for the elevator in the other wing. Once outside, Amos was forgotten. The two professors walked along the pathway around the building. Tom glimpsed a lively shadow darting about like intelligent smoke. Those CIA boys were as dedicated as they were stupid. Even drunk, Tom was still a trained observer. They approached the first parking lot where Tom left his Jeep.

"Can you drive?" Cory asked.

"I'm in the guesthouse on campus." Tom said glad he didn't need to go far.

"Amos was a day late," Cory said, "I'd have hired him, otherwise."

"I know that guy. Saw him in the Badlands on my freshmen year dig. He hasn't aged." Tom was good with faces and remembered the scrawny man's dark, greased hair and waxy skin. "That digger must have discovered the fountain of youth. He should be gray."

"If he found it," Bill said, "I hope he shares the elixir. I'm feeling my age."

Tom and Cory parted where the walkway forked. Tom headed for his Jeep across the lot. That sedan next to his car confirmed it was the CIA with its tinted windows. No one tints windows this far north. He couldn't see inside but it had to be a stakeout. Tom decided it was time to show some balls. He knocked on the window.

"You guys are assholes. Drive an M1 tank, why don't you. Watching me is a waste of government funds."

The sedan's window rolled down a few inches and a voice replied.

"I'm afraid you're—"

"Back off. I'm in, alright. I'll get it for you, then get lost." Nasty wasn't Tom's usual but he had it with the harassment. "I can't believe the CIA pays people to sit and watch a guy who's working for them." Tom pulled the miniature recorder from his shirt pocket and pushed it through the window slit. "I did what you asked. Bug off."

"What about that other guy," the car asked. Tom couldn't see who spoke.

"Professional digger in for an interview. Seen him before. Stop tailing me. Have you considered a less conspicuous car?" Tom climbed into his jeep and started the motor. "You people suck."

Half in the bag, as he was, real cops would have arrested him the moment he slotted his ignition key. Government had his back like it or not. Forced to tolerate them, he didn't have to respect them. He started the Jeep and put it in gear without fear of arrest.

I'll produce results alright and I ain't telling. I'm ready for you. He could quit but he didn't want to. Curiosity had him by the balls. He wanted answers. His ally had played this game before. *Cory knows what he's doing and has the guts to do it.* Mede's way was too careful. Cory's bombastic gales created enough smoke-cover to hide a buffalo.

Tom saluted the car next to him, backed out, and drove off thinking his CIA handlers were in the wrong profession.

"You should be selling used clown cars." Tom yelled as he drove away.

CHAPTER TWENTY-TWO:

MARY

Mary agreed to go with Richard but she didn't expect to go on sneaking. She assumed they, having avoided the Midhurst police, would have switched cars and gone in style. That was her expectation. Richard always goes in style. She liked the idea of riding in a car that didn't smell of French fries and hot dogs. Richard's junker Ford favored the aromas of beer, rust, and mildew. She had inquired about getting a nicer car.

"'We have to travel low-key.'" He had said crossing Midhurst's city limits and he wasn't joking about going low.

Her expectations weren't served. Low-key didn't end at the border. She tried to stop him seeing an irresistible outfit in a fancy-dress shop's window near Reno but he wouldn't risk buying it. 'Hight end shops have security cameras.' Was his excuse.

Richard drove that old, rusted car 1500 miles avoiding people wherever possible. He paid for everything as expected. She didn't expect he'd use cash. He peeled off twenty-dollar bills like a monkey opening a crack-laced banana. Every roadside grease-bucket meal, every cockroach-infested no-telling-who-died-there motel, moldy thrift store duds, and every gallon of regular gas was on him—in cash. He had a truckload of currency and left it behind when they ditched the car near San Francisco. Mary didn't expect that, either. He left a suitcase stuffed with money behind.

"'The car won't last long in Oakland,'" he had said with a chuckle, "'Too bad. I like it, it runs well. I hope a nice family gets the money.'" He popped the truck and walked away.

Mary didn't miss the car. Stealing a Christ Craft runabout and motoring out in a pirated boat to meet his ship parked offshore seemed like business as usual by then. She didn't mind breaking the law. Mary felt alive. She didn't expect that either.

"'Expect the unexpected,'" she said as the little cabin cruiser passed under the Golden Gate Bridge.

In her wildest medication-induced dreams she never boarded *The Finder* although that death-ship often haunted her repose. It loomed just out of sight, a specter of doom below the horizon. The road trip played out like a dream. Her realty bell rang when the good ship, *Finder*, materialized out of glowing mists like a goddess. Climbing the rope ladder felt exhilarating. But once over the gunwale, her road-forged energy switched off. She collapsed into a deckchair exhausted.

A women took Mary's hand and helped her up. "This way Ma'am. Your cabin is ready."

Mary followed in a daze. She took a scented bubble-bath in her luxury cabin, drank sweet wine, and passed out on a flower-patterned bedspread. Hours later, she woke to the knock of a porter at the door bearing the little black dress of her dreams. Her dreams were never this good.

"I wonder when the ax falls?" She said before opening the door.

Richard came at 6 p.m. sharply dressed, clean and shaved. She had gotten used to his stink. He led her toward the captain's table on an upper deck. They walked together along well-lighted passageways which she once knew well. *The Finder* was ship-shape and shiny. No salvage equipment in evidence to induce her nightmares.

"Hope you don't mind the walk. I gave you the aft suit," he said. "Best room in the house."

"After riding shotgun, I would rather be a horse than the buckboard." The vibrating diesel engines comforted her. "It's good we're underway. Moving is safer than sitting like a duck." The silk dress flowing around her knees felt delicious. "I could get used to this."

The satin strip of Richard's tuxedo trousers glimmered as did her dress while strolling past wall sconces making the place more surreal. From road-warrior dirt-bags to king and queen—what a trip.

She had not dressed this well since Tommy was born. Whatever was cheap was it. She forgot how much she enjoyed what Bert had called, "'A fancy night out.'" Her dead husband, as rough around the edges as he was, loved himself a fancy night out and so had she. She resisted indulging that old excitement but it got the better of her. The room provided toiletries and beauty products. Mary made up her face. Thin-bodied, wrinkles few, she passed for younger except when depression drug her through broken glass. She forgot how pretty she was.

And Richard, dapper as a prince in waiting. She hadn't paid attention to his physical appearance. His good looks and matching charm were enough to make any girl rubber-limbed. She hated to admit what a handsome man he is. Well-trimmed graying beard, sharp haircut, tall and fit, any girl should fall for him…but not her.

Richard swept the dining-room door open. She entered first and recognized Doctor Beverly Hess at the table. Deric, the boy who brought her the dress stood by. On the cross-country ride, Richard mentioned Hess was on his research vessel. Mary didn't grasp he meant *The Finder*. Richard pulled out a chair for Mary across from Doctor Hess. A small table was set for three whereas Mary expected a banquet table. Richard didn't take a chair himself.

An announcement came over ship's com. "Six bells."

"Ladies," he said. "I'll let you get acquainted. The chef needs a little more time. Let me see how she's doing."

It was past 6 p.m. when Richard exited. Deric leaned toward the door as if drawn by a magnet. Hess raised her hand, and to Mary's surprise, Deric took Hess' hand.

"You gonna be okay Grandma?" Deric said.

"Yes, yes, I'm sure Mrs. Conley doesn't bite and if she does, I'll bite her back." She clicked her dentures and gave Deric's hand a little squeeze. "Vamoses, now."

He left. Hess wasn't like Mary remembered from the book jacket. Mary had Hess's books in her collection. Bert bought Mary Hess' last book when they were in college. Hess wasn't young then. With wire-rim glasses, snow-white hair, and knit shawl she resembled the quintessential greeting-card grandmother and not the once renowned scholar.

"I'm a big fan…I loved your books, I mean I, I don't know, I, I ah…"

"First order of business, call me Beverly. Let us not indulge in formalities. Secondly, I am pleased you liked When Women Were Gods. The editors came up with the title, which spiked interest, I'm sure. I wrote it for popular consumption, as it were. That you and so many women responded to my ideas so forcefully is why that was my last book-length publication with University Press. You see, the powers don't care for ideas which counter the establishment view, I dare say." Beverly took a sip of wine. "We have much to talk about, you and I."

***

Richard ran up to the bridge. The pilot crew was busy. Two officers plus the captain—all three women were gathered around the radar/sonar station.

"What is it, Gayle?" Richard said.

"U.S. nuclear sub's following. I waited too long for countermeasures."

"Damnit. We'll have to deploy the fish."

"We're still in American waters." The pilot said.

"Let him follow until we're outside," Richard said.

"What! You can't sink a Navy vessel!" The new radar operator said. "That's crazy." She was fresh out of the Navy and still coated with patriotism.

"I'm not stupid," Richard said evenly. "The fish is a trick. It'll attach itself to their hull. They'll think it's a mine and surface, once they do, EMP pulse. We scramble their computers, it doesn't last. I'm not a killer."

"We didn't have anything like that when I was in." The ex-navy woman said. Her voice thoughtful. "Cool idea."

"That's how one stays a step ahead, you out tech the other guy." Richard tapped his lip. Stopping an American sub inside its home waters won't do. Gayle had it right. "Betty, launch the fish but wait for international waters." Betty, the communications officer, doubled on weapons—not the shooting kind. "Slow and steady Gayle, make like we can't see them. But keep an eye on them, let me know when they surface. Meanwhile, make tracks. Prepare for silent running but hold the sails. I'm going to see how chow's coming. Oh, don't forget to blind the satellites after she's up."

Richard exited. He knew his crew, no need to hang on their backs. He made for the kitchen and told the chef to slow down to give Mary and Bev space. Richard started the kitchen computer. On-screen, his guests were deep in conversation. Mary didn't have a reason to trust or take anything he said as fact. *She will listen to Beverly.* The fish will work once, maybe twice before the Navy catches on. This time, no worries, next time the government will be ready.

***

After a short chit-chat and a little wine, Beverly got to the center of things.

"You see," Beverly said, "My book was mass-market but also a serious book with an important message. I showed the power of women-led societies in ancient times. It was a more balanced and progressive social order."

"I've heard that. But, when?" Mary said.

"When war gods replaced the goddesses in the people's hearts. That's when consciousness went awry. Slowly, beginning in prehistory and into the late bronze age, the goddesses' influence was subverted." Beverly took a sip of wine. "It's been a litany of death and destruction since. Today's end-line result is the unnatural relationship dynamics between the sexes. Papers correcting that ideology won't ever be published in this climate. Establishment education is directed by design to hold society askew in favor of the imbalance. It's automatic. It has long been infused into the collective unconsciousness. This may appear good from the men's perspective, but it is not good for humanity."

Beverly took a big sip. "There are timeless forces at work under the surface bent on crushing what powers women have. It is written in ancient records. The agenda, unto this day, bastardized archeology. The warning has been chiseled into stone and written on pottery and yet the message of salvation, the restoration of balance, remains unspoken."

"You proclaimed the truth and they shut you down," Mary said, anger building. "I smelled that rot in acidemia."

"The evidence of egalitarian societies, which exposes the equality of feminine leadership, is routinely ignored as insignificant or misinterpreted when said evidence is impossible to ignore." The old lady's pale face flushed. "I exposed this tainted academic reality, this system-wide war on womenkind. I presented hard evidence. Archeology has long been a man's field. Have the history books been rewritten? No, and they never will be if society continues being driven by man's will. History shows it doesn't work."

"I understand," Mary said. "Men like control, simple psychology. They love the fight. I can't deny their need for domination. No force is behind it. It's a natural social expression. How can there be a grand plan? It just is. It's in the wiring."

"When I wrote, 'life is by design,' I meant it." Hess leaned forward. "We think we know who. There is a who, or a what, I should say, behind our contrived social dynamics. Thirteen thousand years ago Earth's champions lost the war. The males took drastic action and won. I believe they are about to do it again. And soon."

"Who were they?"

Beverly paused for a sip of wine. She took a moment to rub her hands. Mary thought she must have arthritis with her knotted knuckles. Retired prizefighters had better hands.

"My book of twenty years ago, wasn't the end of my research. It was the beginning. Richard, being a fan, has supported my research since my leaving university."

"You were on TV," Mary said. "You were famous. I saw you on talk shows all the time, then you were gone. The media had trashed you, but that only made the book more popular. Can't blame you for bugging out but..." Mary's realizations were piling up. "But...why didn't you fight for your place?"

"I'm not interested in fame, my dear. I am a scientist. Fame doesn't allow one to be anything but a tool. One plays along or else." She sipped again. "I took the second option. And it has been worth it."

"What?" Mary said. "Walk away from fame, I get it, but everybody needs money?"

"To save mankind, womankind, and everything in between, is why." Beverly refilled her glass. "There is a hidden race of men who have, for time out of mind, subjugated women. They aren't like us. They are long-lived and they hate us. Still unconfirmed…They mean to wipe us out as they have done before."

"What! Who, how!?" Mary sprung to her feet. The chair went over backward.

"Homo Ergaster is who. How? Richard is working on that. They are a million years older than us and beyond our technology. They've culled humanity before. Women's Magic is spreading and they can't have it."

Mary clenched her fists. A head-rush came on and it wasn't a panic attack. She uncurled her fingers one by one and placed hands flat-open on the table to steady herself. This was all impossible, but in her bones, she knew Hess was right. The sensation left and she righted the chair. Beverly poured her another glass. Mary let herself down easy. That old, odd feeling of the Earth moving under her hit, and it wasn't the ship. Her mind rocked between realities. Magic, Women's Magic, magic is real.

"Richard has connections," Mary said. "Can he stop them?"

"Did he tell you where he came from? He doesn't know these people but they knew him. He was left to die in a foundling home. Rejected, unworthy. However, Women's Magic was imprinted upon him, to protect him. He didn't know. I don't know why he was gifted. I haven't mentioned my suspicions. Half-breeds are in the scrolls." Beverly released the glass she had been squeezing. "A few more lines of text and we'll know where and how they hide, and with that, a way to stop them."

Beverly explained how Richard discovered that the volcano Bert died on was a machine. The shark too. Only by chance did the beast save Tommy from drowning. She shared what little they knew about the Watchers. Mary listened stuffing down grief.

The door swung open and Richard came in and pulled his chair. "Sorry ladies, food will be right up. Had a little problem, we're good now."

Mary didn't want food. But the wine decided she had better eat. She wanted a clearer head to ask questions. She intended to hold back until the fog cleared and enjoy the meal, but the big question spilled out.

"Where do we go from here?"

"To the belly of the beast," Beverly said, lifting her glass. "I do believe I'm close. With your help, Mary, we will find the rat's nest."

"I knew you'd get along. Food's here. I'm starving." Richard said.

Porters came. The food was excellent and the presentation beautiful. Mary's appetite returned on the first bite. The conversation was light, and oddly, Mary's heart lightened as well. Her perceptions were real. Thoughts and feelings she thought of as mental illness, were not. Messages from the ether, which she had ignored or medicated out of existence, weren't imagined. She had heard the Goddesses crying in the wind and refused to listen. I'm listening now.

"Okay, so, I'm not crazy." Mary said between bites. "Crazy would be better."

CHAPTER TWENTY-THREE:

OFF THE CLOCK

———————

The two CIA men in the SUV had figured their night was over when the super's car parked next to Conley's Jeep. They relocated nearby. When Conley's Jeep left the lot, the driver called in to punch out.

"Base, this is the second watch, copy?"

"We copy, report, over."

"The mark left. We're clear, ready to vacate. Thanks for backup, copy."

"What backup? Over."

The tall one looked at the driver and shrugged his shoulders. The driver swirled his finger around his ear making the crazy sign hand gesture.

"Supervisor just pulled out, copy."

"We didn't send backup." There was a muffled argument in the background. The microphone keyed off without an 'over'. A different voice came on.

"Morons, Conley's bait, not the target. The guy who is after Conley is our guy. You read the job sheet?"

The tall one said to his partner, "What in hell is he talking about? Did you get a new sheet?"

"No," the driver said. "Support clerk didn't have it when I went down. She said it's getting updated. Same job, more details, so I split. We have the original order. Still active or we would have gotten a stop-work."

The passenger pressed the microphone. "Negative, no updated job sheet, SP said new papers are in process, copy." His voice remained professional.

"Goddamn it!" The radio said. Base's microphone slammed into its cradle. The tall one loosened his tie. The driver wasn't flustered either.

"Dispatch screwed up." The driver said. "They should've made sure we had the right profile before we left the shop." He started the car.

"Not our fault." The passenger agreed. "Paperwork's good."

"What about that sedan? Private dick I bet. Cory's wife is on the warpath again." The driver said. They had been watching Cory for a while. Conley was added the day before. "Shouldn't we look into it?"

"I have no need-to-know," the passenger said. "I'm off the clock."

"We could run down that car, it's overtime." The driver said. "Not many hotels around here."

The tall one picked up the mic. "Base, on that unmarked car, we're attempting to locate it. Punch us in."

"Affirmative, base out."

The agent's half-million-dollar bulletproof SUV proceeded to the outskirts of a nearby subdivision. They parked at the White Bear Pub; a ramshackle gin mill haunted by law enforcement types. They were in no hurry to punch out again. Overtime is never challenged. They entered the pub thirsty.

"If there's a private eye around, he'll end up here." The passenger said.

The driver tipped his glass in agreement.

***

Pat Cross, Amos' hired gun, almost felt sorry for Conley. Pat couldn't believe his luck. Conley dropped all the info they needed right into his lap.

"Poor bastard," Cross said, "the CIA's got him coming and going."

They had pulled around back after Conley left and parked where Amos said. The driver, Pat's brother-in-law Ralf, agreed. "No kidding, Conley hates the CIA, too. Paranoia makes people nuts." He had a listening device trained on the CIA's car and marked them leaving. "Nice of Conley giving us his recorder. Amos will appreciate it."

"Scratch that, I'm pawning it," Pat said pulling the data card. He tossed the card out a window. "We just started this job. We get paid by the day, don't we?"

Pat parked in the dumpster alcove off parking lot B to wait. The government car's line-of-site was blocked but it didn't matter. The CIA had gone. Pat and Ralf waited another half hour before the boss showed up. Fredric Amos stepped out of the shadows laughing. He got into the back and slammed the door. They dropped the boss off at his hotel. Boss-man had some gal-pal tied up there.

Amos paid for the night in cash and took the remote ear with him. Amos didn't ask for a report and none was given, no questions asked by either party. Pat wasn't about to upset the cash-cow with unsolicited volunteer info. The pay was good. Pat wanted the job to last.

CHAPTER TWENTY-FOUR:

ALBERT AND KENNY

lbert Dulles had a problem. He and his brother were the last pure Watchers to have lived on the surface and so the last purists to have worked topside. The natural transformation of aging made it impossible for him to go above. Albert had held high honors on the surface and now found it humorous. It was too easy. He had founded America's CIA for the Watcher's advantage. That clever idea had earned him the title Director of Surface Affairs. His spy-master days weren't over. Albert's tentacles reached deep, but without direct involvement, his controls had weakened.

Belloc had called. Something was amiss. The Ancient One was on his way to see Albert in his office. Such a visit was rare and only in the face of trouble. Albert lowered his lights and had Athena turn to the wall so as not to offend Belloc.

His workspace duplicated his former CIA office. Belloc wouldn't appreciate the wood paneling, hardwood floors, drywall ceiling, and Persian carpets. Belloc would think it frivolous or worse, he might think it traitorous. Boric swung the door out. The old coot ambled in. Belloc, twenty thousand years old, appeared much the same as any Watcher except he was hunched over and more deeply wrinkled. The codger's lifespan stretched beyond natural limit. Belloc never rushed. Albert rushed often.

The spy-master stood at his desk until Belloc shuffled across the carpet. "Greeting Ancient One."

The old man stopped. "Dulles," Belloc said, "The prisoner isn't well. Do you know why?"

"He is autistic and has been removed from the environment to which he is accustomed. He will come around."

"No, he will not come around, as you say. He will die and dead bait is no use to us. If he dies…our quarry will not come. I ask again, what of Parks' condition?"

"I don't know."

"I will tell you." Belloc took a big draft of air. "Did you not notice that under the care of our female transportation agent, Parks thrived? Did you not notice that should a male touch him, he becomes catatonic? Have you not read the reports Billings provided?"

"Why would I?" Dulles was indignant. "He's a prisoner, a tool, a dead man walking. Once we have Wailer and his proxies, what does it matter?"

"Fool, the bait will expire before then. He has not eaten. He sits in his cell, shitting himself without moving. He will disease himself and us if this continues."

"You want him on life support, force-fed, bowls tapped?" Albert thought it good. The horror of it was of no concern. "I will arrange it. We will need chemicals to force him awake." Albert's mind raced with ideas. "He could draw Wailer in with a computer."

"If the bait is not naturally functional, it cannot attract our quarry. You are thick, Dulles. Forcing one with his derangements will not work. No computers. We won't risk it. There is a better way."

"Which is?"

"House him with the women. They will revive and enhance Parks and Wailer will hear his cries. The Goddesses are good for more than reproduction. Parks must not be tampered with. Let him be restored. He cannot escape. Think."

This rocked Dulles. Ergaster Women were prisoners reserved for childbearing. Employing their skills was long forbidden. But Belloc was right. Parks was not a man but only a child. Women nurture children. A child is no threat. Women's Magic will preserve Parks and aid his telepathic abilities. Albert should have seen it. The women, as old and abused as they were, still appeared as homo sapiens. Women don't morph as Ergaster men do. Parks will accept them. He won't know they are a different species. Park's life force will attract Wailer.

"Bless your wisdom," Dulles said, "I will see to it."

"Now you are thinking! I leave you to it." With that, the old man shuffled toward the exit but stopped before leaving. "Have the Goddesses washed."

Albert stood until the Old One was long gone. Dulles hailed the facilities manager saying. "Have your slaves cleaned. Send them to the Goddesses with provisions. Have them wash the women's chambers…Make the captives presentable."

Athena was ill-kept. Belloc insisted on a continuous psychological attack. Albert agreed terror is the correct tool. As much as he despised her, having Athena underfoot pressed a boot on her neck. Belloc is wise. Parks won't respond to matted-haired beasts. This was unusual. Uplifting the females only occurred when mating was arranged. Otherwise, the women received minimal sustenance. A hard watch had been kept since the pregnant one escaped in 1898. Artemis was the only one to have escaped. Whose child she carried was never confirmed. She must have killed the Ergaster child.

Albert saw the magic behind the Women's Suffrage movement and later, the Women's Liberation movement which he, as America's CIA director, set about squashing unsuccessfully. But now they had her. His half-breed agent tracked her down. The missing Goddess will return. He looked forward to making her his living footstool.

Treating the women well rubbed him wrong. He feared magic seeping out. No Ergaster man can enter and live. Will Parks survive? Albert made a note to instruct the women to hold Parks in the front chambers. No male can survive Athena's inner chambers. Children and idiots were exempt from her curse. Parks alive and awake was indeed more useful.

"Belloc is wise."

Parks' association with the half-breed created the trap. Parks will project and Wailer will come. The Old One was right. Albert scrawled a note to have his agents inform Wailer's spies of Parks custody. The longer game is better. Albert needed a little more time to finish coordinating the vent system. Alberts's confidence soared.

"Belloc is right again. Boric, remove this dirty rag."

****

Her guard opened the woman's chambers' thick door and pushed her in. Athena tripped into the foyer without losing her feet. Boric withdrew quickly and shut the door.

"Ladies ready yourselves, soften our borders." She said in a soft voice. "The soul of Hermes lives." Athena knelt to meditate. "A child is coming. Make ready."

Fourteen Ergaster women were alive. None young. If not for Women's Magic, Ergaster-kind would have failed. If Ergaster men didn't need them for procreation, they'd be long dead. That the men needed them, kept Athena's plan alive. Belloc believes half-breeds and humans can't reproduce. Ergaster men and sapiens produce mules, but Ergaster women and mortal men together is another matter. It was agreed between them that such a truth must never be spoken lest their jailors learn of their hope.

Athena and her band of near-immortals had long ago agreed to release their souls into the world. Only then would the war end. War requires two participants. Goddesses can only die under the sun, a fact Ergaster man had not forgotten.

"We must unmake ourselves to unmake them." Athena whispered only to reaffirm what she must do.

Athena struggled with her mortality as any living being would. Life is sacrosanct. She and her sisters were life givers. They cannot take it, but they can prevent new lives of her kind. The Goddesses' powers released to the world may give humankind balance…should it ever come. The keys must find a way. Only an unseen champion can free them. Athena knew not how or if She will come.

Athena got off her knees. "The power of three will set us free," she said. The others repeated.

A bang on the door came as expected. Slaves rushed in. The place was cleaned and better clothes were given. The Goddesses were washed and given toiletries—evidence Mother Athena's move against Belloc proceeded. Soap and water were better than a messenger from Zeus. The great washing away begins. But the question remained: will Ergaster wash away humans? Artemis's talisman had escaped the machine, as designed, and found its way into the world. She felt it was near. She wanted to fall to the floor laughing but did not. She held herself quiet until the slave girls withdrew.

"Quiet," Athena said. "Bow your heads, keep the act. Show no pleasure or magic. They are coming. Do not react. Bite your cheeks."

Boric was overlarge, as Ergaster go, and ducked to enter. Seven-foot tall, his jaw massive, his brow ridge so prominent his eyes only knew shadow. The manchild in Boric's arms was a mere trifle to one of Boric's strength. Mother shuttered to think of making love to such a monster as Boric. The feeling was mutual. But he was not there for that. He dropped the poor lad onto a matt. Recently stuffed, the straw was fresh but not soft.

"This is Kenny Parks. Clean him, make him comfortable, see that he eats. If he does not revive one of you will suffer torture. Do you understand?"

None spoke. They bowed instead. Speaking generates wrath. Boric left. Athena did not move until his footfalls were distant clicks on hard, cold stone.

"Water," Mother said. "They turned the water on, we have hot water, fill the blessing tub. Let us bathe him."

The boy was filthy and unresponsive. They brought him deep inside. Their shield did not affect him. He revived in small measures as the Washing Ceremony proceeded. Athena and her cohort absorbed what had transpired from Kenny. He was unexpected. The talisman had hidden itself within the child, a male child. It chose well. One-half of her hope returned but with it came unanswered questions that she could not ask aloud. *Where are the others?*

The vent system had shut off. The keyset escaped on the half-breed's ship as she guessed. Kenny Parks gained power from it which was not intended or predicted as a byproduct of its independence. Never had a pregnant human possessed an amulet and so it abandoned his mother. It could not have come here otherwise. Athena dared not say it. *Artemis's son is not sterile—Wailer could save Ergaster men.*

The boy's mind was hard to untangle. Only bare facts came clear. The plan did not work as planned. Tricking Albert into using the talisman went sideways. It escaped and hid. *But where is the rest? Another woman of The Finder must have it. She must come here. But how? No woman can enter the labyrinth undetected. A talisman had never attached itself to a grown man and Kenny is of age.* Athena's hope waivered. *A man holding one may pass unnoticed but Kenny is not a man.*

Kenny came fully to himself once dressed. They put him in a tunic while his strange clothing dried.

"I'm home, home, home. I have been at here, I seen it, saw it, seen it."

"We are not lost," Athena said the code-phrase not believing it, but that was all she could say under surveillance. Her words were heard and misinterpreted by the Watchers daily.

"I'm hungry," Kenny said in archaic Greek.

"So are we," Athena said in English. "Ladies, prepare a feast. This one requires restoration."

The world needed restoration. Women hungered for it. Athena would set that right. *The boy imbued as he is, cannot know what it is he carries, he cannot know what power resides within. Should he know, they will sense it. All will be lost. What Belloc seeks in the world has been drawn home as intended; this cannot be said. It is not time.*

"We maintain the vow," Athena said so all heard.

Athena stroked Kenny's cheek the way Amy used to. She read the imprint of Amy's life which the talisman preserved. She cooed the soothing words Amy used to say when he was small. The wall in his mind cracked. Kenny became free to morn his mother for a little while. He sobbed openly for the first time in his life. Together the Goddesses cried deeply with and for him.

"I want mommy, where's mommy, mommy. I need mommy…"

The ladies gathered closer around him laying on their hands. They took up his pain and together they remembered Amy Parks and gave unspoken thanks for her sacrifice.

CHAPTER TWENTY-FIVE:

BASECAMP ALASKA

Basecamp setup went slow. Soldiers dogged every move. There wasn't much to erecting tents, but half the students were from the lower states and weren't campers however eager they were. Teaching takes time. Tom's local people took up that slack. Alaska's kids know how to handle harsh conditions. His group consisted of paleoanthropology and archeology students; willing diggers all. Tom envied them as they hammered in the last tent stake. How Cory maneuvered the authorities into an educational dig, Tom didn't know, but it made good cover. The human shield slant crossed his mind. He rejected that idea.

Six tents were set on a broad flat of high ground between hills downrange three hundred yards from the glacier's remnant. Tech student Janis did more of the humpwork than the others. Tom stood by watching for trouble when he would have rather gotten dirty.

Students weren't required to live onsite. The military provided empty barracks built for future oil workers or missile silo builders. Many of the kids camped anyway. Alaskans are especially tough but shovel bums are hardy no matter where they hail from. Lucky the biting flies weren't bad. The dump and its bear population were on the other side of Camp Patten. Bugs swarmed thick over there.

Being two miles out from the newly expanded military's secure inner compound didn't mean they were secure. A rag-tag shanty-town of wooden structures had grown up outside of the base. With the Army's expansion came hard-faced contractors, employment-hopefuls, and conmen. The typical boomtown problems.

"We're all set." Janis said walking up. She pointed at the shantytown. "Camping's better. Boomtowns' suck."

Tom had seen that for himself. "I'll keep my eyes peeled."

The outskirts were under a mile from Tom's basecamp which worried him. Spies could easily hide among Fort Patten's population. Nobody trusted the stores and supply people. Boomtown's fire and brimstone tent chapel was also questionable. Entrepreneurs mashed together with undesirables made a dangerous stew. Trouble could emerge from any quarter.

"This could pass for a last century gold mining town," Tom said.

"Supposed to be safe here, but I ain't feeling it," Janis said waving a hand at the camp.

"Secure or not," Tom said, "I'm not leaving the computers and sat-phone unguarded. Hodges' MPs, true to Cory's deal, cleared out, but I don't trust them."

"They deemed us spy-free. Woopy." Janis said. "I talked with the sergeant. I ain't convinced he's on the up and up. He had too many questions. Something ain't right."

Tom's neck hair stood. The Army was drilling and not for oil. Either Janis had rubbed off on him or he caught Mom's paranoia. *Mental illness runs in families.* More and more his head traveled around in la-la land. Kenny kept showing up in his nightmares such as visions of Kenny trapped in a well. A feeling of doom chased him.

"I agree but I don't think the Army is our problem," Tom said.

"Last tent's up. I'll check it." Janis said. "Keep scratching like that and you'll burst into flames."

"I need to relax. We don't have a production schedule," Tom said.

"Relaxing ain't smart in bear country," Janis said walking away. It wasn't bears Tom worried about.

The comings and goings of glaciers had stripped the landscape leaving the place moon-surface-inhospitable. Even now in high summer, signs of life were few. Only moss, lichens, and stunted weeds held tenuously onto gray rock in the work zone. No food for caribou, bears, or flies. The only consumable was a narrow stream trickling down from the distant dying glacier.

"And we got no place to hide." Tom said following after Janis.

Two days later field surveys were in process. Tom entered the lab-tent to use the satellite phone at the prearranged time. Ignoring the students that milled around, he spoke loudly, the signal being weak. Anyone within a hundred feet heard his half of the conversation. No doubt the government listened on both ends.

"We have plenty of help, more students than I know what to do with," Tom reported to Cory. Cory gave the updates and Tom responded. "That busload from Juneau came early... We're overstaffed...Good idea, grid-search the boulder fields." *This time, without soldiers helping themselves to our artifacts.* "The digitals I sent, have you seen them? They look great, right, good detail...I'll give special attention to where you suggest."

Tom closed the phone. The new students were already circling him. He addressed the crowd.

"This is the scoop. Setup your laptops inside tent one. Don't leave them online. Our satellite connection router is throttled. I'm not running generators constantly. Batteries go dead, you're out of luck. This sat-phone." He held it up. "And my net connection is off-limits. House computer is for site work only."

The assembly grumbled about limited internet access. The computer geeks among them didn't hide their knowing smiles. *Nerds always have a back door.* They'll get online. Given the opportunity many students would spend more time online 'researching' and less time digging.

"Another thing, gentlemen," Tom said, speaking to the men. "Stop pissing in the alcoves. Use the portable john. We have to work in there."

"Yeah right," Linda said to Janis, but everyone heard. "Like boys will walk a mile to the outhouse just to take a leak, get real."

"Neanderthals piss where they sleep, don't they?" Janis said. The girls laughed and some of the boys, too.

Tom suppressed a response. He could go on and on about how sophisticated Neanderthals were, but the joke would go flat. He laughed with them instead. Banter was every shovel bum's favorite pastime. The long, boring hours of brushwork bred smartass remarks like swamps birthed mosquitoes. They were already becoming a team. *This is good.*

Tom had groups organized into search parties. Paleoindian stuff turned up out of the melting ice packs but nothing exciting and nothing older within the glacier field. His handpicked student leaders were briefed separately. He had to trust someone— Janis Graves, for one—Bill hated computers and relied on her. Tom's intern, Linda Cover, had been selected by Cory along with a few other key helpers in advance.

Tom addressed his insiders in a low voice. "The policy is; keep special finds quiet until Cory clears it. He'll take responsibility. If the federals think we have something good, they'll grab first and ask permission later, if at all. Cory doesn't want a rumor-mill spilling our finds. Keep the odd stuff quiet."

"The feds always kill anomalous finds," Linda said.

"I ain't gonna let that happen," Janis said.

"Whatever you find take photos," Tom said. "I have a direct satellite link to the university's mainframe. Whatever passes for Clovis or Neolithic, photo it and send it via my unsecured line whether I'm around or not. Anything older, come and get me. Make sure, pictures first, and if I'm...anything radical happens send what you can into cyberspace fast. Get it out. They aren't gonna screw us this time."

After some questions and Tom's best-guess answers the group dispersed. Linda and Janis were sent to do a visual inspection of the upper slope's permafrost for possible grid search locations. A flat spot looked good from camp. Stone surface finds aren't datable but still provide info about the area's former occupants. The trick was to find items just before they erode out of a thaw. Melting ice packs had produced well everywhere in the world. Safe items were being found everywhere and not too old. The bog where he sent Janic was much older than paleo.

Tom dared hope that his first dig as site director might morph into a normal, productive job without intrigues. By keeping his head low, the taint of Cory might skip over Tom's career. Given a little time and the right soap, such as a legitimate find, it would wash his association with Cory clean. This project might well launch his career...*or kill it for good.*

CHAPTER TWENTY-SIX:

LINDA AND JANIS

Janis and Linda marched upslope for their survey. Shovel bums have much in common. Janis had a mind to dig into Linda. Linda had something hidden under her surface. Was Linda gay like her? Maybe not, wrong vibe. That undercurrent could be something else. Janis's Wonder Woman bell rang, but it wasn't swinging.

"Whatcha think of Conley?" Janis said on the way up.

"Professor's paranoid about something and he doesn't know what," Linda said. "He's like so edgy. Doesn't even register he's stressed out. I bet he's looking for gold. I saw him in the alcoves. Let's put a motion detection eye-cam above pee-rock. I bet he pisses there, too."

Oh, wow she reads emotions, cool.

"Edgy for sure." Janis said, "Not gold. Some things ain't safe to find." Janis said not lying or giving it away. She didn't feel warnings. Her senses had idled ready to rip like a competition chainsaw since arriving. There was danger all around, just pull the saw's trigger and cut it down. But she had to find it first. *Linda's OK, it ain't her.* Janis relaxed her guard. "Yeah, Conley's looking. He wants what shouldn't be here."

"Whatever that is, he isn't the only one," Linda said. They walked slowly watching the ground below the target zone. "Somebody wants whatever it is. The Army doesn't want us to find it." Linda stopped and picked up a pebble, looked it over, and tossed it. "I get a feeling. I sense people wanting, but not what they're after. Weird, right."

"Sister, that ain't the only weirdness around here. Cory's ideas aren't proven, but I know he's right. We need evidence and it's here. If we can find it." Janis explained she worked two years for Cory and recounted some of the strange things she had seen. "Cory's dodging bullets, they hate him."

Janis admitted she had a need to protect Cory without a good reason to do so. Her part-time job didn't motivate: Something else drove her. Linda didn't balk at this weirdness and she opened up, too. Janis shared that that dweeb Conley had grown on her and she felt protective of him although she didn't even like him. Linda knew Cory's tale but not everything. Linda didn't know Conley yet but agreed he needed looking after.

"I wanna know who's screwing with us," Janis said.

"I wanna know what the boys are saying about me behind pee-rock." Linda said with a laugh. "I have a game camera but it doesn't record sound."

"I beat you to it," Janis said. "I put sound-ready motion-detect mini-cameras all over. For bears, right. Got one above pee-rock already. Conley's pissed about people pissing there." Janis and Linda cracked up. "Cory wants cams on everything. I'll send you the link."

"Thanks. Good to know who's hung before accepting a date."

"Whatever floats your canoe," Janis said. *Definitely not gay.*

"Professor's cute for an older man," Linda said, "but I'll take Roger." Linda took Janis's arm stopping them. She lowered her voice. "I'm told…his meat lockers' stuffed. I rather not find out the hard way." This time, Linda cracked up first. "'We have the technology.'" Linda said quoting a ubiquitous tech company ad.

Janis fell out. Linda snorted and choked on laughter. Jains let her bottled-up tension spill. The two riffed on dick jokes for a solid five minutes.

"If Roger's got it going on, we'll know," Janis said wiping a tear. "They'll never see my cam. Sooner or later the bladder strikes."

"How'll you upload without anyone noticing?" Linda said. "You can't put pee-rock on AU's server. We'll get in trouble. Spying is technically illegal."

"Homeland spies on everybody, don't they?" Janis said, a little irritated. "Why shouldn't we? The Army's doing it. Cory wants security. I got cams all over the place. And I don't need basecamp's linkup. I got my very own satellite access."

"You can't put that video out. What if the school traces it? It goes through the schools' computers, right."

"Get real. I use Tina's server. It uploads automatic." Janis said. "I bounce my stuff right outta here under everyone's radar. They can't stop me. Conley's clueless. Cory knows nothing. He thinks it goes directly into AU's system. I only send the safe stuff to school. Spies see what they expect, but my network gets it all." Janis said feeling smug. "I got it under control unless Roger's pecker has devil-horns. I'd have to post that."

Linda busted up laughing first. Once they got their breath, they walked on, eyes to the ground. Janis explained that her convoluted arrangements were done in such a way to prevent Luddite-Cory from getting screwed again. When it came to communications, he was his own worst enemy. She didn't tell him about her secure server arrangements. Janis' plan was to record and secure info before they got the boot.

"He needs a good find badly, although he never told me directly," Janis said. "He trusts me to deliver, but I don't trust AU's data storage. They could shut him out with a click. I told him I'd wire video for everything. Nothing's getting disappeared this time."

"But spying on his own camp is kinda weird, right," Linda said.

"He needs legitimacy. You saw the heat he got for his piece in *Untold Archeology*. He's pissing on the white-shirt's shoes. Admin aims to cork him."

"His credibility is poop. Fame can't protect him," Linda said.

"He should sue Uncle Sam's balls off. He's brave enough but not smart enough. I went overboard a little." Janis stopped. Linda looked on. "I got a cam in Cory's office. He has no idea."

"No webmaster is he," Linda said.

Two hundred yards from camp Janis lit a joint, puffed, and passed it. "All his internet fame and he doesn't know an eye-cam from a bedbug. I'll make him a star on *professorcam.com* and he won't even know it. When I upload, the net's gonna blow up. His lectures are popular. This'll put him over the top."

"Let's do a live-stream," Linda said, "Call it *PeebehindarockAlaska.com*." They fell out laughing. Linda choked on the hit she inhaled and they busted out again. "Maybe we'll get a shot of Conley. I bet he's hung."

"I like Cory," Janis said turning serious. "He gave me a job. He trusts me. I won't put anything out that'll hurt him or his boy Conley."

Janis had eyes on the ground all the while. Something caught her attention inside a small swale. She stopped and bent to the ground. *Silicate sand, river gravel, and fossilized flora—this was a creek bank.* A stark gray bone stuck out of fossilized tundra end-up. *In situ, they'll get a good date.* Janis pulled a sample bag out of her field-vest pocket.

This depression was on the downside of a massive bedrock protrusion. Ice-flows had scraped down the bedrock above and around but not there. It was a virgin spot. Topography had redirected the ice's movements. This exposure was long under a snowpack and could predate the glazier. Impossibly ancient permafrost was left intact. Just the kind of mind-blower Cory needed. Runoff had recently removed the overburden revealing an ancient bog and a snapshot of pristine deposits unseen for eons. Janis understood it with a flash of intuition.

Legs going wacky, Janis fell to her knees. "Get pics of that," Janis said pointing. Linda took shots with her blue-tooth-ready camera. "Something good here, do you feel it? I'm feeling it."

"I do."

Janis wiggled it out of the matrix with Linda filming. Ten inches of petrified bone. The shaft was carved with a gun grip crosshatch pattern. Holes along one side, both ends open. Her relatives, past and present, never carved anything like it. It had to be from the 18th century. She handed it to Linda. Linda gave Janis the camera.

"What'd you make of it?" Janis said running the video camera. Linda rolled it over and looked at it with a magnifier. "You're into bones. Ain't that your specialty?"

"It's a forearm radius of a juvie giant cave sloth. This species never made it this far north. It's extremely primitive, early equatorial." She examined it more closely. Her hands shook.

"This subspecies died out before the first interglacial...ah." The words caught in Linda's throat. "I hope I'm wrong. No way. It can't be, not at this latitude. I did a paper on this sloth."

"It's before people were here, right?" Janis said, talking fast. "Even if it's megafauna, it's still older than, like, say, 20K B.P., right? Before Clovis, right?" Janis felt the nape of her neck tingle. Linda looked sick. "Holy shit, it came from South America. Reverse migration? That means—are you okay?" Janis stopped the video.

Linda's chest heaved. She struggled to breathe before finally taking a big inhale. "This is a flute, it's a fucking flute!" Rushed out. "This can't be Clovis. How did it get here?...I think it...its early Pleistocene, Gelasian, like over a million years...like...I gotta sit down." Linda slumped onto a small boulder and handed it to Janis. "It's a fucking flute. Three hundred thousand...I need a glass of wine."

"Not crude, either," Janis said. "I'm sending this to Tina now."

Janis pulled the data card, unstrapped her backpack, and loaded it into her tabphone. Fearing getting picked up, she shut down the moment the signal cleared sent. "Whatever this is, it's recorded."

"Cory's gonna flip when he sees it," Linda said.

Cory never told Janis everything, just what was safe. Janis got the dope anyway. This bone was exactly what the old man needed. Janis bagged the artifact and a sample of the surrounding frozen dirt. Her tab-phone chimed. The file hit AU's server. She stashed the find inside a hidden pocket.

"This ain't going to the processing tent," Janis said. Linda gave a thumb's up. "It's hotter than a two-dollar pistol."

Janis had a talent for hiding handguns. The MPs didn't find it. She never hid bones before but her .357 had a bone handle and nobody ever caught on. Conley didn't even know she packed iron. Janis reckoned she'd manage.

CHAPTER TWENTY-SEVEN:

GENERAL SURVEY

After two days of a general survey, camp lit with excitement. Working in Alcove One, Tom discovered a cave. The alcove cut deep behind a ten-foot-tall boulder near the entry. The men were using the spot for a lavatory. Further into the cut Tom discovered a door-size stone apparently fit into a cave's mouth. Tom recognized tool marks on the wall. He almost missed it in his hurry to get away from the smell. Tom ran back to basecamp and gathered a work crew. After lunch, he marched them to the spot.

"Come on men, let's get it open," Tom said. "Damn the usual procedures." Tom hated negating proper caution but he felt time ran thin. "Don't be shy, men. Willy, get the pick-ax."

They quickly cleared the foreground and scaped the moss back which fully exposed seams. After prying they rocked the slab loose and out of place enough to see inside. Tom had them work quicker than reasonable. The spot being twenty yards from where Cory found the mortar and pestle had Tom's heart thumping. Tom clamped his excitement although his chest itched like a demon's dog. *Breathe Tom, breathe.*

"Flashlight, who's got a flashlight?" Tom said. Nobody had one. "One of you go, go fast." A student took off running. Tom and his crew backed out of the twenty-yard long cut and into daylight. "Okay, people let's take five."

Finger formations leaving pre-glacier terrain untouched never happens. These ratchets had been on the border between the snow pack and moving ice. Tom had only half-believed Cory but his reservations melted away. Tom's shovel bum heart pumped a geyser given that this manmade cave door was impossibly old.

"I can't believe it," Roger said speaking for the small group on hand. "People were here, this gotta be 250K if it's a year."

The flashlight runner came back. Tom snatched it up and proceeded into the cut with the others following. The alcove passage was narrow but the end opened wider with room for his men. The sky above afforded little light. It didn't take long to pry the slab out a good distance. Tom's adrenalin ran down. He learned against the side-wall, wiped the sweat off his face, and took a deep breath before turning back. He spotted an inner seal. It had been packed with tree pitch which became amber.

"Good God, carbon-14 dateable or too old?" Tom said, "Get samples. I have never seen anything like this, is that hair?"

Billy took out a penknife and sample bag and handed them to Tom. The door and entrance jamb were corresponded with an inner lip carved in to accept sealing material before setting the door slab. The door had been glued into place. This confirms man's far older and advanced than accepted.

"I bet it's a tomb," Billy said as Tom passed him the sample.

"Inaccessible for eons," Tom said backing up. A student must have texted because several more people materialized. "No phones, we can't let the military catch on."

Tom stepped away from the pee smell to gather his thoughts. This area hadn't been ice-free for twenty-four thousand years, minimum. Someone could have done it then. *It could be older.* What if it predates the ice ages? *It'll wreck the text books!* News spread to the others. Tom wasn't happy. His initial elation morphed into overwhelmed as more students crowded into the tight location. Tom had to stop and gather his wits, resist the manic drive to go honey-badger on it. Tom reinstituted his professionalism.

"That's it, everyone out, careful, don't disturb anything. We'll do nothing more until I call Professor Cory." Tom was the last to exit the alcove. He didn't want them to see him shaking. He bounced back to the finds-tent on rubber legs. Janis took the sample off Billy.

The next morning, with Cory's blessing, he and his team pried the slab out far enough for him to squeeze in. Tom, relatively thin, slipped inside with great care although his heart ran on high-idle. Past the rough-cut inner jamb, the walls were polished smooth. A few steps within, he spotted a niche at chest level holding a stone tablet. He blew the dust off it. Odd marks were deeply carved in a Coptic-like script like on Cory's mortar. Tom had trouble holding himself up.

"Mom would go nuts over this text," Tom whispered running a finger over the artifact's flat surface exposing green stone. "Jade? Jade doesn't belong here. Wait a minute." An image of his old amulet rose to mind—same color stone. Tom's legs wobbled. He steadied himself against the wall. "Can't be, can't be."

"What's that? What do you see?" Somebody outside called.

"Pass me a camera, quick, light, give me more lights!" Tom's birthmark sizzled.

Students aimed flashlights in from all around the opening. Others unpacked the lighting gear. A small portable generator was started while Tom took pictures but, remembering proper procedures, he didn't touch the artifact again. The men passed in a setup of bulb sockets in plastic baskets on stands. Power came by Romex wires. Tom spread the first two light stands five feet apart a little way down the tunnel. He ran the cords along the floor and not carefully.

Deeper inside, at the half-way point, Tom found the floor littered with small rust-encrusted objects and polishing stones which resembled what Cory had found. Tom resisted jumping to conclusions, but the evidence indicated to him a primitive people and a more sophisticated group must have worked together. *Slaves and masters.* One rusted item, only and impression in rust, might have been manacles. One metallic object on the floor stood out though covered in a thick layer of dust which had turned into wet muck. He took pictures on the blue-tooth camera. Against normal procedures, Tom picked it up. Students watched from outside but he had his back to them, and the light farther in was dim. He bagged the walnut-sized gold object and stuffed it into the hidden pocket of his safari vest.

Tom thought he'd seen impossible things before but gold working in the Upper Paleolithic? It was possible. If that's the time period represented, even so, it was still a special find. It had to be much older. The idea staggered his mind. Curiosity kept him on his feet.

"I'm going deeper," He called back when he got a hold of himself. He ventured well past the last light stand against normal procedures.

He crept forward swinging his flashlight slow and was careful to avoid stepping on anything. He located another stone door ten yards on at the back wall. This wasn't a simple burial. The dust was dry deeper in. Ancient boot-prints were scattered about. Many around the door. Only one set lead outward. Both doors were made to push out which gave Tom a strange idea.

"Emergency exit."

His digital camera recorded. None of this was acceptable. He could hardly believe what he saw, but facts don't lie. The inner door felt hot. It would take the rest of the season to process the foyer's contents alone. He wasn't going to make Carter's mistake and bash open the equivalent of King Tut's tomb.

"It's the discovery of the century." Saying it made his head swim. "I can't blow it."

He understood what Carter must have felt on the threshold of Tutankhamun's tomb. The promise of greater things lay beyond the next door. *Wonderful things.'* The artifacts in evidence indicated greater things to come, things more dangerous than wonderful. So dazed was he, he didn't think to see if the footprints were recent or old.

Having filled the memory-card he came outside dripping sweat. His itch abated but his mind ran wild. "That's enough for today, back to camp. Upload what we have before proceeding. We gotta slow down, make a plan. Grid-search the floor tomorrow. Plaster casts...the works."

Tom floated to camp on impossibilities. Janis uploaded the pictures and his quickie report into basecamp's computer and fired it off to Cory. Tom dug the bottle out of his footlocker and poured for all takers in the finds tent. The joy of discovery did not last long.

Within an hour of sending the photos, military police swooped into camp halting all activity. They took his computer, phone, and router but nothing belonging to the students. MPs deployed and stationed themselves everywhere around camp looking for trouble. The military police gathered everyone outside the mess tent while the others scoured the area with handheld scanning devices.

"Hey Asshole, I left my camera in the cave. I gotta go back." Janis said to the MP in charge. Tom knew she was lying, she already uploaded, but he didn't see her camera either.

"No one's allowed up there till we clear it." The guard said. Janis moved on him, poking his shoulder with a stiff finger, and to Tom's surprise, the man backed up. "Knock it off, bitch. You want me to cuff you?"

"Try it, I dare you."

Tom stepped in and pulled Janis away. Janis clocking the cop might be entertaining, but Tom had pressing issues to attend. Something big was behind that door and he had to know what. Military police didn't care. Tom wanted to scream, but he couldn't act aggressive with students present. *Why'd Hodges change tactics?* Tom had questions. He didn't get to ask any. A yellow bus arrived skidding to a stop. The same one that transported half his students each morning. The MPs ushered everyone to it.

Security men did a fast pat-down search on each one before boarding. The MPs were in a grand hurry to move AU offsite. Tom's people grabbed what personal items they had at hand and boarded in disarray. The driver wasn't their regular man. Tom didn't know how she did it, but Janis smuggled out the sat-phone. The military took his electronics but not the data card he palmed or the gold item he stashed. The bus rolled out.

Tom dialed the sat-phone. Cory picked up. "Bill, you're not going to believe this. The fucking military just closed my dig! Fuck me!"

Students ceased chattering. Abashed, Tom squelched his speech.

"Sorry gang," he said. "Go on Bill."

Underway the bus motor roared.

"You get the pics?" Tom shouted into the phone. "I sent half hour ago…You didn't?… I have confirmation… What?… You don't have them?… I don't believe this!… That double-crossing bastard! They intercepted our transmission."

Tom cut the signal and lowered his head between knees fighting thoughts of committing bloody murder as the bus bounced its way toward Boomtown with the engine screaming.

"Shift gears you moron," Tom said to the floor.

It hit him: All his hopes were dashed. He fought to contain himself. He didn't know what was better for relief, scream, cry, or punch the first MP he saw. He was trapped. Either work for the CIA or flip burgers. All of his academic life his advisors had said, 'don't quit, work hard, take a chance, you'll go places.' Mom's voice also droned, 'don't take risks, play it safe.' Who was right?

He lifted his head when Janis touched his shoulder.

"Prof, we have a problem." She pointed a thumb over her shoulder at basecamp.

"Goddamn right we have a problem." The bus hit a rut and Tom bounced out of his seat. He took one step and another jolt put him back into his seat. "I'm telling Commander Hodges to fire that asshole driver and get Fred back. BALLS!"

The driver drove too fast for that rough road taxing the bus's suspension beyond its limit. The driver messed with a cell phone rather than shift gears. Tom punched the back of the seat in front of him.

"Goddamn, that smarts!"

Janis raised her hands, her mouth and eyes as round as donuts, and backed up. Tom thought he scared her. He scared himself. The bus bucked and Janis took a seat the hard way.

****

The bus knocked Janis off her feet. She landed next to Linda. Conley tried moving forward between wheel hops with figurative smoke coming out of his ears.

"Better tell him his data went to Tina before he pisses blood," Linda said. "Never seen him upset…this…is—"

"It's coming. Something bad…Shit! Hold on!"

Janis got on her feet, tab-phone in hand. *Save the tablet.* One step forward. An explosion jacked the bus's rear off the ground knocking her to the floor. She anticipated and fell well.

Pieces of trucks and ice rained down mixed with flaming rocks. Gravel hit the rear exit door like cannon-fired grapeshot spidering the safety glass, followed by a green-clad human torso splattering the ruined door. The dead man stuck a second and slid off smearing gore on the emergency exit.

Blood smell penetrated the cracked window. People screamed. Janis had seen worse. Polar bears eat people. A calm came over her. Danger always did that. There was something more, another danger still hidden. Janis's Wonder Woman senses were still buzzing but the vibrations changed.

CHAPTER TWENTY-EIGHT:

RETURN TO AU

Tom moved forward a few steps and was knocked off his feet. The next bump launched him out of the seat he fell into. His head smashed against the ceiling. Kenny's voice echoed inside his ringing noggin, *cell phone, cell phone.* The driver's cell phone? Tom reacted to Janis's cry and turned. She braced gripping a seat with one hand, legs spread, her tablet tucked in. The back of the bus jumped thirty degrees skyward with an ear-splitting roar. Students flew like ragdolls.

Chaos ensued. He rushed to help people. No one was hurt too bad on Tom's first inspection; looking past the bloody rear window, basecamp burned. A smoking mess lay upslope where the cave should have been. Twisted Humvees and armored cars were strewn about like discarded toys. Everything was blown to bits. The bus slowed but the driver kept whining the motor. That last-minute driver didn't know how to drive a stick—forgivable given the emergency. Tom's anger shifted.

"Total loss," Tom cried punching the bus's ceiling; "Those incompetent assholes blew themselves up."

"Chill Prof, sit," Janis said, taking control. "Everybody needs to chill. You stay here, I got this."

She proceeded to recheck everyone. Tom rubbed his aching head.

"That girl's a rock."

Tom's first-aid certification didn't help. He couldn't think straight. He stood to help Janis when several Humvees raced up the creek-wash toward ruin. Sirens bellowed. Tom's ears rang. Students wept. Tom lowered himself back down and sucked the blood off his knuckles. The ride only took a few minutes. The bus stopped at temporary housing. Medical was there waiting. Tom directed the ambulance people away from himself and to the students. He forgot the driver.

Things were quickly under control. His head ached but Tom stormed off to Commander Hodges's office only to be held in the reception area for three hours. They wouldn't let him leave. The explosion had Hodge's office in a whirlwind. All Tom could do was sit and wait and stew. The MPs wouldn't even let him take a leak. When he pulled his fly down and stood before a potted plant one of the policemen took the hint and let him use the officer's john.

Admitted to Hodges' office he twasted no time. "What the hell are you doing?" Tom demanded. "I'm CIA, you aren't supposed to touch us!"

Hodges looked tired. "See here Conley, I have orders. I was told to keep an eye on you, you know that. I don't stand by with a thumb up my ass. I'm guarding your operation—"

"Bullshit. We haven't found any goddamn secrets. This is straight archeology, nothing to call the goons out over. What the hell were you thinking? You monitor our transmissions. You, you…I can't believe you blew up my site!"

"Shut the hell up! I didn't do this!" Commander Hodges bolted up from his desk. "I don't have time for this. Pissing on my boots won't get us anywhere."

"Yeah, sure…Yes sir," Tom said feeling like a fool. "Sorry."

"That's better," Hodges sat. "Here's the situation. We did not, I repeat, did not, intercept your transmissions. But someone else did and sent a virus in the process. Whatever you transmitted via my satellite link is gone along with my dailies. I did not do this. When we zeroed in on the predatory device's location, I sent a squad. Electronic recon said the source of the hacker's signal was on that hill above your project. Someone's spying on my installation using you for cover."

"Security breach?" Tom said amazed.

"We had one," Hodges said, "That explosion took out who and what was watching my installation. Bad luck for you, smart for them to hide on top of you. We didn't know. Recon detected it, so we moved in. We pinpointed them and cleared you out. I can't share how. My MPs closed in as you exited. Recon says detonation was by a local remote signal. The sender was close. We think Bluetooth."

"Holy shit," Tom said. "If you didn't send the bus, we'd be hamburger."

"I didn't send transport, only men to protect you while we searched. This is not over." Hodges leaned forward. "I want you to pack up. Get your civilians out of here. Site is closed. Everyone stays in the barracks tonight. I want you loaded and on the road by 0800 tomorrow morning. You'll drive. I'll send over a motor-pool bus. That one's evidence. Your driver won't be available…once I find him."

"I don't know where Fred is, but that driver wasn't him. I saw him on a cell phone."

"I'll send an investigator over to get your statement and the others."

Hodges picked up the phone and dismissed Tom with a wave. Tom left with his head swimming and chest burning. That emergency driver wasn't right and Tom didn't get a good look at him.

CHAPTER TWENTY-NINE:

TIMING

Fredric Amos chose his timing well. The bomb created ample time for his escape. Eons of Watcher's subversion provided the inroads and means. He was equipped and ready. He got away clean. They will not find the entryway. The second foyer collapsed as planned. Removing the rubble will not expose the stairway or any sign of the machine. The vent network was ready for restart. Best of all, he had the missing Goddess. She had been sent to stop them and failed. Her magic undergirded Cory. He could not have otherwise located the service tunnel.

Artemis is a fool. Her leading Cory was too obvious.

After parking, his passengers were ushered away. Meanwhile, Conley rushed off as predicted. Amos calmly departed in a nondescript rental car with automatic transmission. He gained the highway before lockdown and blended into traffic. Military helicopters were dispatched, but of course, much too late. They flew overhead searching for a car driving madly. He did not hurry.

"Only one thing yet to do," he said to himself, "First a much-needed rest. Belloc will be pleased."

He pulled into a motel, drank too much at the bar that night, and slept late the next day. He had little confidence in his hired men but his captive was secure with them. He wasn't sure if his captive's half-breed child yet lives or not. Belloc will know. The female was one of his mission's objectives. But if the child of Artemis yet lives, finding him would be a bonus. He looked forward to the results of Belloc's interrogation. Amos felt certain there was a child.

"'Torture will tell,'" Amose repeated the old saying. "The child will come next." But first, finish the mission. Amos long suspected Artemis's deception. He could not wait to go home and show Belloc what evidence he had. "But first I must tie a loose end."

Amos had studied Cory's habits. The doctor will be alone in his office. Cory's security employee, the native woman, now unavailable, invited this attack. She has power. That woman could be a problem imbued as she is. Cory left alone has no protection. This will be easy.

"Cory's female is dangerous. But aren't they all?"

Janis Graves was a concern. He had avoided her successfully. No other had the power to stand against him. Amos had time.

CHAPTER THIRTY:

NEXT DAY

Sad news came when Tom picked up the bus. They found Fred's body behind the motor pool. Whoever drove yesterday stabbed Fred in the heart. Tom couldn't leave fast enough. The Two-hundred-mile trip back to ASU with two dozen dejected souls wasn't how he preferred to leave. He wished for the guts to beat the shit out of the first CIA man that came calling and no doubt they will. He had failed. New requests from the CIA won't be offered, or accepted, and he was glad.

Tom stewed in misery over the deaths. He convinced himself he'd tell the feds to stick it. He'd get himself arrested for punching an officer in the snoot. It was a nice fantasy. He had committed himself, not for them, but for himself. He wanted the bastards who did it punished.

It was a long, quiet, all-day ride. Tom overheard Janis and Linda behind him as he drove. Toward the end of the trip talking increased. The kids, closer to home, became less somber. In a side-long way, he thought things would eventually get better for him. *My CIA days are over, thank God.*

"What're you doing on the computer," Linda asked.

"Videos. Having a fresh look at yesterday." Janis said. "These are my videos of the first week. Look at that. It's that weirdo I told you about. He came for an interview. I had a bad vibe when I saw him."

"He is strange, creeps me out." Linda said.

Tom saw in the mirror Janis had her tablet open.

"Got him on eye-cam in Alcove One. He wasn't taking a leak, either." Janis said. "The cops would love this footage but I ain't giving it up."

Tom hit the brakes and pulled off. The bus came swiftly to a stop. They were traveling a paved road having left gravel roads behind.

"That's it," Tom said, "spill it, what eye-cam?"

"Why'd you stop? We're only fifteen minutes from home. I got to pee bad," Linda said.

"We aren't going anywhere until I get the story."

Janis had no choice but to tell him about her spy-cams and data sending methods. Cory didn't share that information because he didn't know it. Tom had no clue either. The sat-phone Tom used belonged to Janis and not the university. Janis didn't link it to the military's system either. Tom thought it good, but what if Janis got hacked? Tom's neck hair bristled.

"You should have told me," Tom said, "you saved the day but next time inform me. What am I saying? There ain't gonna be the next time." Tom took a breath and dialed down. "At least we have pictures. We know who planted the bomb...but why?"

"Can't wait to get my hands on him," Janis said.

"Let the feds chase Amos. When we get back, tell the authorities. Copy that tape and send it to AU. Not all your footage, just the bomber."

"Tape? Oh, you mean video... Sure whatever," Janis said.

This information reenergized him.

"I am profoundly relieved. This venture isn't a total loss. Too bad pictures aren't hard evidence. I wonder how Cory will take it? You saved the bone flute, that's good. We can date that."

"Sorry about spying," Janis said, "Doc told me to watch out for anything weird."

"She sent reprocessed pics an hour ago," Linda said. "Doc Cory looks happy. I really gotta pee. Can we go now, please?"

"He looks happy? How would you know?" Tom said. "He doesn't have a video phone."

"Opps," Janis said.

"Show him," Linda said, "I really gotta go!"

Janis' phone-tablet was connected to her laptop. She typed on the laptop and spun it around for Tom. A moment later Tom was looking at Professor Cory's office via a live-feed and Cory wasn't alone.

"Holy crap," Linda said, "that's the guy on pee-cam. He's got a gun!"

Tom jumped back into the driver's seat, gunned the motor, and dumped the clutch. He raced toward the university barking orders.

"Janis, put up the live feed and whatever pics you have. Blast the web. Put it out, all of it, whatever you have. Tell your nerd buddies...Do it! Everyone, hang on! Someone call Cory!"

"Thank God he drives like a maniac," Linda said as she keyed Cory's number, "I won't wet myself...I hope...Cory's not picking up. I'm calling the cops."

While Tom drove, Janis recorded and shouted out what's happening in Cory's office. A fifteen-minute ride became eight. Linda wet herself anyway.

Staying out of sight of Cory's office windows, Tom jumped the curb into lot B. He saw that CIA sedan and aimed for it. The bus skidded into the dumpster corral on wet cardboard. He didn't stop in time and hit the CIA car pushing it into a cement wall. The car bounced back. Two men dressed like lumberjacks jumped out and ran.

"They aren't cops," Tom yelled. "Let me see that." He ripped the tablet out of Janis's hands. Cory was still at his desk. The back of the killer's head faced the entry door. "He's still alive!" The car's trunk had sprung open, the windshield broke, but he didn't have time. "Janis, check the car for anyone hurt. I'm going after Cory."

He ran for Cory's office trying to work out a plan.

***

Janis had hunted bears and elk. Growing up Inuit provided certain skills. She saw her Wonder Woman powers as a spirit-gift. There was more in her than learned skills. She and her family had faced starving wolves together. She received warnings in her vision. She saw them before they got close. She sensed their defeat. She wasn't scared then, she was now.

Janis was off her game. Normally she'd spring into action. She'd beat Conley to Cory's door easy; such was her power. But another power not hers held her. Village Mother's words came to mind, *'In all things serve the sprint. Hear her voice.'*

"I'm feeling it, Mother."

Conley bolted. Kids were screaming. Linda had pissed herself and was no help. She should forget the car and follow Conley but something stopped her. She took a deep breath and pulled her .357 Magnum out and spun the cylinder.

"What're you doing!" Someone cried. "Guns ain't allowed."

A quarry was within her huntress zone. She moved toward the exit holding her revolver up. She felt calm. *Panic kills you when a bear charges.* She never went anywhere without her bear-stopper.

"Screw the school's rules," Janis said.

"What are you going to do?" Linda called.

"Checking the car. I'm going after them. They ain't here for an education."

Janis left the bus. The call to action came from within. Whoever those two clowns were, they ran for a bad reason. Wonder Woman never lies. This wasn't a chase. She had time. First the car. The closer she got to the open truck the wider her power spread. *Conley's walking into a trap.* That vision warned her, but the car wasn't empty. A voice without sound pulled her to the car's trunk.

A tied and gagged girl was there alive and needing help. Janis untied the lady and helped her out. The lady glowed. Janis was blinded to her features. The lady's power filled Janis and locked her feet.

Rubbing her wrists, the lady spoke. "Sister, find them. They must pay and I must go."

Power like electricity coursed through Janis. The need to protect Conley evaporated. Janis went after the kidnappers swept along on waves of the lady's revengeful desires. Janis, unable to do anything else but obey, began pursuit. When a Goddess speaks the huntress must act.

***

Tom ran the staircase on adrenalin-driven legs. *What am I doing!* Every warning against danger Mom infused into him begged him to stop. 'You aren't a hero, play it safe, don't take chances' Tom admitted long ago he wasn't a hero but not a coward either. Tom had his limits but Cory was in trouble.

He stopped on the top stair. *Keep cool, think, be quiet.* Slowing his breath, he crept forward along the hallway. Opening the anteroom door a crack that the suit of armor was still there. Cory's door was closed. Amos hadn't left. Evil seeped out from under the door. Tom prayed the dagger wasn't rusted into place. He never killed anyone or anything before. *What am I doing? I'm not a killer. I'll make him drop the gun.*

***

Amos had strolled into Cory's office and took the seat opposite him. Cory barely noticed engrossed in the laptop on his desk. Cory raised one finger, a sign to wait. Such drop-in visits were perfectly acceptable. Anyone could do the same. Amos thought to toy with his mouse before the kill. He had time. And he so seldom knew his victims. Time to him had little meaning. No other half-breed had lived so long as he. He was special. A saber-toothed cat would not have hesitated. Megafauna cats killed first and played later. He knew it firsthand. Cats indeed played with their quarries, and why shouldn't he? He was in the mood for sport.

****

Cory looked up to see Amos.

"What can I do for you," Cory said pushing his laptop aside. "You're that digger. I had something for you, not my site, but you never came—"

Up came a black revolver. "I was there at Fort Patten, Doctor Cory. It better served my intentions to remain out of view." The phone rang. Janis's sat-phone on caller ID. Amos pointed the gun at Cory. "Don't answer it. You will have no more need of phones."

"What's this about?" Cory demanded clenching his fists.

"What this is about, my esteemed professor, is your end, but as is the custom of my people, I will tell you why you must die. I have been looking forward to this for a long time."

His people, CIA assassin? Amos was hard to place. Short, thin, dark, maybe Middle Eastern, not CIA? Amos' facial features weren't of any particular race. The man could be from anywhere or nowhere. *Stall him, Conley's on the way.*

"What do you mean your people? What's this all about? Can't we negotiate, what have I done to offend your people?" Cory tried holding back the fear peppering his tone. "Why me?"

"This is not personal Professor. It is my duty as a guardian of my race to protect our interests. We cannot have you digging where you should not. Everyone deserves a last request, no? I will answer a few questions. After you, Conley is next, of course, he is CIA, as you know. Afterword, my business will be complete."

Cory bit his lip. *Keep it cool, keep him talking.* His group nearly getting killed rankled him to no-end. His old Army instincts bristled filling his boiler with steam.

"You, you blew up my find!" Cory wasn't able to keep a tight lid. He stood. "You! You screwed me out of vindication." The urge to roll his desk over bubbled. But his damnable curiosity hesitated. Cory had two hands on the desk ready to go. "You bastard, I should—"

Amos aimed the pistol. Cory froze. "Shall I shoot you now, Doctor?" Amos cocked the hammer. "Or would you rather hear my tale?"

"Hold on now," Cory said lowering slowly into the chair. "You got me. Have your say. I'll listen."

"Good," Amos said, "I rather not kill without confession. Should my end ever come I will pass with honor. The tradition of honor your race learned from mine I will keep. I could answer endless questions regarding our past. My life is long, but thousands of years of explanations are over much, no? I will not spend the time. Humorous, no? I have little time now however endless my life is. The location I destroyed is only one entrance to a…let us say power facility…Access had been blocked for many lifetimes. We thought it unreachable. Inside are vestiges of our glories. You primitives were our slaves, you know, nothing more than animals when we constructed that station."

"Get off it, it was covered in ice two hundred K if it's a week, nobody lives that long."

"You are correct, Belloc is only twenty thousand years old. We built the station in an earlier age. Such devices were never intended for you slaves." Amos spun the cylinder of his revolver. He didn't have Janis's lightning reflexes, but he handled the gun in solid Annie Oakley fashion. "Alas, my people are so few. We haven't many needs. Our devices were farrow and not required until now."

"You talk in riddles." Cory leaned forward, intrigued, his suspicions were filling out. "Answer me this, who are your people?"

"We are your legends, the Gods of the Greeks, Hindu's and Egyptians, the purveyors of your esoteric traditions. We gave Moses the law. Your David slew one of us. My race is two million years civilized. Methuselah's nine hundred years is wrong. He, a half-breed, lived longer. We Watchers live long. When we rose, you monkeys were our pets. We altered you to serve us. We are Homo Ergaster."

"Just a minute, if you're so advanced why screw with us?" Such an idea was outrageous. Cory's theories of successive human advancements and declines were trash if Amos proved right. "I can't see it. What could you possibly have wanted from us?"

"Laborers. But you proved cunning, destructive, and learned too fast. You breed like rats. By fifty thousand years ago, you were as intellectually advanced as you can ever be. Wisely, we gave you no science to expand your minds. You have recently advanced and for this you must… …recede…shall we say?"

"I see," Cory said. He had heard enough and more than he ever imagined. He turned his mind to an attack. *Piss him off. Disrupt his focus.* "So, what went wrong? We beat you. You aren't our masters. What are you, sore losers?"

Amos laughed long. His mirth rained down a cold shower. Shivers ran up Cory's back.

"We are the winners! We run your world but undetected. As you have once again multiplied that is problematic. Given time, too many slaves may over-run their masters, no? Expediency dictates culling. We never stopped programming you. You owe us everything."

Amos beat his fist on Cory's desk with such sudden power, Cory flinched back. Rage came on Amos like a snake strike. It passed quickly. He laughed again. His gun seesawed.

"We utilize means that stem your progress." Amos's face turned serious. "Of late, sadly, to no avail. However, we maintain control yet. We remain hidden. Your technology has grown, but not you. Children with adult toys you are. That will stop." Amos flipped the revolver's cylinder out and back in again.

Cory didn't know where to go next. He had to keep stalling and blurted out the first thing that came to mind.

"What's your role, I don't get it." Cory planted his feet, tensed his back, and gripped the desk. "If you're so well entrenched why bother? You don't make sense. What's your job?"

"Me? I see that we are not discovered. I live among you for that reason. And now my mission is fulfilled. There will be no more finds by you, Doctor. You located our facility. For that you must die ahead of the rest."

"Wait, I'll help you, I got stuff you'll want."

Amos' waved Cory off, his manor more animated. His speech had gained speed in the last minute. Cory realized the killer's internal timer had ticked down. *He's loading up to kill me.*

"Your last words, please." Amos said.

"Why me?!" Cory blurted and nearly jacked the desk but the gun was pointed right at him. *Please wave the gun.* "You're behind it, running interference on me. Why?"

"Only you are brave enough to interpret relics that speak of us publicly. Evidence is otherwise covered even as it lies in museums the world over. The institutions we devised discredit anomalies."

Amos laughed. The rasp of his voice sounded unnatural. He cocked the antique double action Colt revolver's hammer one click. *It's in the safe position.*

"Your colleagues are trained to ignore us," Amos continued. "Funding-whores don't search basement archives. Who openly ventures outside of the orthodoxy but you? That is your answer, Doctor. Now you must die. Your parting words?"

Cory wasn't surprised. Big institutions lie. Curiosity, his downfall, paused action. Rather, he placed a hand on top of the desk and drummed fingers. The clock behind Amos said the conversation lasted seventeen minutes. Amos waited for Cory's parting comment.

"I have long suspected humankind had advanced higher and earlier than accepted. We achieved heights and failed time and again, but I wasn't sure why. If there were others, I often wondered, who could they be? The elongated skull people were one possibility but they vanished. You put the puzzle pieces nicely together. My life's work proves valid. But I have one more question, if I may?"

"One more question Doctor. But then..."

Amos waved the gun.

"I have a million questions, of course, but I'll ask this. Why are you so intent on protecting this, this history of our races? Why this monumental deception?"

"Deception, and deceit. Deception is everywhere," Amos said, "I am not the only player. Such as your CIA..."

No shit Sherlock.

"...you and Mede have seen me before now. The powerful look for what is hid. The governments and I have played this game a long time. They never knew."

"What made Conley cave in?" Cory prompted. The killer was enjoying it. *Cat and mouse never changes.* "I gotta know. I get them going after me, but why Conley? He's harmless."

"Conley has your obsession. To the CIA, he is a pawn to use and cast aside. What better bait to capture him than a well moneyed trap? He could not say no and so he dies." Amos' face faded into stone. "Your government has not the imagination to see that men such as Conley have the poetical to expose us."

Amos smiled with jewel incrusted teeth.

"That ain't fair. He's done nothing."

Cory slipped his hands under the desk. *The first bullet won't stop me. I'll hit him hard.*

"Once you are gone, he will not matter. I will kill him at my leisure. It is time you received your just reward."

Bill Cory did not get his due.

***

Tom listened at the door, fingering the dagger, unsure what to do. He waited for an opportunity but time ran out. He bust through the door, ancient dagger in hand. Amos bolted upright and twisted. Cory flipped the desk. Amos fell backward into Tom's charge. By luck or divine intervention, the dagger rammed home like a flaming spike through rice paper.

Amos crashed forward onto the overturned desk in a heap with his head still twisted backward toward the door. The killer's eyes were wide in surprise but blank. Just black, empty pools. Tom shivered and dropped the dagger. He didn't intend on stabbing the man dead.

"I only wanted to make him put it down!" Tom cried on the edge of hyperventilation.

Tom bent over, gasping. The dead man deflated before his eyes. Amos dehydrated into a husk. His clothing fell away like fly-ash. In only seconds there was nothing left but skin and black bones. Another artifact for Cory's incongruent menagerie. Tom's head reeled. He staggered back away from the body. War films of burned corpses weren't anything like this. Tom leaned on the door jamb hung-mouth until Amos stopped shrinking.

"Christ, I didn't mean to kill him," Tom kicked the dagger away.

Cory stammered, "How the hell?"

"I knew where he was…I need a drink." Tom took a couple of deep breaths. "Janis has a cam on you. I wasn't going to stab him, I swear. I had a mind to make him drop the gun. I'd come in behind and make him…I didn't mean to hurt him. Christ!"

"Nothing you could have done, Son," Cory said. "He meant to kill me and you, he said as much."

Cory pulled a bottle from the filing cabinet and poured two stiff glasses. They stood gulping whiskey as police sirens closed in. Cory poured another and pointed at Amos with an over-full glass, sloshing Wild Trumpet on his Oriental rug.

"All the evidence I need is right there," Cory said. "His physiology's not ours, to be sure. My suppositions were true but also off more than I dreamed. I never expected another living race of men hiding under tree-roots like demented hobbits."

Cory tapped the body's leg with his foot. The body of Fredrick Amos crumbled into dust like an old horror movie cliché. As the dust fell away, so too did Cory's hopes, Tom thought. Cory sucked down his drink and slammed the empty glass on the file cabinet.

"Goddamn, we got nothing! We'll never prove it. No one's going to believe what happened here!"

Tom turned Bill around and pointed above the door with his glass. "I would not be so sure. I think everyone knows. Smile, you're on camera."

Bill took his glasses out of his top pocket, put them on, looked up at the cam and said, "I'll be God dammed."

"You're reaccredited and I am out of a job unless it's government work, no way... Can I stay on with you?"

"I'd love to have you, but this came for you," Bill said. "Came by messenger from the Foundation this morning."

Tom stepped into the outer office. Bill followed. The body, or what was left of it, smelled of mummy-dirt and rotting fish. Cory handed him the envelope. The messenger Tom had met back in the Badlands came to mind, but he didn't take it seriously. The note had said if he cooperated with the CIA, the Foundation would provide a position for him at Berkeley. He didn't believe that job would come through. Getting into Berkeley would take a magician. He used to think magic wasn't real. What happened since confirmed unseen forces were in play, but he didn't think it applied to him. Danger wasn't after him. He stopped resisting reality, but also ignored the signs. He was done running away from it.

"I can't ignore where this is taking me," Tom said, holding up the envelope. He tore it open and sat down to read the letter. "Gotta be another rejection letter."

Downstairs, a police car entered the parking lot with lights flashing. His heart jumped fingering the envelope, but his chest didn't burn or itch. Soon the place would be crawling with police. Tom thought he had better read it before the cops poured in. Why wait for disappointment? He unfolded the note to find one paragraph on a signal page.

"What's it say?" Cory asked.

"The Foundation wants me to run a dig that's closing out in California. The Foundation's been sponsoring another multi-school venture. Not on public land, private property, temporary position. I'm still jobless." Tom didn't restrict the disappointment in his voice. Not a word about Berkeley. "All I want is regular employment, dirt under my fingernails, interesting finds. I screwed your dig up. Maybe the government will leave me alone now."

"Don't count on it," Cory said, "they'll show up whenever the site's interesting. They put you on me, didn't they, and never told you why, correct?"

"I am not supposed to know. My guess, they're looking for high technology."

Tom reached into his pocket and pulled out a plastic bag with a walnut sized shinny-gold metallic object in it. The unknown writing was starkly visible under the reception area's harsh fluorescent lights. He handed it to Cory.

"If I ever found anything anomalous, I'd have to hand it over," Tom said. "I never found any such thing. If you found such a thing, say last year, that's out of my reach."

Cory smiled like the Cheshire Cat. "We have a book to write partner."

"I'll leave that to you," Tom said and handed the note to Cory who proceeded to read it.

Mede gave him good advice. Stay out of the limelight if you want a career. Tom wasn't ready to put it all on the line for a few minutes of fame. Cory got rich from his books and so didn't need the university. He was bigger than life and willing to play the game. Cory was near the end of his professional life. Tom just got started. This wasn't his time to make a radical move.

"You sure, I don't mind sharing credits," Cory said.

I'm not risking my career. The media was all over Cory. Tom didn't want Cory's magnified life although they had a deep curiosity in common. They both needed the truth. But too much truth got people killed.

"I'll pass, thanks."

More police cars filed into the parking lot. An ambulance came in right behind them. They didn't come upstairs right away. The feds will make Cory's office first priority, Tom thought, once they see the video. Cory found his laptop and booted up. Cory's news-feed was blowing up. The murder event had gone live all over the 'net. The world saw Amos melt like the Wicked Witch of the West. The recording was spreading fast.

"This is good," Cory said. "Bless Janis. I smell another bestseller. I'm sure the government's social constructionists will hammer this down like they always do, but that's good for sales."

"I'll go down and see what I could do for the students," Tom said.

Janis had squeezed the private-eyes, and they confessed while she recorded on cell phone. Amos's detectives had held a woman captive for Amos. Janis freed her, but the captive didn't give a name and ran away. The only description Janis could give was that the lady wore a gold neckless with a green pendant. Janis had citizen-arrested the kidnappers. She found them in a girl's bathroom and shot one in the kneecap when he pulled a gun. The evidence to convict Amos's men of false imprisonment ran off, but the cops arrested them anyway.

Tom's people were debriefed by Homeland Security, the FBI and finally the CIA. After three days of interrogations, Tom was released having said nothing they didn't already know. Murphy was the only one he spoke to.

Tom decided to drive down to the new job slow and careful. The official counter-narrative was already in full swing before he pulled out. By the time he crossed into Canada, the event was widely discredited. Tom checked his phone after entering Washington State. Cory's website had ten million hits and no mention of him. Tom's face and voice were blurred out on Cory's website as Tom requested.

"I'm glad that's over," Tom said to himself although he didn't believe it was.

CHAPTER THIRTY-ONE:

FIRE WOMEN

Sofia Wong AKA, Sally, loved university. She loved her classes. That was a problem because she took whatever courses the spirit directed her to take. She took history, anthropology, archeology, and social psychology classes, but she didn't have enough of any one subject to get a master's degree. After four and a half years, she could not graduate with anything useful. They gave her one more semester to get something accomplished…or else.

"I either get my act together or I wait tables." Sally said to the stuffed toys on her bed.

"'Choose a major,'" Her course advisor demanded last Friday, the day before the big camp-out. "'If I don't have a course plan from you by semester's end—and that is in three days—I will withdraw my recommendation for your scholarship renewal. Get on the stick, Miss Wong. This isn't a game.'"

Dad's money ran out and she was up to her ass in loans. If she was to finish, she had to have that scholarship. She had to decide on a direction and fast.

Friends had planned the big camp-out for the first summer session weekend. It was the place to be. That's where the boys, pot, and beer were and Sally loved boys, pot, and beer. Asked to go, she said no. She almost said yes, but something bugged her about it. Self-control didn't stop her. The campfire did.

She had no time for distraction. Campfires pulled her out of herself. No time for campfire-insanity. *I must stay focused.* That longing for fire frightened and excited her at the same time. It had been that way since she fell into a campfire at age four. She didn't remember much, other than she didn't get burned. She put the bonfire party out of her mind, but the fire-lust stayed behind. Home for the bonfire weekend, she read the course guide instead. Sally had to pick a class that got her somewhere. Archeology III jumped off the page for no reason.

"Thomas Conley, who the hell's that?"

The course description included field work requiring camping. Sacramento State, with the Finder Foundation, had a year-round credit-course running near her home in California. Another archeology class would give her a BA. She could springboard into a joint MA/ Ph.D. from there. The description got her attention. She loved camping for the fires. Doing school outside beat class work any day.

"I bet they'll have campfires." Sally read it again and saw a small picture of Professor Conley in the sidebar. "He's the campfire type, rough around the edges, longish hair, outdoorsy face, lanky outdoorsy body."

Sally dropped the brochure on her desk. It felt hot.

"Conley seems…I don't know, Con…ley…" She decided she didn't have the hots for him but something was there. "He's okay I guess." She looked closer. "Sparks… He makes sparks…" She rubbed her eyes and the illusion disappeared. "That's weird."

She hadn't felt right since Grand came in from China. A waking dream came on the thought. She relived falling into the campfire in a flash memory. Her parents refused to speak of that day. It frightened the hell out of them. They never talked about it. Sally wanted to know what happened. Her trances always took place staring into a fire. It never happens while awake, but now it just did. Her visions were never from her own life. She reached for that day, and it played in her mind like a movie.

The family was camping. She is four again at the campfire. Dad keeps telling her to back up. Her stick got shorter with every marshmallow, but she wanted closer. She longed for her stick to burn.

"Dan, will you please push her back. She's too close," Mom said.

Dad forced the old stick from her hand and gave her a new, longer one. "Backup Sally, you're too close."

She and her older brother, Chen, fought over the fresh marshmallow sprig. He had one end and she the other. Bigger Chen pulled the stick sideways hard.

"Chen, let her have it," Dad said. "Let it go!"

Chen whipped her sideways. She lost grip, spun and fell face-first into flames. Her pajamas caught fire instantly burning with blue flame. Time stopped. Giggling, she watched flames dance higher all around, blue, green, orange. Pretty ladies dancing.

"Oh, so pretty!"

The spell broke when Dad dunked her in the creek's icy water.

Mom snatched her, ran to the camper and stiped the charred remains of cloth away. Sally wasn't burned. Dad was crying at the camper's door. His nylon vest had melted. Dad's eyebrow hair was gone, his face blistered.

"Daddy's sad."

"Dan, she's not burned!"

"More marshmallows please, Daddy."

They were all hugging and crying together next. Everyone laughing, even Chen.

"More marshmallows, more marsh…more marsh—"

Sally came out of the vision weeping.

"Sally, you good in there," Mom called.

Sally came fully back to her senses with wet cheeks and a lump in her throat.

"Good Mom, I'm good."

The dream let itself out in broad daylight. That never happened before. She sobbed in real-time, too. *Tom Conley's a bad influence.*

"You sure, honey?" Mom tapped on her bedroom door. "You sound upset?"

"I'm good Mom." Sally managed to croak. "Not really," she said in a lower voice. She wiped her chipmunk cheeks off with a palm.

"Come out, yah, your great grandmother is back from Grandmother's house."

Great-Grand had recently come from China. What motivated the 100-year-old to make the trip, who knows? Great-Grand and Mom got along and that was weird, because Dad's parents didn't like Mom. Mom was an off-the-boat Swede whose genetics made Sally look like a porcelain doll, Asian features with Norse skin and blue eyes. Her hair was thick and black. Unlike Mom, Sally never sunburned. She often wished she had Mom's face bones instead of Dad's puffy cheeks. Sally sopped tears with a dirty sock and used eye wash to get the red out. She always had some because she smoked a lot of pot, and her parents didn't like it. *Maybe that's why I never make up my mind?*

Sally met Grand in the living room. Grand sat in Dad's chair, smoking a corncob pipe loaded with something nasty. Mom gave her a cereal bowl for an ashtray. Only Grand got away with smoking in this house. How someone her age didn't die from smoking had to be magic. She'd dump pipe embers into her hand without getting burned. The ashes vanished. Nobody ever noticed? *That's weird.*

"Come, Sophia, let me touch you, come close," Grand said in broken English.

Grand repeated it in Cantonese. Sally understood the tongue, but couldn't speak it. Grand would mix Sally's proper English name into her Chinese. Grand never used Sally's American nickname.

"Hi, Grand. Nice to see you."

Sally approached holding out both hands. Grand took them. The old lady was half-blind. Sally had to get close. Grand pulled Sally closer still and brushed Sally's hair back with a grizzled chicken-claw hand. Grand resembled a pile of wrinkles dressed in silk. Her eyelids were so heavy they looked closed. The old lady was the size of a hobbit but even so, Sally felt a power radiating out of Grand.

Grand whispered. "I have joy, Sophia. The thread is not lost. A new Fire Women, that is who you are. You must go where our vision points us…protect this Conley."

"Grand, I don't understand." *No way she said the professor's name. I miss heard her.*

Grand didn't answer, rather she breathed into Sally's face. Sally imagined herself facing a wide-open coal furnace and caught a faraway chant within the flames, "Fire cannot hurt us, fire can't hurt us, fire can't…"

Grand squeezed Sally's hands. "Will you take up the brand?"

"Oh, okay, Grand, whatever you say." Sally pulled back from the heat.

"You accept?" Grand released Sally.

"Sure, why not," Sally said. Conley's sparks came to mind. "I better go help Conley…er, Mom in the kitchen." Sally backed away bowing.

Grand had come to America to do something important, but she didn't say what. Maybe to see Sally's little brother off to college. Whatever it was, Sally felt as if Grand's purpose was met. Sally had evidence. Grand appeared lighter, transparent even, like she'd float away. It gave Sally the willies. Dad and her sibs were home and nobody else saw Grand turning invisible? The old lady's contentment spilled over and coated Sally in happy molasses. A great relief came over Sally as she entered the kitchen to help Mom.

"You decide, yah?" Mom asked.

"I guess… I'm taking Ark III." Sally said but it wasn't a guess.

CHAPTER THIRTY-TWO:

NORTHERN CALIFORNIAN

Sally didn't mind the long bus ride out to the ranch. One bus carried students, the other hauled gear. Sally brought her laptop along. Being behind, she updated her diary on the trip. She reserved the diary for stuff she'd never write on her blog.

My advisor crapped a biscuit when I told him I decided to become an archeologist. *He begrudgingly let me take Arc. III. This is my last chance. I'm still not sure if this is what I want, but I never know what I want. Grand had zeroed me in. I'm regretting it. I have this weird feeling, like a foreboding, silly, right? I don't know anything about Conley. I always audit before deciding. But then again, I love, love, love camping. Good timing. I needed this. Home sucks since Grand died. The spirits know best, right.*

I told myself this isn't camping, this isn't fun, this is work. Forget mesmerizing coals and whispering voices. I'm not a kid. No more fire-dreams. I'm serious. I have to grow up. Maturity will kill my obsession. But, so far, it hasn't. Fire still calls. Buckle up, strap your ass in. I have to break this or I'll wind up wanting tables.

Sally closed the diary and opened the course prospectus provided by the funding agency. She downloaded it two weeks ago. "Better late than never."

Field work concerned a shallow cave atypical of northern California. The place was discovered two years ago. Excavation ongoing. The guide explained the deepest layers were already reached and the dig was closing out. Her group would be the last. *Thank God I don't have to shovel guano.* The lower levels could be pre-Clovis at thirty-four thousand years old, if true. That would be revolutionary, but dating wasn't confirmed. A groundbreaking discovery was not anticipated.

"This site is played-out. Nothing left undiscovered." Sally said to a boy wearing headphones. He gave a thumbs up. Older dates would bring new interest. The upper layer's Paleo assemblage wasn't old enough. "We really need an ancient hearth to confirm dates."

"A firepit would be cool," the boy said.

Sally wasn't worried. Old fires didn't take her. Dead firepits never lit her mind. It'd be embarrassing if she fell into a crazy voodoo girl trance. She brought a big bag of pot along to temper her furnace.

They turned off the local two-lane road and onto a dirt track. The site was on a private mega ranch. Flatlands to distant mountains was all one property. Semi-desert with lots of gullies and shallow dead-end canyons plus a dry lake. Mad cool geology, she thought as the bus seesawed along the rancher's rutted track. It took an hour of slow-crawl to reach the offload zone. Basecamp was downhill two miles from bus parking at the bottom of a shallow bowl valley. If not for the distant tents, she would not have noticed it.

Sally and the rest hiked down hauling their packs and one-man tents. An old volunteer guy named Jorge helped setup camp. He told them where things were. Dig crew was still in the field. That evening the diggers came back covered in dust and barking for food. The mess tent was stocked. Everyone pitched in, got food, and cleaned up. It felt like Girl Scout camp. Kids from four different schools were there giving the place that jamboree feel.

"I'm stoked." She said to the guy next to her in the mess hall. "This is great."

He pulled down his glasses and looked at her funny. "Yeah, I love eating dirt."

After dinner, without asking or being told, Sally got the fire going. They had a fire ring and lots of wood. Old Jorge looked on but didn't say anything. Weird, how he watched. They didn't run generators at night, so the fire was the big hang out spot.

After everyone settled in at the fireside Conley gave a welcome speech. Professor Conley looked like the picture accept worn down. Not bad looking, thin-ish, tan, sandy brown surfer-cut hair, and no wedding ring. Sally watched the social dynamics. Two of the girls had the hots for the professor. They batted eyelashes at him so much it bellowed the fire, especially Jill, with her sorority girl edge.

"Can she be any more flirtatious?" Sally said to the flames.

That man was staked with claims. Sally returned her focus on tending the fire. It felt good. She had it burning just right, flames weren't too big. It was a cold night so she got plenty of coals lined up to radiate heat outwards. Big-flame fires didn't give off deep heat, all the warmth went straight up.

Standing fireside, Conley finished introductions of staff and shifted into lecture gear.

"We're lucky," Conley said. This is a special place. One family on this land a hundred and forty years. Nobody screwed with our artifacts. When the owners discovered it, they called the Foundation immediately. Top layers were recent natives, under that Paleoindians, Clovis below that, but who do we have now at 34K BP? That's the million-dollar question. These stone industry flakes are dissimilar..."

Conley talked but the fire captured Sally. She hadn't gotten close to a fire since Grand died. Grand wanted a fire at her services and Sally did the honors. She didn't hear half of what Conley said. She zoned out reaching for something she couldn't touch. She became engrossed in rearranging the coals. The broken ax handle she prodded with didn't surprise her. *These nerds never chopped wood in their lives.* She had a knack for firewood. At Girl Scout camp they always made her the fire keeper. Girls made fun of her and gave her a fake Indian name, 'Fire Watcher.' Sally didn't mind. They almost had it right.

"...These flakes aren't Clovis industry, they're..." Conley kept yammering on about lithics.

Someone tossed a flat stick into her fire. It caught fast. It was as dry as desert bones. Mesquite by the smell. A fire-watching Girl Scout knows her fuel. That mesquite begged for attention. If left alone, it would have made big, fun-fire flames. This wasn't a party fire. Sally arranged it to radiant heat. Wrong wood for that. Time to make a change. *Talk fires need big flames and less smoke...*

"Where're the marshmallows at?" Sally said.

"…About the bone tools and atlatl…they're in the processing tent…you'll see them tomorrow. They're more closely related to…"

"Where did that mesquite come from? Aren't any mesquite trees for five hundred miles? That does burn nice," Sally said.

"…As you will note…" Conley droned on.

"I hope we aren't being tested on this." Something pricked Sally's insides. "Wake up!" Rolled out of her mouth and she didn't say it.

She popped out of her camp chair, reached into the fire, and pulled that stick out like a maniac. *It wasn't just a stick.* 'It doesn't belong,' screamed in her mind. She kicked a crapload of dirt on it fast. The group must have thought she sat on a snake the way they reacted.

"What are you doing, Miss Wong? Can't you see I'm lecturing?" Conley said harshly.

Sally was never one to put up with abuse. She answered in a harsher voice. "Why're you burning a native bowstave dickhead? Aren't you here to save history?"

"What!?!"

Oh, shit I'm screwed. Never insult your professor.

Conley jumped over the fire and grabbed it, still smoldering. "Son of a bitch. Where'd this come from?!"

Before Jill could own up, Sally blurted out. "Down Mexico way. It's mesquite. Locals used junipers, right?"

Conley's mouth hung half-open. He eyeballed Sally as if seeing her for the first time and he wasn't pissed. He snapped his mouth shut and his lips went Mona Lisa. Everyone talked at the same time. Conley stood there rubbing his chest.

After the smoke cleared, Jill said she found it coming down from the parking lot. She used it for a walking stick. She forgot and tossed it in. On quick exam, the stave wasn't that old, less than a few thousand years, but it sure wasn't local. Evidence of trade, perhaps? Jorge came and whispered something in Conley's ear and the professor lowered himself into a camp chair. Jorge ran the artifact up to the processing tent.

Conley stared at the fire rubbing his chest for a time in apparent concentration. After a while, he perked up saying, "Good eye, Miss Wong. Guess what? You're in charge of the campfire. And you, Miss Harvey, first thing tomorrow you will hike your ass up to parking, locate and mark where you found it."

Jill broke out her pouty face and started whining but Conley didn't buy the girly-girl act and shut her down. Bus parking was two miles uphill and Jill ain't the athletic type.

"Can't I use the Jeep, please?" Jill said changing tactics to a silky voice.

"No, walk it. How're you going to survey the trail?" Conley said.

Jeeps were used to get all the big stuff down to basecamp. A vehicle couldn't use the walk-path. The Jeep had to go a long way around and make a lot of trips which was why they packed their personnel stuff down. Of course, Jill needed more help than a stick. The boys carried all her crap. Judging by Jill's *Ralph Lauren* shoulder bag, high-heel Lugs, and sun-kissed perfect cheeks, unlike Sally's chipmunk pouches, Jill was accustomed to lots of help. Conley, to his credit, didn't buy her act. The name Spring-Flower popped into Sally's head.

Later at the fire, after staff had gone to bed, snatches of her old childhood fire-dreams blazed in and out of recollection. Maybe it was the beer and pot. Her first-night camping wasn't a party, but she drank too much on purpose. Drinking drowned out her visions.

CHAPTER THIRTY-THREE:

MARY ALL STOP

Mary Conley lived in the map room. She poured over a select number of ancient scrolls one more time with mounting unease.

Doctor Beverly Hess had collected many texts over forty years. But these were not collected by Beverly alone. The best was provided by Richard. After Doctor Hess had published her last tome, *When the Goddess Ruled*, she was attacked, her place in academia imperiled. If not for Richard's defense of her, she would have lost her position. As it turned out, Hess resigned in the end. The Foundation offered her heart's desire: The study of antiquity in search of what no respectable Ph.D. could touch. Hess and Wailer's like-minds had connected on contact. Hess never looked back.

"Damn the critics' egos, funding, and status," Mary said. She had a habit of talking to herself while working. "We're going where no man has dared to go before."

Hess discovered that women were formerly powerful heads of societies. These ancient elders possessed magic-like mental abilities. Richard insisted technology had been more advanced than known today. He unearthed scrolls dated to 14K BCE. If not for the ink made of pure gold, there would have been nothing left but petrified velum. Such ink cannot be made today.

"I see why you vacated," Mary said thinking of Hess while carefully unrolling another scroll. "This stuff is academic suicide. It'll shoot holes in anyone's sheepskin."

Mary laughed. She hadn't laughed much since Bert died. The velum she reviewed wasn't sheepskin. It came from an extinct Asian red deer.

By chance or design, Mary was glad she joined Richard's team. Coming to the aid of her youthful hero Doctor Hess was a fantasy made real. There was more to this than Beverly's failing sight. Mary deciphered key scripts unnaturally fast. Answers to her came in dreams. Text stuck in her mind like magnetic bubblegum until she cracked it. Her skills grew—skills or something other? That she had once held the medallion made Richard's ship a needful hiding place, but there was more. Mary activated her voice recorder.

"T-13 is certainly Proto Coptic. I'm a specialist in hieroglyphs but I know enough Coptic to get by. Don't quote me, but this content must have influenced Egypt." She stopped recording.

Richard had told her that theses scrolls came out of north Africa but were made long before Coptic times. And he was right. They were made eons before the Pharos. Mary determined the scribes were women. Their story impossible and sad. These scrolls depicted the scourging of the goddesses for the oppression of womankind.

She started her recorder. "Fairy tales, mythologies…It's not. It reads too much like statements of facts. Richard, you must already know this. Why did you have me read it?" She answered her question. "To make me understand. Richard, what is going on here?"

Hess had the basics. Not every word was understood. Mary's effort filled in the blanks. She finished the list of unknown terms and refined the context. These scrolls had been excavated from the bottom of a filled-in stepwell. The scrolls were sealed in primitive stone jars before civilization began, or so Mary was told. She was told a lot she didn't believe before boarding.

"God, forgive me. I believe now."

Mary put aside the text and laid down her voice recorder. Many sections were housed in protective sheets although it had once been a continuous roll. It was a miracle that they had survived. She took up her notebook, but her concentration broke. The engines stopped. They never stop. A feeling of dread came over her.

"Richard has some explaining to do." Mary went out on deck to find it empty. She looked everywhere, no crew? Up to the pilot house, she went. First Mate Stephany Bernard was at the helm.

"Oh, there you are," Stephany said. "I sent Deric looking for you."

"Where is everyone?"

"The lower stateroom, there's a meeting. Go on down. The crew is there except me. I'll watch on video."

Mary ran into Deric on her way, and that was good because Mary had never seen the lower decks. In the past, on that disastrous treasure adventure, she had no business in the ship's bowels. That's why the engines stopped, she guessed. Too noisy for a meeting. Deric disagreed.

"That ain't behind all-stop," he said. "Captain shut the engines down for safety."

Deric split opened one half of the double door for her. She expected to find dirty utility spaces behind the flat metal door, but the room was large, well-lit, and clean. Paneled walls? Such trimmings weren't usual when *The Finder* was commissioned in 1904. Mary didn't expect room for forty women seated at one long table. Beverly and Richard sat at the head.

"What's this? *The Vagina Monologues?*" Mary blurted. There weren't any men on this ship except Richard and Deric and Deric backed out, closing the door.

"This is an emergency," Richard said. "Sit Mary, please."

"Wait a minute, I have a question. I need to talk to you."

"I know, I'll answer your questions, but business first."

Mary wasn't clued into ship's business. Richard provided an overloaded ear full which so stuffed her head with worry it would have fallen off if it weren't spinning. She felt like an out-of-balance washing machine.

The ship rested and not only the motors. Everything was shut down. Richard ordered silent running, but they weren't moving. *Finder* would remain dead in the water until an all-clear was established. Electronic counter measures ran on batteries, all other communications were halted. The fear of danger rippled within the group as Richard gave specific technical instructions. Finally, after him going on about things she didn't understand, he paused and asked if there were questions.

"I have one," Mary called out, "What in the hell are you talking about? Am I a prisoner? While I'm asking, why can't I call Tommy?"

"We'll talk after this,' Richard said. "No questions, good, ladies, you know your jobs, please proceed. Batten down, full countermeasures. Ready rigging."

With that, the crew filed out. None were happy. Stern-faced fear became the uniform of the day. The room stank with it. Doctor Hess stopped and gave Mary's hand a little squeeze.

"I'll be all right, dear. Have faith." Hess said and left.

"Okay bucko, what's going on?" Mary said facing Richard. "Plain language, please."

"They've been chasing me, and I've been chasing them, and I do believe we may meet. And if so, I'm holding the losing hand."

"Goddamn it, Richard, knock off the cryptic bullshit, will you?"

"Fine, we are being followed by an American sub. I tried to disarm it and the attempt failed. They know about my technology. Somebody on the inside must have told them. The Watchers infiltrated the CIA as I expected. I'm convinced they have claws inside the U.S. Navy. That makes sense. To protect the device, what better way is there? I'm about to confirm activation and they've been blocking us and now closing in on us. The clock's ticking down. I must leave *Finder* to give the crew time. I'll slip the blockade...if I can."

"Time for what?"

"Escape. I'm weakening the women's shield. I must go. Deric's gay and doesn't register."

Mary stood out of her seat. A sudden dread pressed in on her and she lowered herself back. Richard took the chair next to her.

"Who are you, what are you?" Mary said.

"I'm human, just not your kind. My kin would like to see your kind end forever and they intend to make it happen. Your husband and I stopped them, inadvertently. I've lately learned who's behind it. That volcano in the Sargasso Sea wasn't natural. It's a weapon. Bert yanked the start key. They want it back but...it doesn't matter." He lowered his voice. "They found another way. Black smokers are rising all over the world."

"Black smoker, ashy volcanoes, so what?" Mary said. "I don't get it?"

"The little ice age, one eruption caused it. What if a thousand like Krakatoa went off at once?"

"Oh lord."

She believed him. Cogs clicked into place. She became stronger after leaving home, her mind clearer, her body youthful. *It's the crew's energy.* Smart, talented women, true, but there was more. Each held power and special qualities. Their protection laid a shaman's shawl on the ship. The Watchers have advanced technology, but they couldn't penetrate the shroud. Richard acted as a seam splitter. The ship couldn't steam away with him. *The Finder* was caught in a fish weir.

"The ship will be sunk if I stay." He repeated.

"How'd they zero in on you? You a machine or a wizard or what?" Mary said. "I can't read you. I'm good at figuring people out. You don't register."

"The Watchers and I are genetically related." Richard leaned forward. "I don't talk about it. I was left in a foundling home in 1898. Abandoned by a woman of the

Watcher's race who I believe is, or was, an escaped captive. I've confirmed my mother wasn't a sapient. She escaped late with child. Me."

"Was or is…She was brave," Mary said. "Who expects a pregnant woman to go on the lam?"

Richard shared what he had pieced together. He spent more than one lifetime puzzling it into form. These Watchers meant to destroy him and all life not under their thumb. Of late, he said, the Watchers were losing control, too many pins in the bowling alley.

"The Watchers will tear Earth apart to save themselves. Are they mad?" Mary said.

"They think they're protected underground, and they are, to a point. Their agents are the world's movers," Richard took a deep breath. "I've long suspected a hidden power. I too have agents in every corner. Cat and mouse to be sure, but the Watchers didn't know I played until Bert recovered that amulet. Where it went wasn't known by them or me on the day. It took twenty years for them to trace it to me. I didn't understand until recently. It gathers and concentrates magic…Women's Magic. The Watchers know we found it. They're after it, after me, and anyone near it. They're after you too, Mary. I'm sorry."

"My Tommy! He had the damn thing. Won't they want him?" Mary said with rising anger forcing herself to her feet. "I swear Richard—"

"Tommy drained you." Richard put his hand out and she backed down. "The other half drained Amy and hid. What better way? It's not made for men. It protected Tommy as a boy. Kenny will always be a boy and thus it remains undetectable. I don't believe any man can handle one. It burned me when I touched it. They know Kenny had half of it…Kenny was kidnapped last week."

"What about my son?"

"They don't know who has it. He doesn't know either. Tommy can't know," Richard said, "Or they'll find him." Richard turned away.

"Say it, Richard. Spit it out."

"Tommy absorbed it. He doesn't know that. They're after you hard. They think you have it. You don't. As long as you run, they'll assume it's with you. Bait, Mary. You're shark bait."

"Tommy's in danger! I must tell him."

"You can't. Not knowing protects him. It's a spell. You translated it, remember? They think I have the other. They traced it to us. This may all be moot. They found a way to start the creation machines. Us running keeps them distracted. They want their trophy back. You can hide here, I can't."

"I must go to him. Get me off this tub!"

"No, I have agents in play. Stay hidden until I find a way. They'll think Kenny lost it. It hid itself by design. They're using Kenny to trap me. This is my fault."

Richard's voice cracked.

"It's alive," Mary said. Realizations came full. "The thing's intelligent… good God."

"Its designers gave it intelligence. It needed a champion, a hero." He spread his hands. "It chose Tommy."

"It chose wrong. Tommy is not a hero. All my life, I implored him to stay safe. You don't know how much I hated him skateboarding."

The weight of parental failure squeezed Mary's heart. She and Bert were adventurers before he drowned. She encouraged Tommy to take chances then. But, after Bert died, she did the opposite.

"Can't this be passed to someone more able?" Mary said in a weak voice. "I taught my son how not to be a hero."

Richard perked up in his seat rubbing his beard. He had slumped while unfolding the story.

"That is interesting, I wonder," Richard said tapping his bottom lip. "A brave man isn't required. Anyone could pass it along…still…"

A new thought lit his face. Mary had seen this before. His eyebrows rose, the crow's feet around his eyes deepened.

"It resides in him unknown." Richard's eyes twinkled. "It chose the unlikeliest persons. That's another level of protection. The key didn't haphazard its way into Tommy. It chose him. It knows how to hide. I was inspired to find that tiny spot in the ocean for a reason, not my reasons. Tommy spotted it first. He's the key holder."

"And we're stuck until a torpedo decides to make a splash," Mary said feeling action ready like the woman she was before Bert passed. "Okay genius, now what'll we do?"

"I'll show you." He checked his watch. "Everything's ready by now."

Richard led the way up to the main deck. There, the crew was stationed at intervals chanting words she didn't understand, but the song woke an awareness. She perceived the invisible shield. Not all the crew were chanting. Some were rigging square sails on three tall masts. *Finder* had been refitted with modern engines but she was built when steam engines were untrustworthy. Steamships of the era also sailed.

"We aren't dead in the water," Mary said. "They're beautiful," she said of the sails.

"We'll be dead soon if I stay." Richard pointed aft.

Richard's wooden sailboat was being lowered on a manual chain hoist. All-stop meant no motors. Mary remembered that little sloop. The craft was a sleek and swift 26-footer. She and Bert had taken it out. Richard had it with *Finder* when she and Bert crewed. It hit home. Richard drew the Watchers. He stays, the ship dies. He— No, they—had to go.

They stood together at the rail as *Little Finder* kissed the ocean. She mounted the ropes to climb down. He put a hand on her arm and stopped her.

"You stay. They'll need your magic. You held the amulet."

He's right, damn it.

"Where too, O captain of the briny seas?" Mary tried to be playful. Richard replied with the face of a starving monk.

"You know the answer," he said. "That bit of interruption you did, that word you translated? It stumped us for a long time."

"Lower Egypt. The Romans called it Hell's Bridge," she said. "Egypt's over 1500 miles. It'll take you weeks to sail there."

"It'll give you time," Richard said. "You located an entrance. The last place they'll look is on their back doorstep. My agents will contact Tommy and tell him to get to

Cairo. Stephany will take care of it once clear. Tommy must get to Egypt. He can't know why. I'll think of something when I meet him."

Richard climbed down, cast off, and set the rigging. Mary leaned over the rail and blew a kiss as he drifted off. She had not forgotten how to sail and envied him. Before bipolar, she ran her one-woman Sailfish on the Great Lakes at every opportunity. She regretted not showing Tommy how to sail. Then again, he refused to go near the water after his brush with the abyss.

Richard's sails quickly became triangles on the horizon reminding her of the shark's fin that followed in *Finder's* wake. *Little Finder* was built for speed and Richard's flag soon dipped below the horizon. Leaving the rail, she turned. *The Finder's* sheets bellowed. The big ship moved off. Mary imagined the submarine's confusion. Richard's wooden sloop won't ping.

Chanting continued. Mary joined. Her intuition provided the words. She felt safe. She knew when the sub changed course. Women's Magic written of in forbidden texts wasn't mythology. For Tommy to accept magic as fact invited danger. His unbelief was another shield.

"Thank Goddess Tommy's an atheist."

CHAPTER THIRTY-FOUR:

FIRE TRIPPING

Sally and the rest hit the dig next morning after breakfast, dragging ass, and nursing beer-bent brains. The cave was a mere rock outcropping overhang thing. Enos ago it had been a deeper, bigger cave but most of it had collapsed. Behind the outcrop lay a depression of low ground which was a part of the defunct cave system. The landscape beyond was littered with depressions and big chunky outcrops that were formally below grade. Such rock piles were peppered over a long topographical decline and up the other side miles beyond.

Geology wasn't Sally's thing although she had been required to take classes. She surveyed the landscape while Conley organized the day. Her almost educated guess was that the standing stones were left after caves collapsed leaving harder rock standing like mesa cores. In the Pleistocene, this area would have had tons of shallow caves for people. Lots of them had been just below or at the surface. The land continually lost elevation due to wind erosion. Rock shelters had withered away. Soil filled the caves' deeper reaches.

"This was below grade for millions of years," Sally said waiting with her group. "Look at them. Wind effects carved them into goddesses."

"Mother Earth's blow job," Roger said pointing. "Looks figurative."

"Good eye, Miss Wong. Interesting observation," Conley said. "Ever consider geology?"

"Not really, Mr. Conley." *Thanks for reminding me how torn I am over degree possibilities.*

For sure, geology wasn't one of her choices. Geology is handy, but it sat on her cold burner. She could apply Arch III to it. She didn't know where she'd end up after the BA, but she had to stick with archeology or lose the money. At least geology was scratched off her list. Sally got into the dig routine of removing the last layers of soil tucked into edges and cracks. It wasn't long before the spirit of discovery captured her. Conley's enthusiasm spread like an underground coal fire. Conley's slow burn teaching held her attention.

A week into the dig, Sally, the professor, and some of the others were dancing between "anthills" talking about what to do next. They weren't real anthills but unexcavated mounds left in place to track soil stratification for dating and height from bedrock.

"I know there's more here, I feel it," Conley said toward the end of the day, flowing around the site, tapping his chest.

The cave floor was a 3-D checkerboard with a dozen small mounds still in place. Level by level select artifacts had remained untouched for context. One lower anthill held the only Clovis point, the overburden above that level had been removed before Sally's group arrived. Clovis rested sixteen inches above bedrock and three feet below the start grade. Theoretically, everything below that point was older than 13K BP. Cave digs generally progress leaving samples in situ until bedrock is exposed.

There wasn't much left not excavated and therefore no hope of finding anything older. Only flakes were found below the Clovis point. Wash down deposits were ruled out so where did that worked stone come from?

"People reach out, use your intuition," Conley said again.

The professor had murmured nonsense on and off all that day as he picked around.

"Kenny said it's here, it's got to be here. I must be losing my mind."

Nobody seemed to hear him except her. Conley wasn't talking about the last stage, which would be excavating those orphaned chucks of matrix. Odds were, there wasn't anything inside them. The kids were convinced this project was over but Sally had a feeling it wasn't. Conley scratching his chest created friction she felt.

"There's more here," Conley said at day's end, but this time his words rippled through her.

Sally guessed the professor had reached the end of his funding rope. He kept scratching all day. The others said it was a stress-tick but Sally thought it a motivation system. Sally focused her attention on him and saw sparks flying off him. She rubbed her eyes.

"Think outside of yourself, anyone? Volunteer your intuition, any wild guesses? I won't bite," Conley said.

People were packing their gear but Sally watched him spark instead. The last thing a science major needed was intuition, magical thinking being the opposite of what was taught in class. But Sally had this intuitive sense she couldn't escape or accept. She didn't trust her inner workings but she opened herself up a little because Conley kept asking. That last ask was when the call of fire smacked her. *Old fires are near.* She never felt fire under these conditions before. Something about Conley lit her fuse. *I'm deluded, it's my bladder—I gotta pee.*

"Don't pack out now people, we got time for one more go-around." Conley said.

While everyone fine-tooth-combed Sally stumbled outside to pee. It felt like an invitation and not the urge. She had a spot behind a chest high boulder and walked right past it. Big rocks were strewn everywhere like free radicals. Soil had filled where sinks had been. A couple of nearby rock walls reminded her of idols and drew her attention. There were lots of places to go but the uprights intrigued her. She could go back to camp where the portable bathrooms were, but she had her camper's funnel. Stick it under, press tight, and pee standing like a boy. She hated peeing on her *Timberlines.*

She let it rip. The sizzle of water spilling on hot coals returned to her. When done, she felt dizzy and leaned on a boulder. For no reason, her head jerked back. She saw it. That big-ass rock she leaned on had fallen from above. A vision came: natives roasting a fawn over an open fire beside her standing stone. *Not the clan I dream about.* The episode passed quickly. She felt compelled to tell Conley.

"Professor," Sally called from the cave's mouth. "I found something."

Conley got off his knees and followed her to the place.

"I found a firepit, see that big rock?" Sally pointed. "It came from there." She pointed up at the overhang which looked like an old lady. "It broke off and rolled but not far. A firepit depression stopped it."

They got down on the ground. Conley didn't mind the smell. She held her nose, and they scratch around with garden shovels. Conley found spent charcoal.

"That's Neolithic. Same age as Jill's stave." Sally said.

"Might be a cookfire, possibly a garbage pit," Conley said. "We got lucky. Good eye, Sally. Maybe geology is your calling."

It wasn't a trash-pit. *Garbage doesn't call me.*

Conley and the boys levered the boulder out. After an hour of brushing and digging, the dinner bell rang. Conley confirmed a cookfire.

"We have charred deer bones and the rest one would expect such as stone knapping debris, no pottery shards," Conley said having reached the bottom. "Just a quicky cookfire. One or two nights used. No megafauna bones."

Sally already knew it was young. The call didn't leave her. That got her thinking and reaching deeper. Normally, when the feeling came, she'd run the other way— that's how she lived with it—but, she didn't want to let Conley down, either. Another fire had to be nearby.

"That's enough for today people. Dinner is on. Let's pack it in."

The group left feeling upbeat. The nerd speak on their way up to camp was relentless. The new find was better than nothing even if it wasn't old. It might keep the dig going a few more days.

Late that night after dinner, she had the fire burning low. Sally and a few others smoked a blunt. The staff wasn't around. Pot was legal but staff wasn't allowed. The weed sparked it. Stoned, beer in hand, a vision struck.

A hearth materialized within the coals as it was thirty-five thousand years ago. It wasn't that Paleo pit. This one was still undiscovered. She'd seen it before, that old crone woman cross-legged fireside dressed in a pullover shirt and a wrap-skirt made of deer hides. Her costume wasn't movie buckskins. The old lady's clothes were better, different in many ways, and more practical. Sally had seen this repeated in her childhood dreams. Sally didn't have the words to describe it as a little girl.

The woman wore two long hair braids, one on each side, duck feathers woven in. Necklaces were layered upon her, each ornament different: one neckless of shells, one of tiny painted fired clay balls, one of bones and teeth. Each material significant. Sally knew why. Half remembered dreams became clearer.

The crone sees me, looking right at me, gave a nod. Why didn't she say anything?

The matron, so old, had forgotten her birth name. Even so, Sally knew her. The Clan called her Fire Women, the plural, because she hosted the souls of her ancestors. The dead spoke through her.

"She's their shaman," Sally whispered. "She looks like Grand."

The clan's hunt leader, Bear Claw, was old himself at forty seasons. Bear Claw said inside Sally's dream, 'Fire Women was old when I was a boy.' *I know. She's too old to chew skins for leather, too old to gather, or net fish, or mate.* Age wasn't why she tended the hearth. She always did. Fire-Spirit gave her magic. None worked the hearth with such wisdom. Clan folk didn't know if past Fire Women had greater talents, but they trusted and respected the old one's skill. Fire is magic and a tool. Sally didn't know how she knew. *Info's coming straight out of my blood.*

Fire Women said, 'Come to me my child,' and Sally drifted unfettered toward her. A chant came to Sally's mind. *Time is a river of flame. I touched brazen waters and drowned.*

CHAPTER THIRTY-FIVE:

REALITY CHECK

Someone pressed a cold beer bottle on Sally's neck from behind.

"Maybe you should slow down, Sally." Charlie said, "You're nodding out. Damn near fell in the fire."

Sally wasn't drunk, but she wished she were. "I'm okay, okay? Give me that beer." She twisted the cap off and gulped.

"If you're gonna do fire watch, do it right," Charlie said. "You'll get us in trouble."

That wet touch shocked her back into herself like when Chen dumped her out of a sun-scorched lounger and right into an icy swimming pool. She was shocked into reality, but her heart still floated in fire. *My soul escaped.* Everything was colored in flame. She took another gulp and touched down feeling offended. Charlie accused her of dereliction of fire duty and that pissed her off. Her vision cleared into normal focus.

Charlie was still talking shit. "If you got burned, we'd all be in deep do-do, they'll shit-can the beer and—"

"Shut up," Came out of her with force. "I'll never fail fire. It can't fail me…can't hurt us. I'm…I'm…I'm. What am I saying?" Sally thrust onto her feet.

"Dude, you're whacked. Here hit this." Phil passed the joint that was hanging on his bottom lip and addressed the others. "Did one of you clowns put shrooms in her beer?"

Embarrassed, she slowly lowered herself back down. "How long was I gone?" Sally said blowing out smoke. "Don't tell Conley, K."

"Chill fire girl, your super powers are safe with me," Charlie said laughing.

"Sorry, I'm snappish," Sally said.

Everybody laughed. Sally finished the seven oz bottle and took a can. She said that, but it didn't come from her. When the joint came back around, she only saw its amber tip. Smoke that smelled of roasting red deer clouded her vision. The joint came to her in slow motion. The rest of the world didn't exist. She held it watching the tip glow. Her eyeballs were fire baked, but she could not look away.

"Dude, are you going to hit that or what?"

She took a quick pull and passed it on. Maybe it was the pot. When stoned, fire had a hypnotic effect on her. The past burned in her like some weird historical Tabasco sauce. She pushed it out of her mind, as she usually did when such thoughts plagued her. That icy can she clamped between knees felt hot. A fire still called. She had to answer. She closed her eyes and walked across a lake of lava. She arrived on a far shore. The cave was a few yards from a creek like the one Daddy had dunked her in.

***

Fire Women sat cross-legged by the hearth thirty paces from the cave's mouth adjusting coals with a rock-wood stick. Her white hair grew life long and yet never tangled. Her two braids, woven with ornaments to assist soul flights, hung forward in the flames unaffected.

Clan folk said of her, 'Your hair never burns. It is Fire Magic.' They were right. *Fire cannot harm me.*

The men came in from the hunt. The elks they drove fell into their pit trap and not a man among the dozen runners was hurt. Not one big cat or bear in sight to steal their game.

"Gather around children," Mother said. "Such a good kill is a teaching opportunity. I will show keeping a smoke hearth to cure meat." She meant to draw any young one interested. She did not yet know who would keep the sacrament after she died and this worried her.

The boys and young men had man things to do. The younger girls looked upon Mother Fire with reverence but hesitated out of fear. Red Dawn, the youngest, showed keen interest but she was yet too young. The hunters, with their excitement still thick, led the clan's heart on kill days.

"There are two elk to skin," Bear Claw's oldest son, Black Wolf, said, "Meat must be racked to dry."

"Without a certain fire, the meat will not dry correctly," Fire Women said.

"That is your concern. I will find sprigs," Wolf said and left.

"Tuber needs clay to make pots," Moss Foot said watching Wolf leave. Moss licked his jealous lips.

Although Moss saw fourteen seasons, and was old enough to hunt, he was not invited. A lame foot kept him from running or using a spear thrower well. Moss joined the women in gathering and became one with them. Moss preferred man work such as digging roots or gathering clay. Moss had found good clay and became the favorite of Old Man Tuber. Even so, Moss remained under women's care as was proper for the lame. Fire Women, being a former consort of Tuber, gave Moss over to care for Tuber's needs.

Tuber depended on Fire Women's magic and he did not care for that as he often announced. *What can he do but flap gums? Women hold greater wisdom. He has no good arguments.* He, at his late age, was bulb-fat and crooked legged giving him the shape of his underground namesake. He was no good for man work anymore. Yet he had a use.

Fitting, Fire Women thought, he makes pots, pots as round and squat as himself. The fermented berries others stewed in his pots kept him in good standing. The lesser magic of Water and Earth were the powers Tuber held which he enjoyed lording over Moss.

The horn sounded. The older boys were called to dig the roasting pit. The males touched their foreheads to show respect before leaving. Fire Women signaled permission and they ran eagerly to help. The women were already busy gathering herbs to flavor the feast. Fire Women's audience quickly reduced. Only the youngest stayed, save a pair of inadequate adults.

"You Moss should pay attention," Fire Women said, "There is more to life than digging. Tuber can't make pots forever. You may take his place someday. You will need my wisdom then. Pots cannot be made without a right fire."

"Fire lore is for Fire Women," Moss said. "This day is for elk. The big one has good horns. I need them for digging." Moss took a flint knife and limped after the rest.

He walks like Jorge.

"Whenever the men kill, learning stops." Fire Women called after him. "Fire is life!"

"Teach me," Sally said. How am I able to speak? They can't see me?

"There is plenty of food, the pots are full. I have time. I will teach."

Fire Women looked to the ceiling and said, "but you, should you not teach me?"

She knows I'm here but can she really see me? Way cool...or maybe not.

Fire Women searched the cave's walls considering the clan's story. All around pictures made by mineral paints spoke of successes. Everywhere depictions of the hunt, men's magic, were in evidence. *Did she address me, or her spirit guides?*

When Fire Women spoke again, she spoke with Sally's voice.

"Time is consumed," they said as one. Turning to Spring Flower, "You are fifteen and not yet pregnant."

She didn't talk to me. She's communing with her imaginary friends.

Sally felt Fire Women's contempt for pretty Spring Flower. Fire Women's disharmony bathed Sally in flames like holy water. *That girl is thickheaded, only good for making babies. Oh, what the men will do for her. Beauty prevents learning. Useless girl.*

"Did I think that?" Sally said.

"This one, I cannot abide." Fire Women said, pointing at Spring. "All the others old enough are doing chores, making the feast, acting responsibly."

Spring is the only adult not doing her share. Hanging at the fire is an excuse to avoid work.

Did I think that?

Fire Women looked at the ceiling then at Spring. "Have you no berries to gather?"

Spring kicked dirt at Fire Women's feet, an insult. "Teach me this magic."

Fire Women turned back to her hearth. The younger girls were still there. She did not address anyone, but fixed her attention on the coals.

"The fire of life resides inside you, set it alight." All the little girls responded, "Yes Mother." Fire Women turned to Spring Flower. "Make babies then I will show you—first a baby for the clan." The magician spread her hands and looked to the ceiling. "We agree."

Holy cow, she sees me.

Sally viewed herself superimposed behind the cave's wall art from Fire Women's eyes. There were handprints and spirals representing Sky Spirits. Stick figures were drawn—sticks for the fire. Zigzags meant lightning, the Sky Spirits' fire. Sally read the pictographs' ageless lore. *Petroglyphs show we're connected through time.* Sally let go and allowed the fire to pull her down. A hazy image of Sally appeared within the wispy smoke just above the firepit's low flames.

"You will fly between stars," she said to Sally. "Your spirit will visit many suns."

Fire Women often made new words. She invented names. Sally knew the naming words from dreams. She named each tree according to its status, if dry, or fresh, or rotten the name was modified. She used each condition of wood as needed. Sally dreamed this over and over in the weeks after her childhood baptism in fire and water. It all rushed back. None of the clan understood fire like this old lady.

I…she knows how to make special fires.

"Mother of Fire," Spring Flower spoke softer. *Ha, trying to get on our good side, not happening.* "Is there no time for both learning and bearing?"

Fire Women answered from a half trance. "There is time for babies and there is time for lore." And we thought: who will know my craft when I am gone? Fire Women had long worried that her art would be lost.

You know the answer. Whose thought is that?

"It is not lost." Mother said drawing up straighter and looking beyond Spring Flower.

The old woman's focus seldom strayed from the coals. She added fuel and the fire flared brightly. The south wall featured a rock protrusion and on it was painted a mastodon which quivered and pulsed as the fire flickers. Sally and Fire Women watched the spirit run. Fire gave it life.

How does she know all of the women's hearts without gathering, or chewing, or pounding grains with them? Making and gathering are how secrets pass between women generation to generation. Men weren't invited, not even Moss. Fire Women's knowing was yet another mystery to the clan. Sally and Fire Women sat at the flames a while, in and out of trance.

Sally held her questions and waited. Meanwhile, Spring Flower rocked foot to foot impatient, red lips pouting. Spring Flower's depth is dangerously shallow.

"Wisdom's spark is in you," Fire Women said finally. "You are worthy."

Spring Flower came close and laid a hand on Fire Women's shoulder. The old woman jerked away as if bitten. "Not you."

She's talking about me, dumbass.

The men came back with long, green, saplings and arranged drying racks. Fire Women busied herself changing how the fire burned. She called for greener wood that gave both smoke and good taste, but she maintained hardwood burning on one side. Coals were raked into place to burn greenwood as required. She got the little ones involved by letting them feed fresh fuel to the hardwood side. Spring Flower paid attention to the men and not the fire. Spring soon left to gather greens with Black Wolf. Spring didn't learn anything. Sally sucked it up. Spring Flower was a loss cause. The old one was happy nonetheless.

"Wolf will earn his namesake this day," Fire Women said to the flames.

Time went on, hours it seemed. Sally learned Mother's meat smoking technique from inside a flavored cloud. Sally was fascinated, and enchanted, and she wanted to stay forever. But reality forced her back. Her eyes had watered like crazy against the smoke. She blinked and wiped tears away not wanting to miss anything.

Sally's eyesight cleared. She found herself slumped in a camp chair. A hot unopened can of beer resting between her knees. The fire had gone out. Here chipmunk cheeks glistened wet. Her eyelids were swollen. Sally had been crying.

"Spring Flower," Sally choked, dry throated. She cracked that hot beer and swigged.

Someone's watching. The dig master, cook, and resident grumpy old man Jorge stood outside the chair ring on the opposite side of the pit in the dark. Sally launched out of the chair startled. A pile of white cigarette butts lay at his feet. Only he smoked cigs. Everyone had gone.

"Welcome back, *señorita*. Your trip meaningful, *sí?*"

He didn't say anything more, just tuned and limped away like Moss Foot. Sally should have been creeped out. An old guy watching a passed-out girl is messed up. But she didn't feel danger. No bad vibes. *He's got my back?* Getting caught passed out drunk was grounds for dismissal. The old man wasn't going to rat. She didn't know why, but it was true. She wasn't in trouble although her internal heat was building.

"Thanks, Jorge," Sally whispered before going to her tent.

The next day, Sally skipped breakfast and ran up to the site early. She normally got sick eating the morning after drinking. She felt fresh and not hung-over at all. The smell of food cooking wasn't why she skipped. She was too embarrassed to face Jorge in the chow line. She checked for vibes before the others showed up and stood outside the cave reaching. She couldn't zero in.

Too soon the others filed in. Students got on with brushing down the remaining anthills. Conley bagged what artifacts remained first. The firepit out back was ready to process but Conley saved it for another day. Each anthill got worked down to baserock pretty fast. Nothing was found inside them. *Good work for hung-over frat boys,* Sally thought. Charlie and Phil were fuzzy-eyed but Sally's mind ran on high-definition all morning. When basecamp's lunch bell rang everyone scrammed. Sally, almost done with her mound of dirt, stayed behind. Conley put on a sick-with-worry face.

Watching Conley, a flash memory of Dad pulling her out of that fire came on. Conley wore that same pained expression. She felt sorry for him.

The site went quiet. She was able to pick up a weak fire call in the air while brushing dirt off a charred snail shell. That wasn't the source. The south wall radiated warmth as she worked closer to it. *Just outside there laid the new firepit.* That's not it. Wrong vibe. Something else was there, just a whisper of hot air.

Professor Conley came and squatted down on his haunches next to her. So engrossed sniffing the vibes, she didn't notice him until he spoke.

"I feel it, too," he said. "Wish I had your talent. I didn't believe it before but... I guess...Looks like Kenny's wrong. I'm mistaken. We're out of time."

"I don't know what you mean." *You're out of time, I'm beyond time.*

"An idea was suggested...but it doesn't work for me. You're different. Close your eyes, reach for it, Sally, follow it." Conley said.

She didn't need instructions. Behind her eyelids she saw how the cave was before. The image flashed off and on like a disco ball projection. Details landed in her awareness. *Oh, that's where it's coming from.* Message received. She popped her baby blues open.

"See that raised floor section adjacent to the south wall? It's not bedrock, it sheared off that wall." She pointed. "It's a dislodged slab, not floor. There's a hearth under it." She got off her knees and approached the spot. "Pottery, too. One of Tuber's pots got left behind when they moved."

"Nobody made pottery at that time," Conley said.

"That's where they fired his pots...I'm sure...weird, right."

Conley examined the wall and floor. "You're right, of course, good geological eye. Keep using that...method and you'll do well."

"I'll change my major…to geology, I guess…if that's your recommendation. I don't know, I…" Her words faded.

She swallowed a tear. Geology wasn't for her. Did the muses decide? She didn't know what she wanted but that wasn't it.

"Two lucky finds, I guess, can make a person's career," she said. "Poop."

Conley scratched around the slab's base as she talked. He pulled out from under the slab a tiny piece of pottery. "Look at that. Here's your vessel, straw too, dateable material."

"Guess I'm doing geology."

"Geology? That's ridiculous," Conley got up and checked around. No one else was there. He spoke lower. "I didn't want to believe it, but this tares it…Jorge tried to convince me. Mede hinted, never said it outright. Cory didn't buy it either, he thinks it's technology. I resisted. I don't trust belief…it might be unknown physics, whatever it is, it's real."

"What's real!?" Sally cried.

"Magic is real. It pains me to say this but, Sally, you are a finder." Conley took a breath. "I lost touch with Kenny. Jorge retired; he only came here to herald a new finder…It's you, Sally. You have the touch."

Heat waves radiated from Conley's chest.

"I don't understand," Sally said quietly. "Yeah, I got this weird thing going on… but…I think…I need a shrink. I'm deluded. I need a mental health checkup."

"Don't bother. I don't understand it either, but it's real. My advice? Go where your talent takes you. I'm at Berkeley this fall, just got word. Tell Sac State you'll transfer. Take my course. Money is available. I need to understand this. Help me help you and myself. If I don't figure this out, I'll never get off this crazy train. I intend to see it to the end. I need you. Give the nod."

She hadn't until then seen the professor so animated. The flames around him sparked something inside her.

"I'm interested in primitive fire use," she said, measuring each word, having never said it out loud before.

Telling somebody filled out her truth. She wanted this for real but no such supporting degree program existed. His brow furrowed with intensity. Easy going Conley had another side, a crazy side, which didn't scare her. It solidified her desires.

"I'd go if they had a program. Nobody's sponsoring hearth studies on the west coast, I checked."

"I'll recommend you, I'll suggest a program." Conley said. "There's doctorate potential in hearth studies. It's a wide-open field. The only American specialist that I know of is in Israel. You'll come? You need this, you're made for it. I need you."

He knows more about me than I do. Her belly pushed against her backbone. What if people find out? He's got my secret. What if he tells Dad? I want a science career. This ain't science but…but it's amazing.

"I'm not crazy?" Sally said. "You don't think I'm crazy?"

"No, just special."

Career stress fell away like scales from a biblical prophet's eyes. Sally had a direction, an offer, and it was right. Yet, behind it, uncontrolled heat. Life with Conley wasn't going to be easy. Danger was coming and she had to face it. Fire Women seek flame and so do the enemies of life. Fire Mothers go where it is least safe. Fear welled up in her. Her jaw quivered. Conley watched, dripping with sweat although the cave felt cold.

"I gotta think," Sally said.

That hearth proves Clovis wasn't first in the northwest. The pots weren't supposed to exist at all. Primitives making wine and storing grains will never be accepted. They weren't supposed to have advanced industries. Such a find will create a firestorm. She saw them. She knew them, but who would believe it? Conley.

There wasn't any evidence to make such claims until now. Whatever is under that slab changes everything. Too dangerous. Ground-breaking finds break careers. But he'll listen. Holding back sucked. Trust poured out from him. That fire in his chest… he needs Fire Women's protection. *Fire consumes him and he doesn't even know.*

"Nobody's gonna believe this," Sally said. "We get that slab off…holy cow, this is gonna piss off a lot of people. What'll I tell my parents when I get kicked out of school?"

"We don't touch it. It's too hot," Conley said. "It's a career ender and better left buried. I have what I came for. Join me at Berkeley. Think it over." Sweat rolled down his nose. "Whatever you decide, never tell how you find things. No one. Not a word to your advisor. The government's watching me."

"I should say no, but…I don't know."

Sac State was close to home. Berkeley ninety miles away. She didn't even know if she'd like his classes. Her anthropology professor said Conley was a 'walking controversy.' He already had a reputation. But Conley's passion was contagious. He had something none of her teachers had. His flames jumped to her. She caught his fire.

"I'm feeling your heat," she said.

"I used to think what burned in my chest was curiosity," Conley said, excitement leaving his voice. "Not sure what causes it, I still don't know. I can't ignore it anymore. It tells me I need you. I don't know why."

"I don't know, either."

Conley gave her full credit for a major find although nobody would ever know it. That tipped her. That river of fire called time swept them together. Time runs out. Her life didn't seem real until then. Societies and people swam in and out of time making it hard to know what's right or real. Fire is true. Fire Women seek fire. *The Goddess made us for it.* Confirmation came at that moment. Everything became clear. '*Seek the fire,*' rang inside her mind.

It was a big, scary, weird step but the echoes bouncing around the cave gave her confidence. The voices droned. Generations of Fire Women chanted and she did, too, inside her heart. "Fire can't hurt us, fire can't hurt us, fire can't hurt me, fire…"

Thomas Conley was surrounded by hostile flames and he didn't know why. A man steeped in flame needs a guide. Conley attracts magic. But he can't use it. He can't see it. He can't control it. Sally Wong saw it. *I have a part to play. He needs our protection.*

He watched her like an expectant puppy. Sally always wanted a puppy.

"I'll go," she said.

CHAPTER THIRTY-SIX:

NEW DEAL

onley's long strange trip finally landed at Berkeley but not a solid landing. AU and the Foundation sent messages saying to expect a federal agent. After Alaska, he thought the CIA would leave him alone. They didn't show up for the ranch dig. His freedom wasn't yet secure. *I got to finish. My choice.* Any logical man would tell the CIA to go to hell, and he would have if not for that escalating feeling of time running out. He didn't know why or how but Tom was sure he was missing something important. He didn't have the pieces to solve this nebulas puzzle. He wanted answers and the feds had pieces of it. The message spilled grains of hope and doubt.

The establishment forced Cory's retirement, the same as Mede. Tom had refused to put himself into an outsider's box. Alaska University asked him to fill Cory's spot temporarily. Conley declined and not for Berkeley's sake. Alaska, the ranch, Badlands, were all stepping stones, and Berkeley, too, he saw the pattern. There was no escaping it. Move forward was the only option.

"I must be out of my mind," Tom said to himself.

"Hey Prof, eyes out," Janis called from the reception area. "Trouble."

He felt it coming, too. Cory's parting words came to mind. *'The world is crazy and getting worse. Expose what's behind it, and it stops. Bad is coming, Tom. Janis has the nose for trouble, trust her.'*

Tom didn't hire Janis. On the day he arrived at Berkeley, she was already there setting up the office. Janis insisted he'd need her hackery, and she was right. He knew better than to argue. Digging for ancient truth wasn't supposed to be dangerous. He needed a guard dog. Janis was good at it. His resistance to such facts had collapsed on the ranch dig.

He despised big university culture within the first week. Enforcing orthodoxy for the sake of reputation rankled his shorts as much as gatekeeping for the security state. *Why can't I just dig holes and provide a few tiny answers?* He lived under a black cloud. Janis Graves and Sally Wong stood ready, but he didn't know where to go. Something was still missing.

"CIA's outside," Janis called from her reception desk. Her security camera hacking skills provided well.

Both doors were open as usual. Tom closed his laptop. *Danger can't hide from that woman.* She had foresights like Kenny, but Kenny needed computers to send and receive messages. What happened to him? Why did he stop? Other than dreams, nothing came from him. Kenny's emails had dried up.

"He's entering the building," she said. "Packing iron, small bore auto."

"Let me know when he's close."

Did her gift work like Sally's or old Jorge's? Between her tech skills and danger detector, he'd keep her as long as Berkeley let him. The money for student employees wasn't explained. Everything in academia had its money bent. Somebody's cash wanted her there. Admin didn't give lowly assistants to the assistant professor money to play with yet they gave him three student-employee slots to fill. He didn't have anyone in mind for the third spot.

"Maybe I'll hire a limo driver." Tom mused.

Janis had the air conditioning set on hard-nipple cold. Small price to pay for her long eyes. Tom drew his wool sweater tighter. He didn't eat well with doom percolating in his guts and lost some weight. The birthmark hadn't inched lately until it broke fast this morning.

"Hey Prof, you see what I see?" Janis said. "It's that guy from debriefing. I'll put it on your screen."

He reopened the laptop. All of his AU students had been interviewed in Alaska. A busload of interrogators showed up. Tom heard about it. Tom only met with the big dog, Director Murphy.

Janis's white noise generator made eavesdropping impossible. She checked for bugs and found a handful on her first day. Planted just for him? Electronics might elude her software, but not her nose. Janis quickly mastered the universities' security system. Tom's video player booted. The man's black suit stuck out. Tom reduced the screen size and backed up the video tracing the man back to visitor's parking. He checked the time stamp. Janis spotted the CIA man before he had gone ten feet.

"What do you make of him?" Tom called out.

"He's one floor below on the stairs," she said from the outer office. She moved to his door. "Cops hate elevators. He's the slimy type. Maybe he's alright. He's ambiguous. Good-cop bad-cop in one package."

"I'll play it by ear," Tom said.

Tom trusted easily and assumed the best of people. A decent man treating people decently didn't smell evil. That was her skill. But even so, he detected hints of it. Bad traveled alongside him but hadn't run him over yet. This felt different. Tom joined her at her desk.

"Something's telling me he ain't a team player," Janis said. She blew up the image.

"Son of a bitch, that's Tod Murphy," Tom said.

"You know this clown? I don't trust him."

Janis pulled her .357, spun the cylinder, and put it back in a blur. Tom had no idea how she did it so fast. Annie Oakley couldn't compete. Tom's chest itched. He retreated to his desk. Murphy didn't knock and marched straight into the outer office.

"That way, he's expecting you," Janis said pointing with her gun's barrel.

The man opened his mouth and shut it. That rattled his cage. Murphy strode in and extended a big, hard, hand. Tom didn't take it.

"Nothing like Cory's office, is it?" He said, "They stuck you in the office pool, huh."

"I'm not Cory. What do you want, Murphy? If it's the same offer; you get the same answer."

Murphy had offered Tom an agency job while in Alaska. Murphy shut the door, pushed a chair in close, and didn't answer. *Janis will get it all on video.* He took a cigar torch out of his jacket pocket and scanned the room. Tom never saw a lighter with blinking lights before.

It was hot outside, and Murphy had time to cool off on his way, but his face glistened with flop sweat. Janis's icebox office didn't slow the man's inner burn. *Murphy is rattled.* Murphy didn't fit the bad-cop description. His Dick Tracy's face and six-two height didn't fit with the pudgy office worker's body. Police met two descriptions, in Tom's mind: Donut cops and steroid cops. Murphy fell outside both types. Even so, Tom guessed Murphy could break him like a tomato stick.

"We're alone," Murphy said.

"You were expecting otherwise?"

"I told them to back down," Murphy said. "They don't always listen. What about the Eskimo girl?" Murphy pointed with his chin.

"She's Inuit. Don't call her that or…" Tom shut up before he said too much.

Murphy laughed. "What's she gonna do about it?"

"Good question. She soundproofed the outer door. We have a vat of acid below the floor under your seat. Bones dissolve fast. What can I do for you?"

Murphy didn't smile.

"I'll be straight. The Company has a find-and-destroy job. Got a tip from Kenny Parks…you aren't supposed to know that. There's evidence of advanced civilizations in Anatolia yet to be discovered. We need to either obtain it or bury it. I rather obtain it. I was told to talk you into going, hang out a carrot, a bribe, anything. We must get it before the eastern archaeologists do. America can't control what we ain't got. You didn't hear me say that."

"What's in it for you? What drives a man to destroy history?" *He is lying.*

Murphy was off guard. He pushed back away from the desk with hurt on his face. He had that bug detector device in hand the whole time and waved it around before answering. He pushed in closer to the desk.

"I'll be honest," Murphy said in a lower voice. "Here's my thing, what I don't tell anybody. I don't know why, but I need to know what they don't want folks knowing. Balls out, I don't agree with the policy." Murphy leaned in closer still. "I believe people have a right to our past—warts, zits, and what-have-you—but not if it hurts them. We're protecting the people."

"Which people? Academic people or 'We the People.' Or inside people?"

"National security." Murphy kicked back with a thoughtful expression. "I can't say who deserves what. In truth, I don't know. However, hiding historical reality has stopped making sense to me. I've seen things I want answers to. Cover operations don't provide answers. We kill them." Murphy removed his fedora and mopped his brow with a hanky. "Christ, I could use a drink."

The Humphrey Bogart act fell away in Tom's eyes and was replaced by Clark Kent having a bad day. *Maybe he's on the level. Curiosity killed the cat, but sometimes the cat kills you.*

"Why drag me into it? What about you? Why are you doing it?" Tom said despite the internal pressure to accept whatever Murphy was selling.

"I'm a geology grad, anthropology minor. I was going after a doctorate when the CIA drafted me," Murphy said, leaning forward. "Here's the thing. I found a two-man submarine buried in an inland field while taking cores, two hundred miles inland. A freshwater inland sea had drained fifteen thousand years ago." Murphy blew on his fingernails like a safecracker. "Big ass lake, too. I'm talking ocean size. It expanded overnight and drained away fast, catastrophic event. A sub washed in and remained."

"What's this to do with me? I'm not into oceanography."

"I told Parks. Parks and I had a little talk. Government has the boy under study, see. You know Parks has visions. This info about Parks is strictly need-to-know and you aren't listed. I was told, 'Get Conley to go.' My neck's out now. I spilled my guts. I have my own needs. I need to know. Parks said there's a, and I quote, "a special gift," waiting there for Mr. Conley. He wasn't specific."

They have Kenny locked up. That's what happened to the emails. I didn't get that message.

"Interesting, any big lakes or rivers near?" Tom said. "Maybe a modern tornado, or thieves, ditched it."

"Lake Van, Turkey, is what's left of the inland sea. 80 miles away, maybe more. There ain't no reason why a sub should be there."

"You're messing with me. Van's a volcanic basin sixteen hundred feet above sea level. Earth's water level was a thousand feet higher twelve K ago, but...hummmm...I hear there's new volcanic activity at Van. Let me see that."

Murphy slid over a job folder containing charts and graphs. "Take your time."

Tom dug in. Van was brackish yet landlocked and fed by mountain rivers. Geologists concluded salts came from upland deposits. Twelve thousand BP water was a thousand feet higher and yet not connected to the Black Sea. The dig site's location was indeed too far inland. Van's elevation was lower now. Papers said the same flood event that destroyed North America drained Lake Van. Artifacts of note were possible. Lakesides can be archaeological boons. Who had a submarine before recorded history? Homo sapiens or someone else? Tom didn't believe it. But Murphy was dead serious. Tom went over the data twice.

"This is real."

If Tom wasn't sitting, he would have slumped to the floor.

"You alright, what's with the itching?" Murphy said.

"Heart burn. Where'd you find it, exactly." Tom said trying for a steady tone.

He had the map open. This kind of stuff never made the periodicals. His birthmark pulsed and burned. *Damn thing keeps growing.*

"Van used to border the Pontiac Mountains when the Black Sea was a freshwater lake on the other side of the range, after the event." Murphy stabbed the map with a big finger. "It flooded. I'm talking Biblical floods. It drained away fast. The gradualists can't stomach change by catastrophe. What about you?" Murphy moved his finger to the dig's location. "That was the shoreline of Van."

"Van's two hundred miles...shit."

Tom took in the possibilities. What a great opportunity. Neolithic shorelines were like shopping malls for ancient people. He stopped scratching.

"I pick my team. Your men stay off. We do real science. I'm not a treasure hunter. I'm not doing politics." *Nice bait. But if this is real...*

"That's fine." Murphy said drumming his fingers on Tom's desk. "This is between us. I shouldn't say why the Company's on this." His voice softened. "It's not just another international archaeological survey. That's our cover. We're replacing the Italians. The Russians come in next. We can't let Russia find it. If we can't have it, nobody's getting it."

He's half lying. Foreign digs are watched. Tom heard the rumors and blew it off as a student. He had since learned archeology is used for more than educational purposes. Money leverages coattail riding scientists into complacency. Why wasn't Murphy simply bribing him? *He's after something he ain't saying.*

"You'll want a watchdog on me," Tom said. "Callahan failed. I'm not tolerating another ham-fisted moron hanging on me. I won't put up with it. You send one like him—"

"Callahan screwed up. Relax. I'm going myself." Murphy leaned in again. "You'll need me given the political situation. Do all the legitimate archeology you want. The fact is you must. America wants that sub. We only need to locate it. We don't extract it. Others do that later, after the survey's over and we're gone."

"Locate it? I thought you know where it is?" Tom said.

"I reburied it in a hurry twenty years ago. Lost its location. You aren't supposed to know. Take the deal. I won't stop you from publishing. You keep your job here. There are other anomalies not too hot for credits. Keep your finds. Publish if you have the balls." Murphy kicked back. "Cory's books are incomplete. Maybe you'll provide another chapter."

"I don't see how you'll let me do my own thing. I'll pass, thanks."

"Factions inside the Company support the Antiquities Department. Some work against us. What I'm telling you ain't for public consumption. Tell no one, not even the next Company man you meet." Murphy got up. "Don't cross me, Conley. Think it over. Call me."

Murphy handed him a slip of paper with a phone number on it. The man took his job file and left. Janis came in once Murphy was away with a screwed expression on her face. Tom crushed the slip of paper and tossed it into the basket.

"No good?" Tom asked. Of course, Janis heard everything.

"It's weird. I can't read him right. He's dangerous but not to us right now. He's okay on some levels. I'll play it back for Sally."

"Sally's paper tanked," Tom said. "She needs to stay and work on it. She can't go."

"We need her," Janis said. "The feds can rig anything. He said you can pick your people. Pick Sally. Make Murphy fix it."

"If you can call what he does fixing things, it's more the other way."

Working with him could kill his team's careers. The idea was gut-wrenching. Damned either way. Unseen movers made this situation. Saying that aloud invited a ride to the loony bin. Discover the wrong artifact and they'll plow him and his people under. *I can't let Murphy do that.*

"Take the offer," Janis said. "Wonder Woman's up for it."

"I'm at a loss," Tom said. "I won't screw Sally—"

"Sally will come," Janis said. "She's got loans. Working part time doesn't pay the bills. You ain't got nothing full time for her. This is a money gig, right. Paid staff. Hire her. I'll ask if she's up for it."

"Without a finder, it's a waste of time," Tom said wishing Jorge hadn't retired. "She's only a fire finder. I didn't say that, did I?" Was Jorge a finder or simply eagle-eyed? "Then again, I'd hate to waste my dig season sitting here."

"Every dig's a good dig, right?" Janis said. "Every little bit helps."

True and if they don't find Murphy's Bain, so what? Whatever they uncover can help assemble humanity's puzzle. Strike-out and maybe Murphy will leave them alone.

"About Sally's loans. This expedition isn't gonna pay a lot." Tom said. "I can't take Sally from her studies. It's all her parents care about. If we go, she'll have to continue online. We'll need satellite access. This going to cost Murphy big money."

"I'll let her know. She'll go. She'll hate you, but you'll get over it," Janis said. "We're meeting for lunch, see ya." Janis locked her desk and left.

Tom didn't see how they'd manage to smuggle out finds like on Cory's dig. The only way in and out of Turkey were by official channels. And the Turkish government doesn't play nice. They recently kicked out a French team working on a Roman Villa due to a political slight. Murphy's arrangements must be beyond local bribes. Big players involved. Tom shivered. It scared him on many levels.

"I'd be an idiot to go." He said aloud to hear pronounced wisdom. His chest didn't burn. It didn't itch. It didn't tell him anything. "Talisman my ass. I'm having it removed after we get back."

Volunteers only. He won't press anyone into danger. Whoever goes gets paid well or no deal. Big projects are prestige generators. It won't cost Berkeley a dime and they'll get the credit. Brownie points go a long way in academia. Tom was nothing to Berkeley but the department's chair-warmer. He hated being stuck on campus. He needed the balm of dirt under his fingernails.

"I talked myself into it."

Tom pulled Murphy's note out of the trashcan.

CHAPTER THIRTY-SEVEN:

TURKEY, TWO MONTHS LATER

Tom stood by as the last local student group's bus pulled into camp for a two-week field study. Tom didn't speak their tongue but a few in each class spoke his, English being the scientific standard. These kids were thirsty for the trade. Archeology was more a trade than a scientific inquiry there. Tomb raiding became a careful art. The scientific methods served thieves as well as educators.

"This place sucks," Tom said.

Two months in the field with no progress. The low valley's soil was deep and remixed over and over like a nine-dimensional puzzle in 3-D. Boreholes showed deep silt, evidence of catastrophic flooding. The general landscape directed seasonal mountain meltwater runoff into the lower grades bringing fresh deposits and more confusion year after year. Conley saw why the region hadn't been thoroughly explored. There weren't any tells nearby. The oldest materials rested twenty feet below grade. Deposits had come from many directions confusing which floods carried what away, or in, and when.

Antediluvian artifacts were mere flecks of spice in a spaghetti pot. Inactive farm plots dotted the valley between stoney open grounds. Such cobbles resembled Neolithic tools, but they weren't.

"Neolithic items mixed with Paleo and every empire since Babylon," Tom said, shaking his head in discuss on yet another unpromising morning.

Nothing interesting or important was found. *If these rocky hills and bedrock exposures could talk, they'd say, 'Tom, you're barking at the wrong tree.'* Turkish Army troops watched from the valley's ridges increasing tension. Cold at night and too hot all day, the military's protection only added more discomfort.

The local town people hated them, too. No beer runs into town. They didn't have beer anyway. No taking in the local culture. Tents and portable toilets were the only man-made structures. Other than black smoke rising from a new volcano on Lake Van, nothing moved in the sky, no jets or birds. Horizons in two directions blackened more each day. Tom's hopes reflected the skyline. He wanted out. Time pressed down on him.

Sifting mixed hard pack was dismal work. Unexpectedly, Murphy had been helpful, polite, and earnest. The man was enjoying himself. He was desperate to find it, but Murphy didn't show it. Murphy joined Tom.

"I'll go and welcome the crew, take a break," Murphy said. Tom stayed behind.

Murphy got the spirit. What a contrast. Callahan's work was half-assed. Murphy, on the other hand, worked hard, treated the kids well, and had a good eye. He ran between student projects. If a groundbreaking artifact popped, Murphy was there to snatch it. Too bad there was nothing discovered worth snatching. Sally walked up.

"Two weeks and we're out of here, thank God," Sally said as the bus unloaded. "I hope they brought firewood."

"I told Murphy," Tom said. "And beer. It's a tall order. He better pull it off."

"He didn't get the day laborers," Sally said miserably. "Look at them toothpick kids, skinny as beanpoles. Don't they eat? That girl has an antique metal detector, how cute. Is that the Ground Penetrating Radar you ordered? I'm going to my tent. I need a good cry."

Sally shuffled off. They had moved tons of soil and got little for it but blisters and backaches. Shoveling and sifting dirt without results all summer took its toll. Janis had spent more time sulking in the finds tent than digging lately.

"Have a good cry for me too," Tom called after her.

She didn't turn but sent up her middle finger. Tom was beat after yesterday's hard dig, but he had to meet the incoming group. Shovel bumming was hard, slow work. Results are what keeps one going and results weren't happening. He looked down at his sore feet. A flint blade lay there. He picked it up. *It's not a blade.* He tossed it aside. *Murphy's wasting our time.*

"At least students get experience," Tom said as Murphy rejoined him.

"You're frazzled," Murphy said. "I'll give the welcome speech after they get settled."

"Any of them speak English?" Tom said. "You're the dig supervisor, what's on the roster? Any hot tips?"

The boy's and girl's tents were separated on opposite sides of the camp. The boys had gotten off first and lined up away from the girls. Many of the girls wore dark hijabs and were well covered otherwise. Even so, one couldn't miss how malnourished they were.

"That crazy girl with the metal detector, she's a language major, speaks a couple of dialects I never heard of," Murphy said. "She'll interrupt. Mother was a UK citizen, Turkish descent, father an Afghani. Both dead. That's what I got on file."

"Great," Tom said. He didn't care about files. "She ain't an archeology student, just perfect. Now we gotta babysit a nut job."

"Think positive. By the way, Aadiya, calls herself Addie. She ain't Muslim." Murphy said. "I gotta check her machine. Not likely but it could be a bomb."

"Sally's beer will never make it past the blockade," Tom said.

Tom walked away thinking the Turkish Army was supposed to check for weapons.

"Don't be so sure," Murphy called after him.

They frisked everyone at the checkpoint on the only road in and out. The military searched his camp whenever it suited them. Maybe Murphy was right. They didn't find Janis's gun. Maybe the beer will make it in. Tom's nearby tent had a porch canopy so he retreated there seeking shade. He watched Murphy between fly bites. Murphy unscrewed Addie's detector face. No bomb, no shit. Even at this distance, Tom judged her metal detector was useless junk.

Murphy and the men unloaded luggage while the girl swung her detector around. The other young ladies huddled together ignoring detector-girl waiting for their bags.

Addie bent and picked something up and handed it to Murphy. He pocketed it. With everyone's gear debarked, Murphy and Sally led them to their segregated tents.

Murphy came back. Tom didn't get up. "That's that," Murphy said.

"What did she detect? Cigarette foil?" Tom said.

Everyone local smoked cigarettes. The grounds were full of butts, wrappers, and modern trash.

"No, just this," Murphy said handing Tom a blackened coin.

"Roman silver, denarius." Tom said. "Not uncommon but unusual here. I didn't know legions passed here." He rolled it around. "Coin's an early one. I wish we had that GPR unit. This is the best find so far. Even a cheap-ass metal detector gets better results than us."

"That thing doesn't work. No batteries. She must have seen it."

Tom's internals alarmed but he didn't let on. Something was not right. But he had a hard time trusting his intuition lately, and he never trusted Murphy. His birthmark throbbed for the first time in weeks.

"What about firewood and beer? Sally can't see without it." Tom said. He felt stupid still believing it. *Win or lose, she's an excuse for campfire beers.* "Did you get it?"

"To borrow Cory's phrase, does Homo Habilis shit in the woods?"

Tom didn't joke back. Why encourage the untrustworthy man? The last thing Tom wanted was to connect with the enemy. But something clicked into place. Detector-girl was clearly not like the others. Tom decided he had better keep an eye on her. *What's her name, Aadiya? Something's off with her?*

"Maybe things are looking up," Tom scoffed.

CHAPTER THIRTY-EIGHT:

THE FIRE

The next morning, after chow and his daily speech, Tom went back for his dig kit and noticed his cell phone blinking. Strange, they didn't have cell service. He hadn't charged the battery in months. Satellites provided communications.

"How'd I get a phone message?" He pressed play.

"Tommy, it's Mom. I have a request, more like a demand. I don't have time to explain. You must meet Richard in Cairo. When the opportunity comes, take it. Love ya."

"What the hell?" Tom tried to replay but the battery was flat dead. "I'm imagining things."

Another long, futile day followed. Field classes were taught, grid-lines set up, scratching took place, and nothing worth mentioning found.

After nightfall, students in bed, Tom set out with his campfire supplies walking into the dark without a flashlight. Sally and Janis went ahead to make a hearth. The spot was a mile from basecamp below an outcrop of bedrock. According to Murphy, it was out of the Army's view. Campfires were a universal pleasure in all cultures, but the new arrivals weren't invited. The local kids can't be found partying with beer-guzzling Americans. Cultural separation worked for him. Normally, incoming groups got his campfire briefing. He had no enthusiasm for it, even if allowed. His dig season depended on Sally's vision. Otherwise, the trip was a waste. A twelve-pack of compensation appeared as promised. Murphy also provided a fat joint.

"I should let up on Murphy a little." Tom said to the stary night.

Tom arrived clean. Nobody followed. He and Janis talked quietly while Sally settled into fire watching. Sally didn't mind background noise.

"I hope Dick-Tracy-Face doesn't come. Sally hates him," Janis said. "Look at that, she's vegged out already."

"I hope this works," Tom said kicking a stone. "It doesn't work unless she's close to an ancient firepit. This feels like the right spot."

He cringed at his own words. As time went on doubts about her abilities increased. Janis lit and passed the joint. He took a puff. He never smoked with students and rarely smoked at all before. He considered it a condemned man's last pleasure. Nobody around but them, the isolation eased his tension. It was nice sitting by a fire, beer in hand, stars shining on a clear night. Cooler conditions were much welcomed after the day's heat. He had not relaxed since arriving.

"Good shit," Janis said and passed it.

He hit it again and passed it to Sally. Sally had zoned out but she took it and smoked.

"Yeah, good shit," Sally repeated, her voice far away.

Sally sipped her third beer absorbed in the fire. The fire reflected in her eyes, but it showed a different fire. Tom saw people wearing skins and dancing within Sally's eye flames. *I doubted her. I'm an ass.* Tom took the joint and hit it.

"Good shit," Tom repeated.

"Better be. Cost the government thousands to fly it out of California," Murphy said approaching the fire. "Turks catch us with weed, it's jail time."

"Fuck a duck, I'm not getting anywhere. I can't hold it. Murphy ruined it." Sally snapped, coming out of the trance.

"Fine, I'll go," Murphy said with a snotty tone.

"Forget it," Sally said getting up. "I gotta pee." She stopped near Tom. "I hate that guy." Everyone heard it.

"This is going well, right Pros?" Janis took another poke on the joint. Sally faded into the darkness. "Fire's gone cold."

Tom replied by opening another beer. *Murphy's magic repellent.* The man took Sally's seat, picked up her stick, added wood, and poked her coals. They sat without speaking until the fire reduced. Tom decided on another beer and why not? This project was a bust. One damn Roman coin. He hadn't gotten a drunk on since freshman year. *One or two more beers ought-a do it.* They sat together in silence a long while.

"Sally's gone an hour," Janis said.

"I'll go get her," Murphy got up with a grunt. "I don't trust the Turks."

Janis popped out of her chair. "She's not in danger," Janis said with fiery confidence. "Leave her alone, Murphy, I mean it."

"I'm the goddamn security here," Murphy spat. His chair went over, his chest expanded. His fists balled. He pressed toe to toe with Janis. "What I say goes. Back off Cupcake, or—"

Janis pulled her revolver, cocked it, and shoved it under Murphy's chin within an eye-blink. Murphy stopped dead cold; mouth open.

"Or what?" She said, "You don't think Callahan disappeared on his own, do you?"

"What about it?" Murphy shot the question at Tom. "If you people—"

"Sit down," Tom said, "Sally's fine. You said you want on our side. Here's your chance to prove it. Trust her. Don't be an authoritarian asshole."

Murphy's emotions took control of him. Janis had never seen the Badlands. She had nothing to do with Callahan. Tom stifled a laugh. Of course, she knew all about it. Tom's team heard everything, such as, things Murphey would like to know. Tom hadn't shared much with Murphy. The man had yet to prove himself. Regardless, Janis' threat did the job. Tom bit his knuckle to prevent himself from cracking up.

"Anything happens to her I'm pulling the plug." Murphy said and sat.

"Here, pull away," Tom said sticking out a finger, "but I might fart."

Janis moved her chair out of Murphy's reach and laid the gun in her lap. Tom didn't know where she got it and didn't care. As far as he could tell, this gig was over. How that girl smuggled guns was a question for the sages and he didn't know any.

CHAPTER THIRTY-NINE:

ADDIE AND SALLY

Sally wandered the rocky fields looking for a bush and didn't find one. Short dried grasses offered no cover. Out of time, she squatted and watered the shoots. Looking back, the campfire was a distant glow. She had TP in her pocket but had left her camper's funnel in California. Somehow, she managed to miss her boots.

"Boy, that's lucky."

She resumed walking. Fires buzzed around her, different kinds, old and new. She skated under the stars sniffing for dead fires. Many people had passed there but she didn't pick up anything super old. That so many had come through confused everything. Age levels were too jumbled to sort out. Older fires entertained fewer people. The people in her dream-vision were who she wanted, but they were a grain of sand on the beachhead of time. She reached and saw camel caravans and sheepherders under the Roman Army layer. Too many small groups came and went for her to pin older ones down. Seeking tribes, she realized the tribe-ness of her current associations.

"Like it or not, Murphy's one of us."

Guilt flooded in about how she regularly trashed Murphy. His vibes weren't terrible. She hated what Murphy represented, but not him, not really. It was unfair of her to hate on him. She decided to make an effort to be nicer. Murphy aside, Sally's other concerns and questions pulled at her.

"Why am I even here? What are we doing?"

Campfires aren't working. Too many ghosts everywhere and nowhere. *Murphy's distracting me but Conley needs him.* The dynamic rolled around in her mind while walking aimlessly. Deep, smooth, currents struggled against rough, surface waves. She gave up trying to untangle it.

"Lots of stars, not too cold, why not enjoy it?" Sally caught sight of Addie's dark clothing ahead. "That's weird."

The local girl swung her broken detector like a *Weed Wacker.* Addie's device didn't work, but Sally suspected it had power. Addie didn't control it. It dragged her along. Sally snuck closer for a better look. Ten yards out, Sally was about to say hi when Addie stopped and scratched around with a hand shovel. She picked something up and held it high. It glinted in the starlight.

"Hey, Addie, what'd you find?" Sally called advancing.

The girl spun stuffing something into her jean's pocket. Addie's olive face paled. Sally had seen that raiding-the-cookie-jar look before. But fear shaded surprise.

"Hey, it's okay. I'm not ratting you out." Sally said, "Chill. What is it, a coin?"

"For my family," Addie said with tears forming. "They…We are quite poor. They are not my immediate family, you see. I am a refugee here. Father was a doctor. American bombs…" She wiped a tear away. "My host family is poor. I help, but they hate me, but they feed me and I…I…" Addie choked on her words.

"Slow down. It's okay really. Sorry I freaked you out." Sally said. "I'm a friend, okay?"

Addie sniffled and wiped her eyes. "I'm sorry to have spilt open, as I did, please don't tell. We need money."

She pulled the coin and gave it to Sally. Gold, a big one, Roman and worth many times its weight. It had to be over an ounce. Sally handed it back.

"Keep it. How are you going to get it out of here?"

"I have an unused orifice, no?" Addie said.

"Every girl has a readymade coin slot." Sally slapped her hands over her mouth. "I didn't say that, did I?"

Sally cracked up. Addie fell in. Addie's deep voice cracked with high squeaks which made Sally laugh more. Both tried to be quiet, but their attempt to hold back made them snort which, in turn, made them laugh harder. Sally welcomed it. Too much tension had chained her soul in place. The release untethered her.

"I like how you laugh," Sally said, wiping crud from her eye. "Girlfriend, I needed that so bad."

"I understand exactly."

They hung out confessing what they could never tell others. Sally shared Firewomen lore, stuff she never spoke aloud before. Addie admitted her detector didn't work. She used it to help her focus. If Addie's village knew how she found things, they'd cut her head off unless a warlord scooped her up first. Grave robber gangsters wouldn't care how she found stuff. Addie getting caught would be big trouble. The townies hardly tolerated her. Nonlocal, different religion, so one misstep and it's goodbye sister. Addie played the village idiot so people would leave her alone. Crazy being taboo. But her adoptive parents wanted that gold. Addie's latitude came with isolation. The conversation turned to the current drought.

"I cannot seek water, which they need. They will not accept me finding a well with this." Addie held up her machine. "They think divining is sinful."

"So, it's not just gold? You can find water. How about campfires, old ones?"

"Yes, I can do this."

"Would you leave Turkey, if you had the chance? What about America?"

"Nothing holds me," Addie said. "I am a UK citizen. I'm stuck here without papers. I would go if leaving were possible."

"Not impossible. I got an idea. Come with me."

Sally didn't see the fire and she didn't need to. Firewomen know fires. Sally led them over a low hill which had blocked the view. Sally spotted the distant embers.

"There they are, let's go."

CHAPTER FORTY:

CAMPFIRE

Tom didn't want to add fuel to the fire. It was getting late. He should have called it a night, but his chest throbbed, and he thought he should wait until it quit. Walking back on unsteady feet in the dark with half a bag on wasn't smart. He tossed on a few small bits of wood. The fire seemed about right.

The verbal hostilities between Janis and Murphy quelled but Janis didn't let up. She performed cowboy tricks with her revolver whenever Murphy opened his mouth. They weren't allowed to have firearms. Of course, she had one anyway. That Janis had smuggled in her piece must make Murphy think twice. *He'd be a fool to attack an expert shooter like her.* How she stashed guns was a mystery. Thing were quiet until Murphy grabbed for the last beer. Janis was saving it for Sally.

Janis recounted a story to mess with Murphy.

"First time I shot a handgun, "Janis began, "I killed a charging polar bear. Small caliber pistol, .38 snub-nose. I was seven. I wasn't allowed to have a .357...yet." Janis turned the cylinder of her handgun slow making each click stand out. "I shot it through the eye, one round. Brain shot. Skimmed its eye socket a little. Not my cleanest shot. I've improved a lot since then."

Her tale was actually true. Murphy didn't know that. The scare tactic worked anyway. Murphy gave up on his beer grab. The night had darkened. Tom's chest felt better and he stood to leave. *Sally must have gone back to camp.* Tom couldn't see to gather his gear, so he put the last of the wood on the fire.

"Great, it's wet. It won't catch," Tom said.

"Here comes trouble," Janis said pulling up her .357.

Tom's knees buckled. He didn't need "murderer" on his resume. Kill a Turk, go to jail. Tom braced for a shot. Janis stood ready. Sally and Addie came into the light. The wet wood Tom just tossed on the embers flared high. Sally had arrived and walked straight up to Murphy with Addie on her heels.

"We wanna make a deal."

"What kind of deal?" Murphy and Tom said together.

"What if I found a finder than can find anything?" Sally said.

"That'd be a big help," Murphy said rubbing the stubble on his cement-block chin.

"Can you get her out of here, make her part of the team?" Sally said. "If she helps?"

"I could make arrangements," Murphy said. "If she's good. Got to have results. We'll need something for the Company or extraction won't fly." Murphy sounded tentative.

"This place is old. I know there's stuff here," Sally said. "You'll see. Addie, what do you feel? Anything cool here?"

"There is pottery," she waved the vintage metal detector around. "Many campfires took place here over many years. Romans, Asian traders, Greeks, more and older, as well. Long list."

"That's bull," Murphy said. "We've already identified such artifacts."

"Shut up, asshole," Janis said. "Give the girl a minute."

"Under that chair, six inches, there is a Bronze Age spearpoint from Ur."

Tom grabbed the firepit shovel. "This is undisturbed soil. Plows can't get in here."

Exposed rock lay below the outcrop where they had set up. Soil eroding from the fields above had washed down filling pockets in between patches of bedrock. Tom dug into a wide crevice clearing away pottery shards until he found it. He rubbed the spearpoint on his pants and looked it over. It was black with age where not encrusted with matrix. It had the right shape. He scratched it with a penknife.

"It's bronze."

Tom didn't know that period well. He handed it to Murphy who said he collected ancient weapons. Murphy's face lit with a genuine smile.

"God help us, definitely Ur. If she finds it, you got a deal. She'll EVAC with us."

"What do you mean e-vac?" Sally said.

"You dump her…Kiss us goodbye," Janis said, "if you live long enough to pucker."

"Sucks when the jackboot is on the other's foot, doesn't it?" Tom said.

Janis slipped her gun into a hidden holster at the small of her back. Murphy's shit-eating happy face washed out. He got the message. Janis is not a finder of things but a finder of trouble. She was no one to cross and it seemed Murphy caught on. The depression of a crappy job lifted off Tom's shoulders. A breakthrough had come.

"Back to camp," Tom said. "Tomorrow comes early. This dig's about to fly."

After his morning speech with Addie interpreting, Tom assigned dig crews. The new group went with Murphy up and over the west ridge into a little swale for a surface survey. The class disappeared out of sight. The student's job was to locate concentrations of pottery shards, set up exploratory trenches, and sift the contents. Students were to practice site methodology. Nothing important was expected within the dead creek's rubble.

Tom stuffed his backpack with wood, tools, and beer for the effort. He, Addie, and Sally went east to a low hill running north and south. Farm fields below, rocky soil above. The difference in elevation wasn't great. They targeted the exposed bedrock band between elevations. Above, previously grasslands, water had stripped most of the topsoil and deposited it below. The farm's fields held that rich dirt. No sign of the dead antediluvian lake was in evidence. Topsoil infusions and blown-in dust had filled the lakebed. Floods relandscaped the basin dozens of times after 15K BP. Plenty of little rolling hills had been laid down like sand ripples on a beach.

Murphy had worked on core sample dating before the CIA snagged him. The lake's pre-flood shores had been tentatively identified until Murphy's Bain's was lost due to a fast exit under duress. The bedrock band was the oldest exposure. Tom stopped on the crest of the ridge to re-read Murphy's field notes.

'Submarine's encased in heavy flood deposits IE jumbled materials. Much of it doesn't belong, mountain and marine fossils. My geology group took cores from the Black Sea to Lake Van. No doubt a massive flood between them transpired. Let's see them kill this.'

"They won't publish flood events. Nothing Bible thumpers can misconstrue," Tom said before pushing on after the girls. Murphy said as much before sharing his old notebook. Tom got that message and another: U.S. policy trumps scientific research. *And the CIA trumps all.*

A mile out from camp Addie stopped swinging and called Sally. Tom dropped the handful of pottery shards he had collected.

"This is a firepit,' Addie said. "Unlike the others which are far older or very young. This fire was made during the marshland period just after the lake receded."

Sally lowered to the ground and put her hands on the spot. "It's hot, Fire Women was here."

"What do we do now Professor Tom?" Addie asked.

"Build a fire," Tom said lowering the pack. "We'll try one overtop the ancient one. I think it'll help."

"The power of three will set us free," Janis said evenly.

"What," Tom said.

She didn't answer. That phrase hit a nerve.

It didn't take long. The girls spread out around the firepit forming a triangle. Murphy caught up to them having seen the smoke. He left his group with a local assistant. Tom and Murphy backed away and sat in the shadows. Sally plopped down on the ground. She didn't finish her beer before going away. This reminded Tom of how Kenny would go away.

Sally spoke of and with whoever she contacted. It sounded like two people inside the same head. Maybe it was all inside her head. Tom couldn't say, except he thought it was real. He still wasn't convinced its magic. There must be a science behind it, such as, quantum mechanics or another physical aspect beyond his line of study.

"Yet to be discovered as Kenny would say." Tom whispered.

Notebook in hand Tom wrote what Sally said from her trance. His voice recorder refused to work.

****

"There's a small band. Male hunters and women," Sally said.

"'The water is leaving. The Goddess drinks it up. Fire tells me.'" Sally narrated. *"That's Fire Women..."* *'The old man, the young Fire Women's father, is proud. The shaman gave her blessing to his daughter. The elder Fire Women is dead. His child keeps the holy fires. Her birth name is finished. She is Fire Women. Lowland has red deer,'"* "Old Man's saying this..."

"'...No more must we eat goat. Again, we may lay our dead inside Mother Earth as before. No more will bird shamans give our dead over to vultures.'"

"He spat on the ground..." *"'I will rest in Mother's arms, in the place prepared for me. Earth and Water I honor. The cloud watchers insult we human beings.'"* "Why...Oh, I see, you came here for him." Sally said in her normal voice sitting up straight. "Fire

Women made him a fire to celebrate his life. He is sick and dying." Sally came out of the trance. "The others are talking all at once. I understand them, weird, right? I got inside her and she knew it. They don't want the elder to die. But it is his time. So sad."

Tears rolled down Sally's cheeks. Tom saw flames within those droplets like streams of lava. He shuttered when she brushed them away. Sally gulped a large portion of beer, moaned, and slumped again.

"*'Hush the fire speaks. She is here with us, he will live.'*" Sally said, rocking back and forth. "*'Wait, no, no that is not why she comes to us from the forward beyond. He will know peace,'*" Sally said to the vision. "*'We are Earth and Fire and Water and so we return. Our fire lives on.'* "I told her. She says they know that."

"*'The ground and wood are wet, and yet, fire cannot evade us. Tree Horn's sharp ears hear the monsters coming up from the river. Now we all hear them. Two with slick, yellow skin and one big eye. They are the hated masters. Bad spirits guide them...'*" "I see them. It ain't skin, it's a suit, a hazmat suit, or something like that." Sally said.

Sally's voice changed when she recited the words of the others. The voices became distant with faint echoes and harder to hear. The effect gave Tom the willies. It felt like Halloween.

"*'The Watchers float over the Earth. The people are afraid. They cry. The tribe runs toward the tomb. I want to run. Fire holds me, Fire keeps me but I must run!'*"

A young woman's voice spoke. It wasn't anything like Sally's voice. Tom shivered.

"*'No, stay, we need to see. We are Fire. We cannot perish.'*" Sally's voice said in chorus with many others. "*'We hear the High Men's words. A language we don't know. They talk to each other as they approach our fire. We panic and are curious. Fire protects us. One takes off his mask. As I thought. His head is too large, his jaw too big. They are people of the corrupted race. Watchers stand before us yet they cannot see our magic. I must run, I will run.'*" "No, you gotta stay, you must listen," Sally said. "*'I will stay though I do not understand. Fire keeps us.'*"

Sally continued another fifteen minutes. Tom listened but Sally lapsed into an archaic language no one knew. She occasionally mumbled in English. The tongue had no modern parallel he ever heard although Sally spoke it clearly at first. The deeper she went the less intelligible. Tom stopped writing."

"Addie's a linguist. I hope she can figure it out," Tom said setting aside his notebook.

Wisely, Murphy didn't speak. Addie continued jotting down whatever she could. Of course, Murphy had his recorder but it didn't work. Sally sat humming and rocking for an hour until her voice returned as the fire burned to embers.

"...the power of three, the power of three...Wow, that was weird," Sally said.

She stood and stretched. "I saw the crew of that sub. They wore environment suits, maybe diving suits, and they floated. Some kind of antigravity device. They were not like us. They removed their helmets and weren't concerned with us at all. They marched uphill." Sally pointed the way. "It used to be steeper."

"Who were they? What were they?" Murphy asked with excitement.

"Hominids, big heads, Neanderthal nostrils, big jaws. Taller than people. Fire Women called them Watchers. That's weird, right. I'm not sure what they were. Not Neanderthal, I don't think. Fire Women didn't know. For sure, they had crazy tech. They weren't gods."

"This is dynamite," Tom said with instant enthusiasm, but his mood soured. "It'll never fly without evidence."

"Murphy grabbed Sally by both arms. "What'd they say, what—"

Sally broke his grip. "Get off me. I don't know. I only know what Fire Women thought. They went up to the tomb," Sally pointed the way. "That's where she said they went."

"You know Sally knows Kung fu. You're lucky she didn't twist your balls off," Janis said.

"Shit," Murphy said. He looked like the wind had been kicked out of him. "That's it. We're done."

"Not yet," Tom said. All he had to do was keep quiet and this venture would be over. "I'm gonna regret asking, but Addie, can you find and follow the path?"

Addie took off swinging the detector. She moved up the rise fast. Tom and the rest followed leaving the chairs behind. Addie stopped a hundred yards upslope on the gentle incline. She stood before a mound of rocks protruding out of a hillside.

"There was a bonfire here, a sacrifice," Addie said. "There is a cave. I can't find a path leading away. Too much eroded." She touched a vertical rockface on the hillside. "In here."

"Great spot for a hobbit hole," Janis said.

"Yeah, a fire," Sally said extending her hands. "Not made by Fire Women. It doesn't have the vibe. It's buried, not deep."

Tom opened his folding camp shovel and tapped the exposed rock until a flat horizontal section rang hollow. Janis' camp-knife made quick work of removing the lichen and moss. The more she scraped, the more the surface appeared to have been worked. The slab's dappled appearance was typical of bashing soft stone with harder rock mallets. Tom put his hands on it.

It was eroded but readable. Such marks were easily overlooked. At a glance, it was not enough to warrant excavation. But a curious vertical line looked vitrified. Faint symbols were written on this glass. It hit him in the chest. Tom staggered back.

"This is a door, a freaking door seal!" Everyone closed in. "Same shit in Alaska, they're connected," Tom said. "Watch this." Tom tapped with his shovel for a small sample but large chunks cascaded off. "Vitrified stone. Too damn brittle. I lost the door's curse."

"The sub must be in the other direction," Murphy said pointing downhill. "We should—"

"Shut up, Murphy." Sally, Addie, and Janis said in one voice.

Their words ripple through Tom's chest.

Sally laid hands on the ground again. "This one didn't have a fire woman. But I can still see it. The ground filled in. The pit's here two or three feet deeper. Right in front of the door."

Tom dug at the slab's base and managed ten inches below the surface very quickly. "Less eroded here," Tom said. Murphy shone his flashlight in the hole. "Toolmarks are unmistakable. It's megalithic, a dolmen of some sort. Murphy, let's get a team up here tomorrow."

It was too late to get started. Tom and the girls didn't have lunch. The sun was on the horizon and Tom's empty gut complained.

Murphy protested. "Let's keep going—"

"That's enough," Tom said, letting his irritation show. "I'm gonna go eat."

Murphy's student team should be done for the day. Murphy never went back to release them. Tom hoped they had enough sense to go back to basecamp when the dinner bell rang. The local assistant prof, who Murphy left with the kids, was afraid of Murphy and might have stayed where put.

All dog-tired, hot, and dirty, they trudged back to basecamp excited but restrained. Chow was a mile away up and sideways. The power bar Tom munched six hours ago ran out of gas. Murphy also showed signs of exhaustion, but had enough get-up-and-go to race ahead of the rest. Tom suspected Murphy ran to call in the feds to shut down the project before the Turks caught on. Half a mile out Tom looked back. The Turkish Army was snooping around his find.

"That's the end of Murphy's sub," Tom said and picked up the pace.

CHAPTER FORTY-ONE:

BREAKOUT MORNING

Tom was site director, but Murphy held the real power. It didn't bother Tom until Murphy pulled everyone off other projects and redirected them to the new find. Student diggers removed the topsoil and big rocks a few feet down around the general area and four feet at the vertical rockface. They plowed right through Sally's firepit. Flat bedrock lay exposed by lunch time. Grunt work done, Murphy sent the locals packing before the bell rang. Tom wasn't pleased.

"This is their land. They should be present." Tom complained. "The edges are melted. These kids aren't stupid. You can't hide it."

"The seeds of inquiry spread fast,' Murphy agreed. "We gotta get in and out quick." Murphy rubbed his chin. "Lunch is good cover."

He didn't find what he came for, but Murphy reacted to the discovery like Callahan would. Time had made the doorway above grade unrecognizable but below grade, the story was plain. Tom confirmed the door's shape. He knew vitrified stone when he saw it. But how? No soot. It wasn't done by any fire that Sally could read.

"Stone doesn't melt easy," Tom said. "It has to be high tech."

Janis escorted the locals back to camp and she would have stayed if trouble was underfoot. Tom had to trust Murphy although, intellectually, trusting Murphy was a bad idea. Tom's latest dream featured Kenny's voice on the wind repeating, 'Trust Murphy.'

"I'm going out of my mind," Tom said tapping the door with a rock hammer.

"Say again?" Murphy asked.

"Forget it." Standing in the hole Tom tapped top to bottom to be sure. "This looks good. The top is thicker. Break it open here, waist level?"

Murphy examined the spot. Tom hated to admit it but Murphy the geologist proved handy. Tom stuffed his resentments although it still galled him how a trained scientist could turn his back on progress. And for what, national security? Nothing in history was secure. Nations are temporary. New finds change historical perspectives every season.

"It is weaker," Murphy said in agreement. "Whatever did this wasn't primitive." Murphy backed up scratching his chin. "No doubt vitrified. This info can't get out."

"But it's a tomb," Sally said. "I know it."

"Many such melted walls are known. The Roman fort in Shrewsbury, UK, for example," Addie said.

"We gotta see what's inside," Tom said. But breaking the protocols of archeology pushed against his training. "We need to do this fast, damn it…but careful, easy—"

"Fuck that, bust it open," Murphy said. He called Janis on the walkie-talkie. "Janis, let them eat, after, bring them back but not fast. Stall them."

"Okay, fine," Tom said.

Tom began chipping the door at center just above the hole's bottom. Brittle materials fell away quickly. The seal crumbled altogether as he pounded. Murphy shoveled glass heaving it onto the refuge pile. With the evidence gone, Tom wacked away at the door harder. At three feet from bottom the rock became too thick for his rock hammer. Tom had cleared enough side to side in fifteen minutes to get his head inside. Murphy, on hands and knees, pulled Tom back and crawled forward with a flashlight in hand. Murphy lit the cave and immediately scurried back.

"Something's moving!" Murphy rolled to his feet, dropping the flashlight. "What the hell!"

"What, a ghost? You scared?" Sally said from the lip of the excavation. "What a puss. Bullies are always pussies."

Murphy's hands trembled. Tom's curiosity drove him. He snatched the flashlight and peered in.

"That explains Sally's observation," Tom said. "Antigravity footwear and it still works. A pair of boots seem to be floating above a table slab."

The team each took a turn looking inside. Artifacts were coated with dust laying on a rough-cut floor. Primitive items: stone-caved bowls, hammerstones, stone blades, the usual Neolithic assemblage with startling exceptions. Baskets that age were only known by tiny scraps and yet a reed basket survived. The interior's preservation was uncanny. Yellow boots hanging midair over a stone altar was beyond wild expectations.

"No body, or bones," Tom said. "Muslim students will be fine with it."

"Forget that," Murphy said, "we'll scoop up everything and git before they come back."

The debate began. Twenty minutes of heated discussion between Murphy and Tom ensued. Conley defended science while Murphy responded with political reality. Meanwhile Sally and Addie chipped the hole bigger.

"What about radioactivity," Tom was saying when a clump of dirt hit him from behind.

"You two dickheads need to shut up," Sally said. She wiped the dirt off her hands. "There's an Army truck up there and it's coming this way." She pointed at the top of the rise.

"This gets buried," Murphy said. He grabbed Tom's arms and got in his face. "You can't publish this! Anyone sees this, game over. The Company will jump all over you, all of you." Murphy stink-eyed Sally who was recording him on her cell phone. "I got explosives. I'm not giving this to the Turks. We can't."

"There is no we, Murphy, you're going back on your word," Tom said shouting. "What about the locals? This is Neolithic, maybe older. It's the most important find of this region. Way beyond politics. It's important…It's, oh hell…"

Tom crumpled down onto a low bolder with no idea what was right. He had nowhere to go with this. He felt like a rock surrounded by hot lava. He had to stand up to Murphy. Killing this find was more than he could stand.

"No bombs, Tod. We must save what we can."

"They're calling in their bosses," Sally said. "Military's looking to scoop up treasure. That's okay, there ain't no gold here, just an unused grave. Nothing they'd want, right? So let them have it."

"We gotta give the Trucks something," Tom said. "You said that going in, Murphy. Sending them back set off alarms."

"I know, I know…let me think," Murphy said. "Crawl in there, remove the high tech." Murphy said. "Let them have the typical stuff. That suit you?"

"That or blow it all up." Tom's chest burned so bad he couldn't stand it. He didn't know if it was a warning or approval.

"You aren't supposed to know, but if we don't bring the Company results, it ain't good but…if you play ball, they will back off."

"If that's copper, the ax head stays." Tom said speaking of what he saw from the entry. "It's anomalous for Neolithic. A lost moment. Maybe the first attempt at copper working. Give the Turks something sensational. Pushes the copper age closer to where it belongs and takes the heat off us. It won't hurt your stupid establishment narratives."

"I can live with that," Murphy said. "It'll cost me."

"Let's do it. Grab the boots and run." Tom said.

Tom helped Sally into the chamber. She called out all that she saw quickly. Addie recorded. The chamber wasn't big yet full of pristine primitive afterlife stores. Some items were never seen before in this context. The only high-tech items were the boots, which Sally quickly handed out. Murphy snatched them before Sally had time to squeeze out of the hole. The CIA man ran for the Jeep and drove off before the Army's truck rolled downhill toward them. The hole they bashed wasn't big enough for a big man. The local students would manage it. Sally brushed herself off while Tom followed Murphy's Jeep racing over the ridge and out of sight.

Addie closed in. Sally, Tom and Addie spoke in low voices fearing the Army's remote listening devices.

"There should have been two yellow suits in there," Tom said. "You said they had helmets."

"Disintegrated into dust," Addie said. "Nothing is left. You saw that yellow dirt."

"Nothing iron or plastic could have survived," Sally said.

"The boots' power pack must have preserved them." Addie suggested.

"We'll leave everything else, it's fair and good cover," Tom said. "Great, I'm thinking like a spy."

"Yes, that is wise," Addie said.

Tom's thoughts raced in circles. Antediluvian plastic? The only evidence just got sucked into the CIA's black hole. Cory's idea again proved true. Advanced people, not us, had ruled the Earth. Tom saw why governments can't let that fly. Government career killers keep everyone in line. Tom wondered how many amazing things have been hidden. Murphy wouldn't dare share this. Anti-gravity being a CIA man's dream find. Murphy was in for big accolades.

"What about the dirt, won't they sample it?" Sally said.

"It'll pass for mineral deposits. No time to remove it," Tom said. "The Army will step all over it." The girls locked on him. Their unspoken question was his, too. "What we do now is nothing. We wait. Play it like any dig. Follow the rules, and keep quiet."

An Army personnel carrier arrived. A dozen armed men spread out. Addie explained the site to the man in charge. The Turkish captain got on his knees and looked with a flashlight, which satisfied him, but he and his men didn't leave. The soldiers were too big to enter wearing their gear. Tom, skinner since arriving, didn't fit either. The soldiers searched Tom and found nothing. They didn't search the ladies. Tom's team continued clearing material away from the entry while eyeballing the guards who eyeballed them right back. After an hour the boss guard got into an argument with Addie. She translated that the Army wanted site activities stopped. The Army's mistrust boiled over.

The tension broke when Murphy returned with a busload of excited students followed by a military staff car. The kids hurried downhill toting shovels and big smiles. Addie spoke to the Turkish commander while Tom organized students.

"What'd you tell him," Tom asked Addie.

"I said, 'The Americans aren't taking our heritage away.' He thinks I'm Afghani and I naturally don't trust you. He knows I've been here the whole time."

A bit of glass ruble still covered the doorsill. Students removed it and widened the whole excavation pit so more people fit. Murphy's show of good faith was working. The Army backed up but not out. Managing became problematic. More Army people swooped in as the kids slowly removed soil and began sifting. Before long, servicemen took over student activities. The Army made short work of the remaining overburden. Every shovel full should have been sifted and cataloged. The Army pushed the kids back giving them room to swing hammers and bashed out the rest of the door. Chunks flew inward contaminating the site. Tom hated the lack of professionalism on display.

"I got no room to talk," Tom said to Murphy. "At least Turkey gets credit for screwing this up."

"This is good," Murphy said. "I need them distracted. The bigger the better."

The University of Turkey landed their A-team by way of helicopter within two hours. That anomalous ax head won't be dismissed, Tom thought. Turkey would enjoy new fame. Addie and the other women were forced farther back. When the big shot Turkish archaeologist arrived, he took over. The Army usher Tom's people off the dig site. Tom was disgusted. No professional credits would come of it and that was just one of his problems.

"Send out what we have?" Tom asked Janis in the finds tent. "Put out the word, upload video to the internet? Cell phone video sucks but it's not nothing."

"Do polar bears crap on the icepack?" Janis said and it wasn't a joke. "I'll need everyone's phone, whatever's recorded, all the raw footage."

Janis's quickie report and pictures got around fast. The news spread within the hour. Tom feared he'd get the hatchet job like they did to Cory. But that won't happen to an acceptable find and his name won't be on it. Mede was right, things do slip out. Nobody in academia accepted Cory's material from that Alaska dig. The media worked overtime to discredit it. Cory made bank off the publicity.

True to his word, Cory's new book didn't mention Tom Conley. Tom's precarious position remained safe. All the same, this experience provided questions he never thought to ask. Maybe Amos told the truth. Amos didn't need to spin lies. And why would he?

This project was over although Tom had a good idea of where that sub was buried. Tom decided to keep that to himself.

"This is the grand distraction Murphy wanted, but why?"

CHAPTER FORTY-TWO:

JAIL BREAK

Murphy called an end to America's involvement at breakfast with a Turkish general at his elbow. The Turks took over. The Army watchers remained suspicious. The general openly accused them of stealing. Thus, the Army formed a wide ring around basecamp. The Turkish students were told to pack it in as well.

"No American is to leave," Were the general's last words which surprised Tom.

"I'm getting us and it out," Murphy said quietly, poking Tom in the ribs. "Real soon, get ready. Pass the word. Wait for my signal. I'm working on something."

"What signal?" Tom said miserably.

He didn't get an answer. Murphy took off out of the mess tent. Murphy was hot to get his prize out of country, but the Turks tightened security. Tom didn't see any way out. By noon, tents had been searched. Personal items rifled. A soldier stole Callahan's silver eyepiece out of Tom's kit. *Murphy's working on 'something', working on what?* Bribes were Tom's guess. At four p.m. the answer came in the form of three U.S. Military helicopters. Two Cobra jet gunships and an armed Huey. They appeared in the distance out of nowhere flying up over the rise.

"Run Mr. Conley, run," came Kenny's voice clear as white glass out of Tom's own mouth. Tom didn't move.

The choppers came in fast and low out of the sun and straight into camp. Dust blinded the sentries. One gunship hovered over the guard station forcing them to take cover. They didn't touch down. Armed men in black uniforms jumped out of the Huey. Tom stood at his tent petrified. *Run Mr. Conley, run! Oh yes run, run, run...* The few Turks there were overwhelmed but for how long?

Murphy jogged by yelling, "Get your gear, let's go!"

He headed for the girl's tent. Murphy had pushed everyone to get packed. Tom brushed him off and wasn't ready. He felt like an idiot stuffing his duffel bag. He expected a long, slow, dusty truck ride to a half-ass airfield fifty miles away and not a sudden escape. Tom exited straight into a whirlwind of dirt and chaos. Sally, Janis, and Addie were ahead of him hauling backpacks. Beyond the scene, Turkish military vehicles raced toward basecamp. Tom ran for the Huey. Addie swung her duffel up to the door gunner as Tom arrived. Murphy came with a Marine and helped Tom up.

"Get in, they're shooting!" Murphy shouted.

The Marine stood station swinging his gun. One at a time the girls climbed in with the help of Tom and Murphy. Murphy held Addie back. The noise was tremendous and worse when the door gunner let go a burst. Tom's head rang. Addie's face screamed dejection. Tom hung out the door, reached and grabbed Murphy by the collars and yelled into Murphy's face.

"What're you doing!?"

The door gunner opened up with a longer burst. One chopper lifted off, circled low, and returned fire.

"She can't," Murphy shouted over the rotors. "I haven't made arrangements."

"Why" Tom shouted.

"Overloaded."

"I'll stay." Tom yelled.

Tom swung his legs out. The Huey revved its motor. The men who came with the Huey raced toward them. Tom dropped down and stepped away. The soldiers scrambled in. Murphy grabbed Tom's face and yelled.

"I'll stay. I said I'm with you. You go!"

Murphy waved Addie forward. Tom's heart burned. Taking Addie without a visa was illegal as hell. Tom climbed in after her. The chopper's engines whined and screamed as it gained altitude. It dawned on Tom that Murphy wasn't on anybody's team but his own until now. Maybe Tod Murphy wasn't so bad after all.

"See you at Berkeley," Tom called.

Murphy didn't hear. The airship pitched sideways with Tom's legs dangling. Addie and Janis pulled him in. The bird tilted nose first and gained speed. They made straight for the Black Sea flying low under radar. Tom worried about the hilltops. He leaned close to Addie's ear.

"Your notes. You saved them? Can you transcribe?" Tom said.

"Sally annunciated well. I am a linguist. I will know what they said."

"Don't tell Murphy," Tom said.

She passed the message to the others. He wanted a lid on it until they reached Berkeley. Whoever these people were, and whatever happened to them, he didn't know but he wanted to. He'd bet Amos's ancestors made the boots. The ground raced by while Tom sat rejecting his suppositions one after the other. Conventional didn't account for this. Distant smoke billowing in several directions filled him with dread. War or fires? It didn't seem natural.

Tom's relationship with the CIA wasn't natural either. But Tom and Murphy shared a connecting obsession: to understand the past. Same goal, different agendas. What drove Murphy was simple patriotism, Tom thought. Tom didn't have Murphy's reasons. Tom's internal drivers had no Earthly source. Desire came from deep within unlike Murphy. He didn't trust the man. Murphy had answers and Tom wanted them badly enough to tolerate the CIA.

I'll face down the devil if that's what it takes.

Finding Amos's masters would prove everything. Tom felt he had to solve it or lose his mind. He rejected adopting Mede's slow methods to preserve a career which was failing anyway. Cory's method is dangerous. Are intellectual shackles worth the price? Yes or no, he wanted whoever sent Amos punished. Tom dreamed of Kenny's prison. Who took him? Murphy's CIA buddies or Sally's hidden High Men. *Amos's people.*

Tom didn't understand how it worked, or why, but unseen forces stood in opposition. He had to overcome them. *'To reach the bottom one must enter the well.'* That quote wasn't his, but he accepted it. The burning stopped. His mind flashed danger and he didn't care.

I either lost my mind or Pandora's Jar broke wide open.

CHAPTER FORTY-THREE:

MEDE REVISITED

om returned to Berkeley with a black cloud over his head and he wasn't the only one. A volcano had risen off Catalina Island, though many miles away. Its smoke hung thick over the Bay Area. The same condition had developed in many places around the world. The world outside his Berkeley office had gone monotone gray.

TV news downplayed the danger of new oceanic volcanoes. The internet blazed with debates and religious doomsayers. Fundamentalists called it "The End" and few disagreed. Geologists argued the why and how of black-smokers covering the planet with no resolve. Tom wished he knew more about volcanism, but he never had an interest. Dad died on a submerged oceanic volcano. Dark skies brought back Dad's death. In the wee hours, he'd bolt upright sweating, guts churning, chest-thumping reliving himself hanging over *Little Finder's* rail only to blink and find himself in sickbay with Wailer's bad news. He had no memory of diving in.

"I hate volcanoes."

He returned in time to set up classes for the coming semester. He had his first lecture hall time slot secured, a dream come true, but it was not to be. Coastal evacuations weren't yet called for although on everyone's mind. Classes were canceled that morning.

"Look outside," Janis said standing at his door.

Tom spun the chair. Gray ash flakes fell and not for the first time.

"Snowing again, so what?"

"Look down."

Dr. Mede stood in the parking lot with an open umbrella covering Sally and Addie. Sally pointed up at Tom's reflective window. On impulse Tom waved, but they couldn't see him. Tom's mood improved. Mede was the right man to talk shop with. Tom needed a break from building worries. He missed the man. Tom had learned a lot from Mede. Tolerating Mede's crazy ideas was the cost of riding the doctor's coattails. Mede's ideas weren't crazy after all.

Mede entered Tom's office bustling with energy, his over-white dentures reflected the fluorescent lights. He hadn't changed.

"Tom my boy, good to see you, very good, good indeed!" He thrust out a paw. Tom took it. *He's as strong as ever.* Mede's touch charged Tom's batteries. "I'm hearing good things about you. That middle east project, simply revolutionary. That's how you chip away paradigms. Copper ax, 15K BP. They can't scratch that off the record, ha!"

"Doctor Johnathan Mede, as I live and breathe. Have a seat, drink? I got whiskey." Tom said.

"Love one. Two fingers, please. I don't have time for three. Murphy is on his way here. Ladies, come in, shut the door, you too Janis." Mede said.

That was just like him, giving orders people wanted to follow. The same words out of Murphy's mouth would have caused a protest. Mede slugged half his drink and set the mug down carefully.

"Small talk later," Mede said. His happy expression faded taking a chair. "I've something you folks need to hear. I'm not sure where Murphy is on this line. I don't trust him, not yet. At any rate, I've been in touch with Richard Wailer and—"

"Wailer! Hold on, I—" Tom's gut reaction burst out.

Mede slapped the desk hard. "Stop! Listen, will you, listen," Mede yelled.

Tom's mouth snapped shut.

"That's better. Me and Rich, that's Richard Wailer, been working on this a few years." Mede lowered his glasses. The girls moved closer. "You don't approve? Get over it, Conley. We're old buddies. I'll cut to the conclusion and support it later. We have evidence, you've seen some of it."

Mede downed the rest of his drink.

"He ain't messing around," Janis said.

Everyone leaned toward him.

"Amos didn't lie," Mede said. "There is a human group related to us. They live underground, literally under the surface. They have topside representatives with claws into everything, world governments, spy agencies, the highest places. They, via prox- ies, control us. They kidnapped your boy, Kenny Parks, right out of the government's hands. That's power."

"What! Murphy lied! He said the CIA has him," Tom jetted out of his seat. "That's why communication stopped. I thought the government…Oh, no." He low- ered himself back down.

"Feds had him. No longer and Murphy knows it. This they don't know. Kenny's has Women's Magic. We don't know how, or why, but that's how he does it. That boy is dangerous. Wailer parked him at a group home and invited the CIA for safety. The Watchers nabbed him anyway. Murphy was involved with research on Kenny."

"But, but…but Murphy said…" Sally cried. "He told us his history, okay, but crap—"

"Shut up, let him talk," Janis said.

"Murphy lied, fine. Doesn't matter now," Mede said. "Rich has men laced into the fabric, men like me, lawmen, you name it. Insiders take Watcher's money, too. Some of them rather take Rich's money, even Murphy, although he may not have known it. Rich dug out a lot of facts the clandestine way. His people, anyhow. Rich is also missing, by the way."

Mede motioned Tom to pour and he obliged. Tom sat back down. He doubted Mom had sent that message about Cairo. It read like Wailer wrote it. Mede took a sip and continued.

"These puppeteers, these Watchers…nasty people. They're behind the volcanoes. You know this, Tom, deep down. You were with Rich at the first one. He told me the story. That amulet's a device. It concentrates magic. If Bert didn't grab it, we'd all be dead by now. Your dad stopped the machine. Unfortunately, he passed the problem to you. Watchers mean to kill humanity off. First attempt failed. They aren't finished."

Tom rose, staggered backward and leaned on the window sill. His internal merry-go-round wouldn't stop. His chest burned with a new kind of heat, a fire without pain. Intuition screamed, "truth," but his mind wouldn't give up on logic.

"Where' the hard evidence?" Tom said. I don't see how this can be…I can't…I don't want to believe it…but…I know you're right."

"Them black smokers are machines lad, believe it," Mede said.

"Doc Mede ain't lying," Janis said. "Am I right ladies?"

Addie put her hands out. Sally lit a cigarette lighter before her eyes. Tom waited for their judgment. He accepted these women were special before Turkey. Now he trusted them without reservation. Each one nodded approval.

"You'll have to smoke them out," Mede said. "There's more."

Tom said, "You have the floor, Doctor."

Mede explained how he pulled together the idea and how he confirmed these hidden men exist. Tom had provided evidence and clues without knowing the implications. Wailer's agents delivered, too, such as Kenny's captured emails which were sent without touching a computer for two weeks after his disappearance. The timeline made sense. After Kenny's kidnappers went underground, email messages dried up. Soon after, Tom's nightmares of Kenny's captivity began.

"The pieces fit," Tom said.

Mede chuckled. "That had me going, computers, that boy don't need 'em. He must have accessed his captors' phones while on the lam. He's been cut off. They put a block on him."

"If there's a way to save him, I'm in." Tom's blood boiled.

"Cory broke it open."

Mede went on explaining and spoke of how Wailer backed Cory. The Finder Foundation, Wailer's organization, pulled strings to place Tom. Tom chastised himself for not seeing it. The Foundation, to him, was just another of the funding entities floating around universities. Wailer's researchers had concluded Tom's amulet was an ignition device. The idea never crossed his mind.

"A starter key makes sense," Tom said. "I thought it had a purpose as a boy."

"Them smokers were built to vent internal pressure for planet wide stability. They must have used them millions of years ago," Mede said. "Run them all at once and it's goodbye Mabel. Takes two keys like our nuclear missiles. Ted's ROV photos IDed two on that alter. Too bad they found a way around it." Mede pointed outside and tipped his mug. "The Kraken's been loosed."

"How do we stop it?" Tom said.

"Women's Magic," Mede swept his hand toward the girls. "But them bastards have lady repellent. Kenny can't help. Too bad. The boy transits through time. He might have gone and got the thing but it's too late now. I wish Rich figured it out sooner." Mede spread his hands in surrender. "Rich thought you'd be good for the boy. He had a premonition about you."

"Yeah, really good, I got him kidnapped," Tom said in a miserable tone.

"That's not true." Mede came back quick. "You did well. His talent would've gotten noticed eventually. Rich screwed everything sideways. They didn't catch onto you, did they? Kenny distracted them, maybe that's his job. The Watchers took him for bait. Rich is their quarry. They want him. They expect him. They won't see you folks coming."

Janis walked to the window. "Murphy's pulling in."

"What'll we do?" Tom said.

Mede slid an envelope across the table. "It's from Rich's girl Sam. It's info on where to meet him. You must get to Africa before air travel's shut down. Trust Murphy or not, I can't say, you'll have to figure that out, but he's your ticket out of here. I gotta git before he sees me."

Mede made a quick exit. Tom read Wailer's note. It gave an address and nothing more. The writing wasn't familiar. He didn't have time to wonder.

Murphy came straight in with a folder in hand. He slapped it down on Tom's desk. The folder said, 'Eritrea, Africa' written large on the cover.

"Good to see you all. Take a look, tell me what you think?" Murphy backed up a step. "You'll get full credit, of course."

Tom kicked back in his chair. Tom's dearest interest was paleoanthropology. Younger archeology was a secondary interest. He dreamed of digging for humanity's ancestors. He saw forgotten Calico as his opportunity to carve out a career within Berkeley's human origin studies. Places like the Rift Valley, Djibouti, and Ethiopia were reserved for top men. Cracking the mysteries of Calico was his best shot of finding a big puzzle piece. Nobody but Berkeley would touch that site and they wouldn't either if they hadn't been bequeathed the Calico assemblages. That basement full of orphan artifacts gave Tom elbow room and hope of a big discovery. Africa was not even a remote career possibility for him and yet, it fell out of the sky.

"What I think is you're playing me. You almost got us killed. Damn it, I'll read it."

Tom flipped through the pictures, maps, and text without seeing much. Eritrea is stabbing distance from Egypt, and also, very near to where Louis Leakey uncovered his greatest finds. Eritrea edged humanity's beginning. Tom's mouth watered at the prospect. The world's best homo deposits within a spear's throw and Tom couldn't do a damn thing about it. Wailer said to meet him in Cairo, Egypt.

"Interesting," Tom said sliding the folder back to Murphy who snapped it up. Tom decided to go but first he played Murphy. "Unusual cave paintings. So what? That's not my specialty."

"This ain't no cake-walk," Murphy said. "Harsh conditions, hostile locals, the usual. This trip will be as hard as petrified camel turds. I swear this is the last time the Company will ask. I told them you've had enough, ready to break. Okay, I lied, you still got juice. You up for a little adventure?"

"Do I have a choice?" Tom said. "I'll go if the girls go." Each one indicated agreement. "Let me see that again."

Murphy slid the folder over. Tom calculated. Site was close enough to Cairo to dive if no other way. They'd give Murphy the slip. Murphy couldn't be trusted. Who else bought Murphy's allegiance? Cairo is two thousand miles from the dig. What to expect wasn't in Wailer's note, only one address, a tourist bar. Tom had his passage overseas. Riding shotgun with the devil was his only option.

Murphy's file wasn't enough to convince Tom. The site wasn't worth the effort. Murphy designed the file to capture Tom's attention. There was more unsaid in it than said. Thinking of Wailer's note, Tom realized it was written in Mom's handwriting. If Wailer is in Cairo, so is Mom. What Dad had said on the day they boarded *The Finder* came to him. 'If it was easy, everybody would do it.' Dad spoke of diving adventures. The same logic applied. North Africa is rough in the best of times and the times weren't good. Driving north, if it came to that, was going to be a bitch.

"Okay Murphy. We do this my way or forget it," Tom said.

"I can live with that," Murphy said.

"Or die, "Janis said.

Tom got up and poured a round of Old Triumph for all. Murphy wiped his sweaty brow and slugged it down. Maybe Murphy wasn't such a good liar after all.

CHAPTER FORTY-FOUR:

AFRICA

Tom didn't need his birthmark to tell him time was short. New volcanic black smokers were rising everywhere. But there, in Eritrea, the sky remained clear. Two volcanoes had popped in the Red Sea and another in nearby Sudan but the winds favored Tom. Murphy was in and out and away most of the time arranging a caravan. They had to cross a dune sea to reach the project location. This allowed time to relax, but he couldn't. Janis and Addie used Murphy's excursions away to make other arrangements. The effort to escape Murphy was on. So far, Janis struck out on locating an airplane.

The Red Sea lay below his hotel room's balcony. Many shallow water ruins dotted the crescent-moon bay. Former stone docks, buildings, and jetties abounded. These waters were never properly explored. This bay had been the world's gateway to India and beyond since Alexander the Great. Greek and Roman merchants knew Eritrea well in their day. Shipwrecks aplenty, with many holding priceless artifacts, remained untouched.

"Wailer's wet dream," Tom said of the sea beyond his hotel room balcony.

The bay's hidden riches juxtaposed the extreme local poverty. His brand-new hotel was built in preparation for a tourist industry yet to come. Eritrea had recently been confirmed as the ancient Egypt's legendary land of Punt. Archaeologists from around the world were called to free Punt of its sands and watery graves. A hot sea breeze brushed Tom's cheek as he sipped his morning tea.

A knock came at his door. Tom yelled, "Come!"

Sally met him on the balcony with a miserable look on her face.

"What'd you find out?" He asked.

"Murphy's an asshole," Sally said. "He's supposed to get us out to the caves, but he's been sneaking around talking to crooked salt traders, and bandits, and not the military. This is a military dictatorship, you know. Nothing happens unless they let us. They got the trucks and stuff we need. Murphy's full of poop."

Sally was right. Three days there and nothing happening. The folder said the U.S. government joined Berkeley on this. The local officials knew nothing of the government's involvement. Murphy scurried around like a rat bribing the cat. No other Americans were housed nearby. Tom smelled something rotten and it wasn't dead fish.

"Something's off." Tom opened the job folder. His travel version was thinner than what Murphy first presented. The maps and photos were gone. "Why's the government interested in a petroglyph site anyway, what's the point?" Tom tried to remember the images but he had only glanced at them. "The real action's here in Massawa. No matter, we get a plane, we're gone."

"Murphy never did say how he wiggled out of Turkey," Sally said. "Claiming 'state's secret' is bullshit. I thought he's on our side?"

"What side he's on is doubtful," Tom agreed.

Tom had lost confidence in the man since arriving. Leaving Murphy behind was the right move. Tom would shoot the camels and steal the Jeep if that's what it took it to get clear of Murphy. The folder gave coordinates. Basecamp was sixty miles inland. Tom thought it a great place for early hominids, but not a good place to launch north from. They didn't need Murphy. The needed air travel but nothing was flying. Did liar Murphy get supplies dropped as he said? They could get whatever food and water needed for the trip and drive it. Tom decided he'd risk driving north without Murphy's supplies if that's what it took. First, they needed transportation.

"We gotta go today before Murphy returns," Tom said. "We'll skip the site and get what we need on the way."

"Get any visions? Messages? What about Kenny?" Sally asked. "I'm feeling heat up in Cairo, less here, it's totally like a nuclear bomb or something."

"I got nothing, and that worries me. I get pieces most nights, little dream snatches but...I don't know. One thing is certain—we must leave before Murphy comes back."

"We gotta get outta here with or without him. I hope Janis gets the airplane."

Over the balcony's rail two stories below a faded black SUV pulled up and parked. Janis and Addie got out in a hurry. A few minutes later Jains burst into the room.

"You guys, we need to go like now."

"I gotta pack—" Sally said.

"Forget it! Get your bug-out bag. No room. I got us an airplane. It ain't gonna wait." Jains said.

Tom grabbed a small backpack and stuffed in the essentials. He left the bulk of his things behind to make it look as if he was still around. Murphy might think they were out sightseeing. Tom left his prized dig kit in plain view. He never went afield without it. But he took Dad's old pocket knife. The rest didn't matter. He removed his wristwatch adding it to the deception. Everyone knew that watch had belonged to his dad.

Tom, Sally, and Addie took the back stairs. Janis met them behind the building. The SUV was a twenty-year-old Ford oil-burner with a nasty valve tap.

"I hope you filled the oil and checked the gas," Tom said.

"That'll never make it to Cairo," Sally said and slid into the back seat. "I hope the airport is close by?"

"We ain't going to no airport," Janis said from the driver's seat. "Got us hooked up with smugglers. Gave them all our American money. It's cool."

The car didn't have air conditioning and it had already hit 100 degrees.

"You spent all our money? How are we going to get by?" Janis ignored Tom and drove off.

Janis didn't know. Her Wonder Woman powers were on the fritz. Even so, power flowed from the north and even Tom felt it. An evil radiated out of the north forcing his team's abilities off-center. Janis smelled rats everywhere, but couldn't zero in. And she goes and hires a crook?

They took one of the few decent paved roads over the hills. Hill country held forests which were thicker on the coast side. Descending the far side, a dessert spread out before them. The highway edged the desert's flatlands splitting north and south. The tarmac could melt iron.

They stopped at the cross road. The smugglers' airfield was west of the pass according to Janis. Her GPS acted sketchy and Janis couldn't exactly locate the spot.

"Salt flats do make decent landing facilities." Janis said to quell the groups' complaints.

Tom wasn't comforted.

She drove north a few miles first, then made a U-turn and went back the way they had come. She repeated several times before pulling off into the sand to let a truck go by. Janis, both hands on the top of the wheel, rested her forehead there. Addie, up in the front, asked the big question.

"Do you not know the way? Did they not tell you where to go from the hill road?" Her tone was snotty.

"Sister, that's your job. I'm not good with directions, okay?" Janis snapped.

"Me? Did you not get instruction? I did not hear them give directions. How can I find when I do not know where to look?" Even tempered Addie let her inner bitch out and crossed her arms. "Is this not your responsibility? I find old thing. Airplanes are not old. Paaaa!"

"Should have brought your detector," Sally whined. "I'm dying for water." Sally turned and reached back into the rear compartment. "Water's gone, fuck a duck!"

"I do not need that device to use my talent," Addie said in a hard voice. "My skill is fine."

"That's bull," Janis said. "None of us feel right since we got here. I can't tell friend from foe anymore. Your talent sucks." The argument escalated, all three talking at once.

"Shut up, all of you," Tom said. He got out of the car. "I'm waving down the next car that goes by."

He slammed the door in frustration and walked away from the argument. He felt drawn toward a hollow hosting a clump of gnarled trees and thick brush off the roadside. Uphill had foliage, but the desert side of the road was barren except there. He spotted nothing else green except that patch. He walked toward it.

"That's curious. Must be water." He said arriving. He stood scratching his chin wondering if it was worth the effort to dive into the thicket for water. "Not an oasis. If there's water, it's too deep."

The place reminded him of a famous 19th CE. book, The Golden Bough, and Fraser's work on sacred spaces in nature. Such places were associated with nature goddesses and the Tree of Life. Tom stared into the thicket until the image of a woman formed within its leaves and branches. The foliage pulsed on heat waves. The mirage pointed out into the desert. He rubbed his eyes and she vanished.

"Heat stroke. I'm seeing things."

A particular dead branch grabbed his attention. Janis had shared Inuit shaman practices. Addie studied the languages of the deep past which spoke of magic. Tom's work on ancient cultures revealed numerous ancient people held feminine spiritual concepts in common. Such spirituality may have been universal in prehistory as witnessed by the Venus figurines found world over. The Golden Bough took many forms, springs, groves, tree stands, rock formations. Magician's wands were made of wood from sacred grounds.

"Magic sticks, I wonder." Tom touched the Y shaped branch. "It's a divining rod."

Old-timers used them to find water. Tom snapped the dry, dead branch off and trimmed it with his pocket knife. He returned to the car banishing his stick. The girls had exited and huddled together on the shady side of the car still arguing about where to go.

"Here try this." He handed the stick to Addie. "Direct from Mother Nature."

"What is this? I do not understand." Addie gave it back. "That cannot work."

"People used them to find water." Tom showed how they used to handle divining rods. "I thought it was a scam. Maybe not. You can't fool Mother Nature. But people get hoodwinked."

Addie took up the Y stick and it pointed at the car. "Open the door, please."

Sally obliged. Addie went in with the stick. The long end dove hard at the floor. Tom got on his knees and searched under the seats and pulled out three bottles of water.

"The damn thing works," Tom said. What else can Mother Nature find? How about an aircraft?"

Addie walked away from the car and worked the stick as if it was an old habit. It pointed out into the desert with force.

"It is that way. I see it. It is there, the airplane. Trouble lies there as well."

Janis faced that direction with her hands out.

"She's right, I feel it, I think, it's strong, but I'm not sure…To many conflicts to sort out." She pulled her revolver and checked it. "We could get killed. Get in the truck. Let's go."

"Easy on the water, Sally," Tom said. "We're going."

They proceeded into a sea of sand and waving heat. As the miles clicked away, the desert sands became flatter and mixed with salt. After an hour, they reached the salt flats proper. A makeshift runway came into view after another hour of speeding over stark-white salt. Their black Ford left them no place to hide.

"We slipped Murphy but good." Janis said. She slowed the Ford.

An airplane sat a quarter mile ahead along with several light trucks parked near a fuel truck. The Toyota had a 50-caliber machine gun mounted on its bed. Tom looked over Janis's shoulder from the back seat grinding his teeth. Their truck's gas was nearly gone. The motor was overheating. Janis slowed more and fingered the revolver in her lap.

Kenny's words came loud into Tom's mind, trust Murphy, trust Murphy.

"Sorry Kenny, Murphy's not here." Tom whispered. He wasn't heard over the crunching tires.

Janis slowed to a crawl. "Told ya it's cool. Nobody's shooting, right? Am I right?"

"Nobody's here," Sally said. "I don't feel good about this."

No one in sight. Janis parked next to a box van and shut the Ford down. Everyone got out. A four-passenger Cessna sat with its motor running. Janis holstered her gun.

"Where are those who drove here?" Addie said.

A man in black robes and headscarf came out from behind the cargo van. He yelled and shouldered an assault rifle. The intruder advanced, pointing his weapon at Tom. Janis turned, drew, raised her arm to fire and collided with Sally. Janis fell, face first, gun in hand. She pulled the trigger on her way down. The intruder went over backward while Janis face-planted.

Her gun produced an ear-splitting report. Sally clamped hands over her ears.

Tom rushed to the downed man calling, "You alright, you alright?!"

The man's face had a new hole where his nose belonged.

"He's dead," Tom backed up spewing bile. Walking a few steps, he fell on his knees retching. "I hate this! I fucking hate it! I'm a fucking archaeologist. It's supposed to be safe, Jesus!" Tom dry heaved.

"Crackers! Here comes another," Sally cried.

"Don't shoot! It's me! Hold on. Christ, you killed the pilot," Murphy said. He wore the same black robes as the dead man.

"He drew on us," Janis cried. "Point a gun my way and you're dead."

"That's fair," Murphy said. He pulled off the local coverings and covered the body.

"I warned him and he did it anyway, poor bastard." Murphy helped Tom up. "Said I'm with you, didn't I. Sent you a message. Thought I'd meet you here. Found it, I see. That was fast." Murphy pointed at the body. "Told him, no guns. We use these guys on the regular. He should have known better."

Someone handed Tom the last bottle of water and he rinsed his mouth before a draught. "What now?" Tom said. "There must be enough gas between these trucks to get us north."

"The Cessna is fueled. Come on. Let's go." Murphy started toward the plane.

"You fly?" Tom asked.

Murphy chuckled. "You might say that. I once flew ultralights for geological surveys. I'll figure it out. The owner of that pickup will act badly when he finds his partner dead."

The group moved into the airplane squeezing close together. Body odor mingled with fear. Murphy managed to get it off the ground. But he didn't know the way. A few degrees off in 2000 miles might land them in Libya. Murphy aimed for the coast. Once there he flew just high enough to avoid hitting trees to stay clear of radar. Murphy used the regular CIA rout with gas stops. Crossing into Yemen's airways attracted potshots but no hits. Tom was lucky to have lost his lunch on the ground. Watering the cabin with his guts would have been awful. Their flying sardine can's odor was bad enough.

Murphy beat tail out of the warzone. Addie directed them toward the Nile River. The engine noise made it hard to talk without shouting, but Tom had to ask. When Murphy leveled off over the Nile, the motor no longer throttled up, Tom relaxed and popped his question.

"All a ruse, not real. There isn't any petroglyph site, is there?"

Murphy handed a folder over his shoulder from the pilot's seat.

"Here's the real file. You tell me."

Tom opened Murphy's folder marked Top Secret. The file was thick with notes and detailed photos he hadn't seen before. Tom's dig prospectus lacked this info. Murphy's pictures were beyond odd. One petroglyph stood out although most were strange to begin with, but nothing like the usual cave art one expected from North Africa. The caption dated it 24K BP and said the paint is non-organic. Tom rubbed his eyes. No mistaking it. One painting featured a smoking volcano and on either side stood a Venus figure. Each held high an amulet. Each amulet resembled the one he dove into the Sargassos Sea to recover. Above the pinnacle, another amulet floated which represented a third, but unseen, goddess.

Tom opened his mouth thinking he had something to say. Rather than speak, an urge stopped him. He closed the file. Kenny's voice droned with the aircraft's tiny engine. *I told you…I told you…I told you.*

Tom thought it best not to mention it.

CHAPTER FORTY-FIVE:

CAIRO

The back bar was dusty, hot, and dark although the building's front was open to the street. It could have been a Hollywood set. The inner sanctum was for western tourists only. Tom half expected Humphrey Bogart to walk in followed by Peter O'Toole although he didn't see a Borough Superior motorcycle parked outside. Laurence of Arabian and his motorcycle were long dead. Old men in rickety chairs wearing turbans or Fezzes drank tea and played dominoes at the curbside tables under the building's extended canopy. Rick's Café served traditional tea. Locals didn't indulge in the bar's wares.

The game players stopped to watch a dust devil of volcanic soot swirl in the street.

"Here's to simplicity."

Tom lifted his glass to the locals who didn't see it. Television movies didn't capture places like this. He loved those old flicks as a boy. His perception of archeology then had been that of a dangerous and exciting profession. Later he found that untrue. Tom had expected his line of work would be a safe, careful profession. The hope of rare finds kept a man traveling this career road. That danger followed and preceded him was the last thing he expected.

"'If it was easy, everyone would do it,'" Tom said quoting Dad. He had his back to the bar hoping for a breeze.

"What's that?" Murphy said.

"Nothing," Tom turned around. "You never said how you knew we were coming here. Why are you so hot on this?"

"Let me tell you a little story," Murphy said rolling whiskey around his dirty glass. "Anatolia wasn't my first clash with these people. My old man taught me you don't run, you face things. You dig the truth out."

"The sub's still there, you know," Tom said. "Addie followed the trial away from it, not toward it."

Tom sloshed his ice-melted drink around and set it aside.

"I thought so." Murphy took a sip. "My team will get it. Not my job. I find and confirm. Specialists extract the big-ticket items."

"You weren't surprised when Sally described the Watchers," Tom said. "Did she get it right?"

"I was here twenty years back," Murphy looked around and lowered his voice. "I found an entrance. Egypt's underground labyrinth is known by certain people. Nobody goes inside. Too dangerous. The government here is on the payroll. Nobody in academia is supposed to know. I blatantly trespassed on Egypt's most restricted property. That entry is still active. Henchmen gotta come and go."

"That doesn't answer," Tom said. He swirled his drink around. "Who are they?"

"I was on a survey team," Murphy said, speaking with far-away eyes. "I snuck into that restricted area and followed the grade. Curious geology. I found a cut in exposed bedrock made to channel water runoff. I traced it."

Murphy picked up his drink with a shaking hand. Whiskey sloshed over the side. He set the glass back down without a sip. Tod Murphy's protective hedges were crumbling.

"I found a stairway going deep into the ground. Crazy deep, I couldn't see bottom. Stepwell, I guessed, but it wasn't buried. It was maintained, no trash or debris." Murphy picked up his glass and slugged it. "I went down. Found a well and a cave. Caves don't belong. I jumped over the water and into the cave. Rough stairwell outside, smooth walls inside."

Murphy waved the barkeep over. "I need another."

The bartender's face was hidden in dim light behind a bushy beard and turban but seemed familiar. The barman poured. Murphy gulped his water and wiped his mouth with a sleeve before taking a little whiskey. Murphy resumed.

"Way back, I saw a faint light. That's curious, I thought. Shouldn't be any illuminating fungus in local caves. Pulled a flashlight and proceeded deeper. Fifty yards in, the floor sloped down. I saw a silhouetted figure way ahead. He came at me fast. Goddamn it." Murphy took a drink. "I only told one other person this. Seven-foot tall, big head, deep eyes, giant brow ridges, massive jaw, wore a robe like a priest. Scared the fuck out of me."

Tom touched Murphy's arm for encouragement. He had seen Mom crack up enough to know Murphy was on the edge.

"Slow deep breaths," Tom said. "It's fine, you're fine, you aren't in danger. Easy slow breaths. That's it, breathe."

Tom continued talking him down. Murphy buried his face in his hands. It was some time before he could speak. Murphy struggled to pull himself together. Nobody asked. The barkeep topped off Murphy's drink. Tom pushed his away. Murphy straightened up and wrapped both hands around his glass.

"Anyway," Murphy said, his face two shades whiter than when he started. "He warned me…his voice…so strange, thick with age. The monster described his handiwork. There was this Egyptologist found in the desert a few weeks earlier alive, buried up to his neck. Left there to die…horrible. Why that bastard didn't kill me, who knows."

Why indeed. *Cultivating new agents?* Tom considered his drink but thought better of it. "What did you do after?"

"I went to the consulate," Murphy said. "Talked to a CIA man. Told the whole thing. He didn't think me insane. Fact is, he offered me a job. I didn't take it right away…but here I am."

"I didn't think Tod was crazy either," The barman said in perfect English. "I'd have hired him if I got the recording sooner." The man pulled off his turban, light brown hair, not a local.

"What the hell?" Tom tilted off his barstool. "I know that voice. Wailer!"

Wailer turned on an overhead light.

"Moms with you, right? Where is she?"

"Safe for now. They want her. She held the amulet. They're after me as well. We split up. It was safer."

"Start talking, Wailer." Tom said with aggression.

"Hold on Conley," Murphy said, "I have questions—"

"Thanks, Tod, I'll take it from here," Wailer said. "Don't look so surprised. The Watchers aren't the only ones with men in high places. Tod doesn't mind a little side work now and again himself. Mr. Murphy, if you will, please mind the store. Come with me, Tommy."

"It's Tom, not Tommy, I'm not a kid anymore."

"And just in the nick of time," Wailer said.

Tom followed Wailer to a back room. The room had air conditioning. Tom wasn't ready or willing to dispel his internal heat. The bar's temperature didn't seem to bother Wailer. Tom had the impression Wailer operated beyond weather conditions.

"Mede sent you; I know. I tried to reach you a couple of ways." Wailer waved Tom to sit. "Took some convincing."

Unlike his ship, Wailer's office was a mess. He cleared off a chair laden with old magazines. Tom remained on his feet.

"Murphy stumbled into one of the Watcher's doors, true," Wailer said. "I didn't know who they were until recently. I heard Murphy's story years ago which got me thinking. It took a long time…I know how to get in. I need you to get Kenny out of there."

"That's why I came. Driven is more like it," Tom said, realizing his situation. "Now that the great Richard Wailer is here with all his money, why don't you handle it? You handle everything, even Mom. What's Kenny to do with this?"

Wailer's easy demeanor transmuted into dead serious. The wrinkles of his forehead became canyons, his merry crow's feet, crevasses. Wailer tapped his lower lip in concentration. Another man would have blown his top at Tom's accusing tone.

"There's a lot to say. It'll take weeks to tell you what took me a hundred years to ferret out. We don't have time. If we don't stop them now, humanity goes extinct."

"A hundred years…Who the hell are you?" Tom shivered.

"I'm a half-breed and I can't go near the place. They'll detect me. They want me badly. They took Kenny to bait me, due to my association with him. Kenny's mother, and yours, were on my ship."

"Why Kenny?" Tom crocked out.

A sly smile crossed Wailer's face. Tom clenched his fists.

"Spill it."

"I'm supposed to be sterile." Wailer continued calmly. "They haven't figured it out. Covered in magic as he is. Kenny is my son. Even so, they took him to trap me. You aren't expected. You're the blind spot, a wildcard. You both possessed an amulet and yet they can't read you. You're shrouded in Women's Magic. I don't know how. I believe Kenny is a keyholder. He can shut the doomsday device down, but not alone. He needs guidance. He trusts you. You must help him…it's the only way."

Tom fell into the old oak office chair with his mind reeling. "You let your son fall into a trap!"

"It's the only way." Wailer said evenly. "I'd do it again if that's what it takes to save humanity. Time has run out. You must go."

Tom's chest pulsed. Wailer told the truth. The fibers of Tom's being vibrated. Kenny's dream-messages proved real. The amulet gave Kenny power. Tom's birthmark changed the day he lost his half of the talisman. Tom never got power from it. He couldn't ignore the cogs snapping into place. The amulet's influence attracted women of power to him. *I'm the fulcrum.* That idea scared the stuffing out of him.

"I can't, I'm not a hero," Tom said.

"That's the point. They expect one and you aren't it. No need for heroics. If your team can get you to the backdoor, simply go in and get him. There aren't many Watchers. They won't know you're inside. All you need to do is get Kenny out. He'll stop the device. Transport in time and stop it before it starts. He can't project within their energy field. He doesn't know how, why, or what until you tell him. You must spring him first. You two are connected."

"I know," Tom said thinking of connections. "I sensed it. I've never understood. I need time. I've never made a snap decision in my life."

"In few hours…" Wailer's hands spread wide. "We act now. Save Kenny and we might save the world. What do you say?"

What difference did it make—die in the caves or die on the surface? News of the world was grim. The device, as Wailer called it, ran full bore. Volcanoes were erupting everywhere. Toxic gasses pouring out, huge numbers dead. Lava flows and earthquakes to follow. The Siberian Traps reopened and new rifts were developing elsewhere. Black smokers will soon blot out the sun. Tom's only choice was how to die.

"Kenny's thread is pulling," Tom whispered.

"Watches intend on killing everyone," Murphy said entering the backroom. He had Wailer's wall-hanger long gun he took from the bar in hand.

"I'll go," Tom said. "No idea where to begin."

"Tod will see you to the general location." Wailer handed Murphy a box of ammo. "Your ladies will pinpoint it. Tod can't go inside. He's marked. They'll detect him. The area is shielded. The Watchers have technical abilities well beyond us. But you have magical protections. The Watchers don't know that."

Wailer checked his watch. "If that machine isn't stopped in two hours, we're dead, all of us. Mary, too. Slow death, but dead is dead."

Tom proceeded on rubber legs to the bar's open front. It was as dark outside as inside. The game players had gone. He hedged. *This natural disaster ain't natural.* Images of Dad materialized within Tom's mind. Dad's confident voice rang, *'Never give up son, be brave, be strong, you can do it,'* Behind it echoed Mom's weaker voice, *'don't take risks.'*

"I can't," Tom said to the blacking sky.

His words chocked him. His chest burned like thermite. His heart danced on the edge of stopping. He fell to his knees gasping for clean air and tasted only soot.

"Alright, I'll do it, I'll do it!"

The burn ended. Tom got up on stronger legs. Murphy and Wailer rushed to him.

"Fine now, I'm fine, fine," Toms said as they held him, one man on each side. "Come on. Let's do this."

"I'll cover the rear guard," Wailer said.

Tom and Murphy took off for the hotel. Arriving, the lobby was empty. Soot coated everything. *Nobody goes to work on doomsday.* The elevator was off-line so Tom ran the stairs. The fire door was locked. He banged on it and yelled. Janis didn't take long to open it.

"Jesus Prof, where the hell have you been?" Janis looked grizzly-bear dangerous dressed in the local black on black garb.

"No time, we got to go," Tom said. "Where's Addie and—"

The other two came around the corner ready to travel. Addie had another metal detector. All were dressed in local attire.

"Going native?" Tom said.

"Janis's idea, blend-in. We'll move faster this way," Sally said.

They set out. The girls' long skirts made descending the stairs a slow-motion balancing act for Janis and Sally. Addie flowed like a ghost in her long, black dress.

They loaded into Wailer's Jeep and took off on local roads to avoid traffic. The highways were clogged with animals and stalled cars. Panic and soot filled the air. They made for the place Murphy visited years before. He knew each landmark along the way. Houses were shut tight while others were abandoned and left wide open. In only a few hours, the sky went from light-smokey to black. People were running or hiding or looting. Old ladies wailed prayers on street corners. Janis needed Tod's directions. Her Wonder Woman powers were better than GPS normally, but it failed her. Police cars weren't evident. Janis drove the Jeep hard. Once out of densely populated areas, they took a residential street bordering the desert.

Near a closed girl's school, Murphy pointed, "It's there, right there."

Janis veered and didn't stop. She accelerated and rammed the restricted area's chain link gate. The gate went down taking some fencing with it. She K-turned and parked just outside the crashed barrier.

"I'll cover your back," Murphy said.

He pulled his pistol with a quivering hand. The man looked like Tom felt, scared witless.

"What're you going to do with a .38?" Janis asked.

"I got Wailer's carbine, too," Murphy said.

Inside the fence, distances were hazy although no soot fell. The air glowed yellow. Tom, Sally, Addie, and Janis walked forward into the badlands without equipment or supplies. It seemed a long walk. Only minutes passed before Tom felt exposed. The inner lands became brighter as they proceeded. Turning to look back, there was nothing behind but a shimmering wall. Nothing in sight, no Jeep, no town, nothing but an electric waterfall.

The air within the energy field was clean and clear of soot. The Watchers didn't allow volcanic poisons to penetrate their shield. The further inside, the better the air, but Tom's girls struggled to breathe. Their steps slowed. They squinted for focus, although Tom could see fine. He cursed himself for forgetting the flashlight.

Addie left her detector at the hotel. She made an impromptu dowsing rod out of a clothing hanger found in the Jeep. Addie stopped swinging. Sally stopped, too, her skin glowing yellow. Janis managed one more stride before she stopped and stood there shaking violently. Addie let her divining rod fall. Janis didn't drop her gun.

"What're you doing?" Tom said. "We got to keep going."

Sally pushed her hands out in front. "I can't, the fire is…all consuming…evil fire, the devil's flames. I can't see, I can't." She collapsed onto the ground.

"I cannot go any farther," Addie said. "They will know we are here. They have protections. They eat our magic."

"She's right," Janis said, "I've never feared…this is freaking me out. We can't go…It's on you, Prof."

Tom felt fine and took three steps forward testing. He checked behind. The women were immobilized. Tom gained new resolve. His energy surged. Whatever zapped the ladies gave him strength.

Quitting was logical, but logic didn't count. What he'd never accept before proved true. Immutable reality meant nothing. Power such as he never knew poured out of that stepwell. A mix of evil and good, the feminine and masculine, magic and cold reality tumbled into his awareness. He leaned forward scared, shocked, excited, and exposed. Yet, he could not turn back. Would not.

"I got this," Tom said over his shoulder. "Go back, help Murphy."

Tom sprang forward. He didn't need directions. Nothing lay behind him but a shimmering haze. Pressing on, he reached the well's threshold. The pit extended on grade seventy-five yards downrange, an eight-foot wide slit in the Earth, just as Murphy said. Tom balanced on the stair's stone still. The way down disappeared into gloom. He stumbled on the first step. They weren't made for people. The rock-cut stairs were steep and uneven. The walls were rough without handrails.

The bottom was as Murphy described except the water had dried up. Jumping distance wasn't bad. Where's the bottom? He dropped a stone. If it hit it, it landed out of hearing range. The cave's interior shone light deep within. Tom wound up and jumped with all he had. He hit the deck, rolled, and layed sprawled on the floor forcing air into his lungs.

I should have taken Janis's gun.

Tom got up and proceeded. He jogged dragging one hand on the wall fearful of unseen junctions. The floor ran black under his feet. Fear banged his heart. Eyes wide, ears open, there was no sign of the enemy. The odor of seawater grew stronger. His chest gave no comment. Creeping along, he found a side tunnel. There, a massive hand clamped down on his shoulder driving him to the ground.

A man mountain picked Tom up by Tom's safari vest and held him aloft one handed. The creature was uglier than Murphy described. Its head was twice the size of a normal man. It's jaw that of a mountain gorilla. His breath stank of seaweed.

The creature spoke. "I have an intruder. Shall I dispatch him?"

"Wait!" Tom cried. "I know where Richard Wailer is. You want him, don't you?"

The giant's communication device answered. "Yes, we do want him."

There was a muffled conversation in the background.

"Boric, put him with the prisoners. Stay there, watch them. Our most critical moment is at hand. Full power countdown has begun. Albert out."

The giant tucked Tom under an arm and set out at a remarkable pace. Tom got jostled, ribs squeezed and bruised, but nothing broke although he hurt badly. At the end of Tom's endurance, the creature set him down before a wooden door. The light was better and he could see. Tom examined his jailer with professional fascination. Wax museum cavemen didn't wear gold trimmed tunics and Greek armor.

"In you go," the monster said.

He pushed Tom inside and closed the door. Tom grabbed the doorknob to pull himself up and the knob turned.

"Aren't prisoners kept locked?" *Not when there's no escape.*

He stood short of air to find a rock-cut anteroom, good light, carpets on the walls and floors. A tight group of five old women stood nearby. Tom's instincts said they were the Watcher species. *Morphodynamical.* The women appeared human. Haggard expressions and rags for clothing spoke of their captivity.

A desire to fall on his knees in worship came over him, but he couldn't move. The oldest of them came forward. She was bent by a third. Her blouse and long skirt were strips of once-bright fabrics joined by shredded pleats. Her skirt flowed like gray ghosts in a tattered forest. A gnarled hand reached for him. He took it in a daze.

"We expected a champion. Not you," she said. Tom swooned.

She led him into a maze of rock-cut galleries. The place was empty except for minimal furnishings. Pity filled him. Oppression hovered above like a smothering blanket. Women's Magic pushed back. His heart warned him not to speak. Her magic beat back Watcher men but was he safe? The march ended before a small wooden door of gray planks.

A dozen women joined along the way and gathered around him at the door. They came to shield him. He swung the door open. A person stood in the shadows. Kenny rushed to Tom and embraced him.

"Kenny! Kenny," Tom cried full of joy.

Tom hugged him hard enough to stop a bear and Kenny hugged right back.

"The joining begins, ready your hearts." The elder said.

The ladies moved in surrounding Tom and Kenny. That thing, that birthmark pressed hard against his skin. It wanted out. Tom's chest burst. Sparks exploded. He felt it in Kenny, too. Together, for only a moment, they existed in fire. All harms seen. All things revealed. The powers of these women filled him. He saw the doom generator. He knew where it was and how to shut it off.

"I gotta get the other amulet." Tom said, breathless.

An explosion of light blinded him. They fell away from each other. The women caught them. Where he and Kenny stood moments before, two bloody amulets lay on the floor fused together. Tom put a hand over his heart and felt hot wetness.

"It's gone," Tom said between heaving breaths.

"We have two," The old lady said. "It is not enough. You, Tom Conley, you must shut off the shield. We cannot leave."

"I need a weapon," Tom gasped.

Their power flowed through him. He had come to do what no one, not even he, could do without their blessing. The amulet had chosen the unlikeliest advocates. He didn't know until then what he had carried. Kenny was bait, alright. But the snare caught him.

"We have prepared this," she said. "We imbued it."

It materialized out of hard rock. A polearm with ax-head, hammer, and point configured such as a Bec De Corbin from medieval France, a gruesome thing.

"I got it, got, I got it," Kenny said. "Oh yes, I went in time and got it. No more time trips, that's not allowed. Oh no. Heavy shield, too heavy."

"You did good, Kenny," Tom said testing its weight. Its massive head weighted nothing under the Goddess's power. "This will do."

Tom wasn't a fighting man. He never punched, kicked, or bit anyone. He ran from trouble. Even so, he understood this medieval weapon. He admired blacksmith made things, even deadly ones. He didn't need training. Polearms were designed for unskilled surfs.

"If a farm boy can do it, so can I. But I need practice," Tom cried.

"Our magic won't last under the shield." The old one said. "They cannot defeat this pike while the blessing lasts. Use it before Magic fails. You must go now."

"It's them or us," Tom said.

The ladies ushered Tom to the door. Dad had cleaned fish. Tom never had the stomach for gutting fish or people. Exiting the women's quarters, Boric was twenty yards away. Tom had room to swing in the main tunnel. Tom took a stance. Boric closed in four steps and kicked Tom's feet out from under him. Tom fell face-down and lost the poleax. Tom gasped for air while searching for the pike with a blind hand.

The giant loomed over him.

"Funny little man," Boric said. "Shall I dispatch you now?"

Boric unsheathed his sword. The shaft found Tom's hand. He grabbed it and thrusted upwards one handed. The spike-end tore a hole through Boric's chest plate. Impossible without borrowed powers. The blow drained Tom's energy. The wounded man staggered and fell. Boric's toppling released the spike. The giant rolled onto his knees. Tom sprung hewing and struck the giant's helmet with the hammer head. A bell clang echoed. Boric fell over in a heap with his dented helmet skewed sideways. Alarms sounded.

"Damn it, I killed a man! Horrible."

Under the joining Tom learned how spread thin his enemies were. They must keep track of each other. Tom's power faded more by the second. The weapon gained weight. He had to fly. But first, Tom yanked the communication device off Boric accidentally activating it.

A voice came over the device. "Boric, what is happening?"

Tom imitated the voice. "The prisoner escaped."

"Protect the generator."

Tom took off jogging, hauling the heavy weapon. His vision had provided directions. He'd soon be on his own as the blessing ran down. Without help, Tom didn't have the strength to swing his polearm. It became an anchor. Running wore him down more. His doubts gained ground as power drained. His sense of direction remained clear only because the magic he carried compressed under the strain. What magical strength he gained evaporated. Only his fortitude remained.

I'll never make the control room.

He ran on anyway. One turn more to reach destination. He stopped, breathing hard. With his adrenalin spent, he readied for the last push. The smell of oil and ozone tinted the air. Machine noises filled the tunnel. *Boric's communicator locates him. They'll think I'm him.* Tom had no magic, no fighting skills, nothing left but a cheap trick. He peeked around the corner. A guard stood at the machine room door. Tom banged on a wall.

"Boric, is that you?" Came a voice out of sight.

"I am wounded. Help me," Tom said.

He crouched low on his hunches in the dark. Two hands on the staff. The beast rounded the corner. Tom thrusted upwards blindly with the last of his reserves unsure of a target. The pike's dagger blade ripped the guard's neck. A higher or lower thrust would have missed. The giant toppled backward spewing a fountain of blood. Pike in hand, Tom turned for the door. The downed man grabbed Tom's pant leg and dragged him backward. Tom stuffed the urge to scream as he was pulled close.

Tom back-kicked the creature's massive face and he let go. Tom scrambled away slipping in blood. Regaining his feet, Tom jammed the spearpoint into his attacker's eye socket and withdrew it. The body began dehydrating. Tom, exhausted, dropped the staff. He took a long-handled war ax off the body. It was heavy but lighter than the polearm.

Tom burst into the control room swinging. He hacked the old-timer seated at a control panel until the operator's head fell off. The body spewed gore falling over. The dude crumpled into dust while Tom gasped for air.

Alarms rang anew. Tom ripped a pull ring out of the board which held the amulet he saw in his vision. He stuffed it into his pants pocket. An Ergaster man moved toward his location on one of the many screens. Tom hauled back with the ax and smashed the control board. He pounded, hammered, and stabbed until the lights went out. The machines stopped replaced with silence. He slumped to the floor feeling powerless in the darkness.

"I'm dead but the damn thing's off." Tom whispered.

No way out. Ergaster men were on the way. No reprieve. *They'll kill me. I can't stop them.* The door was open. Tom heard footsteps. He pulled himself up, hoping to get one good shot in. Footfalls closed. He readied the ax, aiming high, thinking to target the head. No light to swing by. He guessed the neck's height. *Close now. Why don't they use a light?* The air changed. Tom swung. He stuck the door's arch.

"Oh no. Not good, not good, oh no. Mr. Conley, we have to go."

"Kenny! What the hell!"

"Kenny don't need lights to see," Kenny said. "Magic lights…yes, yes…it's light. Lady magic lights of the world. Take my, my…hand."

Tom held his hand out. He didn't know where Kenny was. Kenny acted completely unlike himself. *Amulets made us family.* Kenny's hand was warm, calming, serene, and yet energizing. What Kenny experienced filled Tom. The boy had cat eyes. They moved out jogging. Tom followed using Kenny's sight. Tom stopped for the pike hoping he had enough strength to use it.

The way back seemed endless. Time moved slow. Every minute lessoned Tom's hope of escape. As they ran, Tom's resolve wore thin. Fresh fears chased him. Earth tremors slowed their retreat. Tom might have laid down and died in terror if not for his need to save Kenny. Tom couldn't give up. The kid didn't know fear. Tom, on the other hand, carried enough for them both.

"We gotta save the ladies, save the ladies," Kenny repeated as they progressed.

Tom ran on and didn't answer.

CHAPTER FORTY-SIX:

MURPHY AND THE LADIES

Prof Conley left Janis and her partners behind. He pushed forward into the simmering fog of death. Janis had never been so terrified, not even when she shot that bear with a peashooter .38. Star Trek shit was sucking her gift out like a cosmic vacuum cleaner. She stayed where Prof left her. Ice queen sculptures had more mobility.

"Where's Frosty the Snow Man when you need him?"

Hot as it was, Janis shivered. Her bravery vacated under this attack. Her magic flowed away. Visions of her ancestors appeared before her closed eyes chanting encouragement. Grandmother had first recognized her heritage. Janis never shared the facts of her abilities until meeting Conley. Sharing power made her love it more.

"I won't let them take my gift!"

Sally and Addie were a million years away a few steps behind. Shadow voices begged her. *'Janis, go back, go back.'* Winds howled with shaman ghost voices. She heard them on the tundra as a child. The ancestor's song gave her strength. She was able to turn her head.

"Janis, Janis, do you hear me, come on," Sally yelled against the fog.

"Run, you must run." The dream-speaker's voice came from Janis's lips.

She moved one foot back against a sucking riptide. It wanted her dead. She forced another step. The next came easier. One more. Janis reached. Sally's hand clamped on. Half a step more and Addie's touch brought more power. Finally, with the other's support, together they reversed course. *The power of three.* A few yards on normal perception returned.

"Which way? I can't find it…I'm lost." Addie yelled into the gale. "No sun or landmarks. How can we leave?"

"Footprints," Janis said. "I got this."

The group's tracks were visible, but disappearing fast under the force of wind-blown sand.

"This wind ain't natural," Sally said.

"They're dragging energy in," Jains said. "We gotta get the hell outta here."

Janis led them the way they had come. Every step was an effort. Prints were nearly impossible to see. Ancient mother shamans encouraged her. Janis had learned the craft young. Her brother, a top tracker, taught Janis well. Survival depends on sharing skills. In older times, she would have been made shaman. People can't choose. The Spirits chose. They picked her.

The fog faded as the footprints ran out. Addie sighted the crashed gate ahead. Janis pulled her gun and cleared the sand out of it. She holstered it by way of a slit in her local clothing at the small of her back. Together as one, they proceeded.

Addie mumbled, "'the power of three will set us free.'"

"A woman alone in that vortex can't survive," Sally said. "What'll we do now?"

"For sure, I thought that," Janis said. "I'd go after Conley if I could. Not happening. Dang, I gotta pee."

The Jeep was half in and half out of the entrance. Murphy watched the road resting that old rifle on the front of the Jeep for stability. The fence had skewed out of plumb when the gates went down. It was hard to see with soot swirling. The sky had darkened more. Janis couldn't see thirty yards. But her senses detected danger in every direction. *A full bladder's no good in a fight.* Jains ignored Murphy's shouts and ducked behind the back of the Jeep to pee. She hiked up the long skirt and pulled down the cargo shorts she wore under it.

"Murphy, stop! What're you doing!" Sally yelled.

Janis stood half up tangled in clothes. Sally and Addie's hands shot up. Janus turned. Murphy had the carbine pointed her way. Janis's gun got lost in layers of clothing. She struggled for it. Bang. Bang. Bullets whizzed past her ear. A body crashed into her knocking her to the ground still tangled in her skirt.

"He came up along the fence," Murphy cried.

Murphy and the others pulled the dead man off Janis. Her outer dress was wet with blood. She stripped it off and pulled up her shorts. She had worn her regular clothes underneath.

"Thanks, Murphy," Janis said. "What's that?" She pointed.

Five bodies littered the road, military people. The spent casings under her feet said Murphy had been busy.

"Who the hell were they?"

"Local Army on the payroll. Where have you been? Where's Conley, you've been gone two hours?"

"He's inside," Addie said.

"Car's coming, take cover!" Murphy cried.

Mixed feelings about Murphy vanished. Vibes told Janis he wasn't dangerous to them but still dangerous. Something was off. Trouble coated that guy in layers. She watched him while fingering her .357. She didn't register danger from the approaching car.

"Here he comes," Murphy said, "heading straight for us."

Murphy raised the rifle. She stepped over the dead man and took a firing position. Janis signaled the others to duck. She tracked as the car progressed toward them. It rolled slow avoiding debris in the street.

"Who takes a limo to a gunfight?" Janis said to Murphy.

The car stopped a little way down the road. A shadow got out, one man. He walked forward with hands up, black robes and salted beard blowing back. Sand goggles covered his face.

"Suicide bomber!" Sally cried.

Murphy tried to shoot but that WWII wall-hanger's bolt stuck. Janis felt it jam in her teeth.

"Shoot, Shoot!" Murphy cried.

Janis' impulse didn't agree. "He's not armed." She let the man come on.

"What if he's got a bomb, they do that ya know," Sally said.

"Shoot, damn it!" Murphy smacked the rifle with his palm. Sand fell out. "Sweet Jesus!"

"It is Mr. Wailer," Addie said. "He cannot be here."

"They'll find us, no doubt," Murphy said.

"Wailer?" Sally and Janis said together.

"With us…he's with us," Addie said.

"That's an understatement," Wailer said lifting his goggles. "They're busy and I'm outside. I'm expected at the front door." Wailer fluffed soot out of his beard. "Me drawing attention here might distract them and give Tom cover, but…" A gust pushed back his robe. "I brought AK-47s just in case." Wailer kicked a dead body. "Good I came. Janis doesn't have enough bullets. That carbine you borrowed isn't trustworthy…Next time ask."

"Next time, next time?" Murphy said.

"These assholes might have an army," Janis said. Wailer did good. Come on girls."

Janis and Wailer crossed over with the others behind. Wailer popped the limo's truck. It was full of arms and ammo. Janis chanted a prayer to the Hunting Spirit asking a blessing for Sally and Addie. They hadn't handled a gun before. Janis shifted into defense mode.

"Wailer, bring the limo up. Park V-shape with the Jeep."

Wailer complied and pulled the limo in. They took the rifles and shut the trunk. Janis gave Sally and Addie a quick firearms lesion before slamming a magazine into each long gun. Janis clicked on the safety before handing them over.

"Don't point this at anyone you don't want dead. I put my whammy on it."

They settled into positions. The wind dropped. An unnatural calm descended. Janis remembered Alaska's morning fogs within snowfalls. Such events transformed her childhood world into muffled white stillness. This was a black calm. Corpse-gray soot sawed down in big flakes. The cliché proved true. There is a calm before the storm.

"What'll we do now, Mr. Wailer?" Sally said.

"We wait and hope," Wailer said. "I'll fill you in."

Wailer talked, and they listened. Strange tales sprang out. *He's a regular Wizard of Oz.* Wailer had pulled leavers, spun dials, and sent adversaries chasing false trails. He pushed women of power forward all the while. Always hiding and avoiding the adversary's detection. Conley would have shit himself if he had known who backed him. Wailer admitted to having hidden help, too. Janis caught a whiff of Goddess on him. Conley had no clue. It had to be that way. Conley was a witless catalyst. This game had been in motion since before Janis was born. Wailer figured it out. But he didn't know everything.

As he confessed, Janis pulled the pieces together. He was born to free the Goddesses. His mother was hidden, too. That woman Janis sprung from Amos's car in Alaska was her. Janis had no idea what that woman looked like. Janis was under a spell. The captive must have been his mother, a goddess.

"When this is over, I got news for you Richie Rich," Janis said. "If we live."

CHAPTER FORTY-SEVEN:

ESCAPE

Kenny repeated over and over as they ran, "Save the ladies…save the ladies…"

"Wait, I need air," Tom said.

That desperate swing in the dark took a lot out of him. His reserves finally dissipated. He let go of Kenny's hand and dropped the weapon. Blind in the dark, he slid to the floor taking deep breaths.

"I'm not here to save your ladies." Tom said panting. "I came for you."

"The ladies will make them…Make them stop…only the ladies can…can…can do it, do it…do it."

Brushing his pants pocket, the stolen amulet he stashed gave Tom a jolt. He pulled it out of his pocket and kissed it, before depositing it in his shirt's top pocket. His heart lit with hope but not energy.

"Mr. Conley, we gotta…gotta…go…we go…go. Find the ladies! Save the ladies!

"You feel it? Bad guys are coming," Tom said. "I can't see. How do I fight?"

Raising a hand in front of his face, Tom found only blackness. Images of tunnels had filled his mind's eye upon removing the control room medallion. It showed many ways out. A side passage well beyond the women's jail being most direct, if only they could reach it, if only he could see normally. The shortest path to the surface took them past the women's quarters. Death awaited there. An evil presence blocked that way.

"Kenny, you're right." Tom got up. "Take us. We'll save your ladies."

"Oh yes! Yes, yes. Kenny counts in the dark…One step, then two and three. Trust Kenny, oh yes. Hold hands. That's the way. Follow the thread."

The two reconnected. Kenny's hand was hot with sweat. Kenny's cat sight switched out. Now, Kenny's second-sight engaged. Energies rippled in the form of flowing, colored strings. Spatial images became mere shadows. One current was not like the others. A whisper of kindness, surrounded by torrents of destruction, found them. One thin thread led to the ladies. No way to test it. Was this extra perception or delusion? Tom had to trust Kenny.

"We'll need the poleax," Tom said. "It's gotten so heavy, but I'll try."

Tom wasted precious minutes searching for it. It had no living energy. Kenny couldn't see it. Tom found it by crawling. Once in hand, Tom led them along the corridor through Kenny's senses. Tom, with the ax in one hand, and Kenny's hand in the other, proceeded quietly. The thread brightened as they got closer. Tom slowed as the thread pulled harder. They crept forward until that string stopped just ahead. Tom couldn't see why. Kenny's sight became hazier from Tom's perspective.

He questioned in his mind, where is he?

Kenny answered inside Tom's head. *Around a corner, a corner...Bad man on the other side...Oh no, oh no.*

"*Where is he?*"

"*Low, bent over...Bent. Aim for the legs, the legs! Aim low. Low, low.*"

In another life, Tom would have fallen on his face begging for mercy. That amulet in his breast pocket refused cowardness. Its lust to live poured into Tom. He didn't need that encouragement. The boy's protection was motivation enough to face Goliath.

They inched forward. Kenny quivered and shook more violently with each step. Tom could not swing one handed, but he was blind without Kenny. Closer, the Ergaster's breath became a seaborn wind. So close. The smell of seawater, blood and rot, instilled panic. Black energy covered the white thread. Tom dropped Kenny's hand and his sight vanished. Tom strained his ears.

Where is he, how close?

Tom creeped another foot and wound up. Kenny's actual voice came from behind.

"This way, Mr. Conley. Oh yes, this way. This is the way...the way."

The air changed. Tom swung. He hit a side of beef.

"Oooofff."

The Ergaster man fell backward, ripping Tom's weapon out of hand. Scuffling sounds. A flashlight came on. *Kenny has a flashlight!* The Ergaster man had crouched in duck-walk position. The hammer end of the war ax crushed Boric's chest. Tom meant to use the blade which was useless against armor. By luck the mallet struck a sweet spot. Tom pulled on the handle but it snagged. The monster still breathed. Weaponless, Tom couldn't finish him off.

"He's alive, he's alive," Kenny whined.

"No time, Kenny. Where's the ladies? Show me. Let's go."

Tom took Kenny's hand and clicked the flashlight off. They passed several open intersections and each time, the odor of Ergaster man flowed outward. They moved deeper into the maze and returned to where they had started. Thirteen women waited, huddled in the front room. Emergency lights cast a dull, yellow glow on them.

"Generator is dead. It's time to leave," Tom said. The women made no move. "Come on, we gotta go," Tom said.

"We cannot," the head woman said. "The exit has power. We cannot break it. The amulet is in parts, we have two. The power of three sets us free. Thank you for—"

"Will this help?"

Tom pulled the one out of his pocket that he took from the generator and handed it over. The bent lady straightened. She kissed it and held it up. It shone, lighting her face. Age fell off of them all.

"She's beautiful," Tom said marveling.

"Shield your hearts. We go." The lead woman said.

"Athena, we cannot! They are not done. They will find us," one said. The others spoke rapidly in a language Tom didn't know. "No matter where we go, they always find us."

"They have not found Artemis. She is on the surface. Is that not so? We have the final way. Release our spirits and they cannot harm us. We must disperse our power before they destroy it."

"But Mother! It will be the end of us."

"It will end them," Athena said with sadness in her voice "We go!"

"What's the problem?!" Tom cried. "Let's get the hell out of here! They're coming!"

Athena turned to Tom. "In the light of day, if ever we see it, we will have our revenge. This, they never suspected. It is the way."

"Whatever the way is, I don't give a rat's ass. I'm going, come or stay, I'm outta here."

"We go, all of us, now," Mother Athena said.

"Oh no, oh no! They come, oh no! Close…They're closer," Kenny cried.

Thirteen women in ragged robes, and Tom holding Kenny's hand, proceeded with speed. Athena led without a weapon. Tom had no doubt she knew how to fight. Kenny marked black energy approaching from behind. No Ergaster ahead. They ran as a unit, moving fast like a covey of quail. Negative energies poured from every crossroad, yet Ergaster men were not near enough to stop them. Luck held so far.

They reached the stepwell's long branch tunnel. Tom's heart jumped glad for that glint of natural light at the far end. He picked up the pace and let go of Kenny. The group broke into a flat-out run. Athena's group, a few steps behind, egged him on.

Tom didn't slow at the end. He jumped over the pit and landing on the stairs. The clouds far above were black, yet yellow sunlight filtered through. Soot snow reached the bottom of the stairwell. The shield had gone down. Kenny jumped last. Tom climbed with the rest just behind, not believing he was still alive. He paused after clearing the top. Tom was relieved at the change. Normal perception returned, but ash clouds aren't normal. Still, shafts of sunlight found Earth. The border fence was only a few hundred yards on. Tom thought he had walked miles to the entrance.

"We can't stay here. Let's go," Tom grabbed a woman's hand.

She in turn took another one's hand, and another, until a chain formed.

They linked together for the last push and moved in a huddle compressing power. The men's shield began to reform. Waves of power radiating from the group distorted the air making a bubble around them. Ash didn't touch them. Tom didn't need Kenny to see the war between forces in play. The Goddesses' power revitalized him. Together they proceeded. Arriving near the gate, Tom released the hand and ran ahead. Wailer was there holding a rifle. The others were armed and under cover. Dead bodies and bullet holes told the tale.

"We aren't saved yet," Tom said. "We got to get them outta here."

Addie and Sally, behind a black car, sprang forward dropping their guns in the dirt. Janis laid her AK-47 respectfully on the Jeep's hood. The three marched forward and joined the coven. His partners received the group's embrace with songs of joy. The peace didn't last.

"We must hurry," Athena said backing away. "They know we are here. We must act before they can stop us."

The women formed a circle, hand in hand. Janis, Sally, and Addie stood outside in a triangle formation at a little distance. All but the men chanted. As their voices increased so did their power until a thick, white light poured down from above.

Tom squinted. The women became transparent within shimmering white. They radiated young and beauty, clad in gold girdles, silver kilts, wearing crowns or helmets of gold. Athena held high a spear which cascaded sparks from its point. Tom lost her in the shower. Then, the light withdrew slowly into the sky. Tom imagined the finger of God dipping into vanilla light. He watched transfixed unable to move until the light rose high and blinked out.

"Gone...they're gone," Tom whispered.

Only scraps of rags remained. Wailer stagged and dropped to the ground. Murphy swooned, holding onto the Jeep. Tom and his ladies remained upright. Sally's face ran with tears. Addie's head bowed. Janis used her T-shirt, exposing her bra, to wipe her eyes.

"Where...Where'd they go?" Murphy stammered. "I don't get it."

"Gone," Sally said, her voice quiet. "Not suicide. They released their life into the world...They gave everyone a gift."

"Them assholes down in the hole are still alive." Jains said. "Watchers can't make more of themselves except half-breeds." She pointed at Wailer on the ground. "He's different. His daddy ain't one of them. I really hate those guys."

"The elder race will die out," Addie said. "The Goddesses sacrificed—"

"Not all. There's one left, his mommy." Janis pointed at Wailer. "We'll—" Janis spun, pulled her revolver, and fired two rounds toward the well. "Son of a bitch, I winged him, damn it."

Tom saw an Ergaster running for cover in the distance. Wailer got up and brushed himself off.

"Best we go while we can," Wailer said. "Son, it's time to go home." Wailer reached his hand to Kenny. "Sorry, things had to go this way. We together would have been a beacon."

"Dad? Dad...Dad, can I sit in the front...in the front, the front is best...the best." Kenny shook Wailer's hand, pumped it a few times, and let go. "Mr. Webber showed me how to shake hands."

"Sure, you sit with me. We'll get you a driver's license someday," Wailer said. "You're upfront from now on."

They climbed into the limo leaving the rifles behind. Janis, with her senses restored, said guns won't be needed. Wailer backed the car out and made a wide turn. He drove half a mile before the stepwell blew up. No doubt the Watchers' own handiwork. Rocks the size of cement blocks rained down pelting the limo. Of course, Wailer's car was armor plated. Even so, Tom cowered like a beaten dog. Rocks smashed all around. The downpour only lasted seconds.

"America won't be attacking by that door," Murphy said. "CIA's been after them a long time, I'd bet. That's my qualified guess. Don't worry, Wailer. I'm not telling the Company diddly."

"Even if you do, the authorities won't bother me," Wailer said. "I have my...supporters. Besides, the government has better things to do. It'll take years to dig them out. My security company may be of service." Wailer chuckled. "The Watchers aren't finished. Actually, Tod, the CIA hasn't been looking. Corruption's claws run deep."

Wailer continued on slowly, weaving around gray-coated abandoned cars. The rock-rain stopped, but the soot redoubled. Wailer picked his way with caution while Tom's inner voice screamed 'go faster'. Cairo passed for a post-apocalypse movie set.

"Where are we going," Sally asked.

"*The Finder* is moored in the Mediterranean off lower Egypt or she should be by now. Air traffic is shut down. She's the only way out of here. You folks need a ride?"

Murphy agreed to tag along, claiming he needed a vacation. Tom had no idea where Murphy was really coming from given his record. The CIA man proved to be a good liar. Tom appreciated Wailer for using every tool money could buy to get at the truth. He hired or bribed or financed many helpers in his quest. Tom had suspected Murphy was on Wailer's payroll. Which one of Murphy's stories were true, if any?

They arrived at the marina to find no ship. *The Finder* wasn't there, but Wailer's 26-foot sloop sat docked. It didn't look shipshape. Port was too far upriver for a deep-water craft such as *Finder*. Wailer's sailboat may have been seaworthy, but it wasn't built for six people.

The gunwales rode low in the water with all aboard. It became terrifying to Addie when the boat entered choppy waters. She stripped off the local attire and donned a life vest. The bilge pump ran overtime. How long can it keep sucking ash? The sea's tossed surface didn't provide confidence as they exited the delta into open water. Underway against thrashing waves, Wailer gunned the small outboard motor. He tried to hail *Finder* on the marine band radio but got nowhere.

"Radios don't work during the apocalypse?" Tom said. "Never saw that in the Bible."

"Typical man," Sally said. "Technology ain't the answer."

Volcanoes generate electromagnetic interference. The compass didn't work. Wailer didn't know which direction they should go. Wailer steered his overloaded boat where Addie pointed and straight into a mud storm.

CHAPTER FORTY-EIGHT:

THE RETURN

The sky broke clear on day three and *The Finder's* billowing, fresh-laundered sails dazzled on the horizon. Tom spotted her as the sloop limped along on one ragged spinnaker. The outboard motor was gone and the sails ripped to shreds. Wailer's refit antique craft sported a new transom for the outboard, and Tom thought the man was a purest. Wailer pushed it overboard when the fuel ran out although that little engine had saved them. Tech and magic happy together.

Wailer's sloop wasn't the only craft of his to receive an overhaul. *The Finder* was sleek, orderly, and polished, the exploratory equipment and cranes were gone. Rigged and stripped for speed, she appeared brand-new despite her 1904 manufacture. She had not encountered soot or if she had, it didn't stick. *The Finder* had its version of a power shield with its all-woman crew. The ship's reconfiguration amazed Tom. He had never seen *Finder's* masts rigged.

"Wow, majestic," Tom said, as they moved closer.

"Yes, like your mother," Wailer said.

Mom waited on the rail as *Finder* closed. Even at a distance, Tom saw Mom had put on weight and shed worry. Once on board, after many hours of hugs and talks, Tom found Mom's mind and body sharp and balanced. The long trip home gave him time to experience a side of his mother he never knew. Tom's need to coddle her evaporated.

Three months later, *The Finder* floated free near the spot where this started. She drifted like a ghost ship in the Sargasso Sea. Richard wanted to make sure the first and last black smoker had sunk. It had. The Sargasso Sea was foggy and dead flat on the day *Finder* pulled down her sails and started the engines. The volcano's sinking had created a hundred square mile fog.

Tom spotted Richard on deck looking over the bow railing before dinner. Water droplets fell from Wailer's trim beard onto his tux. Tom halted to build his arguments. Electronic piloting didn't care about fog. Human lookouts weren't necessary but Wailer had posted watches there each day. He wasn't at the bow looking for icebergs.

He's checking for that shark. It's time we talk.

Tom avoided Richard. Yet Tom happily mixed in with the crew. Richard Wailer sleeping with Mom was hard to take. Tom had no right to complain. He had slept with two of the crew himself. Another of Wailer's team had asked him to dinner. The all-girl crew didn't seem to mind sharing the only two free men aboard. Deric wasn't on the menu.

Tom snaked up to Wailer intent on releasing the angry words he had choked down for three months. Ready to pick bones, Tom met him at the rail. Wailer spoke before Tom could spit venom.

"Tom, good to see you." Wailer's smile was bright and real. "Good, indeed." Wailer's eyes twinkled love which took Tom aback. "I never thought…Half-breeds weren't supposed to be fertile. We tested. No doubt Kenny's my son. I didn't know for sure. It felt right, but evidence is foremost. Doc Smith confirmed it. I'm a family man." Wailer shook his head as if in disbelief. "Now, about Mary—"

"See anything?" Tom asked, diverting the topic. Richard's goodwill doused Tom's smoldering fuse. "I've spotted that big shark a few times, too."

"It's not a shark. It's a guardian spirit," Wailer said. "I once thought it's a machine. It's not. She's a manifestation. You're free of the amulet. Mary imbued it. The amulet took her powers to hide itself in you. She received special protections for the loan."

Wailer paused. Tom didn't speak.

"Women who handle power keys are blessed." The captain turned back toward the sea, elbows on the rail. "Madame Shark escorts your mother. Call it an honor guard. Mary's a baby goddess herself, so to speak."

Tom didn't think Wailer had it exactly. Some women are born with magic while others make it. Maybe it came down from older generations.

Tom quietly stood watch with Wailer for a time. Tom spied a fin off port running a little ahead. Tom wouldn't have believed it a year ago, no doubt the same fish that saved him. The amulet had drawn the guardian. Did it choose him or was it the device? Tom's beef faded with the clearing fog. Love is its own magic and Wailer loves Mom.

"That shark's purpose is finished." Tom said to fill the silence. Sadness caught him. "I'm done too. What'll I do now, flip burgers? What's left for me in archeology? My career's over."

Richard Wailer laughed with his deep baritone. "This isn't over. There are a million pieces to humanity's puzzle yet to be discovered! You can't stop looking, Tom. I won't. Too many unanswered questions. There's a lot more to learn."

"What about Ergaster? They'll want me dead."

"The Watcher's aren't your problem anymore, mine either. Murphy contacted his bosses. The government is on top of it and I'll keep an eye out, too. What about Berkeley? You have your teaching job."

"There is that," Tom said without enthusiasm. He had time to think. Classroom teaching wasn't what he wanted, shovel bumming being his bliss. "How'd you manage it? Jobs at Berkeley don't come easy. They want Ph.Ds."

"I funded the Calico program, free money to them, but they treated my project as an embarrassment. Imagine an important school doing tinfoil hat research." Richard laughed. He laughed a lot lately. "Berkeley needed an out without losing face, or money, so I offered them a win-win: Take my friend Tom and I'll fund another project. I wanted Calico studied, important clues there, but I diverted the funds so they'd hire you." Richard spread his hands. "There remains much to be discovered."

"Yet to be discovered." Tom spoke Kenny's favored phrase.

"More than we know," Richard agreed.

Tom bit his lower lip. He wanted Berkeley to get to Calico. That was his dream. That site wasn't popular. Wailer stuck his neck out and asked nothing in return. Richard Wailer made good his promises. *You don't punch a man's gift-horse in the teeth.* Tom decided he'd keep his mouth shut about Calico. The dream was over.

"Berkeley lets people ride skateboards on campus," Tom mused. "Old U thought I was a terrorist."

"There is that," Richard said. "Take the doctorate's program. It's free for employees."

"Whatever gets me outside and into the field is what I'll do."

"That's the spirit, smart man. As my old acquaintance, Josh Campbell used to say, 'follow your bliss.'" Richard put a strong hand on Tom's shoulder and gave a little squeeze. "I'd offer you a job, but I don't hire family, company policy. Speaking of company, here comes Wendy." Wailer patted Tom's back.

"She's my date," Tom said, "Question. Why didn't the Watchers go after me?"

Tom held a digit up at Wendy and mouthed to her, *One minute.* She stopped a few yards away.

Richard straightened up. "Mary was bait…she didn't know. She held the amulet, which they detected. Running with me, from their perspective, was evidence we had the amulets. Watches assumed wrong. I pulled Mary out just in time. They went hard after us. We had a hell of a hide and seek time." He turned back to the rail. "After Amy died, they pulled cautions. That's when they took Kenny, not knowing he had it. We can't make Women's Magic, but we can carry the Goddesses' device for them." Wailer chuckled. "The Watchers were misguided. Poor Kenny…"

The fog didn't cover Wailer's sadness. Tom felt for him. Had Tom known about Kenny's plight, or that he, too, had absorbed a power key himself, the game would have been lost. Kenny had suffered much and his mother more.

"So, the amulet killed Amy," Tom said.

"She was a willing decoy," Wailer said. "Human females can absorb talismans. Hiding inside a pair of young boys was unexpected." He opened his fist and flexed his fingers. "They poisoned her. That lit my ass. They defiled her body looking for it. Thought I had Kenny protected, but…" Richard spread his hands.

"Amulets operate in pairs, and threes," Tom said. "Mine's a half. I wondered about the other. Three amulets overcame the door seal but one wasn't complete. The control room key was only a half. Three did the trick, I guess."

"It took four," Richard said. "They couldn't have transmuted otherwise. They didn't have it. It's why I couldn't enter the Wachter's house. You and Kenny had one. Men aren't supposed to hold them, but children are different. Half-breeds are different. They never suspected you. They suspected me and Mary for good reason."

Richard drew out a long, gold chain from under his shirt. He wrapped it around one finger. Stretching out his hand, the amulet-half hung on a gold chain, glowing unnaturally.

"I had this when I was left at the foundling home. The asylum wanted it, greedy bastards, but it hid itself. I've never been able to remove it."

Richard lifted it over his head.

"Look at that, it came off."

Richard held it over the side. It dangled, glittering over the sea. "It won't stick to me anymore. Letting go is good. I have one more thing to do." He lifted it higher. "Power's gone out of it."

"Don't do it," Tom said. He signaled to Wendy. "Keep it. It was your moms, whoever she was."

"Her name was Artemis. No doubt dead," Richard said. "I'd keep it but the guardian needs it."

Wailer let it go. Tom sensed that truth as it fell.

"Don't keep Wendy waiting. Enjoy." Richard turned back to the sea. Tom didn't move. "I'll be along shortly."

Tom left him at the rail and proceeded to dinner. He and Wendy were joined by Tod Murphy, Doctor Hess, and several of Wendy's shipmates. Murphy was in a talkative mood and spent most of the evening trying to impress the ladies. The more Murphy drank, the more he fell into confessions. There was something about *The Finder* that made people honest.

Murphy spoke of his suspicions. Higher-ups at the CIA knew about Watchers all along, he guessed. Murphy fingered undeclared inner agencies of off-grid operators. The Company hosted rogue factions he knew and others he heard rumors of. Murphy mentioned Billings who took a bullet after the kidnapping. Murphy thought it was an inside job.

"Corruptions everywhere. Everyone's on the take," Murphy announced slurring.

He had worked side-jobs for Richard with and without knowing it. Moonlighting wasn't usual. Pro Watcher groups and anti-Watcher factions were mixed into the batter. Murphy was drunk. But it was Tom's head spinning.

"Right don't know what the left's doing, ha!" Murphy took a deep drink. "It'll take years to pry them interlopers out. Count me out, too dangerous. I'm a geologist for Christ's sake."

Murphy's level didn't reach into the CIA's bottom, Tom assumed. Tom left dinner alone, sober and thoughtful. He and Wendy agreed on another date. The next time, they'll dine alone. He had time. The Sargasso Sea was a long way from the Panama Canal and the trip north to San Francisco.

They motored on running slow. *Finder* had everything onboard, research lavatories, library, gym, game room, and talented women with sharp, liberated minds. Plenty to engage him. Tom enjoyed learning how to rig sails. He made the crow's nest climb several times. The only thing the ship didn't have was an answer to his question:

What do I do now?

EPILOGUE:

Tom finished his morning lecture at Berkeley and ambled back to his office. His sparse assigned space felt antiseptic. Cory's office was stuffed with things the old explorer had recovered. All Tom had was a dozen borrowed boxes full of Calico cobbles to sort and catalog on his own time. Which ones were tools, or rocks, was hard to say.

"I see why Leakey's critics had issues." He lamented into his voice recorder. "I'm not a lithic expert."

He shut the recorder off. Tom knew his career wasn't going anywhere. Third string assistant professors don't get choices. His lecture hall was as empty as his own collection.

"I could teach this course from inside my camper."

This morning's class hosted more than the usual, having been attended by eight students and one dark figure auditing from the back row. Life at Berkeley didn't meet Tom's expectations—too safe, too easy, too constricting, too conventional.

"Boring as hell." Tom slumped in his chair and pushed a stack of test papers away.

He had to grade them for the boss's class. *Why hurry?* He kicked back and put both feet atop his gunmetal desk. His new pair of Hi-Boy skate sneakers were too tidy like everything else in his life. He had bought a new skateboard, too. Californians don't laugh at grown men riding skateboards like at Old U. His new board rested in a corner untried.

Tom left his doors open in hope of colleague interactions. From there, he could see way down the hallway. Students might have questions. His fellow department members avoided him. His association with Cory left a stink. Cory mentioned Professor Conley in his latest bestseller.

"Hey, anybody back there?" A voice sung out.

"Crap, here comes another gonzo reporter."

A backlit, longhaired, bearded man marched toward him. Too old to be a student. Tom pushed his hair back behind both ears. Tom needed a haircut six months ago. He never got around to it. He hadn't shaved in three days either. The department head hated longhairs. Tom enjoyed agitating the bastard. The visitor walked straight in. Tom stood and stuck out a hand.

"What can I do for you, sir?"

"Sir, you never called me that before. Asshole a few times. How're you doing, Tom?"

"Tod Murphy, as I live and breathe! What's with the hair, you undercover?"

"No, nothing like that. Where're your girls? I hear Sophia got accepted for a doctorate program." Murphy took a chair. "This place looks like a funeral home for pet-rocks."

"Sophia? Oh, Sally. Her proper name. Janis went to Nome. Addie went with her. It seems they're a going concern. Gold prospecting, if you can call it that. It's more like gold finding. They don't know what else to do with themselves."

"Too bad," Murphy said. "I got something. I'd like to have a word with them, but the clock's ticking."

"Word, what kind of word? Weren't we interrogated enough? The damn feds were supposed to back off. That's why you're here? Delivering more government bullshit."

"Relax, Tom. It's not like that." Murphy chuckled without the usual undertones of malice. "I resigned. Screw the CIA. I'm out. The Antiquities Department is on its own. I'm doing…er…freelance geology now. I'm thinking to expand. I've come across an interesting site. I've got a foundation revved up for it. They'll finance the dig. But first I need a lead archaeologist and backup people. The whole deal."

"Interesting," Tom said. "What kind of backup?"

"Addie sure as hell, and there's a need for security, especially where I'm going, so Janis, too. How many oil surveys can a man stand? I thought you might know a shovel bum looking for work. Too bad Sophia's tied up."

"Wailer's not behind this…is he?" Tom said feeling suspicious.

Tom hadn't yet adjusted to the fact Mom and Richard got married. *46 and knocked up, wow. I'm 26 and can't get a date.* He needed distance and time to let Mom's pregnancy sink in. "If he's got anything to—"

"Wailer, hell no!" Murphy put a shocked look on his face. "He's pissed at me, wanted an inside man at Antiquities. There's a world of lost history 'yet to be discovered,' as Kenny would say. That kid's a pisser. Nobody on *Finder* could beat him at ping-pong."

"What exactly is interesting enough to exit a good paying job?" Tom said. "You're draining the bathwater before the baby arrives."

Murphy had worked in government for eighteen years, two more would have gotten him a full pension. Changing career in one's late 40s is risky. There had to be more behind it. Why would anyone give up retiring at age fifty? Berkeley's benefit package was great, too. 'Hang in long enough and you'll have it made.' Richard said. *If I don't die of boredom first.*

Murphy looked around and behind him. Tom half expected him to take out that gizmo which detected listening devices. Rather, Murphy hopped his chair closer to the desk, leaned over, and spoke in a low voice.

"Ever hear of the Gueld Formation in North Africa? It's in the Sahara Desert. Commonly called the 'Eye of Africa.'"

"No clue."

"A lot of people won't touch it. It's known by another name you might know, a Greek name." Murphy leaned way over. Tom leaned toward him. "Plato called it Atlantis."

Murphy thrusted back into his chair with a big, toothy smile.

"I know, ridiculous, but I have evidence."

"You'll have to lay that out for me," Tom said. "Your bait's rotten."

Murphy told his story. He had followed up on leads he got from the same smugglers he had hired to get the Cessna. He went back to pay them off and convince them to stay on the Company's payroll. While there, he snooped around and got chummy with oil people. One thing got him into the other. He explained the details. Tom was intrigued. If Murphy was right, this was huge. The kind of discovery that made careers and enemies.

"Sounds like academic suicide, I like it," Tom said.

"Recent eroding exposed location. Trapped materials released. I found something in a hidden cave. A civilization had washed away…but not everything." Murphy laid a gold coin on the table. Athena's face was on it along with an unknown script. "A golden opportunity, I'd say. Nobody's willing to take the risk, careers, hardships, and whatnot, not to mention danger, a very unstable political situation. Know any hungry young shovel bums willing to face the tempests?"

Tom flipped the coin over. On the other side was a person with an elongated skull.

"You know, Tod, Mom warned me to steer clear of pirates like you."

Tom got up, went to a filing cabinet, and took out a bottle of rye. He poured two. *Murphy's a whiskey man. He's got that going for him.* Murphy accepted.

"What's this? Too early for happy hour."

"Makes it easier. I'm handing in my resignation." Tom upended his glass. Murphy followed. Tom poured another round and held his glass high.

"Here's to the Eye of Africa," Tom said.

They clicked glasses.

"I'm moving on this today," Murphy said. "Shoving off this afternoon. You'll need time to write your resignation, get your affairs in order. Meet me in Africa?"

"I'll go now," Tom said. "I'll need a few things out of my camper, it's parked in self-storage. We'll stop on the way out."

"You don't want to burn this bridge, Tom. You should give them proper notice. I don't want you to screw over your career. What if this is a bust?"

"I'll be gone months before Berkeley notices I left," Tom said.

Tom dug a fast-food napkin out of the garbage can and wrote, "I quit," on it. He showed it to Murphy and laid it on the desk. He loaded his backpack with his new, and unused, homemade dig-kit and what little else he had there. He walked out with Murphy.

Outside, Tom realized he had forgotten his skateboard. Having crossed the threshold, Tom had no desire to go back.

THE END

ACKNOWLEDGMENTS:

TOM CONLEY

Many of my fellow writers have given me input and ideas for this novel. My thanks go to the pool of writers I've associated with over the years and especially my friends at the Greater Lehigh Valley Writers Group (GLVWG. org). A special thanks to Gayle F. Hendricks, my formatting and book design guru. Thank you, Angel Ackerman, for your excellent proofreading and line editing. Angel Ackerman has been a longtime friend, mentor, and teacher who helped me on many of my writing projects. She taught me a lot. My greatest thanks go to Lisa Cross, my partner in life, who tolerates my writer's life and is instrumental as a story critic and proofreader. Without Lisa's support, I could not write. Last but not least, thanks to my real-life friend, Tom Conley, a former wreck diver who lent me his name for my character and put some good ideas into my head. The real Tom Conley bears no resemblance to my fictional adventurer.

ABOUT THE AUTHOR

Rachel Thompson, writing as R.C. Thom began her writing career after surviving a near death motorcycle accident in 2003. She published nonfiction and cartoons in newspapers and magazines before working for several years as a freelance community news reporter. Her quirky short stories have appeared in various anthologies, among them those published by the Greater Lehigh Valley Writers Group and Parisian Phoenix Publishing. She has six novels in print, this one included, and two anthologies. Thompson was born and raised in Ocean County, New Jersey and later spent many years living in the Lehigh Valley, Pennsylvania, before moving to the Deep South. She now resides in the heart of a national forest where she paints and plays guitar when not writing.